HER

HER

L.J. DIVA

★ Royal Star Publishing ★

Chances is an imprint of Royal Star Publishing
www.royalstarpublishing.com.au

First edition paperback published in 2025
All Rights Reserved, Copyright ©L.J. Diva 2025

Trade Paperback ISBN: 978-1-922307-84-2
Large Print Paperback ISBN: 978-1-922307-85-9
Dust Jacket Hardcover ISBN: 978-1-922307-86-6
E-book ISBN: 978-1-922307-83-5
A catalogue record for this book is available from the National
Library of Australia.

Cover design: Royal Star Publishing and ©Designed with Grace
Cover photos: Female silhouette: MS207/shutterstock.com
Cityscape: 4LUCK/shutterstock.com
Typesetting in Minion Pro by Royal Star Publishing

DEDICATION

This series is dedicated to the crime fighting Reagan family, especially Sean. Sometimes, *Blood* is not thicker and definitely not *Blue*, and the truly wrong will always pay for their sins.

PART ONE

Chapter 1

Die, bitch, die!

The silence in the room was so thick it could have been cut with a knife. But considering the three words, a weapon of any kind would not have been welcome in that suffocating moment.

"Well…" she finally said, looking up from the paper in her hand. "It's not like I haven't received notes like this before."

"What!" The woman sitting on the sofa in her New York office shot upward. The champagne in the glass in her hand barely moved with the action even as she slammed it onto the glass and chrome coffee table in front of her. "What do you mean? You've received other death threats? Sydney, what the hell? You should have told me."

"Calm down, CC. You'll get your Chanel in a twist." Sydney dropped the note onto the coffee table next to the glass. "You know all about L.A. and why I moved here. Clearly, crazies are everywhere." Heaving a sigh, she slumped into an expensive armchair and eyed off the group of disapproving women before her with a wary gaze.

CC Charleston was the publisher extraordinaire with New York's top publishing house, *Pulsate Publishing*. The CC stood for Chanel Cleopatra, thanks to her mother's love of Chanel, and her father's love of ancient Egypt, hence the shortening and legally so, but the woman was Chanel from head to toe. It was all she wore, breathed, and smelt like. And it was why her high-rise office was smothered in the label.

Olivia Sutton, agent to the stars, had her own agency ranging from authors to actors to musicians and singers. Celebrities of the highest calibre and earning status were the only types Olivia took on. That was why she had Sydney on her books.

Gemma Madison, editing phenomenon with CC's publishing house, had done wonders whipping Sydney's ten novels into shape.

And Emerson Lake, producer, director, show runner, show writer had done it all in L.A. for twenty-five years and had moved to New York when Sydney had because she'd not only needed a change, but was Sydney's best friend.

"Sydney." CC sat back calmly on her Chanel covered sofa and smoothed her black skirt over her elegant narrow knees. "Please tell me you're taking this seriously. You're not the first author here at Pulsate who's ever received death threats." She glanced sideways at Gemma. "That we've had to deal with."

"Look, CC." Sydney crossed her legs and flipped her shoulder-length brown hair back. "You know full well what happened in L.A.; you know full well I received many death threats while I was there, but I never took them seriously until that last time. I left just days later. You also know, full well, why we're keeping that quiet and I never mention it." Fatigue overcame her and she felt the exhaustion full bore. "I think it's time to go home. I've been tired a lot lately."

"Probably the stress of L.A.," Gemma told her. She eyed her client and noted the dark circles and bags under her eyes, then gave CC and Olivia a knowing glance. "Or is it the stress of staying up late finishing off the new book you're supposed to be writing?"

"Or it could be a new man," Olivia murmured and sipped her champagne. "Are you getting what we're not, Sydney? I'd like to live vicariously if you are."

Sydney scoffed and looked at her forty-something brunette agent. "Hardly, Liv. I haven't had a man in two years."

"I thought it was three," Emerson interrupted and giggled at her best friend's shocked expression.

"Hey! Don't make me sound that desperate and lonely," Sydney chided. "It's only *two* years and he was a very hot and needy lover. He's Italian after all, and you know what they're like."

"If only," CC muttered and sighed. "How about a bodyguard? Do we know if the person caught in L.A. is actually the one that was stalking you? Could it be him who sent the letter? Or do you have another stalker? Seriously, Sydney." She picked up her glass and raised it to her highest selling author. "Do we need to get you a bodyguard? Oh, and when's your next book coming?"

Sydney deflated. That was the whole reason she was there. To talk about her next book which was *not* forthcoming. After ten years of writing under the pen name of Cassandra Kingsley, Sydney Kingston was a successful international best-selling author with ten number one novels, five number one novellas, and ten years in Hollywood bringing her books to life in movies, but it was a stalker who'd ruined all of that. In order to keep it under the radar as much as possible, and wanting to get out of L.A. after that night, she'd headed for the gritty streets of New York City and all its fabulous glory to try and write her next novel; a psychological thriller. She had the bare bones of an idea, but nothing had come to her since setting foot in The Big Apple. With so much exploring to be done, she'd barely slept in four weeks, let alone written one word.

"I've been busy exploring the city which is why I don't have a book for you." Sydney cringed and gave a grim smile. "Sorry, CC, but I just haven't had it in me to write what I started a couple of months ago. But," she brightened, "I've been taking a tonne of photos and recording a tonne of notes on everywhere I've been so there's a few ideas floating around. I just need some time to settle in and settle down—"

"So, you do have a man," Emerson said. "How come I don't know?" She brushed aside a long dark curl of hair and flashed her blue eyes at her best friend. "How dare you not tell me!"

Sydney huffed and waved a hand. "Hardly, Em. With all the time we've spent together this last month you would've seen one. You haven't because we were too busy moving me into my new home."

"That's right," Gemma cooed. "A gorgeous Queen

Anne brownstone in the fancy Upper East Side. What's it like? You haven't posted pictures on social media yet."

"That's because I'm not finished moving in." Tucking her hair behind her ear, Sydney uncrossed her legs and took a sip of champagne. "Fully modernised by the previous owners, but the old-style brownstone charm still remains. Wood floors, warm colours, lots of stuff to unpack and I should be done this weekend."

"Great! Then you can get on with that book," CC told her. "But only after you have a house warming party because I want to see it myself."

"Ha! I knew it," Sydney replied. "You just want to be nosy and party."

"Hardly, darling." CC waved her glass through the air. "I just want to see what type of security system it has. How many deadbolts, bars on the windows, back doors…"

"I'll be fine, CC." A sigh left Sydney and her mood slipped. "I'm not going to let what happened in L.A. stop me from living my life. The brownstone is very secure. I have Amy with me a lot, or I'm with Em, so I'm not alone and I know some basic martial arts to defend myself."

CC aimed her finger at the note on the coffee table. "But the letter—"

"That's a sick and twisted arsehole's way of trying to get to me?" Sydney's Australian accent came back strong. "I'm not going to let anyone do this to me again. I've had letters before, I'll have letters again. Besides," she stole a glance at the note, "cut out magazine letters on a white piece of paper. Hardly original, and it's not as if DNA would be found."

"You don't know that," CC cut her off and glanced at the other women for support. "You're our number one best-selling author and we need to keep you safe. So, I'm going to give this to a detective or call someone in and see if they can find anything on it. There would be fingerprints he left behind."

"Or you left behind, or I left behind," Sydney added. "I know you mean well, CC, but I'll be fine now."

"We could get you a bodyguard," CC repeated. "You ignored me a minute ago when I said it."

"Make it a hot one and you can fall in love with him," Emerson joked, a twinkle in her eye as she finished off her champagne. "And if he's *really* hot, maybe I will too. We could share."

"That's gross, Em." Sydney groaned. "Just gross."

"Well, you can't let Whitney have all the fun. They got it on, even though *The Bodyguard* is a movie. Who knows what adventures you two could get up to with an illicit affair?" Gemma realised what she'd said and quickly scribbled in a small notebook. Even though she was an editor, she was also trying to write her own novel.

"Then feel free to get yourself one for the final cut," Sydney said, before turning to CC. "Is this the only one?"

CC's crinkled grey eyes widened. "Should there be more?"

Sydney shrugged. "How should I know? That's why I'm asking. Look…" She slid forwards in her chair. "If that's the only one in the last month or so, then there's no need to worry about it. But if there's more, then say so now. Otherwise, let's not worry about it until there is.

So far, it's just a letter and nothing to worry about. I'll let Amy know. We'll figure something out, and I'll keep my eyes wide open every time I enter and exit the house. How's that sound?" She found the strength to shove herself up from the chair. "In the meantime, I'll try and come up with a way of finishing the book, or even start writing another one. Stop worrying about my deadline because I don't have one, remember? You know you have the rights to the next five books anyway."

After the success of the last ten novels, she'd received twenty-five million in a contract for the next five books, with no actual date for delivery. That way, she could write at her own leisure, as fast or slow as she wanted. And the deal was only for the print and foreign rights. She owned all electronic and audio book rights as she'd started out as a self-publisher eleven years earlier, reaching success few indie authors achieved, drawing the attention of one of the world's biggest publishing houses. After much back and forth, Sydney, as Cassandra Kingsley, signed one of the biggest hybrid publishing deals in publishing history. And that continued every few years with a new deal as the audience grew and her stories claimed number one position year after year, selling millions of copies in all formats.

"Yes, I know, darling, that's why I want to keep you safe." CC stood as Sydney threw her bag over her shoulder.

"You just want to keep me alive so you can keep making money out of me." Sydney let out a chuckle and gestured at Em. "I'll head home after lunch and have a scavenge through my notes and old manuscripts that I haven't touched in ages to see if I can resurrect them. If not, I'll try and come up with a new idea and see how that goes."

"I'll give you a month before I expect *something* at least." CC walked them to the door of her twentieth floor office. "And darling," she added as she laid a gentle hand on Sydney's arm, "you went through a lot in L.A. If you need a bodyguard because something's starting up here, then for the love of God, let's get you one."

Sydney glanced over her boss, taking in the crisp grey curly hair in a short, soft style, crisp Chanel white blouse, matching pearls, and black skirt suit. Even her shoes were Chanel. "How about I write the story of an amazing publisher who only ever wore Chanel and was strangled with her own pearls? I'll call it," she waved her hand in the air, "Death by Chanel."

Gemma and Olivia burst out laughing and hustled back to the couch for more champagne, and Emerson clasped her hands over her mouth and hurried off to the elevator.

CC's perfectly plucked brows rose and her lips pursed. "As long as it's good and I can sell it, darling, kill away."

Sydney smiled and walked out.

"I can't believe you said that," Emerson told Sydney when they entered the lift. "That was hilarious."

"And she was right." Sydney hit the down button and the doors silently closed. "Any idea, if written well, should sell. Even if it means killing off my publisher."

Emerson shook her head and gave a last breathless chuckle. "That was funny and I'd like to see you write it. But what *are* you going to write?"

"I don't know," Sydney mumbled as they arrived on the ground floor and the doors opened. "But since you're the one who's made movies from the last five, they'd better be good, huh? The book I started writing before I left L.A. was okay. The idea was really good, I thought. But everything that happened just turned me off it. Almost as if the experience tainted it even though the book had nothing to do with it."

"Why not write a book based on what happened?" Emerson waved her hand to hail a cab and one stopped almost immediately. They climbed in and Emerson gave the driver her address, which was closer than Sydney's.

"I could, but it feels too icky to do that. As if I'd be reliving it and I don't want to do that."

"I'm not saying relive it. I'm saying take the basics of what happened and craft a story about a fictional character around it. Isn't that the way you authorly types usually do it?"

Sydney glanced at her and laughed half-heartedly. "Authorly types? Who are you kidding? How many authorly types have you met?"

"Quite a few, actually. I meet them every time I turn their books into movies and TV series. God, the stories I could tell you." She tucked a wayward strand of curls back into her topknot bun. "You're not the first, Syd, and you won't be the last."

"And here I was thinking I was your only," Sydney joked and slid off her seatbelt as they pulled up outside Emerson's apartment building. "How much stuff do you have left to unpack? I want to get home early and try and figure out a new book. Or an idea, at least."

Emerson paid the driver and they alighted. "Not much, but with the two of us, it should be an hour or two…it's only…" She glanced at her phone for the time. "Twelve. We can work a couple of hours, have lunch, and then you can go home. Who knows, maybe you'll come up with an idea while we work."

They waved at the doorman and collected the mail before going upstairs. Emerson's apartment was a spacious loft with walls that only went halfway up to let in the light between rooms. It was painted stark white with large windows from floor to ceiling that framed a view of the East River and downtown. Emerson had decorated it with large bright prints of Caribbean life, warm throw rugs, and cushions on colourful couches and chairs.

"Looks like you've already finished decorating, and Christ, look at that view." Sydney stood gaping at the Manhattan skyline. "Why the hell don't I live here?"

"Because the backstory of your brownstone being a brothel only ten years ago was too tempting a story for you to turn down." Emerson chuckled. "I've done everywhere but the office. Come on. I need a good dozen boxes unpacked."

While they sorted out what went where, Emerson brought up the idea of a bodyguard. "Is it something you'd want?"

"No," Sydney said, point blank. "I didn't get one in L.A., and I won't get one now."

"And look how well it turned out," Emerson muttered and lined up Golden Globes for her TV work on a shelf. She'd received quite a few awards over the last twenty-five years, from Globes to People's Choice to Oscars, SAGs, and many overseas awards.

"Emerson!" Sydney held a signed baseball in a glass cube in her hand. "Bring up L.A. one more time and this'll go right out that window," she threatened.

"Don't care if it does." Emerson shrugged, took it from her, and placed it on a shelf. "But you can pay for a new window. Will you not even consider it?"

Sydney stood still while staring at the tropical print on the wall in front of her. She didn't want to live in fear, or anyone else's fear, and being Australian gave her a certain type of chutzpah. A fighting spirit. She didn't get upset and cry, she got pissed and wanted to fight. And she had. All the way to the end when she had blood on her hands. She knew she could defend herself, but this note…just the one so far…wasn't going to make her quake in her shoes. She hadn't before; why would she now?

"At this point," she finally said. "There's no need for a bodyguard. One letter doesn't require it."

"But if more letters come?" Emerson had studied her friend while waiting for an answer.

Sydney finally glanced her way. "Only then will I consider it."

*****

He stared up at the windows of the apartment and could see them at the window he knew was an office. He had seen something in her hand be taken away. He wasn't worried about being noticed. The street was fairly busy with people heading out to lunch for an hour in the sun before drudging back to their office buildings or stores, and he had his camera with him and took photos of architecture, street signs, buildings, knowing people would just see a photographer in average clothing. There was nothing special about him. A little taller than average, he didn't stand out, but blended in nicely. He raised the camera to his eye, zoomed in on the woman in the window, and snapped away.

*****

Sydney glanced at her watch. "It's two o'clock, time for lunch and then I'm off home. Have you got a stocked fridge or do we need to get takeout?" She saw Emerson place one last item on a shelf and fold the empty box up flat.

"Don't have much in the fridge." Emerson shrugged and set the box on the pile with the others. "But there's a great Chinese restaurant down the road. I've eaten from there a few times already."

"Chinese it is," Sydney agreed and picked up her bag.

After a hearty meal and a quick cab ride home, Sydney closed the door to the vestibule, leaned wearily against it, and sighed. Her body slowly deflated, bending slightly, head hung low. It had been a long day, and it was only mid-afternoon.

The door to the house opened and Sydney's head shot up. She looked into the surprised brown eyes of her assistant.

"You look like shit. What've you been up to?" Amy

asked, pulling the door back and stepping aside for Sydney to enter.

Sydney slowly trod through the door and into the front room. "Not a lot, actually, but damn, I'm exhausted." She collapsed into an easy chair by the front window. The late afternoon's rays breaking through the curtains were enough to cover her in their soft yellow glow.

"It has been a long few weeks." Amy stood staring at her. "Why don't you take a nap and take the rest of the day off? It's Friday, so have the rest of the weekend off. Spend it in bed, catch up on sleep, start fresh Monday morning."

A sigh heaved Sydney's body up out of the chair. "Sounds good. Here I was thinking New York was going to invigorate me. New scenery, and all that. But all it's done is make me tired."

"No, that would be because of the crap we ran out of L.A. for. It was emotionally exhausting and you've been unpacking since. Your emotions *and* your stuff. Either way, I'm done for the day and everything's locked up. So, send me off, lock up, and go to bed." Amy grabbed her bag and light jacket from the coat rack and opened the door. "Don't forget to lock the door and set the alarm. It's important."

"Yes, ma'am." Sydney saluted. "Everything's either got deadbolts or bars. I'll be fine."

Amy frowned. "I'll see you Monday."

"Yes, Amy." Sydney locked and bolted both front doors and set the alarm, then headed into the kitchen for a bottle of water. She glanced out the back French doors into her old English garden, and closed the curtains over them. She padded upstairs, freshened up, and changed into comfy house clothes, plugged her phone in on her bedside table, took a swig of water, and settled down in the massive four poster bed.

She was asleep in moments.

*****

He lifted his camera and took photos of the brownstone. Upper East Side, nice neighbourhood, rich, artsy type folk. Colourful trees dotted the street and he took a few snaps of the one he was standing under as a couple emerged from their home. He didn't want people to notice; needed to be inconspicuous. He snapped a couple of pictures of the gargoyles on the front stairs of the brownstone behind him, and then of the crack in the bottom stair. He wanted, *needed*, people to think he was just photographing the world around him. Which he was. They just didn't need to know why.

He took a few snaps of the brownstone and left minutes later.

Chapter 2

Sydney didn't wake until Saturday morning. She stretched her arms above her head, heard her back crack, and yawned. Relaxing back in place, she breathed deeply and reached for her bedside clock.

Eight o'clock on the dot.

Her body always knew what time to wake. Always eight. Rain, hail, or shine. It took her half an hour or so to actually get out of bed, but she always woke at eight. She was surprised she didn't sleep later, considering she was an artist. Creative types worked into the night most times, got to bed late and so woke late. But Sydney wasn't one to work *too* late. Her usual typical writing day started at nine, stopped at one for an hour lunch, started back up at two until six when she stopped again, and started back up at seven going until eleven if she was thoroughly immersed in what she was writing. Some days, she didn't write at all, and others she worked through until bedtime, forgetting to eat, sometimes forgetting to sleep. But she always forgot the world outside her door. Because the world inside was much more exciting. A world of characters, sex, and thrills. Hot gorgeous insatiable men with a bad side and a wild streak, and hot gorgeous insatiable women who knew how to kick-ass and never get their asses kicked; who knew how to defend themselves and stand up to the men of the world.

"If only I knew how to do the same thing," Sydney muttered, and stretched out her ankle and calf muscles. "It's what my brand is based on. My signature kick-ass women, two or three in every book, showing that women could and would stand up for themselves and never let the man control them. But here I am, cowering in my brownstone."

Not exactly cowering, her brain said.

"Yeah. That's true. One letter, that's it. And it was sent to my publisher and not me. That's a new one."

In L.A. the letters had been found in her mailbox. No stamp, so not sent through the mail, but actually *placed* in her mail box. That meant the person delivering them knew where she lived and had been stalking her.

"Don't have to worry about that now, though." She rolled over, facing her bedside table, and saw her phone silently flash with a call. She saw CC's name and chose to ignore it. She was taking the weekend off and that was it.

After further contemplation about her life and her writing, she finally hauled herself out of bed, showered, and went downstairs for the first coffee of the day. Sitting on the back porch, she watched the sun filter down over the flowers and trees. The previous owners had created a very nice garden that had caught her eye when she first saw it. But what was even more interesting was the history of the house and who the owner before the last owners had been.

I just wish the garden didn't back onto an alley and there was a house instead, might be a bit safer. Anyone can jump the fence and find their way in.

She gazed at the back fence taking up half the width of the yard. A single car garage took up the other half. Still enough space for someone to jump over. And while the view to the fence wasn't clear, that meant anyone who jumped it could sneak their way to the back door almost sight unseen.

Sydney shivered. Her bare feet hit the timber of the porch and she slowly stood, her gaze riveted to the back fence. The path wasn't any clearer, and that meant she wasn't going to see anyone entering from the rear unless she was looking out an upstairs window.

"Fuck! Maybe I should take some of those bushes out, or trim them down." A shaky sigh left her. "I can't have anyone sneaking up on me, especially when I'm here alone. Fuck." The realisation hit her. "Like right now." She hurried inside and bolted the French doors shut, staring out towards the fence. "Maybe I shouldn't be on my own," she murmured, and then burst out with a maniacal laugh. "What the fuck am I doing? Cowering from my own shadows now all because of one note. No! I'm not going to let this get to me. L.A. is over, the stalker is gone. I'm not letting one stupid letter get to me."

Shaking off her fears, she ate a hearty protein rich breakfast then sat down at her desk in the first floor full-length room she'd curated into an office library.

To the right of the door as you entered, were poster sized framed covers of her books on both the walls, and two turquoise easy chairs either side of the bay window facing the tree-lined street, with a small coffee table between them. To the left of the room, were light pine shelves on both walls lined with books, hers and others, with a desk top in the built-in unit along one wall. Awards sat on the shelf above it, and her desk sat in front of it and faced the wall opposite. Two more turquoise easy chairs were either side of the bay window overlooking the back yard and mirroring the opposite side of the room. The carpet was a soft salmon pink; the walls a soft white. It was a library, lounge, and office space that the previous owners had created for the arty types they hoped to rent to.

When Sydney had seen the online photos, she'd wanted to see the brownstone immediately. At five storeys, the whole top floor was a master suite, with the next floor down for the other bedrooms, followed by the full length room she now called an office. Lounging and kitchen was ground floor, and utilities were in the basement along with a storage room and a huge entertainment area.

It suited Sydney perfectly and she'd bought it upon learning its history, which she found quite amusing.

Laying out her notes on the latest novel, Sydney pored over them to get herself back in the story. She reread what had been written, and tried to get the creative juices flowing again. But they wouldn't. The juices were dead. They had gone off in the last months after a hurried pack and move to New York.

She sat back and thought about the issues with the story. Realising there were none, she knew her excitement for the story was gone and clearly not coming back. She rubbed her forehead and rested her elbows on the desk, her chin in her hands.

"Not the first time I've started something and not finished," she muttered.

The story arc was planned, the beats in place; everything worked except for her. She just wasn't interested.

"Okay." Sydney gathered the papers into the file, and along with the notebooks she was writing the story in, threw them into their storage case, and clipped it shut. She put it in the lower cupboard next to the rest of the books she'd started and not finished, and slammed the door shut.

Sighing, she sat back in her seat. Fifteen A4 containers. For stationery technically, but she'd used them for finished and unfinished manuscripts until she had them bound in leather. Fifteen unfinished books. She swung around to her desk. Ten published novels and five published novellas, fifteen stories unfinished. Bloody hell!

Rubbing her eyes, Sydney wondered if she should look through the rest of them to see if she could resurrect one. Maybe the inspiration would hit this time?

Her phone rang out in the silence of the room and she jumped. "Bloody hell! Hey, Em."

"Hey. I received a call from an old college friend today. We haven't seen each other in years, but she saw our photo in one of the local papers, I think she said." She paused. "Or it could have been online, she wasn't sure. Anyway, she invited us over later for drinks and a chat. She's read a couple of your novels and wants to meet you. Apparently, her son does too. He's into writing and she gave into his hounding. What do you say?"

"Later?" Sydney checked the time. "As in today, later?"

"Yep. Her husband's out all day and it's just her and her son. She'll do lunch."

"Where does she live?"

"Brooklyn somewhere. I'll pick you up. Half an hour, okay?"

Sydney rubbed her right eye and knew it was time to put her glasses on. "Sure. I'll get changed and meet you outside. Anything I need to bring?"

"Besides your sparkling personality?" Emerson snorted with laughter. "No. See you in thirty."

Sydney sighed and looked at her phone. Half past twelve already. By the time they made it there it would be an hour or more. Stay a few hours, head back. Maybe they could make it back by dark, but she doubted it. She shut both sets of curtains and hurried to change.

The house was locked and sealed tight by the time Emerson arrived.

Sydney hurried down her front steps and into the four-wheel drive, hearing the click of the door lock. She belted up and turned to Em. "Tell me about this friend and how she just happened to call out of the blue. Don't you think that's weird? And how did she get your number? Your personal or business?"

"Questions, questions," Emerson muttered as she drove off down the street. "We went through four years of college together, were roommates the whole time, but once we both left, we only kept in contact every now and then. I did a Google search of her after the call." She paused to look for traffic at the intersection before driving on.

"And," Sydney prompted.

"And she went on to become the doctor she always said she was going to be. Finished med school top of her class, went on to become a paediatrician, married a hot cop, and had a son."

"How do you know all that? That's pretty private information. Was it on her socials?"

"Some, but no. The reason it was easily found is…get this," she glanced at Sydney, "the hot cop is a son of the Police Commissioner."

Sydney's brows in surprise. "The PC of New York, PC?"

Emerson nodded. "Yep. Can you believe it? And then, of course, there are all those photos of the family and *all* four brothers are hot!"

"Married?" Sydney asked curiously.

Emerson burst out laughing. "I knew *you'd* be interested. Two are married, two are not. But they are most definitely *ALL HOT.* Capital *H.O.T. Hot!*"

Sydney quickly googled the family and saw a photo of all four brothers with their father. "Fuck! They *are* hot." All were tall, with darkish brown wavy hair and sparkling sapphire blue eyes.

"Told you," Emerson said smugly and drove across the Brooklyn Bridge.

Sydney read the article aloud. "The son is seventeen. She's married to the third brother. The eldest is the Attorney General, the youngest is a lawyer, and the middle two are detectives. So is the son of hot cop number two." She finally looked up. "Must run in the family."

"The genes?" Emmerson turned right and drove into Brooklyn.

"The good looks, *and* the law enforcement genes."

"Yep. Pretty solid family. Irish catholic decent on grandma's side, American catholic on grandpa's side. Everything runs in their blood." Emerson turned into the street mentioned by the GPS. "Her name's Laura, did I mention that? She's read a couple of your books so may want an autograph or photo or something. You don't mind, do you?" She pulled to a stop in the driveway of a white clad Hamptons style two-storey home.

Sydney peered out the windshield at it. "Quaint. The seaside cottage vibes are strong. And no, I don't mind. It gets me out of the house and might get some ideas brewing." She slid off her belt and opened the door.

"The book isn't happening?" Emerson asked before climbing out.

"Nope," Sydney said as they walked up the drive. "I'm pretty over it. The well for that book is well and truly dry."

"What number unfinished manuscript is that?" Emerson teased, and rang the bell.

"Fifteen," Sydney remarked dryly.

The door flung open and a huge teenage boy started freaking out. "Oh, my God, I can't believe you're here," he gabbled, hands flapping excitedly in front of him. "I'm such a big fan. Oh, my God. You're Cassandra Kingsley. Oh, my God."

Sydney stared at the boy. He was hitting six feet or so, with wavy brown hair like his father and grandfather and the same sapphire blue eyes. He was on the heavy side, baby fat he hadn't grown out of, and his rounded face made him look even younger.

"Okay, Sean, God." An exhausted looking blonde

woman came up behind him and pulled him away. "God, I'm so sorry," she told them. "Come on in. He's like an excitable puppy." She closed the door behind them and hung their coats on the rack. "Em, great to see you. Ended up becoming that bigwig director producer you always talked about, huh." She hugged her old friend and shook Sydney's hand. "Sydney, nice to meet you." She motioned for them to go into the living room. It was as white and coastal as the exterior and there were decorative plates of fruit, cheese, crackers, and meat, and bowls of olives and cherry tomatoes on the coffee table.

They took a seat and Emerson said, "Yeah, yeah. I did. Just as you became that bigwig paediatrician doctor, top of your class you always talked about."

"I did." Laura popped open a bottle of champagne, making Emerson and Sydney exchange a glance. "I did. But not so much anymore." She handed out glasses and slugged hers back, refreshing her glass before sitting back on the couch.

"Why not anymore?" Emerson asked and took a sip of her champagne. She'd recognised it as an expensive label and wondered what the occasion was.

"Well, you know…" Laura fluffed her short hair and sighed. "Like you, I turned fifty-five this year and I've been doing this for over thirty years. After all those years at med school, then specialist training, getting married, having Sean—it was time for reflecting and I reflected that I didn't want to do this anymore. So, I took a sabbatical and have been doing other things." She downed the rest of her drink and poured another, noticing Sean excitedly hovering near their guests.

"Guess someone wants a book signed."

Sydney looked over her shoulder and her gaze travelled up to see Sean towering over her, holding the trilogy of her books. *The One Who Loved, The One Who Lied, The One Who Betrayed.* Surprised, she said, "You read *those*? Not exactly for teenagers."

"No, they're not," Laura said and picked up a cracker with a slice of cheese.

Sean sat himself beside Sydney. "Oh, Miss Kingsley, these were the first three I read and I was hooked, so I read all of your others. Will you sign them please? They're all first editions." He thrust the books and a black Paper Mate Flair at her.

Hesitating, Sydney glanced at Emerson and Laura, noticed she was pouring her fourth drink, and said, "Ah…okay. And it's Ms Kingston. Cassandra Kingsley is just my pen name." She quickly whipped her signature on each half title page and handed them back. "There you go."

Sean looked at the one on top and disappointment rained down. "Oh…you didn't personalise them."

"You didn't ask me to," Sydney said point blank. "You just asked me to sign them."

He brightened and thrust the books and pen back. "Can you add my name to them?"

Sydney breathed in and stretched her neck. She hated pushy fans, even if they were seventeen-year-old kids. She quickly added *For Sean* above her signatures and handed them back. "That's me done." She turned to Laura. "Em says you've read some of my books too."

Laura finished off her drink and stabbed a couple of

olives onto a toothpick and ate them. "I've read those three and two others, but that's it so far. My father-in-law and his father are big on your books, though. Not sure why; they're not crime thrillers or anything." Laura popped a cherry tomato into her mouth and poured a fifth glass, draining it. "Damn. Need another bottle. Sean, sweetie, can you get us another bottle from the fridge and then leave us alone to talk?"

"But Mom—" he started protesting.

"No buts, Sean. The adults are talking." She waved him off.

He grumbled under his breath and headed for the kitchen.

"Teenagers." Laura rolled her eyes and picked up a cube of cheese, noting they hadn't eaten or drank their first champagne. "Eat up, eat up." She waved a hand at the food and picked up the bowl of olives, throwing them into her mouth two at a time.

Sean came back with a fresh bottle straight from the fridge.

"Great, now piss off and leave us alone." Laura unwrapped the top and popped it.

Sydney exchanged a concerned glance with Emerson and watched Sean slink away in embarrassment.

Laura topped up their glasses. "Drink up, you pussies. You haven't even finished one glass and we're onto our second bottle already." She filled up her own glass before sitting down.

"Ah, Laura, I know it's Saturday, but you're a doctor. Should you be drinking?" Emerson sipped her drink, and dipped a cracker into something off white in a bowl, before popping it in her mouth.

Laura waved a hand. "I told you before, I'm fifty-five and I'm on a sabbatical. I can do what I want and that includes getting fried with old friends and new if I so please. So, Em, what'ch'ya been up to in the last thirty-five years?"

Emerson gave her a quick rundown of her life. She listed movies and TV shows she'd made, and what she had coming up. She snacked on some cheese and cherry tomatoes.

"And Sydney, what about you? Apparently, you've moved to New York to write a thriller or something." Laura stretched out on the couch and put her bare feet on the coffee table near the food. Emerson stared at them and Sydney gulped. "I mean, your books aren't that great. They're not even good. God knows why my father-in-law reads them, or his dad for that matter. They're chick lit at best." She flicked her hair and stared at Sydney. "Definitely not thrillers and definitely not crime."

Sydney knew a grade-A bitch when she saw one, and Emerson's old college roommate was clearly one of them. "Yeah, well, they're obviously not to your taste and that's fine. Different people read them for different reasons and since you're ten sheets to the wind you probably won't remember me calling you a fucking bitch when you wake up tomorrow." Sydney watched her expression sour and looked at a shocked Emerson. "*This* is the type of person you shared a room with for four years? Jesus, Em, glad she didn't influence you."

"Hey…who you calling bitch?" Laura finished her

sixth drink and waved the glass around. "This is my house."

"And we're your guests and you're already pissed off your face." Sydney stood up quickly. "I need your bathroom."

"Down the hall turn right," Laura slurred and reached for the bottle.

"Em, I'll let you two reminisce." Sydney saw her friend shake her head, her eyes lasered on Laura. "Righto." She wandered towards the hall and to the left, stopped, glanced into the living room and saw Laura wasn't looking her way, and quietly dashed up the stairs. After looking into each room, she found Sean sitting on his bed, a sad, lonely, depressed expression on his face. "Having a drunk for a mother must suck." She leaned against the door frame. "But at least you got three books signed. Your mother told Em that you're into writing."

His desolate face brightened at that last word and he jumped off the bed. "Absolutely. I'm not as good as you, but I've been writing through high school and my teachers say I'm really good." He pulled out a drawer in his desk and rustled through some papers. "I saw the picture of you in the paper and hounded Mom to call up Emerson. I was hoping she'd invite you over so I could talk to you about my work. Ah…finally." He pulled a notebook from the drawer and held it up. "I was hoping you'd have a look at some short stories and give me advice. You're a professional writer. You do it for a living so you know what editors and publishers want. If I'm good enough then I might pursue it, but if not…" Sean held the notebook to his chest and became glum. "Then I'll have to find another class to take in college."

Sydney considered the moment. Here was a young kid asking for help and advice. It wasn't something she normally gave for free, but what would it hurt to read something. She looked around the room. Unlike the rest of the house's Hampton's style white and beige vibe, his room was typical teenager. Posters on the walls, clothes on the floor, double bed not even remotely close to being made, and here he was, a seventeen year old boy lurching in at six feet plus, baby-faced, and eager like a puppy.

She sighed. "I'll give them a flip through. Don't think I have time to read each one. A page here and there to see the scope of your work will be all. Here." She held out her hand and he eagerly thrust his notebook into it.

"Oh, my God this is so exciting. Cassandra Kingsley is going to read my work. Oh…" He spun around looking for a place for her to sit and grabbed his desk chair. "Here."

"No, I'll stay here in the doorway so no one can say I was in a teenage boy's bedroom." Sydney leaned her back against the door frame and flipped open the book. She started reading the first page and found herself so quickly engrossed that she finished off the ten page story and started another. When she finished that, she flicked through the book and read passages from different worlds and times and places. Finally, she closed the notebook. "They're great. You absolutely need to study writing. You should publish these."

"Really?" Sean bolted up from the bed where he'd been anxiously watching her face. "You mean it? You really mean it? They're great?" He grabbed the notebook from her outstretched hand and bounced up and down.

"Calm down." Sydney put her hands up and waited for him to stop. "Yes, they're great. You seem to have a natural storytelling ability and use your words well. You also write tight prose. In fact, it's like you've already learned it all."

"No, no, I haven't." He shook his head violently. "I haven't taken any courses or classes other than school. But my teacher said I write well and my stories are great."

"Then I definitely think you should pursue it at college if it's something you want to do. Maybe take a part-time job at a publisher, or do some work experience with an editor somewhere. You could even get a mentor to guide you."

"Could you mentor me?" Sean jumped at the chance. "I know on your publisher's website it says that up-and-coming writers can win a chance to be mentored by one of the authors and you're one of the authors."

"Oh, no, no, no." Sydney put her hands up and backed into the hallway. "No. I don't mentor anyone under twenty-one. It's too risky, age-wise, and I don't want complications. Besides, you write sci-fi fantasy. I don't. You'd be better off with mentoring from someone who does."

"What if I change genres?" Sean took an excited step towards her. "I could give romance or thrillers or crime a go. You got a mix of all three in your books." His hands went to his chest. "I'm from a crime family. I know procedures and the call signs for each crime. I hear about crime all the time from my dad and uncles and grandpa and pops. I could take notes and craft an outline."

"No." Sydney sighed and shoved her hands into her jeans pockets. "You're underage and I don't write children's stories. I wouldn't be helpful."

"What if I get my mom or dad's permission?" Sean stood in front of her. "Would you do it then? I'm sure Grandpa and Pops would tell them to say yes."

Sydney gritted her teeth. "It's up to the publisher. They have their contracts, not me."

"Okay, so I'll contact them. You can put in a good word and I'll get permission."

"I'm agreeing to nothing," Sydney said with a shake of her head and walked off. When she got downstairs, she found Emerson and Laura laughing hysterically. "You two are having fun."

Emerson flashed her a dark look. "Yeah. But it's time to go. I didn't realise we've been here for four hours. It'll be dark soon and I gotta get us over the bridge safely." She noticed Sean standing behind Sydney, a huge grin on his face. "So, guess we'd better hit the road."

"Already," Laura complained, reaching for her glass. She knocked it over and burst into laughter. "More champagne."

Emerson shook her head. "Yeah. Positive."

Sydney looked over her shoulder and saw the disappointment on Sean's face. "That must suck."

He nodded silently and watched his mother knock over the bowl of fruit and go diving for pieces as they rolled over the floor.

"So, Em…" Sydney looked her friend's way. "You fit to drive?"

"Absolutely. I'll drop you off and head on home."

They gathered their coats and watched Laura stumble over to them.

"Had a great time, Em. Good to see you again." She grabbed her into a big bear hug. "We need to do this again."

Emerson glowered over Laura's shoulder at Sydney. "Ah, sure, Loz. But right now, we gotta go. Good to see you again." She detached herself and spun around to find Sean had opened the front door. "Sorry to be leaving you with that."

"Not your fault," he said grimly. "Nice meeting you both. Ms Kingston." He nodded at Sydney and closed the door behind them.

They got in the car and backed out of the drive, waiting until they were some distance away before speaking at the same time.

"You okay to drive?"

"Where the hell were you?"

They burst out laughing and Emerson pulled over to the side of the street.

"How much did you drink?" Sydney asked.

"Barely a glass. She kept filling it and I sipped. Made sure to eat a lot so I don't feel like dinner. And where the hell did you get to? Toilet, my ass."

"I went in search of Sean to see if he was okay. Told him his mother had mentioned his writing to you and he showed me some."

"Any good?" Emerson hit the indicator and drove off.

"Very." Sydney swiped a hand over her face to get a stray hair out of the way and leaned back against the seat, resting her head. "Very bloody good. I recommended taking classes in college or getting a mentor and he asked me."

"What!" Emerson glanced at her in surprise before turning the corner. "I hope you turned him down. He's underage."

"I explained that to him, but he's seen the publisher's website. I told him to get permission and email the publisher."

"Was he the eager puppy he was when he answered the door?" She laughed.

"He was. Full of youthful exuberance."

Emerson turned on the radio as it hit six o'clock.

"In this news bulletin, there's a stalker in New York taking women's panties off their clotheslines."

"What else is new," Emerson muttered, and steered her way over the bridge. "There's always a stalker in New York. But seriously, don't use the word panties on the radio. Blech!"

"There's been a rash of prostitute killings on the Lower East Side. Police are warning all sex workers to stay away, but fear many won't listen."

"That's because they all believe they can make it big in The Big Apple and when they don't, they're too proud and vain to admit it and leave to make a better life for themselves elsewhere. That old adage about New York, if you can make it there you can make it anywhere just ain't true. It's absolute bullshit!" Emerson turned into Sydney's street and pulled to a stop outside the brownstone. "Home sweet home. I'll wait until you're safely inside and have checked the house out. It's all deadbolted, right?"

"It is." Sydney slid out of the car. "Thanks for the lift."

"I got my phone out; call me," Emerson yelled and locked the car doors. She watched Sydney hurry up the stairs and unlock the front door before going inside. Then saw the front and hall lights come on, and then the lights in the living room and upstairs. Every floor lit up, and she saw Sydney wave from the front window. Her phone went off. "Yeah?"

"Alarm hasn't sounded, system said all is shut and locked up tight."

"Great. Now get yourself a guard dog or a hot guard man and then I'll feel safer."

Sydney laughed. "Just make sure you get home safe as well. You have to park a car."

"But I have private underground parking with security guards."

"Doesn't mean they're not stalkers and rapists."

"Thanks for the nightmares," Emerson said dryly.

"Night, Em, sweet dreams."

"Fuck you. Night, Syd."

Chapter 3

During the week, Sydney got out and about doing other work. She secretly signed some of her books in stores, recorded a few audio snippets for CDs and did a photo shoot for updated headshots, plus one for her new home where she sat behind her desk and pretended to write. She lounged on her oversized sofa watching TV, pretended to choose an outfit for her next party in the walk-in closet, and pretended to make a hearty meal. So much pretending, so little time.

The photos would be in some future edition of a home magazine.

On Thursday, Sydney met up with CC, Olivia, and Gemma in CC's office.

"We've seen the photo shoot of your home. It's divine." CC handed her a glass of chilled water and gracefully sat on her Chanel covered couch. "When's the house warming party?"

"There isn't going to be one." Sydney took a sip of her drink and placed the glass on the coffee table between them.

"What do you mean there won't be a house warming

party?" Olivia demanded. "It's a must."

"Not with stalkers stalking around it isn't." Sydney shook her head and crossed her legs. "Besides, I'm not into house warmings. It's not a thing for me."

"Don't you Aussies have house warming parties?" Gemma asked.

"We do. I just don't like great gads of people in my personal space." Sydney took a slow breath. "More so after L.A."

The silence in the room was only interrupted by the ticking of the wall clock, so Sydney went on. "No house warming, not interested. The head shots looked great."

"They did," Olivia agreed. "We'll be using them on our promotional items and the website. You can too. We thought since you're here in New York now we'd go for a different vibe."

"And vibe they did. But as for books, I need to tell you I scrapped the last book I was working on." Sydney shook her head. "I went over it last Saturday, and while it's a sound outline and story, I just have no excitement for it anymore. The well has run dry on it."

"Then what are you presenting to us?" CC asked, her glass paused in mid-air.

"Nothing at the moment, as per my contract. You know there's no time frame built in, CC."

"Oh, darling, I know, but—"

"No buts," Sydney said, watching her face crumple. "I'm currently out of ideas and need a mental break for stimulation and fresh ideas. The last book only came out a couple of months ago. I have time and need it badly. One idea is to use the history of my brownstone as the basis of a book, but nothing's happened past a general first idea."

"That would be an exciting book," Gemma said. "Murder, sex, intrigue, money, cops, prostitution. You said you wanted to write a psych thriller."

"I think that would be more of a general crime thriller, but still. I want to get out and about in the city and find new ideas for inspiration. They need to be different and unique things I haven't seen before." Sydney shrugged. "Got any ideas?"

"The Amityville house," Olivia offered. "You know the story, but maybe the house itself could give you a couple of ideas."

Sydney made a small noise while thinking. "Yeah, but I'm not writing horror or demon possession."

"We have abandoned asylums and hospitals," Gemma said.

"Still horror," Sydney replied. "Look, I don't know what I'm going to write next, but I hope it will strike like lightning and I'll speed through it till the end. Considering I've got fifteen unfinished manuscripts in the cupboard..."

"Is that all?" CC remarked dryly, and topped up her glass. "While we're speaking about writing, a young man has applied to have you as a mentor. He made the application on Sunday and says he has his parents' reluctant permission, but that his grandfather and pops, both police commissioners of New York, encouraged him to apply if teens were allowed."

A deflated sigh left Sydney. "I told him I wouldn't. That he'd have to apply."

"Who?" Olivia asked and adjusted her green blouse before changing positions in her chair.

"Sean Ryan, the Police Commissioner's grandson. His mother was Em's college roommate, and Sean said he harassed her into inviting us over so he could show me some of his writing. We were there last Saturday. I haven't heard anything since."

"Those sons of his are hot!" Gemma declared. "Have you seen them? Tall, dark, and bloody gorgeous. Shame two are married."

CC flashed her a smile. "Back to the conversation. We've gone over his application, and judging by the sample he sent in, he's already very good."

"That's why I suggested taking writing in college, or getting a mentor." Sydney threw her head back and sighed. "How was I to know he'd want me to be his mentor? He's already so good. I have no idea how I could help."

"We could refuse." CC tapped a fingertip to her chin and stared off into the distance. "But we have accepted teens before because we made the age limit sixteen."

"Why the bloody hell did you do that?" Sydney asked.

"Because we have middle-grade and young adult authors. They suggested being able to mentor up-and-coming writers."

"When I told him I don't write sci-fi or kids, he suggested writing adult so I could be his mentor. The kid seemed desperate and that's a turn off. I don't want to be accused of inappropriate behaviour with a minor. Or anyone else for that matter. Which is why I don't mention it. In fact..." She leaned forward and said pointedly at CC.

"Take my photo of the mentor page because I don't want to do it."

"I suppose we could," CC mused and noted the dark circles under her client's eyes. "Are you getting enough sleep, darling? You look tired."

"Yeah, thanks for that," Sydney quipped and stood up. She was tired and ready to leave.

"One thing before you go," Olivia added. "As your agent, I am pressing on you again to get a bodyguard, or at least a security service that can check your house all day or sit out front at night."

"And what good would they do if someone sneaked in the back way?" Sydney argued. "I don't need a bodyguard at this point. You've received one letter and that's it." She picked up her bag and slung it over her shoulder. "That's it. End of discussion. CC, Gemma, I'll see you whenever. Olivia, I'll see you when you have another gig for me." She headed for the door.

"But darling—" CC started.

Sydney cut her off with a wave over her shoulder. "No, CC." She opened the door and left.

Arriving home after a spot of shopping, Sydney paid the cab driver and ascended her stoop stairs. Laden with bags, she spied the white square gift box on the doorstep and set down her shopping with a nervous glance around. After quickly digging in her bag for her key, she unlocked the vestibule door and carried her bags in. "Amy," she yelled, and locked the door. "Amy." She unlocked the house door and set her bags inside the living room parlour facing the street. "Amy."

"Yeah." Amy ran down the stairs. "I was working on

your website. What?"

"There's a gift box on the doorstep. Did we have a delivery?" Sydney slipped off her coat and peered out the window facing the door. "Did you hear anyone? Did anyone knock or ring the bell?"

"No." Amy shook her head and stood beside her, looking at the stoop. "Where is it?"

"On the doorstep."

"Then why are we standing here?" Amy said, exasperated. "Why didn't you bring it in?"

"Because I don't know what it is." Sydney watched Amy open the doors and stare down at the box. No wrapping paper, just a plain white box. The only decoration was a wide white ribbon tied in a bow. "Don't touch it," she cried when Amy reached down. "That could be anything."

Amy rolled her eyes and straightened. "Seriously?"

"We've had no delivery people and you didn't hear the bell. That means no one rang the bell, so it can't be a legitimate delivery," Sydney said. "It could be a bomb."

Amy glanced at it and stepped back, closing the door. "Only one way to find out." She grabbed an umbrella from the stand, opened the door, and thrust the pointy end towards the box, pushing it away from the door. It slid a few feet and left a red, bloody trail.

"What the hell is that?" Sydney screwed her face up and covered her mouth.

Amy walked over to it, crouched down and pulled the ribbon undone. She flipped the lid off and stumbled back.

"What…what?" Sydney demanded. "What is it?"

Ashen faced, Amy turned and ushered her inside.

"It's time to call the cops." She hurried for her phone and quickly made the call, finding Sydney still in the same position she'd left her in, against the wall of the vestibule. "They're on their way. They thought it was a joke at first, but when I mentioned the blood, they said they'd send someone."

Sydney inhaled a shaky breath. "How long?"

"Don't know." Amy looked at her boss. "Could this be to do with the letter CC had?"

"Don't know." Sydney gave a slight shake of her head. "I don't know. Or it could be something else. Previous tenant or owner thing."

"If that's the case, they clearly don't know she's left and the house was bought and sold."

"Maybe," Sydney mumbled, and saw the cops pull up. She let out a sigh of relief. "That was quick."

Amy opened the door and greeted them as they came up the stairs, pointing to the box. They examined it and asked questions. She answered them before turning and pointing to Sydney.

Sydney took a breath and stepped outside. "Hello."

"Ma'am." The male officer, a young Latino about five ten with short black hair, nodded. "Can you tell us what happened?"

Sydney gave a sharp nod and said, "I came home a while ago and found this box on the doorstep." She looked down at the bloody streak before her. "I let myself in and yelled out to my assistant, dropped my bags in the front room, and told her when she came downstairs." She drew a shaky breath and stepped back. "What is it?"

The officer exchanged a glance with his blonde female

partner. "It's a dead rat."

Sydney's brows slowly furrowed, her gaze darting back and forth between the officers and Amy. "What? A dead rat? Who the hell would leave me a dead rat? Why would they leave me a dead rat? Who the fuck does that to people?" She threw up her hands in exasperation. "I know this is New York, but Jesus fucking Christ, a dead fucking rat." She stared at all three of them. "You can't be fucking serious?"

"Unfortunately, we are," the officer said. "We'll file a report and take that with us." He pointed at the box. "We'll just get some gloves and a bag." They hurried down the stairs, and stopped at their car to call headquarters.

Amy moved next to Sydney. "Has this something to do with L.A.?" She kept her voice low and glanced at the police.

"I doubt it. That was all over before we left, and I doubt there's anyone to carry on that crusade."

"Do you know who that is?" the blonde officer, Victoria Velensky, whispered to her partner as she pulled on gloves.

"No, who?" Vasquez asked, pulling gloves from his pocket.

"Author Cassandra Kingsley. I've read all of her books, but it's just a pen name. That's why the name on the house threw me. Her real name's Sydney Kingston." She shook out a large evidence bag and hoped it was big enough for the box.

"Ah. I wasn't sure if she was familiar or not. Think she'll take some photos with us?"

"Seriously," Victoria hissed. "It's not exactly the time and place."

A black muscle car came screeching to a halt beside the cruiser and a tall, good looking man in dark blue jeans, a white t-shirt, a worn, dark brown leather jacket, and matching leather boots stepped out. His dark hair was swept back off his face, but a wavy lock fell forward, adding a boyish charm. He removed his mirrored aviator sunglasses and loped up the stairs.

"Who the fuck is that?" Amy muttered, mesmerised by the man.

"Hot Ryan number two," Sydney replied, her voice low as he stopped before her. "And you are?"

He pulled out his badge. "Detective Ryan. I was in the area and heard the call, recognised the address, and thought I'd come on over and have a look at the old girl." He eyed Sydney up and down. "I checked the name of the owner and recognised it." He put his badge away and rested his hands on his hips.

"How's that?" Sydney stared at him, unable to move from his electrifying good looks and the way his sapphire blue gaze roamed her body from head to toe.

Ryan grinned. "You're the author my nephew Sean wants to mentor him. Your friend is Laura's friend or some such. We heard all about it at Sunday lunch." His gaze turned to Amy. "And you are?"

"Amy Aldridge, Sydney's assistant. I was home but didn't hear anything. I was working upstairs in the office. The bell didn't ring, and there were no knocks."

Ryan gazed at the package, the trail of blood, the spot where the box had sat before Amy moved it, and watched the officers bag it up. "Got security?" He looked at them and they both pointed up simultaneously. His gaze travelled up and saw a small security camera either side of the door. He nodded. "Good. We're going to need that footage."

Amy went inside to make a copy, but Sydney stayed where she was.

"So…" Ryan chewed his gum. "You're gonna mentor my nephew in writing, huh?"

"I never said that." Sydney shook her head. "I told him to apply to the website and get his parents' permission. He'll be mentored by an author who writes in his genre."

"Yeah, well, they weren't too happy about that." Ryan chuckled. "The old man and Gramps convinced them to say yes because they've read your books and think this will be a good experience for him. From what my niece says, his writing is crap, so good luck with that."

"Have any of you read what he's written?" Sydney was fast becoming annoyed. As an author, she'd received stupid insulting comments about being a female author, and the genres of her books, so felt a little defensive on behalf of other writers.

Ryan cocked his head and huffed. "Why would I? He's a kid and Sierra says his writing is crap."

"So's your attitude," Sydney snarked, glaring at him. She was about to say more to his cocked lip when Amy appeared beside her.

"Detective. A copy of the footage. It shows a man in black. You can't see his face." She handed over the disc and noticed the cool vibe between them. "Did I interrupt something?"

"Yes," Sydney told her. "Detective Ryan being an insulting

dickhead about his nephew."

He stepped towards her and lowered his head until their eyes were even. The electricity crackled between them. "You'd better watch your mouth this Sunday; language like that isn't welcome in the Ryan household."

Confusion rained down over Sydney. "What *are* you talking about?"

"Laura was told to invite you and her friend to lunch." He straightened and watched the confusion. "Guess your friend hasn't told you."

"Or your drunk of a sister-in-law didn't call her," Sydney retorted. "Fine performance she put on last Saturday."

Ryan shoved his finger in her face and roared, "Don't you dare use that language against my family."

Sydney slapped his hand away. "And don't you fucking dare come to my place and fucking threaten me for pointing out the truth, you pathetic shit fucker. Get the fuck off my property." She looked past him to the two stunned officers. "Get this arsehole out of here before my lawyer files a complaint with the city." She looked coldly at the detective. "*And* the Police Commissioner."

At the mention of his father, Ryan backed away and had a complete change of attitude. "No need, see you at Sunday lunch." He pointed his forefinger at her, his thumb straight up, his other fingers curled, and clucked his tongue and winked before loping back down the stairs and screeching off in his car.

The officers glanced at each other in shock, then at the scowl on Sydney's face and followed suit.

Sydney and Amy watched them go, looked at each other, and walked inside. "Fucking arsehole," Sydney spat. "Who the fuck does he think he is?"

"The hot as fuck second son of the Police Commissioner," Amy quipped, and went for a bucket of water and a scrubbing brush. "Wish I was going to lunch on Sunday."

Sydney called Emerson.

"First thing I've heard about it," she said. "I've heard nothing. And his attitude sucked."

"Do we worry about it or not?" Sydney watched Amy give the porch a quick scrub.

"Since we didn't know about it, no need to worry about it. We haven't been formerly invited and she hasn't contacted us. So don't worry and get on with your life."

Sydney watched Amy swish the water across the stoop. "I wish I could."

*****

Sydney spent all day Friday trying to come up with new ideas for books. She scoured the internet, flipped through her idea thesaurus, picked up a random book, flipped to a page, and stabbed her finger at it hoping to find something that gripped her. But there was nothing. No ideas. No inspiration. Zip, zilch, nada.

She watched TV all night hoping the movies and TV shows would do the trick, but fell asleep on the couch instead.

Chapter 4

On Saturday morning, Sydney met up with Emerson for brunch and then an afternoon of shopping. "Heard anything yet?"

"Nothing." Emerson sipped her chai latte iced coffee. "The gall of the woman!"

"Well, she did only call you up because Sean saw you were in town with me and hounded her to. She probably wouldn't've otherwise." Sydney shrugged. "And she's a drunk. If she's like that all the time, it's no wonder she forgot."

"Tell me again how hot Ryan number two reacted to you saying that?" Emerson chuckled. "And tell me again how hot he is."

"Oh, for God's sake." Sydney rolled her eyes and stabbed at a piece of five cheese ham, bacon, tomato and olive omelette with her fork. "Fucking hot," she muttered before shoving her food into her mouth.

"And if we *do* actually get invited to lunch on Sunday, I'll get to see for myself." Emerson moved her fried halibut tossed salad around, but didn't take a bite. "You know, she hardly drank at college. We went to a party once a month, and got drunk sometimes. It certainly wasn't a thing." She let go of her fork, leaned back, and tucked a stray strand of hair behind her ear. "She was never like that and you certainly can't be like that as a doctor."

"Some have been, though." Sydney studied her friend as she sipped her juice. "Maybe it's just been since her sabbatical. The stress of being five years past fifty already, just five years away from sixty, plus whatever else is going on in her life. Maybe her home life ain't that great."

Emerson's brows rose in thought. "Maybe you're right. It can't be easy being married to a cop. Both would've had long hours, long nights. Maybe the marriage is falling apart and it's all exacerbated the casual drinking into heavy drinking."

"Did she say anything the other day? Drunk people sometimes can't keep their mouths shut."

Emerson picked up her latte, the straw stopping at her lips. "You know, she kind of did. It wasn't a full on confession or anything, just the usual whinging of a husband not coming home, and when he does, he reeks of alcohol or perfume." Her eyes widened. "Fucking hell! Do you think he's having an affair?"

"Well, if it ain't her perfume he's reeking of, then maybe." Sydney scraped up the last of her omelette and savoured the flavours. Setting her cutlery on her plate, she wiped her mouth and hands with her napkin, and washed her food down with her orange juice. "It's not our business, though. So, what if we do get invited to lunch? It's going to be awkward."

Emerson shrugged. "We still haven't been, and you're

right, it's not our business." She finished off her latte and ordered another, eating the rest of her salad while she waited. The moment the waiter placed her drink on the table, her phone rang. She looked at the number. "Ah, it's her. Took her long enough to remember. Hello, Laura."

"Em, how are you?"

"Good. Just finishing off brunch." She cocked an eyebrow at Sydney.

"Great. Well, I completely forgot to pass along a message. I've been busy all week and only just remembered that my father-in-law's invited you and your friend Sydney to his house for Sunday lunch. He mentioned it last week, but I completely blanked."

"Lunch tomorrow? Well, I don't know. I'll have to check my schedule and call Syd to see if she's free. Can I call you back?"

"Ah," Laura mumbled. "You know you can't turn down the Police Commissioner, Emerson. You do as he says."

"How high when he says jump kinda thing?" Emerson muttered. "I don't care who he is, I need to call Syd to see if she's free and check my own schedule, especially considering how last minute you're informing me. I'll call you back." She ended the call and relayed the message. "The cheek of the bitch."

"She's probably been drunk all week," Sydney huffed. "Imagine dictating that we turn up to the PC's home for lunch. Fuck off!"

Emerson checked her calendar on her phone. "Well, I'm free. How about you?"

"Of course I am, it's Sunday." Sydney chuckled.

Emerson's phone rang. "It's Laura. Nope. Don't

care." She declined the call.

"Not going to answer at all?"

"I am, but I need time to call you to see if you're free, and time to check my own schedule." Emerson patted her mouth with her napkin and called for the bill.

"How long are you making her wait?" Sydney slid her chair under the table and flexed her back.

"Oh, an hour or so." Emerson's phone beeped. "Now she's sending me texts. Banal bitch."

They laughed and left the restaurant, shopping for an hour until Emerson finally called her back.

"Laura, Emerson. I don't appreciate the language in the text messages, nor the rate at which you sent them. I had to call Sydney and find out if she was free. I also had to take other calls." Pause. "No, don't take that tone of voice with me or you can fuck right off." She listened. "Look, Laura. You don't get to dictate. The only reason we're agreeing to lunch is that it might be highly amusing. What's that?" She looked at Sydney. "We need to make lunch?" Pause. "The person who's invited has to make it." Pause. "What do you mean it had better be good? Listen, Laura…" Eye roll. "Fine. Text me the address." Pause. "What do you mean why do I need the address? So, I can bloody drive us there, you idiot."

Sydney rolled her eyes and shook her head. "Fucking Christ what a dickwad."

"Fine, we'll see you tomorrow." Emerson hung up and quickly texted her assistant. "She's sending through the address, but I don't think we got the whole truth. I have a feeling she might be setting us up, you especially." A text came through. "She sent the address."

"Why would she be setting us, or me, up?" Sydney watched her face as she read the next text.

"Mmm, different number," Emerson muttered, and finally looked up. "I just texted my associate here in New York, or one of them, anyway. He knows the mayor and the PC; powerful people, and asked for the address and phone number. He asked why." She sent a quick text back. "I just told him because his daughter-in-law invited us to lunch and I think she gave us the wrong address and I wanted the right one. I think we should call and confirm with the heads of the family, don't you, so we don't make fools of ourselves." She quickly tapped in the number and turned away from the crowded street. "Hello, Commissioner? My name's Emerson Lake. I'm Laura's friend."

"Oh, yes, hello, Emerson," Douglas Ryan said. "We've been talking about your friend Sydney Kingston all week. Sean's very excited to be mentored by her."

"Well, that's fantastic. Laura's finally gotten around to inviting us an hour ago, and I thought I'd confirm with you that Sydney and I can make it for lunch tomorrow. I also wanted to confirm any other details there are, such as if we need to bring food or wine."

"The guests always bring or make lunch," Douglas told her. "It's a tradition."

"Fantastic. Anything anyone's allergic to, or doesn't eat?"

He chuckled. "We're an Irish American family, anything goes."

"Sydney's here with me now. How many people do we need to cook for?"

"At least fifteen people."

Emerson asked Sydney what she'd make and got beef ball hotpot in return. "Sydney's going to make a beef ball hotpot. I've had it, and it's amazing and will definitely feed a large family. Does everyone eat beef?"

"We all do and it sounds delicious."

"Great. We need at least two massive soup pots."

"Got those and we'll grill the bread to go with it."

"Dessert?"

"Pies and cakes are fine. Pumpkin, walnut, key lime. Anything."

"Ooohhh, I do love a good key lime pie." Emerson's mouth watered. "We'll bring four different pies. Wine?"

"We've got plenty."

"Being Irish I bet you do. What time is best to arrive and start cooking?"

"I was thinking eleven. That way Cormac and I can chat to Sydney about her books before the family turns up. We have a feeling Sean might dominate the conversation once he gets here."

"Okay then." Emerson gave Sydney the thumbs up. "Four pies, beef hotpot for fifteen at least. And can you text me your address please, so I get it absolutely right."

"Of course. We look forward to seeing you tomorrow, Emerson, and tell Sydney the same thing."

"Thank you, I will. Goodbye." Emerson closed down the call and sighed. "I think I was right."

"About?" Sydney leaned against the building next to her friend.

Emerson's phone beeped and she looked at the address. She checked it against Laura's text. "I was right. Laura gave us a different address and didn't even mention a time."

"Why would *she* do that?" Sydney mused. "But also, why only call today?" A thought hit her. "Maybe hot Ryan number two has seen her since Thursday and she remembered."

"Why would she see him?"

"They're related."

"Yeah, but…" Emerson trailed off, but then her eyes widened. "Affair?"

Sydney's brows shot up. "I wasn't even thinking that. I was thinking she was jealous. Of what, I don't know."

"Sean's attention for you? Her father-in-law's attention for you? She's left work and become a drunk. If she's having an affair with number two, then that's not something she'd want to broadcast, and *if* she saw him since he met you and found out he blabbed about lunch, that's four Ryans giving *you* attention." She poked her best friend in the chest and chuckled. "I wonder how drunk she'll get tomorrow when Ryans one, three, and four meet you and number three's her husband and if *he's* having an affair…" She paused a moment and her eyes glazed over. "Fucking hell!"

"What?" Sydney quickly glanced around. "What's wrong?"

Emerson tapped her temple; something she did when an idea was forming. "If the husband's having an affair, and she's fucking his brother, and he raved about you along with her son and father-in-law, she could get plenty pissed. The mad *and* drunk varieties. God knows what could come out. You'd better be prepared for a barrage, *and* she thinks she's tricked us with the wrong address. But we'll get there before her. Fuuuuck. Her life must be falling down around her ears, but getting drunk won't help."

Sydney sighed. "Would you have contacted her at all? Did you think about it when you chose to move here with me. Would you have called her?"

Emerson leaned against the wall of the building they were in front of and crossed her arms. "Fuck no. We knew each other for four years, and went our separate ways. After what she said about your books, she's definitely got issues."

"With them, with me, with you?"

"With them, no doubt, but for some reason she's foisting it onto you."

Sydney scratched her head then patted her hair back in place. "Well then, tomorrow's gonna be a riot. Guess we'll have to stop off at the supermarket before going home tonight. I don't have the ingredients at home."

Emerson linked her arm through Sydney's and they headed down the street. "We can do that. But first, we shop for ourselves. Know a good place to get pies?"

"Don't you have an assistant for that?"

"Oh, yeah, I do." She quickly sent a text to her assistant with the suburb of the PC's house, and asked if he knew of any good pie shops in that area.

He texted two names back and said they had the best in New York.

She put in a call to the closest and ordered four pies to be picked up in the morning. By the time the call was done, they had arrived at Fifth Avenue.

Chapter 5

On Sunday morning at ten, Emerson picked up Sydney and her bags of food, and drove off for the bakery in Brooklyn. "So, are you excited, or what? We're having lunch with the NYPD Police Commissioner and his family of hot law enforcement sons."

Sydney grinned and rubbed her lips together. "First time for everything, and it is a bit weird. Considering all the rich and famous people you've met and the few and far between I've met, I don't even come close to meeting the stars at your level. But…he's just the PC and his sons are cops and lawyers. It's not going to be a big deal. Is it?"

"It very possibly could be." Emerson pulled to a stop outside the bakery and turned off the engine. "Would any of this have happened if not for Sean harassing Laura to call me? No, I highly doubt it. Have you ever seen the PC and his father at a book signing?" She tucked her hair behind her ear and pulled her purse out of the centre console.

"No, I don't believe so. Not that I knew what they looked like until I googled them the other day. So that tells me they're not mega fans, the type to stand in line and wait for an autograph." Sydney opened the door and stepped out, shivering at the cool breeze. "My beef ball hotpot will be just the thing for a chilly autumn day."

"You mean fall, sweetie." Emerson slid her hand through the crook of her arm and escorted her into the bakery.

"I mean autumn, sweetie," Sydney replied tartly.

Ten minutes later, they came out with four fresh pies and carefully placed them on the back seat. With the GPS directing them, they pulled into the opening of the driveway of the PC's home at five to eleven.

Two men approached, wearing dark suits and trench coats, and listening devices in their ears. One stopped beside the driver's door, the other at the passenger door. Emerson and Sydney rolled down their windows.

"Ma'am, we need to see some ID," the man at Emerson's window said.

"Of course." Emerson opened her purse and pulled out her driver's licence.

"You too, ma'am," the man beside Sydney said.

She jumped a little. "Ah, sure." After rummaging around in her bag, she flashed her licence and both men nodded.

"Move on, ma'am," the one on the driver's side said. "You're expected."

"Thank you." Emerson rolled up her window and slowly moved up the rest of the driveway, coming to park at the closed door garage. "And we're here."

They unbuckled and opened their doors as Douglas and Cormac Ryan came out of the kitchen door to greet them.

"Cassandra Kingsley in the flesh." Douglas strode up to Sydney as she opened the back door. "Or do you prefer Sydney?" At ninety-two, he was fit as a fiddle with thick grey hair, bright sapphire eyes, and a police commissioner stance. He shook her hand vigorously.

"Sydney's my real name, and I'm not in author mode now." She extracted her hand from his. "Commissioner." She nodded at him before looking at Cormac. "Commissioner Ryan."

"Please, call me Cormac." He shook her hand and then Emerson's. "Ms Lake. Big fan of your crime thriller series, *Twisted Minds*."

"Thank you, Commissioner, ah, Cormac. It was a big hit for me and with a lot of the police forces around the country." She took in his six-four broad-shouldered stance. The brown hair and blue eyes were definitely passed down, and he was still fit and healthy for seventy.

"Well, it was certainly a big hit in this family," Douglas told her and then looked at Sydney. "Is there anything we can help you bring in?"

Sydney reached into the car and produced two pie boxes as Emerson said, "You can carry the pies. We bought four and hope it's enough."

Douglas took the boxes from Sydney. "As long as we cut them up right, we should be able to have two pieces each."

Sydney pulled out the other two pies and handed them to Cormac. "And there's those two and we'll grab the cooler bags." She handed one to Emerson and took the other, shut the door, got her bag from the front seat, and followed Cormac and Douglas into the house with

Emerson behind her.

They entered the old-style, but appliance updated kitchen, to the scent of freshly heated bread. "Smells good already." She placed the bag on a bench beside the oven and saw two huge soup pots ready to go.

"I wasn't sure what else you would need." Douglas turned from the pie box where he'd placed the pumpkin and walnut pies to keep warm.

"The soup pots are fine. The hotpot is only three ingredients and I have all of them." Sydney shucked her coat. "Do you mind if we freshen up before you start with your barrage of authorly questions?"

Cormac reached for their coats. "Of course not. Just down the hall on your left." He pointed behind him. "I'll hang these on the coat rack in the hall."

"Thank you." Sydney and Emerson hurried to the bathroom, freshened up, applied a layer of lip gloss, and fixed their hair.

"Planning to impress?" Emerson pointed to Sydney's turquoise blue knitted top with rhinestones around the neck and sleeve cuffs.

"Aren't you?" Sydney nodded at Emerson's low cut red blouse and wild mane of black curls held back with gold combs. She grinned. "Let's go."

They found their way back to the kitchen where Cormac and Douglas presented them with glasses of wine.

"Oh, sorry, I don't drink," Sydney quickly said. "Should I have mentioned that earlier?"

"Not a problem," Douglas said. "I'll have this one myself. Is there anything else you'd like now?"

"Not right now, thank you." Sydney noticed the tins of soups on the counter. "You emptied the bags?"

"I put the beef balls and the vegetables in the fridge. Unless you want to start cooking now. Are they not supposed to be in the fridge?" Douglas asked.

"No, that's fine. They weren't quite defrosted, so it didn't matter," Sydney replied. "It will only take half an hour or so to cook. Lunch was at one?"

"Yes, so, no need to start cooking just yet. Please, let's sit in the sun room." Cormac gestured to the room next to the kitchen and they stepped into a masculine styled room with an amazing view of the river and city of New York.

"Wow." Sydney moved over to the French doors. "Amazing."

"It is at night when the city lights up." Cormac stood beside her. "Makes you realise just how small you are."

"And just how big a city is to police," Sydney returned, looking at him. "That must be an overwhelming job?"

He signed deep from his gut. "It is. It can be. It always will be."

She noticed the greying hair at his temples, and a few in his moustache. Lines crinkled at the corners of his eyes, and a heavy burden showed on his still attractive face. His hair was left free to roam and a wavy lock fell over his forehead.

"I guess it takes a person made of strong stuff to do that job."

"It certainly does, but you're not here to talk about my job—"

"Oh, I don't know. It might give me inspiration for

my next novel," Sydney said.

Cormac gave a hearty laugh. "Is that so? Let's sit and talk then." He led her to one of two masculine, deep chocolate leather couches and sat in his matching easy chair.

"So, tell me. Before we get into your novels, about mentoring Sean. He's very excited."

"And I haven't said I will," Sydney replied. "I'm not comfortable doing so."

Cormac and Douglas exchanged puzzled frowns.

"And why's that?" Douglas asked. "Are you too good to mentor Sean?"

"I'm too *old* to mentor Sean, and *he's* too young." Sydney's gaze flicked back and forth between them. "He's already very good and doesn't need me, an author who writes in an adult genre. I don't feel comfortable mentoring a teenage boy. I don't want to be accused of inappropriate behaviour. I'd rather not take that risk. There are younger authors who do write in the same genre as him that he'd be better suited to."

"And that's a very mature thing to be up front about." Cormac nodded. "And as a cop, and Police Commissioner, a noble stance to make. What age do you mentor?"

"Twenty-one and over," Sydney replied. "And considering he's from a family of cops and lawyers, that just feels like a very heavy burden if something did go wrong, I'd have you all on my doorstep breathing down my neck."

"And what would go wrong?" Cormac asked, straight and to the point. His blue eyes bored into hers.

"An over-eager seventeen year old boy could potentially

believe that his crush was something more," Sydney shot back. "Hormones make teens and adults do stupid things. Is Sean mentally old enough to know the difference between a mentorship and a crush?"

The Ryans exchanged another glance. "Why?"

"He was very over-eager last week when we arrived at Laura's," Emerson said. "It was pretty clear he already had a bit of a crush."

Cormac gave a slight nod, and thought it through. "You said he was already very good."

"He is," Sydney said.

"So, you wouldn't need to do a lot of mentoring them. Just guide him through the process of becoming an author and getting published." Cormac watched her.

Sydney's eyes narrowed. "What are you getting at?"

"If he doesn't need a lot of mentoring, just some guidance, could you still do that in a controlled environment?" Cormac pushed. "Look…" His meaty fingers tapped the arm of his chair. "He was so eager for it and we," he waved a hand at his father, "pushed his parents into giving their permission because we've read your books and thought it would it be a great thing for Sean, to give him some direction for college, but," he glanced at his father, "it could be a chance for us to meet you as well and talk about your books and meet Emerson." He motioned to her. "Have two celebrities here for lunch."

"So, it was more for you than Sean." Emerson raised a brow. "How sneaky!"

Cormac have her his best grin and Douglas laughed. "I guess it is," Cormac agreed. "Will you give it some thought, Sydney?"

"Will you wait until you've seen Sean this afternoon to make sure I'm not picking up on the wrong signals? Because if you think his behaviour today is harmless, then I'll consider. And then I can blame *you* if it all goes arse over tit."

"Is that an Australian saying?" Douglas asked.

Sydney's head pulled back and she looked at Emerson. "British descent, but don't you say that here?"

"Some of us do; don't listen to him." Emerson waved him away with a flirtatious smile. "Silly."

"Oh." Sydney blushed and gave a small shrug. "Ten years in L.A. and I'm still getting used to the language."

"English?" Douglas asked.

"American," Sydney quipped and raised a brow. "Two completely different things."

Everyone laughed and they changed the subject to crime thrillers, Emerson's TV show, and Sydney's books. At twelve, they moved back into the kitchen to get lunch going.

"Do you need help?" Douglas asked, handing the bags of food to her.

"I need utensils and a bin for the rubbish." Sydney turned on the stove, ripped a bag of balls open, and poured them into one pot. "It won't take long to get ready." Three bags of balls went into each pot and she stirred them to coat them in oil, tapped the spoon on the pot, and laid it across the top. "They'll take about ten minutes, then I'll add the veggies and soup."

"No fresh vegetables or stock?" Douglas stood looking in the pots.

"The veggies are the freshest because they're snap

frozen, and the soup adds the flavour and a few extra veg. No need for watery stock." Sydney watched him write the ingredients down. "Three ingredients. Very quick, very easy."

"I'll have to add it to the meal rotation." Douglas nodded and slid the paper into his recipe file folder.

"I'm here, lunch ready?" was yelled from the front door.

"In here," Cormac called out, and told Sydney and Emerson, "My son, Connor."

"Ah, Ryan number two," Sydney said just as he walked into the kitchen. The electricity crackled and changed the air between them.

"Number two?" Douglas asked.

"There's so many of you we numbered your children." Emerson chuckled. "It's hard to keep up; you're such a large family."

"Hey, author chick's, here." Connor grabbed a beer from the fridge and cranked the lid.

"Ryan number two who shoved his fat finger in my face for no reason is here." Sydney raised a brow; a sly smile lifted the corner of her lips.

"You did what?" Cormac turned to his son.

Connor shrugged. "It was nothing," he told his old man and glared at Sydney. "Just some fun."

Sydney nodded. "Mmm, so was you turning up to my house because you recognised my name on the call and came for a nosy. Find the guy who did it yet?"

"Did what?" Cormac and Douglas asked at the same time.

"Left a dead rat on her doorstep," Connor said. "All wrapped up in a pretty white box with a pretty white bow."

"And then you brought up Sean talking about me at lunch last Sunday, and that we were invited this Sunday, except Laura hadn't called Emerson yet, and for some reason you shoved your finger in my face and told me to mind my language this Sunday."

"Yeah, and then you slapped my hand away. I could have you for assaulting a cop." Connor sneered.

"And I could have you for threatening a civilian for no reason. Bet that would go down really well with the Police Commissioner," Sydney slyly said and glanced at Cormac to find a thunderous expression on his face and Connor white as a sheet.

"You what?" Douglas's voice was low. "You had no right to threaten a victim of crime."

"Hardly a crime, Gramps," Connor said, recovering. "Someone left a dead rat on her doorstep. Couldn't even get face recognition off the surveillance footage. Besides, I wasn't threatening her." He shrugged. "Just told her she'd better watch her language."

"Shall I tell them what you *actually* said and threatened me over?" Sydney wasn't to be pushed around. PC's house or not.

Connor breathed deeply and glanced from person to person. "Nah. It was nothing. Has the game started yet?" He moved into the living room to get away from the glares.

Sydney turned back to the stove and gave the balls a stir. "Ready for the veggies." She ripped open the first one kilo bag of defrosted vegetables and then poured four bags into each pot.

"Would you care to tell me what my son said?"

Cormac stood beside her and pulled the tin of soup from her hand. He cracked the lid and handed it back.

Sydney shrugged and poured the soup in. "First he insulted Sean and his writing, then had a go at me for something I said about Laura." She took the second tin from him and emptied the contents into the pot.

He sighed. "And what about Laura?"

"Just that she must've forgotten to call Em about lunch because she was drunk." She emptied a third tin.

Another sigh from his gut. "We've noticed. We've been limiting the alcohol at lunch for a while." He opened a tin and handed it to her. "And he probably thought he was protecting her. But that's no excuse for bad behaviour. I taught my sons better. The academy taught them the law."

Sydney took a slow breath. "I'll let it go, but I won't tolerate harassment."

"And what about the rat?"

"Well, it's not going in the hotpot, if that's what you're thinking."

He gaped at her open mouthed and watched her shrug and pour another tin into the pot. "*Not* what I was thinking."

She gave a breathy chuckle. "Joke."

"Was it?"

"On my side or the perp's?"

"Both."

"I was joking. But as for why the perp did it, no idea. Maybe they had the wrong address, or it was for a previous owner."

"Possibly. Do you have any enemies?"

A freezing tendril snaked through Sydney's body as she thought about L.A. "Not anymore. And none here except maybe your son or daughter-in-law."

"Anymore?"

Another shrug. "Sometimes, singers, actors, authors, get crazies sending them weird stuff. I had some in L.A., but it was dealt with."

"How?"

"Quietly." Sydney dipped each soup can under the tap and poured a bit of water into each. She swished the cans around and tipped the liquid into the pot. "All it needs is a good mix and to simmer for about half an hour."

"Dad…Gramps…we're here."

"So are we."

"Is Sydney here?"

"Get off it. It's not about her."

Sydney turned from the stove. "Sounds like one, three and four are here."

"Along with Sean." Cormac raised his brows at her and they heard Sean before they saw him.

"Is Sydney here? I saw Emerson." He stumbled to a stop in the kitchen. "Oh, my God, you came, you came. We have Sydney Kingston in our house."

"Whose house?" Cormac gave him a clap on the arm in greeting.

"I know, I know, your home. But I can't believe she's here." He bounced in excitement, his blue eyes sparkling. "And now we can talk about my mentorship. I got my parents' permission and filled out the online application, so this can happen now."

"And I didn't say I'd do it." Sydney turned back to the stove and put the lids on the pots.

Sean's face fell. "But why not?"

"I told you why not. I don't write in the same genre, so I don't think I'll be of any real help. You'd be better off with someone who does." She saw multiple Ryans converge on the kitchen for beer.

"You must be Sydney Kingston. I'm Alec, the eldest." A tall, broad, good looking man with slicked back dark hair, shook her hand. "My kids are Brandon and Sierra, who are here."

"Hello, Ryan number one," Sydney said and then shook Ryan number four's hand.

"I'm Kieran, the youngest," he said. He was a spitting image of his older brother.

"Number four. How are you?"

"Number one and number four?" Alec asked and took a swig of beer.

"There's four of you, it's easier," Sydney told them and saw Ryan number three staring at her. "And you're Declan, Sean's dad. Also number three."

He sneered at her, said, "Cute," and walked off.

"Rude," Sydney returned, and wandered into the living room to find Emerson who was regaling them with details of her crime show.

Sean stood behind her and quietly said, "Sydney. Can we talk in private about it? I really want to do it."

Sydney glanced over her shoulder. "I told your grandfather I'd consider it after today."

He gave her a great beaming smile and hovered by her side.

"I'm here. Did I miss lunch?"

"Hey, Ethan, come and meet the author who's going to mentor Seany," Connor called and slung his arm around his son's shoulder.

"I hate being called that," Sean muttered under his breath, his face dark with hatred.

Connor pulled Ethan over to Sydney. "Sydney Kingston, my son, Ethan."

Sydney's brows rose. "Ah, Ryan number five. And what rank are you in this crime family?"

"That would be law enforcement family," Cormac reminded her as he passed by with glasses of wine.

"Sometimes it's the same thing," Sydney returned and shook Ethan's hand.

"Ah, detective, like my old man," Ethan said, eyeing her off. He was the same height as his father, and his swimmers build made him lean and fit, but he was yet to fill out to the extent of his father and uncles. His eyes were a blue green mix and his brownish red hair curled more than waved.

"Better watch what you say boys and girls, Sydney's looking for inspiration for her new novel," Douglas told them from his spot on the couch.

"Another sloppy romance of the average kind?" Laura asked, swigging back her beer.

"Do you remember what I said to you last Saturday in your house?" Sydney asked her.

Laura's eyes were already glazed from pre-loading on alcohol before she'd left home. "What? Ah…no, why?"

"Be glad you don't," Sydney said, and noticed Emerson hide a grin. "But I will remind you that my novels are not sloppy romances and most definitely not average."

"No, they're not." Cormac glared at his daughter-in-law. "I'm glad they're not romances. I'm also glad they're not full on crime thrillers. The level of crime is just enough for this seasoned veteran to guess whodunit, but then be shocked by the twist at the end. They're an enjoyable read at the end of a long day."

"And it's always nice to hear that I can surprise even a seasoned officer." Sydney gave him a nod. "I'm going to check on lunch." She hurried back into the kitchen with Sean hot on her tail.

"So, are you going to mentor me?" He stood beside her breathing in the aromas of the food. His stomach grumbled.

"You actually don't need a mentor, me or otherwise. You're already good." She stirred the food in the second pot. "What you need is guidance on how to get your material to publishable level and then apply for submissions. In fact, you could probably do that now, and if your English teacher can help you with your writing, all the better."

"But that's part of the mentorship with Pulsate Publishing. A possible contract at the end of it."

"That is true." Sydney placed the lids on the pots. "But we also have sci-fi and young adult authors who mentor, and they would be more appropriate, if not the best ones for you."

"But I don't want any other author to mentor me. I want you." He grabbed Sydney's arm, but she casually shook free. "I love your books, and Grandpa and Pops love your books. I want to write like you, and just because

I'm writing YA and sci-fi now, doesn't mean I will be in a couple of years, or once I turn twenty-one. I might want to spread my author wings and write in other genres. Write normal adult, instead of young adult."

Sydney's gaze darted over Sean's shoulder and landed on Cormac in the doorway. "Your grandfather mentioned it earlier, and I told him, if, by the end of the day he thought it was still a good idea, then I'd think about it. But I want you to think about someone else as a mentor." She glanced at the wall clock. "It's nearly lunchtime."

Cormac turned to the living room. "Kids, time to set the table. That includes you, Ethan."

"But I'm not a kid," he complained, his leg swinging over the arm of the easy chair he was lounging in.

"You are in this family," Cormac said and watched his four grandchildren pull out cutlery, napkins, placemats, and pot holders. He looked at Sydney who stood beside him, noted her raised brow, as if to say, see what I mean, and nodded at her.

The table was set in five minutes, the bread re-heated, and bowls of beef ball hotpot were ladled.

It was a mad house as everyone found their place at the extended table.

Cormac and Douglas sat at the heads of the table, and Sydney found herself three seats down from Cormac with Emerson and Laura on her right, and Sean, his dad, and uncle to her left. Everyone else was on the other side.

"Everyone have their plate, their food, their drink?" Cormac asked. There were a few yeses, and he reached out his hands. "Let's say grace, unless one of our guests wants to say it."

"Ah…" Sydney and Emerson exchanged amused glances.

"Did Laura not tell you?" Emerson said, glaring at her friend. "I'm Jewish."

"And I'm atheist," Sydney added.

"How can you not believe in God?" Douglas asked, astounded.

Sydney's head spun towards him. "Quite easily," she quipped.

"We have no problem with you guys doing your thing, we'll just sit here quietly while you do," Emerson said. "Nice and simple."

Cormac considered it and gave a nod. "That's fine. Everyone else." They held hands, he said grace, and fifteen seconds later they were eating.

"Oh, my God, this is so good," said Sandy McRae, Kieran's girlfriend, and a lawyer at the law office where he worked. "The flavour's so full. What is it?"

"Beef balls, frozen vegetables, and soup," Douglas told her. "The soup adds the flavour. I wouldn't be able to replicate this with stock, or herbs and spices."

"That's why I use it," Sydney said and dunked some of her toasted bread into it.

"The beef balls are amazing," Sean managed around a mouthful of food.

"Don't talk with your mouth full." Declan slapped his son up the back of the head, making Sean choke on his food.

Shocked, Sydney turned to Cormac. "Was that necessary?"

Cormac looked at her. "What?"

"A slap upside the head when you're being chastised. Being embarrassed and humiliated and abused in front of your guests." Sydney cocked her head. "Not the sort of lunch I thought I was coming to. A violent one."

Cormac, stunned by Sydney's forthright manner, put his spoon down and chose his words. "Declan, leave your anger issues at the front door. Hitting Sean was unnecessary, *and* we have guests."

Sean looked from Sydney to his grandfather. The rest of the table was quiet. And curious.

Declan just stared stonily at his father. "So."

"We have guests in the house and we don't bring physical violence to the table," Douglas said quietly.

Everyone else stared back and forth, waiting for the outcome.

Declan leaned back in his seat, picked up his beer and took a swig. "Yeah, yeah."

Douglas slammed his hand on the table. "No yeah, yeah. Apologise to your son."

Glaring at his grandfather, Declan put his bottle down, looked at his son, and rubbed the back of his head, but Sean pulled away. "Sorry, Seany. All better now." His tone patronising, he glanced at Sydney behind Sean's back. "All better now?"

Sydney's eyes narrowed. "Thank you *so much* for showing me what type of person you *really* are." She turned back to her meal. "So, who else has read my average sloppy romances, or seen Em's *Twisted Minds* TV show?"

The conversation went on and became boisterous as lunch was finished and the pies were served.

"I came home from shopping to find a mysterious white gift box wrapped in a white ribbon on the stoop.

When I asked Amy, my assistant, if she knew about it, she pushed it with an umbrella and we saw the blood trail. That's when she called the cops and this one," she waved her fork at Connor, "came screeching along in his muscle car."

"Of course, when I heard the address of the call out, I recognised it and went right over. The owner's name had also come up, so I thought I'd go and introduce myself," Connor regaled the family with his version of the story. He was opposite Sean at the table but pointed at Sydney with his beer bottle. "This one here's feisty and put me in my place."

"How'd she do that?" Sean asked, annoyed at the attention his uncle had been showing Sydney.

"Slapped my hand away and called me," he glanced at her, "what was it, a pathetic shit fucker. Whatever the hell that is."

"Exactly what it says," Sydney told him and raised a cocky brow. "That's what you were being. I calls 'em how I sees 'em."

"You certainly do," Connor replied. "And for the record, even though I haven't admitted it until now…" He looked around at his family before returning his gaze to Sydney. "I have actually read some of your books and they're pretty good."

Laura swigged back her wine, silently pissed off at the attention he was giving Sydney and how she was flirting right back. "How can you like them? They're sloppy romances."

"We all know how you feel about Sydney's books, Laura." Emerson looked at her old roommate. "You've mentioned it quite a few times today. But I'm actually beginning to wonder if you've read them at all because they're not romance novels. They've won multiple awards in the thriller and crime categories and could be considered comedies as a tertiary genre. I've also made five into movies. That's how Sydney and I became best friends." She watched Laura's expression sour before Laura thrust up and out of her chair.

"I need some air," she said, and stormed off through the sun room into the backyard.

"You tell 'em, Em," Connor said. "They're definitely not sloppy romances, otherwise I wouldn't've admitted to reading them."

Light laughter went around the table and they resumed eating their pie.

"Have we inspired you for a new novel yet?" Alec asked as he swiped up the last of his pie. "Although, New York is a highly inspirational town."

"It certainly is." Sydney pushed her plate away and picked up her glass. She'd gone for the lemon lime spritz they had for those who didn't drink.

"Especially your brownstone," Connor butted in. "I recalled that address from a long time ago."

Sydney laughed. "Yeah, yeah. She does have history and maybe it was that history that led to a rat on my doorstep."

"What's the history of the house?" Cormac asked, refilling his cup with coffee.

"Do you remember the Madam X case?" Connor asked everyone.

Cormac's eyes widened as he thought. "Josephine

Pompadour? Madam to the half of New York who serviced the other half of New York?"

"Yeah." Connor grinned. "That's the one."

"What's that got to do with it?" Cormac turned to Sydney for confirmation.

"I bought the brownstone," she told him, an amused half smile on her lips.

His thick set brows rose. "You bought Madam Josephine Pompadour's brownstone?"

"Technically, it wasn't hers," Sydney reminded him. "It had that colourful history before I bought it from the last owners. They got it cheap, renovated it, and rented it out. Little did they realise what Josephine Pompadour was or did. Once you lot raided the house and ripped it apart, it was sold off, the couple spent a lot of money renovating it and then rented it out, but a lot of people just came to look and gawp at it, and they finally had to sell it. Once I saw it, and read about the history, I grabbed it."

"I remember that story," Douglas said. "She had a sex room in the basement."

Sydney blushed and everyone turned to her. "What?" She hid behind her glass and took a sip of spritz.

"Is it still there?" Connor asked.

"Is what still there?" she asked innocently.

"The sex room in the basement." Connor's lips slid into a dirty grin. "Still got it?"

"Not that you'll ever see it," Sydney returned.

"There were also rumours of hidden money and jewels," Alec added. "I didn't get the case, but I know all about it."

Sydney noticed Alec's wife, Sonja, send a wide-eyed look his way and wondered why. She'd been silent for most of the meal, but Sydney had learnt she was an interior designer to the stars and bigwigs of New York.

"Maybe that's why the rat." Emerson pulled on her friend's sleeve. "Have you told CC yet? Here I am just finding out today."

Sydney shook her head. "She'll freak out, so why bother. We called the cops, it's now up to Bozo the Clown here," she pointed at Connor, "to actually find the guy and find out why."

"Who you calling Bozo the Clown, sloppy average romance author," he quipped.

"Oh, so it's like that, is it?" Sydney grinned. "Game on, pathetic shit fucker."

"Back to the brownstone," Kieran interrupted. "Was there anything left behind?"

Sydney shrugged and wondered why the Ryans were so interested in the details. "Don't know. Whatever you lot took, the owners removed, or her girls snagged as they left, who knows. But since I've been there, everything is deadbolted and triple locked. More so now."

"Tapped on any walls, or pulled up floorboards?" Sean asked. "It'd make a great story."

"Yeah." Sydney thought about it. "It would if it hadn't already been told multiple times."

"Yeah, but you'd make it into a novel, not a non-fiction book about a madam getting arrested," Sean added.

"By *this* family, mind you." Sydney raised her brows and grinned. "So, what secrets would *this* family have to hide about Madam Josephine Pompadour, aka, Madam X? You know what, that's actually a really good idea right there. Police Commissioner's family arrest mysterious Madam X, but what do *they* have to hide?" She noticed the scared expressions on several Ryan faces, including Sonja's, and her interest was piqued.

"That'd make a great movie," Emerson said. "Or a TV series. What do you say, Cormac?" She turned to him. "Wanna go on the record?"

He beamed at her and gently laid his hand over hers on the table. "What I say is, let's retire to the living room so the grandkids can do the dishes."

"Oh, man," Sean complained, pulling a face.

Sydney giggled at the expression. "Let's retire."

Once they'd settled into the living room, the conversations continued.

"So, Sydney, how'd you become an author?" Kieran asked, sipping his bourbon.

Sydney nodded at the question. "The way most authors become authors, I guess. Wrote stories in English class at school, was encouraged by my English teacher. Took some classes once I left and became a content and copy writer. While I was doing that, I started writing short stories, did some more classes, and showed my stories, and started a novel. I went into self-publishing and managed to make it big with my e-books. Then Pulsate Publishing came along and offered me a deal I couldn't refuse." She grinned. "It was for the print and foreign rights. I kept the rights for e-books and audio, and once that happened, everything skyrocketed and I now have ten novels and five novellas in electronic, print, foreign, and audio. I just have to find inspiration for the next fifteen."

"Start with your brownstone and the mysterious Madam X." Sean lumbered over and sat beside her, a little too close.

She waved him back. "Boundaries. You take up too much space; no need to sit on my lap." She crossed her legs and glanced at Cormac with a raised a brow, seeing him thoughtfully watching Sean. "Is there any way I could get the info you guys have on the case?"

"You can apply via public records, but it won't be everything," Alec said. "She died in jail."

"Oh." Sydney's brows rose in surprise. "I didn't know that. Maybe I'm being haunted by *her* ghost."

"You could put that in your story," Sean said, and turned to see his mother walk through the French doors. "There's pie in the fridge if you want it."

"I don't need pie. I need wine." Laura moved into the kitchen and no one said anything until Sydney spoke up.

"So, Madam X is dead. In jail. I could add that in. In fact, I feel the tingle of a new idea now, so I'll probably get some ideas written down when I get home."

"Is that how it starts? With a tingle?" Ethan asked. He'd noticed the attraction between his father and Sydney and wondered if something was going on. "Isn't that how love and attraction starts? With a tingle. Is it the same kind, or different?" He'd also had a few tingles for Sydney during the afternoon as he found her incredibly attractive.

Sydney considered his questions and intense stare before replying. "Most times, yes, that's how it starts.

And yes, I guess it can be the same for attraction. It can be a title, a line, a picture, an idea out of the blue, and the ones that cause the tingles are the ones that progress and end up being novels. It's just the way it works. As do the other tingles."

"When I come up with an idea, I just get this driving force in my head to write it down, and I end up writing until it's done. I don't stop. I can't sleep. Is that bad?" Sean asked.

"Why would it be bad? It's different for everyone," Sydney told him.

"Yeah, but it's like a pain or something behind my eyes, or in my brain, and it drives me to write and when I'm done it's all gone."

"Maybe you need an MRI or CAT Scan to make sure there are no issues." Sydney frowned, curious as to the mechanics of Sean's brain.

"All it'll prove is he's got nothing in there," Declan said.

No one said anything, just glared at him until Sydney spoke.

"Make you feel good, did it? Make you feel like a big boy? Make you feel big and brave insulting your son?" She glared at his stunned expression. "Why? Why did you feel the need to insult him? He's actually very talented."

"Talented!" Sierra exclaimed. "His stories are crap."

"*So's that attitude*," Sydney retorted, staring at her until she shrivelled. "And what *is it* that you've *actually* read?"

When Sierra couldn't reply, Sydney turned to Sean. "What stories of yours has she *actually* read?"

Sean shrugged. "I have no idea, but she loves to say it's crap."

Sydney turned back to Sierra. "Exactly what *have you* read of Sean's in order to call it crap? Do tell us so we know why you insult your cousin all the time."

Under the microscope, Sierra finally spoke up. "It was ah…something about robots from outer space or something, really crappy stuff."

"Robots from outer space?" Sean frowned. "I haven't written about robots from space since elementary school. Oh, my God, is that what you read? And you've been telling everyone my writing is crap because you read something over ten years old?"

Sierra gave an embarrassed shrug. "Um, I guess so."

"Well, *that's* pathetic," Sydney said. "You read an old story and made the assumption it's current and that gives you the right to bring your cousin down and insult him. Is this what this family's like?" She looked from person to person. "You insult each other and put one another down? That's really incredibly sad." She looked back to Sierra. "His teachers have told him he's very good. *I've* told him he's very good, and my publisher, from the sample he submitted, said he's very good. If multiple experts are saying he's very good, then clearly *we* know what we're talking about. I've read two of his stories and glanced at more, he has a natural storytelling ability. But clearly *you* don't care. *You'd* rather just insult him. But is that what this family's about?" Again, she looked at each one. "You're so tied up in dealing with crime you'd rather insult and put down instead of encourage and support. That's pathetic."

"I agree," Cormac spoke up. "There's too much nasty behaviour going on out in the real world and no need for insults. You should be encouraging your cousin, not insulting him. Same goes for you, Declan. Stop with the bullshit. Sean deserves a better father than that and that's not the way your mother and I raised you."

"Yeah, yeah." Declan waved him away. "He's my kid."

"Don't yeah, yeah me," Cormac roared. "Stop abusing my grandson!"

Shocked, no one said a thing and Declan sat straight in his chair and turned bright red.

Cormac turned to Sydney. "You said he was good. Could he go all the way?"

Sydney took a beat to breathe. "You mean published?" He nodded. "Yes, it's a part of the mentorship, but if Pulsate turns down future writings, he should absolutely submit to other publishers. He's very good."

Cormac nodded. "Then this family will support and encourage you all the way, Sean. Sydney, I'd like you to mentor him, help him get on his way, and Sean," he looked at his eager grandson, "I'd like to read some of your current stories if you don't mind."

"Ah…" Sean's mouth dropped and he glanced at each family member who were all just as shocked as he. "I…guess. I could get some to you. I don't have any on me."

"Well," said Cormac, giving him an encouraging smile, "when you do, send them. I can print them out if it's easier, if you have them on your computer."

"Ah…yeah. I've been typing some of them. Either I write on my laptop or my notebook, but yeah, I'll email you a file when I get home."

"That's great, thank you, Sean." Cormac glanced at

Sydney and nodded and she nodded in return.

It was done.

*****

Emerson dropped Sydney off at home around six. It had been an eventful day and both were eager to change into comfortable clothes and veg out.

"I'll wait until you're locked inside and you call me," Emerson called and locked the door after Sydney alighted.

Laughing, Sydney hurried up to her door and quickly found her way inside, checking the alarm, locking the doors, and turning on the lights. She called Emerson and waved out the window. "No one's here. I'm fine, you can go now."

"No studs hiding in the sex dungeon?" Emerson asked.

"Ha! I wish," Sydney retorted. "But alas, poor Yorick, I am barren of males."

"What! That doesn't even sound right." Emerson laughed. "See you next week."

"Bye." Sydney waved. "Sweet dreams about studs in sex dungeons."

"Ha! I wish," Emerson retorted and drove off.

Sydney shut off her phone and sighed. It was Sunday night, when she either worked or relaxed, but an idea was niggling at the back of her mind. She had a quick shower, put on a turquoise tracksuit, and dashed down to her office to get the idea on paper. It had grown while she showered, and now demanded her full attention.

She grabbed a notebook, and quickly penned down all of the notes, thoughts, and ideas she'd had about the house; the commissioner's family being involved, Madam X, and the sex dungeon. Once it was all down on paper, the whirling dervish in her brain stopped. That's what came after the tingles. That's what she'd had since everyone dismissed it at lunch. The tingles merged together to create a dervish, whirling furiously in her mind at the base of her skull until she got the idea down on paper. But now the dervish was still. The idea was down; the idea had taken life. Even if it was on sixteen pages of paper.

The front door bell rang and she startled. "Who the hell?" Sydney checked the time and saw it was almost nine. Who'd be ringing her bell this time of night? She hurried to the door of the office and clicked the monitor on the wall. The camera showed a man at her door, his back to her. She clicked another button. "Who are you?"

He turned around and stared at the camera. "You gonna let me in?" Connor asked.

Surprised, Sydney said, "Be down in a moment," and hurried down to unlock both doors. "What are you doing here?"

"Ah, come on, kitten." He leaned against the door frame, his head close to hers. "Don't pretend you didn't feel the sexual chemistry between us at lunch. I thought I'd come for a nightcap and see your sex dungeon for myself."

She breathed in his musky alcoholic scent and leant against the frame. He was so close to her he made her tingle. "Don't call me kitten, and it smells like you've already had a nightcap."

His left forefinger slid along her jawline. "We got

merry at the old man's and I'll call you whatever I like." His finger slid into her mouth, brushing against her teeth and lips.

She grabbed his coat lapel and pulled him inside, locking the vestibule door against the world. "You wanna see the sex dungeon, huh?" She pushed him into the house, and locked the main door. She was already throbbing between her legs, and her stomach was twisting and turning with excitement and shaking inside. Men she was physically or sexually attracted to were few and far between, but even she could admit that the Ryans were damn good looking.

Connor pushed against her, leaning them into the door. "You feel it, don't you?" His lips brushed her jawline, then his tongue brushed her lips. "You feel it between your legs, the exact place I want to be." His hands slid over her hips, under her jumper to her breasts that nestled in a sports top with an under bra. The soft cotton material was no match for her straining nipples that delighted in the advances of his thumbs.

She groaned against his neck. "We really shouldn't be…"

"Shh." He pushed her jumper up and she raised her arms for it to slide off. His fingers slowly found their way down the soft warm flesh and placed her arms around his neck before his fingers went back to her nipples. "Let's just fuck."

The moment was quick, and Sydney didn't even register it. Her pants were down and he was lifting her onto his cock and pushing her back against the door. "Fuck," she cried as he thrust swiftly. It knew what it was doing, and it did the job extremely well.

His mouth was over hers, sucking, slurping, over her face, her neck and chest. It devoured her breasts as his hands held her hips to his so he could thrust harder.

She was fully naked; he was fully clothed, so she pushed off his jacket, one arm at a time, pulled his top up and over his head.

He crushed her to his broad masculine chest covered in soft dark brown fur. It was a manly chest, and one she very much liked the feel of against her body.

He came to a grunting stop and heaved a sigh, leaning against the door, her body between his and the wood. "I knew that would be good." He breathed heavily into her neck. "You're so fucking hot, Sydney. I've had a hard-on all day just thinking about you and what I could do to you and when the sex dungeon was mentioned, fuck, I had to go to the bathroom and jack off."

"Ew." Sydney lowered her legs to the floor. "Well, you can get out now and tell me what you're doing here." She stared into his blue eyes, their noses almost touching. The man was attractive and she'd just fucked him against her front door.

"I came to see you." He tried to catch a kiss but she avoided his mouth and pushed him away, feeling him slip out of her.

She stood completely naked, trying not to feel embarrassed. "And you're still half-dressed because?" She watched him push off his boots and shove his jeans and jocks down.

"There, the problem's fixed." He pulled her towards him and they both sizzled as naked flesh touched naked flesh. "Ready to do that again?"

"So, you just came here to fuck?" Sydney's fingers slid their way up his arms to his chest and caught hold of his nipples, twisting them.

"Ow, you little!" He slapped her hands away and pulled her close, nuzzling her cheek. "Is there anything wrong with wanting to fuck?"

She melted into him, the throb between her legs starting up again. "No, so let's go do that because it's been awhile and I need more." Her hands moved to his penis and found it standing to attention. "Come and say hello, detective."

He lifted her onto him and carried her into the front room where he laid her down on the couch and fucked her till she cried out.

Out on the street, he took the final photo and pulled back on the zoom. He'd been watching her house when *he'd* arrived. Watched them flirt, watched her pull him in, and then watched him carry her into the room with a view.

A very nice clear view thanks to the curtains being open and the sheer netting letting everyone see since the light was on.

His insides seethed with anger, hatred and resentment. That a man she barely knew could be allowed into her house and then into her body!

His hands started shaking, followed by his stomach. Tremors rumbled through his body and he put his camera into his bag so he didn't drop it. His hands gripped one another trying to stop the shaking, but he knew the only way the shaking would stop would be to fix the problem. And he couldn't do that yet. For now, there was only one way to fix it and he had no time to waste.

He strode off down the road and made his way to the Lower East Side. He kept his zip up hoodie low over his face, his gaze darting around to all the girls on the street, looking for the one he normally saw. After a block, he found her, stopped close enough for her to notice him, and took off after her when she nodded in the direction of the alley.

Honey Syrup, a name she'd given herself, made it half way down before turning, and beckoning him over to a spot against the wall hidden by pipes and bins. "Hey, baby, good to see you again. Got a hard-on?" Pushing him against the wall, she unzipped his pants, pulled out his cock, and roughed it up between her hands. She never saw his face, not fully. Never saw his body, just manipulated the one part of him that she did get into doing what she wanted. "Do you want to fuck or suck?"

"We fuck, and then you suck. Are you clean?" His hands covered her breasts, squeezing them together in their tight leopard print crop top. He liked the way she looked, rounded and curvy. Big lips, big tits, big mouth that did the job. His hands pulled her breasts out of her top. Big nipples too.

"Okay, big boy, you want me doggy, or against the wall?" Honey pulled up her short skirt that barely covered anything, and ground her coifed pussy against his flesh in her hand. His penis was wide and long, and did the job regardless of the position.

"I want you every way," he replied, gripping her face. "I want to own you, whore. I will show you what I want and you'll give it to me. You got that?"

He could see shaded terror in her eyes.

She knew he had no reason to kill her, even though she'd figured out he used some type of device to deepen his voice. They never kissed, just fucked, and he always paid well. He pushed to the brink of exquisite pain, but never went to the point of violence.

"I've been a bad girl, baby," she said. "I need you to punish me." It was all part of the play between them which made him her best fuck any night of the week.

"Then you'd better get ready to learn your lesson, Honey." He watched her roll a condom on him and give him a quick suck.

He picked her up under the arms and thrust her back against the wall.

She hung on while he entered, hooking her stiletto heels into the handles of the bin either side of them for leverage. "I've been so bad, baby," she cried. His grunting thrusts sent his dick all the way to her insides. The orgasm didn't stop. Her arms flung over her head and grunts came from her.

"Then you'd better learn your lesson, bitch." He withdrew, set her down, and spun her around to face the wall. He grabbed her by the hair and with her hands on the wall, bent her into him. His thrusts were hard, grunting, with all the power of his anger, hatred and resentment. He imagined it was her. Naked and on top of him instead of that fucking cop, and thrust using his knees and powerful thighs.

Honey's high-pitched squeals came in time with his thrusts. "Harder, baby, harder."

He ejaculated and rocked to a stop. "Ah, fuck!" They panted in time, leaning against the wall to catch their breath. "Was it good for you, Honey? 'Cause I know it was good for me." He breathed in her scent, sex, sweat, and other men.

"Oh, baby, it was good for me, just like always." Regardless of how rough he could get, he titillated her more than any other john. He had a fondness for roughness and she had a fondness for him, guessing he was on the young side or inexperienced.

"Good, now you can suck it," he growled into her ear, spun her around, and pushed her to her knees. While she rolled the condom off, he pulled a Ziploc bag from his sweater pocket and nodded as she dropped it in and proceeded to suck his dick like a lollipop. He shoved the bag into his pocket and leaned against the wall with his left hand, while grabbing her head with his right. "Suck it. Suck it, bitch," he murmured, giddy and lightheaded. The tremors were long gone and now he was weary. His body was losing energy, wanting to sleep to rejuvenate so he could do this all again. His breathing regulated, but pulsated when he came in her mouth with jerking actions and his hands slid through her honey coloured hair, all natural and pure, and slid around her throat. "Suck it, you bitch."

Chapter 6

On Monday morning, Sydney wandered downstairs after her shower and turned on the TV to watch NBC's Today. Connor had left at six for his shift and promised to be back that night to be her bodyguard.

She told him she didn't need one.

He called her a liar and reminded her of the dead rat.

She reminded him that all he wanted was to fuck.

He agreed.

She saw the hosts talking about the latest attack in the lower east quarter.

"Another prostitute was found murdered last night in the Lower East Side. Police say she'd been strangled to death, stripped naked, and left in a garbage bin. Authorities are warning all sex workers once more to stop working, but if they refuse to, then to be safe and congregate in pairs, or small groups. Essentially, to look out for each other. In other news…"

Sydney zoned out until the news was over, contemplating all of the stalker news she'd heard recently. A chill travelled down her spine. She'd had her fair share of stalkers in L.A. and didn't need another one, having moved across the country to get away from the hell she'd ended up in. Fortunately, Emerson had agreed to move with her, having also had enough of the L.A. scene. She had a few ideas for New York style movies and figured it was best to live there to experience it firsthand.

But now there was the letter in magazine cut outs and the dead rat in the gift box; something that was no closer to being solved. *That rat can't be for me*, she thought. *I haven't been here long enough to warrant a dead rat in a gift box. Who the fuck would do that?* She'd watched the surveillance footage and didn't recognise the man who'd left it. His black hooded jacket was zipped up tightly, the hood pulled down low so there was no face to recognise, and he wore black gloves so he left no fingerprints.

She sighed, and a little tremor of fear snaked its way around her stomach. *I can't do this,* she thought. *I won't do this again.* Her phone rang and she jumped at the shrillness in the silent house. "CC it's too early for a call."

"Sydney darling, I want to check in. Can you come downtown?"

"What time?"

"When you're ready, darling. We have much to talk about."

"I don't have a book, if that's what you're after."

"No, darling, it's not. Come soon."

The call ended and left Sydney frowning at her phone. "Okay…that's weird." She finished watching Today, had a quick breakfast, and dressed. After strolling out of the elevator at Pulsate at twelve on the dot, she walked into CC's office and saw Gemma and Olivia. "Okay." She baulked. "Is this an intervention?"

CC laughed. It was light and delicate like her. "No, darling. We just have a few things to catch up on. Sit, sit; do you want champagne?"

"You know I don't drink." Sydney settled into an easy chair, crossed her legs, and pushed her hair back with both hands. "Right. What's going on?"

CC leaned forward in her seat. "Where's your book, darling? Tell us if you've got an idea, something at least."

"I have an idea, but I only wrote it down last night. I would need a tonne of research, but I suppose Amy would help with that. I don't know about the legalities." She went on to tell them her idea.

"Sounds intense," Gemma said. "It could work."

"The fact you bought the house because of the history would be a bonus," Olivia said.

"So would the dead rat in the gift box," Sydney teased, forgetting she hadn't mentioned it. When she got three shocked expressions in return, she told them the story.

"Jesus, Sydney, darling." CC was as white as a ghost. "Didn't we tell you to get a bodyguard? Didn't we tell you to be careful? Didn't we tell you?"

Sydney stopped her with a raised hand. "You told me a lot, CC, but I'm not hiding anymore, not here in New York. The threat was extinguished in L.A. and won't resurface, so I have nothing to fear from that. I'm thinking it's someone who's after the previous tenant, or owner, and doesn't know they'd moved, or been in jail and died. I've only been there barely a month. He could just be confused."

"And he may not be," CC scolded her. "Did you call the police?"

"We did, and two officers turned up and then guess what…" Sydney's brows rose in amusement and she looked at each face. "Hot cop Detective Ryan number two turned up because he recognised the address and my name because, wait for it, his nephew is Sean Ryan who's applied for mentorship and the whole Ryan family discussed it around the lunch table. He told me they had, and that Em and I were invited to lunch yesterday, but Laura hadn't even rang Em yet."

The ladies were instantly excited.

"You mean the commissioner's family? The *Police* Commissioner's family." Gemma gaped at her. "Hot commissioner, hot sons."

"And a desperate grandson," CC said. "He's emailed again. That's one of the reasons I called you in. He emailed and said you'd agreed to do it at lunch yesterday, and when could he start."

Sydney deflated, mumbling under her breath before sighing. "I talked to his grandfather and great-grandfather. They both suggested to his parents to let him do it. But they also admitted to saying yes so they could meet me. They knew Laura was an old friend of Em's, so they had a motive for him getting it as well."

"Do they know how you feel?" Olivia asked, sipping her champagne and nibbling on a cookie from the tray CC had set out for them.

"I was completely truthful. That I wasn't comfortable with mentoring anyone under twenty-one. That I believed things could go wrong and what if they did? They both understood my viewpoint, agreeing that it was sensible and a wise thing to do. But…" She rolled her eyes and sighed. "They still wanted me to do it. I told them I'd only consider it if they watched Sean's behaviour through the day and if they still thought it would be appropriate, then I'd do it."

"And have you considered it?" Gemma poured herself another champagne. "Is he good?"

"Very. So, I don't know exactly how much I could help him. Or what I'd mentor him for. But…" Sydney grimaced. "I could kick myself because after lunch at the house, well, actually, during lunch, and then after, I got stuck into the family about their treatment of him. It was pretty appalling. His father insulted him and slapped him upside the head at the table. His cousin called his story crap. I had a go at both *and* the family, and Cormac agreed."

"Cormac?" Olivia blanked. "Wait, you mean the Police Commissioner? You get to call him Cormac?" Her jaw dropped in surprise and her eyes widened. "First name basis with the PC of the NYPD, *and* invited to lunch. Well, how do."

Sydney laughed lightly. "Yeah, surreal it definitely was. But it was on personal time, so first name basis. And, of course, Connor was there, as was the whole family and he regaled them with the rat story."

"Flirt?" Gemma inquired.

"Are you calling *me* one or him one?" Sydney asked.

"Did the two of you flirt?" Gemma elaborated.

A small sound came from Sydney. "We might have…"

A chorus of oohs went around the group.

"I've seen pictures of the family. Definitely good looking, and I wouldn't mind meeting Cormac myself."

CC opened another bottle of champagne. "He is rather dashing."

"Definitely," Sydney agreed, and waved off the alcohol. "Have you got spritzer in the fridge?"

"Of course. Help yourself."

Sydney grabbed a bottle from CC's drinks fridge and opened it, hearing the effervescence sound out like a sexual sigh. She drank a few mouthfuls and walked around the office before stopping at the floor-to-ceiling window and its palatial view of the city. "He suggested somewhere public. The library or the precinct."

"1PP? For what?" CC asked, puzzled by the change of subject.

"For mentoring Sean. I agreed after I had a go at everyone, but I didn't mention it last night." She turned from the view of the Freedom Tower, shivering at the images of the twin towers galloping through her mind. She hated being in tall buildings, and tried to never enter one. She couldn't go higher than three or four floors.

Pulsate was the exception, and the building it was in was only twenty floors high. Still, the shiver of remembrance slithered through her anyway.

"If you agree to it, I can mentor him here. We can give him information on publishing. What houses want in stories these days, those most appropriate for him, things to look out for, those types of things. How to submit to agencies for an agent. Maybe just a couple of weeks and have others take over. I could give him ideas for writing general fiction. He did say he wouldn't be a teenager for too much longer and would probably start writing general."

"Would you want us to publish him? It's part of the mentorship, if they're good enough by the end of it," CC said. "Would that be problematic?"

"Probably not. You could publish one book of stories, and see how it goes. I'd really prefer he be mentored by a man, but I'm stuck with it."

"Until it goes wrong," Olivia said. "How long does the mentorship go for?"

"Three months," CC told her. "You get one meeting a week, an editor to look over your work, and if it's good we'll move it along for publishing. If not, we hand out a packet of information on classes to improve their writing and to give it another go in a year or two. We try to keep it short and sweet."

"Sounds good for potential writers," Olivia said. "But how many teens do you have applying?"

"It's three or four out of ten. Mainly because the age limit is sixteen."

"Doesn't help me though, so I guess it's happening here at Pulsate." Sydney put her drink on the coffee table. "Set it up, CC, we can start this week. Anything else we needed to discuss? Or was that it?"

"Just you getting yourself a bodyguard, darling," CC replied.

"Any more notes?" Sydney asked, staring at CC.

CC didn't blink. "No, but that doesn't mean we're not worried. You need someone."

"I need a man and a good fuck," Sydney stated. "Not a bodyguard."

"Who doesn't, darling," CC retorted. "But that doesn't mean you can't have them both."

"Wait…you didn't fuck hot Ryan number two?" Gemma chastised. "After all the flirting at lunch I'm surprised you didn't have all the men panting after you."

"Who said I didn't?" Sydney slid her bag over her shoulder. "I certainly had Douglas and Cormac eating out of my hand. Alec and Kieran were eating up every word I said, Sean all but eating off my plate, and Connor eating up my pussy last night. As I said, who said I didn't?" She watched jaws drop and then said, "Toodles," waved her fingers at them, and left the office, leaving them speechless.

*****

"So, what's the plan for tonight?" Connor asked as he strode through Sydney's doorway and into the house.

She closed the vestibule door and followed, watching him shed his leather jacket and throw it over the stair railing. "Who said we had a plan?" Sydney locked the house door and stood before his strong muscular frame.

His hands on hips stance made him look broader, pushing out his chest muscles and pecs. He flexed. "You want a piece of this, don't you, Syd?" The boyish grin spread across his face. "Just admit it; you missed this body, didn't you."

Sydney tried to suppress a grin, but couldn't help it when he pulled her into his arms and kissed her soundly on the mouth.

"Just admit it, Sydney," he said against her mouth. "You've missed this body and want it badly. Because this body has definitely missed you." His hand thrust between her legs, his tongue thrust into her mouth and with his other arm around her, bent her backwards.

Even though she was wearing jeans, Sydney's hand joined his between her legs, thrusting it back and forth, exciting her. Unable to wait, she unzipped her jeans and pushed them down, along with her knickers, and allowed his manhood entry.

He glided back and forth, pushing her against the door, just as he had the night before. Her legs wrapped around him and she thrust against him. The climax left them both gasping.

After a few moments, Sydney slid to the floor. "We need to stop meeting like this and actually make it to the bedroom sometime. And so we can use some condoms."

"Who said I need a bed?" Connor asked and lifted her back up. "Take me to your dungeon. I want to fuck you wildly all night, like a madman."

Her hands slid through his brown hair, over his stubbled jaw, and her thumbs rubbed against his full bottom lip. He was still fully dressed and that needed rectifying. "So, what do you want me to do with you?" she asked, her voice low and sultry, her lips brushing against his.

"Everything," he said and walked down the hall to the basement stairs. He carefully descended and Sydney flicked on the light.

A lavish room for entertainment met them. A huge surround sound TV and a leather u-shaped couch. A drinks bar, dart board, and pool table sprawled around the room.

"No, this isn't it, keep walking, down the hall to the

two doors."

He glanced over her shoulder and made his way down the hall, stopping at two heavy wood doors, both deadbolted, chained and locked tight.

"Turn me around. Better yet, put me down," Sydney said and landed lightly on her feet when he let go. She reached up to the frame of the door to the left and pulled a small section of it away. Inside the hollow was a key. She pulled it out and replaced the wood. It took but a few moments to unlock everything and flick on the light.

Connor stepped in behind her. "Fucking hell!" His eyes took in the red velvet walls and the black cement floor, the roulette wheel for spinning people, to the stretching rack, the whips, the chains, and the BDSM paraphernalia. It was everything you would find in a sex room and then some. "This can't be all of hers? Madam X's? Did she have all of this?" He pointed at it and looked at Sydney in surprise. "Is this hers? Did she get it back? Wait…no…" He frowned and thought about the case. "She died in prison, so did the owners get this back? Or did you say there were tenants before you?"

Sydney locked the door. "All of this is a copy of what she had and where she had it. As far as I know, her items are still in custody unless you lot got rid of it or took it home for yourselves. The owners after her certainly didn't have it."

"How did you get this?" He shook his head and thought it through then grinned. "Wait… You bought it? But you've only been here what…five, six weeks? When did you have time to—"

"The first week." Sydney pulled her top over her head

and dropped it to the floor. She was fully naked and aroused. "Are we getting on with this? You're still dressed."

His gaze roamed her voluptuous body and instantly hardened. His shirt and jeans fell on top of his boots and his penis strained for release as Sydney led him to a narrow bed with shackles and a bondage mask. "And what are we doing with this?" he asked and was pushed down onto his back.

Sydney straddled him. "Your hands are cuffed under the bed; you put the ball in your mouth and the mask over your face."

"So, I can't touch or see you?" Connor planted his feet, stretched his back out, and dropped his hands down. "Okay, let's do this."

Sydney leant against his fur covered chest and cuffed his hands together. She snapped them in place. "Too tight?"

He moved his hands and found they fitted nicely. "Just fine."

She placed the ball in his mouth, and when he nodded, pulled the leather mask over his face and zipped it up. He could still breathe, just not see or speak. "Nice and snug?" she asked and bent down to cuff his ankles to the bench so he couldn't move.

He bucked up, mumbled behind the mask, lifting his head, trying to lift his arms, but couldn't. His dick hardened.

"It's okay," she soothed. "It just stops you bucking or trying to get off." Sydney picked up a whip from the rack above the bed. "And we don't want you getting off the bench." She slid the whip across his balls and shoved it into the spot where his dick joined them. He bucked. "We just want you getting off." The whip cracked across his balls and he yelled behind the mask. "Make as much noise as you like." Sydney mounted his penis and whipped his thighs. "Because no one can hear you scream."

*****

When daylight broke, Sydney unlocked him and removed the mask. "Time for you to get back to work, detective."

"Fucking hell!" He managed to sit up and his back cracked. "Argh. What the fuck did you do to me?" He watched her pull her top on. The rest of her clothes were still upstairs.

Sydney pointed to his clothes. "Get dressed. I'll make coffee." She unlocked the door and looked over her shoulder. "I thoroughly fucked you all night. That's what the fuck I did to you. Get dressed, detective." She left the door open and walked away.

He slowly got to his feet, every muscle in his six-four frame crying out in pain; especially the one that had been used most. He inspected his penis, and found it to be red, a little raw, but generally okay. While it had had a thorough fucking, the whip had left its mark on his body. Red angry streaks flared across his thighs, abdomen, and chest. It was a warning about what this room could do to a guy if they found themselves in it. He wondered if it was Madam X or her girls who had used the room. Maybe it was her secret? Maybe she used it to punish the rich and powerful of the city of New York. Mayors, congressmen, law enforcement from every level…men of industry.

"Anyone who could afford it, I suppose," he muttered, looking at the machines and paraphernalia in the room. "They come to have their asses whipped, and then whipped hers into jail." He wondered about the story. Madam X had never given up her johns. Some had said she hoped they would protect her, and show leniency, but no one had, and for all anyone knew, she had died with her mouth firmly closed on all of her debauched secrets. He slowly dressed, grimacing at each straining burn of his muscles.

"Fucking hell!" he muttered, and recalled more from the file. The house had been ransacked from top to bottom by the cops, furniture moved, floor boards pried up, and walls torn down with axes. No one had found any proof linking her to her clients; no ledgers, journals, paperwork—nothing. She paid her rates and taxes in full, and lived very well in her extravagant Queen Anne brownstone.

The house had remained in disrepair until a couple bought it on the cheap and renovated it.

"So, if there was anything the cops missed, maybe the couple found it?" he murmured. A thought sprang to mind. "Maybe I should track them down and ask? Or…" And another thought. "Maybe Sydney has already done that which is how she knew which sex shop to buy the items in the room from. There are no photos of the room or house except in the files. The dungeon was never made public."

He pondered this information as he finished dressing, and with a last look, flicked off the light, shut the door and went upstairs, finding Sydney in the spacious white kitchen with silver hardware and white built-in cabinets. "Nice."

She poured two coffees and handed one over. "It is. The couple I bought it from did an incredible job of the renovations. Judging from the pictures they took, they had to take a lot of walls back to the studs and re-lay the floors. You arseholes did a bad job of searching for whatever it was you were looking for. The destruction was atrocious." She sipped her coffee and sat at the table. "You want breakfast?"

"What I want is a new dick. I think you broke mine." He leaned against a stool at the island bench. "And who you calling asshole? We did our job searching for her little black book; the higher ups wanted all evidence of the activities found before it got into hands unknown." Connor gulped a mouthful and let it burn his throat. "Whoo, I don't think my dick is ever gonna be the same."

"Well, if it plans on doing that again, it'd better be." Sydney studied his pained expression. "Is it your dick or your throat that's sore because that coffee's hot and you're drinking it like cold water?"

He grinned. "Just the way I like it. But I gotta get going." After another mouthful, he slammed the cup on the table and leaned over Sydney. "We up for tonight?"

Sydney glanced away demurely. "I really should get back to writing…*something*. Are you sure your broken penis won't mind if I use it again?"

"Who said you're going to be using it? I might have my way with you tonight." His phone beeped and he stood up to pull it out of his jeans pocket. He frowned at the text and made a mumbling sound in his throat.

"Everything all right?" Sydney checked the clock. It was six a.m.

"Fine." He shoved the phone into his pocket and took another gulp of coffee. "I'll see you tonight."

"Well, your penis might," Sydney quipped, watching him strut down the hallway towards the door.

He wiggled his ass and opened the vestibule door. "My penis can't wait," he yelled over his shoulder and saw her coming after him.

"Yeah, yeah. Just get out." Sydney grumbled and stood at the front door to wave him off. She locked both doors then tidied up the kitchen and went upstairs to shower and dress. An hour later, she entered her office and pulled out the notebook for her latest novel ideas; the one about Madam X. After reading through them, she made a few more then went to the corner of the room and pulled back the carpet. Underneath was a floor safe which she unlocked and from which she removed a black metal box. She carried it to her desk, unlocked it, and stared at the contents.

These comprised of wads of folded paper tied with ribbon, multiple medium-sized ledgers in multiple colours, and a small hand sized notebook bound in black leather.

Sydney picked up the black notebook and breathed in its scent before opening the cover and end paper. From the first page she silently read the title.

The Clients of Madam X.

Chapter 7

On Wednesday afternoon, Sydney was in the meeting room at Pulsate Publishing, papers spread out across the table's surface, all detailing different aspects of writing, editing, and publishing. Her phone alarm rang out for her four o'clock appointment right as Sean walked through the door.

"Am I late?" he gasped, letting go of the door and striding down the room to where Sydney was standing. "Am I on time?"

"Apparently," Sydney said. "My alarm went off as you arrived, so let's get on with this, shall we?" She motioned for him to sit to her left. She was at the head of the table and the view of New York's Freedom Tower was out the window to her right. She shivered. "Okay, I have no idea how to help mentor you about your actual writing. You'd probably benefit more from an editor than me on that, and as part of your mentorship you get to spend some time with one here at Pulsate. They'll go over your writing and give you advice."

"What type of advice?" Sean gazed adoringly up at her. *She's even more beautiful than at the family lunch,* he thought, noting that her light pink knit sweater brought a rosy tone to her cheeks and the blue and pink scarf holding her hair back brought out the blue in her eyes. "You already said I was good."

Sydney noticed his glazed puppy dog eyes and her stomach clenched. "You are. But an editor will help pinpoint anything that can be improved, and tell you what they look for in new authors or new acquisitions. Now…" She glanced at the papers to get away from Sean's unnerving gaze. "These are writing tips and tricks that editors and publishing companies look out for." She picked up a stapled stack of paper and handed it to him. "All very basic and simple. The editor will go over most of it when you see them."

"Can't you?" he asked, skimming the papers.

"Yeah…not really my forte, you'll get more out of the editor, and this stack…" She handed him another one. "Is information on writing. If you haven't read books on writing all of this is very helpful. It covers every aspect, and has lists of qualified websites and blogs to read, books to read, and anecdotes from authors." She handed him a third pile of papers. "And this stack, is on publishing itself. The ins and outs, how books are published, what they look for, how it all works. So, if you want to submit to others, the info's all in there along with a list of publishing houses and their submission pages. All mentees get the same info along with sessions with an editor, and a tour of Pulsate."

"Will you take me on the tour?" Sean asked, sitting up eagerly. "Can we do it today? Or don't we get the tour yet?"

"Ah…" Sydney considered it while looking out the glass wall dividing the meeting room from the offices. "There's no rule to say it can't be done today."

"Great!" Sean motioned at the paperwork. "If this is all there is, can we take the tour now and you can tell me about the program while we walk." He slid the papers into his bag, stood up, and hiked it over his shoulder.

Not sure what to say, Sydney picked up her bag and pushed her chair under the table. "Okay, um, let's go." They walked out and started the tour.

"Pulsate Publishing takes up three floors of this building. The top floor, where we are, has offices and boardrooms. The heads of Pulsate are on this floor, along with the head acquisitions editors." They stopped to chat with Gemma and CC before going down a floor. "The second floor is the rest of the editors and designers, basically anyone who creates the books." They watched a few graphic designers work on covers and took the lift to the floor below. "And here's everyone else," Sydney said. "Junior staff and part-time workers. It's also where you stop to check in when you come to Pulsate, and London will do that for you."

"Hey, Sydney." London nodded and raised a brow at Sean. "Your mentee?"

"Yes, he is." Sydney introduced them. "London's been here five years and CC says she's the best receptionist she's ever had."

London laughed. "She's lying. She also says I'm the worst."

Sean eyed her high, offside blonde ponytail with spikes of coloured hair snaking out of it, and her bright pink lips. *She's attractive*, he thought, *but not beautiful like Sydney.* "How old are you?"

"Oh…" she stuttered and glanced at Sydney. "Ah… twenty-five."

Sean nodded in thought. "Are there lots of young people working here? Or working in publishing in general? Is it something I could get into as an intern or something?"

"CC's rule is twenty-one and over," Sydney informed him. "Especially if doing a degree in English or writing. It will help you get your foot in the door."

"And help with college bills," London added. "I'm still paying mine off."

"Is it good money?" Sean asked. "I take it all levels of workers are on different levels of income." He gazed across the room full of junior staff.

Sydney's brows rose in surprise. "Why would you be worrying about that?"

He shrugged his free shoulder. His bag was over his right one and he clung to it like a life raft. "I'm seventeen. I'm not exactly relying on my parents to pay my way through college. Even though Mom's a doctor and earns far more than my dad, since taking her sabbatical she's been blowing through money like it's going out of style." He nodded to a private corner of the reception area and they walked over. "I want to earn a living and will probably have to pay my way. But if my writing is good enough to be published, maybe that'll give me a good chunk of money to pay off my debts. And if I'm good enough for Pulsate to publish me after this mentorship, then I'll choose English and writing courses for college to get that foot in the door you were talking about." He was a good head taller than her and could smell the fresh apple scent of her shampoo.

Sydney chose her next words carefully. "How *is* your mum?"

"Well…" He sighed and looked at the framed authors on the wall in front of them. "Drunk most of the time. Angry, loud; she and Dad are fighting when he's home. She's drunk whether he is or not. But something's changed in the last few days. I don't know what, but she's angrier than she was, and has been drinking more. I'm not relying on her to pay my way, as I said. I think she spends a few thousand a week on alcohol, especially champagne."

"Is she doing drugs, or anything? What about an intervention?"

His head shook slightly. "She's the doctor. Ironic, isn't it. She knows better, but she doesn't care. So, what would an intervention do?"

"What about your grandfather, or your great-grandfather? Aren't they able to do anything?"

Sean finally looked at her. "They're cops. What would they do? What *can* they do?"

"For the sake of the family's reputation, they could do *something*. The family has money; your mother would have money. Quietly get her into a facility for the rich or famous who want to keep it quiet. Is there one at the hospital she works for?"

Hysterical laughter burst out of Sean. "Can you imagine my mother's shame and embarrassment if she went to the rehab clinic at her own hospital? She would die before she did that. Besides, I asked her not long ago why she was drinking so much now she'd left work, and you know what she told me?"

Sydney shook her head.

"She told me that if I knew what she knew about my father, I'd be drinking too."

Sydney's left brow rose and she clicked on her mental note taker. "Did she explain what she meant by that?"

"Nope." He shook his head and gripped the strap of his backpack until his knuckles turned white. "But I questioned her and she told me nothing. So, I started thinking, they're clearly having problems, now she's not working and is home more. Dad's angry that's she's there. Angry that she's drinking. Angry that he doesn't have dinner on the table. Angry that she's blowing through money. '*But it's my money,*' she screams back. '*I made it with my own two fucking hands on my feet fifteen hours a day, six days a week for three decades. I fucking earned the time off to do everything I couldn't in the last thirty years.*'" He took a breath, and tried to shake off the embarrassment making his face red.

"Bloody hell!" Sydney murmured. "Maybe your mum taking time off has brought all the problems to the fore. It's shone a light on them. So to speak."

"Yeah. I reckon that's it. Because I never saw problems when Mom was working."

"Maybe they were too exhausted to fight before, but now she has the time and sees how things really are and has the time to fight. Sucks for you, though."

Sean huffed. "Yeah, sucks for me. Not that they give a fuck about me. You saw how they were at lunch. Grandpa and Pops had to talk them into giving me permission because I'm under twenty-one and still in high school. I don't go to college until next year, or unless I excel and move up classes to graduate early. They don't care about me. Mom's a drunk, an alcoholic; Dad's an abusive asshole who uses being a cop to lord it over me. Always has. His only son and only child. I'm going to do what he wants me to or so help me."

"Seriously?" Sydney was mildly shocked. "I saw what he was like, figured him to be a Grade A Douche, only second to Connor. Kieran and Alec seem to be the sensible ones. But if it's one thing I cannot abide, especially in a family of cops, it's abuse. Whether of each other, or of minors. That's why I said something to your grandfather. Emerson and I were guests in his house, and one of his sons was abusing his grandson. That's not on in my book."

"Thanks for defending me," Sean told her. "I appreciated it so much I actually cried that night when I went to bed." A raging blush raced across his cheeks. "Not that I should be admitting that. I'm a grown man after all."

Sydney snorted with laughter. "Oh, little boy, you ain't no grown man, but at least you behave in a more mature manner than your father. *And* your mother. They clearly raised you well before turning into dickshits."

A small grin lit up his face. "Yeah. That's one thing this family did. Raise me well. Even though I'm still seventeen, I definitely act more mature than my parents. *Or* my cousin. Thank you for standing up for me with her, too."

"She's a snarky little thing, isn't she? Is she older? Yet

she behaved so rudely and arrogantly tarred all of your stories with the same brush just because she's read an old story and believed that's what you'd been writing. Quite pompous, really." Sydney turned her nose up. "Maybe you should get yourself published to prove her wrong. To prove your parents wrong. To prove your whole freaking family wrong."

"That sounds like a plan for revenge." Sean was intrigued. "Are you into revenge, Sydney?" He hoped she was.

"I can be if I need to be. I get revenge in my books all the time." She wiggled her brows.

"Ah…that might come in useful." He nodded. "Very useful."

A group of workers stopped at the elevator doors and Sydney glanced at the clock over London's desk. "Damn, it's already after five. Time for you to go. So…ah, same time next week? You can obviously get here after school okay."

"Yeah. I take the subway, so it's pretty quick." Sean hefted his backpack higher on his shoulder. "Same time next week is fine. What will we be doing?"

"I'll hook you up with an editor and they can go over some of your stories. Can you send me some via email and I'll pass them on so they can read them before then."

"Okay, but I'll need your email." Sean crossed his fingers that he'd get it.

Sydney mentally berated herself for mentioning email as she moved towards the lift. "Ah, send it to me via the pub house email and I'll forward it on to the editor. That way it's on the house system. You'd better get going."

"I guess." He reluctantly hit the button. The glut of workers had already departed.

The lift dinged open and he entered, hitting the button and facing her. "Bye, Sydney. Same time next week."

"Wednesday at four," she agreed and watched the doors close. She sat down in the waiting area, pulled out her phone, and hit the record button, repeating everything she could remember of what they just talked about.

*****

Sydney spent the rest of the week working on an idea, writing everything down, making notes about how to wrap scenes together. A full book idea wasn't yet formed, but she could see it was shaping together nicely.

She was in the middle of coming up with a new way to take her story on Saturday night when Connor arrived at her door. "Ryan."

"Kingston." He wearily passed her, came to a halt in the foyer, and slumped on the stair railing. "So, what's the plan for tonight?"

Sydney mentally scrolled through her week and when she'd seen him last. "We didn't have plans for tonight."

"Yeah, I know." He sighed and slid his leather jacket off. "It's been a long couple of days and I'm worn out."

"Then why are you here?" She hung his coat on the rack behind the door. "Why aren't you home in bed getting a good night's sleep?"

"Because I just got off work and your bed is closer." He reached for her hand and held it between his. "I'm just not sure I have the energy for the dungeon."

"It's not a dungeon, but I'm not in the mood for it either." She brushed his hair back from his face and tucked a few stray curls behind his ears. "What I would like is a normal night in bed with a man, and not raucous fucking in the sex room, or on the couch in the living room."

"A normal night of normal fucking." He nodded. "Sounds good."

"Anything you want before we go to bed?" She pressed her body to his.

"Just you, Syd." He kissed her lightly and slid an arm around her, escorting her up the stairs.

They stopped by her office to turn out the light before continuing to the master suite where they undressed each other slowly, kissing and caressing hot naked flesh. She rubbed her face in the nest of brown curls on his chest; he buried his face in the tangle of auburn waves draping her shoulders.

Their mouths found their mates and their tongues danced. Their hands found their way to private places to unveil them. When they were naked, he lifted her onto him and then laid them on the bed.

Slow sensual mating. Low guttural gasping. They made their way to a climax that left them both exhausted.

*****

Sydney's eyes slowly opened. She blinked a few times to get used to the light and her surroundings. She was in her bed, as usual, but she wasn't alone. A smile slid across her lips and she breathed in the masculine scent of the man next to her. They were wrapped in each other's arms, and damn did it feel good. It had been some time since a man had been in her bed, and she didn't mind it one bit. She didn't mind that he was the son of the Police Commissioner; didn't mind that he had an adult son also in the force. And she really didn't mind that he was into kink and had enjoyed his time in the sex room. She snuggled into his chest and his arms moved around her. She was glad she'd set the sex room back up, it had come in very handy.

Connor yawned and grumbled under his breath, coming out of REM state with a vague notion he was with a woman, but it took him a moment to realise he was in bed. "Hey, Kingston. Been here all night?"

"Well, it is my bed, so yeah." Her hand made its way through the curls on his chest and up to his neck where her fingers danced across his jawline. "It's been a while since I woke up with a man in my bed."

"Yeah? How long?" He breathed in and her apple scented shampoo tingled in his nose.

Her fingers paused halfway through their dance. "L.A."

"And how many men did you have in your bed in L.A.?"

She thought a moment. Should she tell him or keep it to herself?

"Or, for that matter, how many men did you have in your sex dungeon in L.A.?"

She gave a breathy laugh. "It's not a dungeon; it's a sex room. And I didn't have one in L.A. The place is basically a cesspool of debauchery anyway."

"Is it? Haven't been there in some time. Clearly I'm missing out."

"Not on much." Sydney lifted her head to look at him. "Drug addicted people on the streets. Homeless in your backyard, producers ruining young women—the whole town needs to be razed and rebuilt."

"Sounds like my kinda joint," he quipped, and yawned again. Stretching his arms over his head, he pushed his body up to stretch out his back and held the pose a moment before relaxing back in place. "It's Sunday. I have the day off. What do you want to do?"

"Write. And besides, you have family lunch at your father's."

He groaned. "We don't always go, you know. Sometimes we just can't make it."

"By choice?"

"Of course. Unless you want to come with? But then I could stay here in bed with you and sleep and fuck the day and night away." His fingers tangled themselves in Sydney's hair. "You feel good, Syd. So good. So different. So different to the other women I've had fun with."

Her brows slowly rose. "You have fun with women? What! No relationship? No long-term something? Just wild, animalistic mating with all the women you can get?"

Connor chuckled. "Yeah, yeah. I make my way through life like a stud. I think the only long-term relationship I had with a woman was Ethan's mother. We were together two years and then went our separate ways. She had Ethan in our second year, but we stayed amicable and reasonable for his sake."

"Is she welcome to family lunch?" Sydney's fingers walked their way down his chest and under the covers. "Any of your conquests welcome to family lunch?"

"You certainly are." His hand dived under the covers to grasp hers and held it over his penis while she did the job. Moments later, he groaned and rolled her over to finish the job inside her.

*****

He watched the man leave the brownstone and ducked down behind a car. Thank God he was on the other side of the street, otherwise he would have been seen. Except for him and his grunting Trans Am, the neighbourhood was quiet. It would be on a Sunday evening when everyone was winding down from their weekend out. Kids would be having baths and getting ready for school tomorrow, and their parents would be having a wine or three and be all ready for the work day starting in just a few hours.

Just the way he liked a neighbourhood when he was working. Although he preferred it if everyone was out, having everyone mellow and complacent was just as good. Today's weather was warm enough to have windows open as evening changed to night, and the rays of the last sunset turned from brilliant oranges, pinks, and purples to black. It gave him cover, and the lack of street lights helped immensely.

Bobbing his head up to check for people, he rose slowly, stayed in stealth mode, but relaxed enough to move. His plan was to walk down the street, cross over, and walk back down the other side. Keep it casual, nod to everyone passing, and pretend he was out for his nightly proverbial.

He moved on, hands in pockets, one foot in front of the other. His gaze darted left and right, making mental notes of which houses had front lights on, and which didn't. He came across no one, heard no cars, no dogs, no traffic in general. It was a quiet neighbourhood, and the only noises were screaming kids and they were few and far between. He came to the end of the street and crossed over, making his way down the other side in relative peace until he made it to the end. Turning left, he walked the block until reaching a small alleyway where he turned left again and walked quietly down the path.

The alley backed onto the yards of houses on both sides. Gardens easily showed who was in the kitchen, the back rooms, the bedroom, any room that overlooked the back yard he could see into. The only great joy of alleys like this was that they gave him easy access.

He came to a few houses with no back lights and peered over the fences as he walked past. He found what he was looking for, a person or family that hung their washing outside and hadn't taken it in yet.

He glanced around nervously, his blood racing through his veins, the pulsating beat of it drumming in his ears. He saw no one, heard nothing, and with a quick step and a jump, deftly flew over the fence without a sound.

*****

Sydney was ten pages deep into a scene when banging landed on her door, startling her out of her writer bubble. When the banging happened again, she cocked her head, held her breath, and didn't move. The doorbell rang out.

Sighing, she removed her glasses and walked to the office door. "Yes," she said into the intercom.

"Ma'am, it's the police. There's been a robbery next door and we're canvasing the area. Can we speak to you for a few minutes?"

"One moment." Sydney padded downstairs, reaching the ground floor to see red and blue flashing lights bouncing off the walls in her hallway. She checked the security camera and unlocked the door, pulling a lever on the side down so the door couldn't slam shut on her. She opened the vestibule door to two officers. One of them had turned up the day her gift arrived.

Officer Velensky's face lit up. "Ah, Ms Kingston. Good to see you again. We need to ask you if you saw or heard anything suspicious within the last few hours? Your next door neighbour had some clothing stolen from her yard. She had a rack of clothes drying on the back terrace."

Sydney's gaze flickered between Velenksy and the other office. "You weren't here last time."

"Ah, no, he had the week off," Velenksy jumped in. "This is Officer Rotrain. Can you answer the question please?"

Sydney shook her head and gazed next door. "Heard nothing, saw nothing. I've been in my office since evening, head down in my work."

"And what do you do?" Rotrain asked. A multi-racial young man in his late twenties, he'd been on the force for five years, but was still just an officer. His superiors kept rejecting him for sergeant due to what they said was an attitude not befitting the New York Police Department. Once it had an adjustment, and he got some more years under his belt, he could advance.

"I'm a writer." Sydney glanced at Velenksy who stared at Rotrain in surprise.

"What type of writing?" Rotrain's pen paused on his notebook.

"Novel writing." Sydney nearly smirked, but kept it in check.

"And would I have read anything you've written?" he continued.

"How the hell would I know, I'm not a fucking mind reader," Sydney snapped. That was one of the stupid questions many people asked her. It had no yes or no answer because how the hell were you going to answer it? If you said yes, then you were a mind reader, or lying. Same thing if you said no. How the hell were you supposed to know if a complete stranger had read your novels? You wouldn't.

His attitude shot up, so did his hand. He lunged forward and his mouth shot open and out came, "And maybe—"

"Enough, Rotrain!" Velenksy stopped him with a hand on the chest. "Don't you know who this is?" When she saw his blank expression, she added, "Best-selling author, Sydney Kingston." He gave her a shrug and a sneer. "She writes as Cassandra Kingsley."

He looked from Velenksy to Sydney and his eyes widened. "Oh, my God. Seriously? I've read all your novels."

"So has Cormac Ryan, the Police Commissioner, who probably wouldn't be happy with your attitude towards me just now," Sydney told him. "I had lunch with his family last week. When I see him again I'll tell him what a wonderful hard working officer Ms Velenksy is." Sydney's brow rose as she looked at her. "So friendly."

Darkness slid over Rotrain's face. "Well, if you're going to be like that—"

"Yes, I am, and I'll finish speaking to Officer Velenksy," Sydney snapped. "Go and speak to someone else." She watched him sneer and trot down the stairs and to the house on the right. "God, what a douche!"

Velenksy giggled, but quickly recovered her composure. "He can be, but back to the robbery. It was about an hour ago, in the backyard."

Sydney shook her head. "My office might overlook my backyard, but it's the next floor up and the windows and curtains were shut around five. The person clearly made no noise."

"No, he didn't. The neighbour found the missing clothes only when she remembered the rack was out there. She found her underwear missing."

Sydney's brows rose in amusement. "You're kidding? Knickers? Bras? Both?"

Velenksy lowered her voice and leaned in close. "Just the knickers. And between you and me, I'd say it's a pervert with a penchant for ladies' knickers."

"Transsexual?" Sydney asked. "Not something I'd put

into a book. Especially what I'm writing."

"Can I ask what that is?" Velenksy asked eagerly.

"Just a little something I'm working on scene by scene," Sydney answered. "But lunch with the PC and his family was very illuminating."

"Right. I remember Connor Ryan turned up last week when we were here." Velenksy nodded. "I think I heard him say something about lunch."

"He did, and I went with my friend Emerson, who created the *Twisted Minds* TV show."

Velensky's eyes widened once more. "Oh, my God I love that show. The whole precinct watches it. It would be great if we could get you both in for a visit."

"And it would be great if I could get back to work," Sydney said. "I was head deep in a scene when one of you banged on my door."

"Oh, that was Rotrain." Velenksy turned to see where he was and found him glaring up at her from the pavement.

"Guess you'd better go and I'd better get back to it. I hope no more creepy crimes happen in this street. Goodnight." Sydney stepped inside, locked and bolted both doors, and hurried upstairs to write it all down.

Chapter 8

On Wednesday afternoon at four, Sydney met Sean in the boardroom at Pulsate.

"You'll be meeting with Victor today. He's an acquisitions editor of young adult and he's looking for new talent. No idea what he thinks of your stories, but we'll find out today." She noticed his excited demeanour. "You seem happy. Good week?"

"Not really, but I've got another hour with you and I'm getting my stories edited with an acquisitions editor. Why wouldn't I be excited?" He'd been nervous for the last week after hitting send on the email to Sydney with five of his stories attached. He'd laboured over which ones to send, and finally decided which were his best. If they weren't going to get him published at the end of this mentorship, then nothing would. His heart raced every time he'd thought of Sydney and seeing her again, and now he was standing next to her and there was so much he wanted to say.

Victor Brothers walked into the room. "Hey, Sydney, and you must be Sean." He pulled out a chair and sat at the table. "Take a seat and let's get into this so you guys can chat about it." He settled piles of stapled paper in front of him and laid them out neatly, waiting for Sean and Sydney to take their seats.

"So, what did you think?" Sydney jumped in. "Good or what?"

"Very," Victor told an eager Sean. "You're actually very good already. Have you studied, or is it just high school English?"

"High school English and lots of books on writing, lots of courses and videos on writing from and by famous authors." Sean fidgeted in his seat, anxious for the rest of the critique.

"Okay. Well, you have talent and some skill. With some editing advice you'll definitely improve to a point we could publish these at the end of your mentorship."

"What!" Sean's head pulled back in shock, his body rigid. "Wait…what?"

"Isn't that what you wanted?" Sydney asked. "An honest opinion and a published book at the end of the three months?"

Sean gaped at her blankly. "Ah…yeah…I guess so."

"No guesses about it." Victor slid a pile of paper over to him. "I've written notes on each story, suggesting where to tighten phrases, use different words, or to avoid more description, but overall, you're far more advanced than most teens your age. Are you acing English?"

"I am." Sean flicked through the pages and saw red pen on a few of them.

"Great. Let me go through each story with you." Victor spent the next forty minutes giving advice to Sean that was invaluable to young or new writers, and something

Sean could take forward into future writings.

"And I think that about covers everything." Victor glanced at the clock. "We've got ten minutes left. Anything you want to ask?"

"Ah…" Sean slowly shook his head. "Not off the top of my head. But what if I come up with a question later? Or more than one?"

"Then email them to me via the publishing house and ask. It comes with the mentorship." Victor pushed his chair back and stood. "Sean, Sydney, until next time."

"Thanks, Victor." Sydney watched him leave and sighed. "If that wasn't helpful, I don't know what else will be. You're already so good you might not even need a three-month mentorship."

"What if I started writing adult?" Sean asked, laying each stack of paper on top of the other. "It's all well and good to talk about these stories, and maybe have them published, but what if I start something adult and got a critique for that?"

Sydney thought about it. "Why not work on them for the rest of the month, and then try something else? But…" she dragged out the word. "You're good at YA, why change?"

"Because I'm going to *be* an adult in a year," he said earnestly. "Why shouldn't I write it?"

She watched him. "Didn't say you shouldn't, just said you're good at YA, so why not stick with it for now and wait and see what being published gets you. You may end up with a contract for more books. What then?"

Sean pondered for a moment, biting his bottom lip. "Is that possible? If it is, then I can do that for a couple of years and earn my writing chops. Prove to my parents and cousin that I *am* good enough. Make some money to pay my way through college, and then when I'm in my twenties give adult a crack." His head bobbed up and down. "I could do a four-year plan. Seventeen to twenty-one, college years, a young adult author popular at college. But wait… If I'm already good enough to be published, would I even need to get a degree in writing?"

Sydney considered the question. "That would definitely be one for Victor. When do you apply for college?"

"At the end of the year so I have time to find out. It would give me a degree and my first book would be considered by publishing houses as a part of the course. But if I'm already published by Pulsate…"

"What if your book doesn't sell? And is only the one? The one book, the one contract?" Sydney asked. "A degree would be another leg up, another useful link in the resume. You'd be considered above others, but then struggling to get a book picked up."

"True." He made some notes in his notebook before slapping it shut. "Our time's up, but this has been incredibly helpful." He shoved his book and paperwork into his backpack.

Sydney stood up and picked up her handbag. She was overly warm in her lightweight knitted star pattern sweater in blue and pink, and the heaters spewing God knows what temperature air into the room didn't help. "Apart from getting the normal advice from everyone else, I really have no idea what kind of help I can offer."

"Help me write adult stories." Sean pushed his chair under the table and hefted his bag onto his shoulder.

"I've gotten advice about my YA stories; now you can give me advice in adult novels. Stories for kids and teens are one thing, but stories for adults are a completely different animal."

"Not really." Sydney led the way to the elevator bank. "The outline is the same. The acts, the beats, the arcs. Every story is laid out the same. It's how you tell it that makes the magic."

The bell dinged and they stepped into the lift, the doors closing just as the second onslaught of workers leaving for the day reached them.

"Okay. So that's all the same, but what about *making* it adult? I don't write sex or romance, but I'd have to in adult."

The doors opened and they stepped into the lobby, stopping by the side of the front glass doors.

"It helps if you've had experiences, you can make it authentic that way, but if you don't want to write romance or sex, then go for crime thrillers, psychological or domestic, action adventure, or something else completely. You could just take a story or two you've written and see if you can adultify it. Change the ages, or something."

A light bulb went off and he nodded. "That's a good idea, but still not quite adult. And while crime would be a natural move, considering my family and all, maybe a thriller might work."

"Let your deepest, darkest secrets out and see what happens." Sydney shrugged. "Doesn't matter if anyone reads it; just use it as an exercise for trying adult."

"Another good idea," he said. "And this is why this

mentorship is a good idea. You have suggestions I wouldn't think of—"

"Then you'd better start thinking of them if you want to write adult fiction when you grow up." Sydney saw Amy pull up outside. "Because sometimes when you're stuck for ideas, you have to reach far and wide for something to write. It doesn't matter if it's wacky and too far out there, give it a try and see what sticks." She motioned for them to walk outside, and they stopped on the sidewalk next to the car.

"Another great idea." Sean waved to Amy and turned his attention back to Sydney. "Considering the family I'm in, you'd think I'd be all over crime, but I can't stand it most of the time. Maybe a medical drama, but there's plenty of those on TV."

"Again, reach far and wide and see what ideas stick." Sydney opened the door and dropped her bag on the seat. "We can talk about it more next week."

"If I write something can you read it and let me know if it's good enough?" Sean stepped closer, but Sydney stayed behind the open passenger door, keeping it between them. "I can whip up a few pages, or few thousand words, and have it ready for next Wednesday."

"Think it's that easy, do you?" she mocked. "Just you wait." A memory sprang to mind. "You said at lunch that you get pain behind your eyes or something and it won't stop until you're finished writing."

"Yeah, it's horrible," he complained. "My eyes throb and my brain pounds."

"Then use that as an indication you've picked the right idea," Sydney suggested. "If an idea does that to you, go with the flow."

"Another great idea." He waved a hand. "I'll do that. Take care, Sydney, see you next week.

*****

"Tell me what's been happening since I saw you last," Emerson said on Saturday morning. "When was it?"

"Lunch at the PC's," Sydney reminded her. "And a lot has happened."

"So spill!" Emerson linked her arm through her best friend's and they walked off down the street for a spot of shopping in the mild autumn weather.

"Well…" Sydney acted nonchalantly. "Hot Ryan number two came to my house later that night."

"Wait, what?" Emerson pulled on her arm to bring her to a stop. "He came over later. What for?"

"Well…he just wanted to get me naked and plant his massive cock inside me," Sydney said. She noticed a few passersby glance their way and raised her brows at them.

"What!" Emerson exclaimed. "Are you fucking joking? You can't be." She noticed Sydney's expression. "Oh, my fucking God. You fucked him."

"Bit hard not to when he got me out of my pants and onto his cock pretty damn quick. In fact, so fucking quick I didn't realise how quick." Sydney started off down the street.

"But was *he* quick?" Emerson asked, hurrying to catch up. She slid her arm back through the crook of Sydney's elbow. "Or did he take you all night?"

"Oh, he did. Mainly on the living room couch, but

the first time was against the front door he was so quick and to the point."

"Fucking hell," Emerson breathed. "And was that it?"

"That night or since?" Sydney pulled her to a stop out the front of a clothing boutique and looked in the window.

"You mean there were more times?" Emerson's mouth dropped. "Oh, my fucking God. What's he like? Is he big? Is he furry? Is he hot naked? Did you orgasm?"

"Jesus, Em," Sydney chastised, and pointed to a bondage style dress in the window. "Think I should buy that?"

"So, you can wear it when you whip him? Have you taken him down to the sex room yet?" Emerson pulled her along. "How many did you try? Did he like it? Did you orgasm? Did he orgasm?"

"What is it with you needing to know about our orgasms?" Sydney stopped again, pulling her friend close to the store window. She lowered her voice. "What is it with you?"

"I need to live vicariously through you," Emerson said. "We've been here what, a month and a half, and you're already fucking a hot cop. And he's been in the sex room. Meanwhile, I'm not getting any action and no orgasms unless I use a toy. And that ain't got a hot male body attached to it."

"Jesus. I did not need to hear that." Sydney shook her head to clear out that information. "I'm surprised you haven't received a call from the hot PC himself. He seemed very smitten with you at lunch a few weeks ago."

Emerson blushed and turned away. "Who said I haven't?" she said coyly, and batted her long black lashes.

"Fucking hell." Sydney pulled her close. "Cormac

called you? Did he ask you out? Did you say yes? Have you gone yet? Have you fucked? Wait, you just said you hadn't had a man, so no to that. But the rest of it?"

"Jesus, Sydney. Now *I* need to say what is it with *you?* No, we haven't gone yet, so no we haven't fucked yet. But our date is for tonight."

"Ooohhh. That's why you called me up and said let's go shopping. You need a dress." Sydney nodded her head at all the thoughts running through it. "Maybe we should go back and get that bondage dress for you. You'll probably get lucky if you wear it."

"Oh, for God's sake." Emerson's face grew scarlet and she moved out of the crowd's way. "Do you think it would fit?"

"Only one way to find out." Sydney led her back to the shop and walked through the door. "Hello, my friend would like to try on that black dress in the window that looks like something an escort would wear."

The assistant gaped at Sydney, asked Emerson her size, and hurried to the rack for another dress. She handed it over and said, "Changing rooms are back there."

Emerson took the dress and quickly changed into it, admiring her curves in the skin tight satin and latex type material in the mirrors. Her hands slid over her hips. "I don't know, Syd, is it appropriate for dinner? Especially one with the PC?" She flung back the curtains and walked out, glancing in the mirrors on the wall opposite the changing rooms.

Sydney's jaw dropped. "Fucking hell, Em. That dress was *made* for you." Her friend's killer curves curved in all the right places. The dress showed off her shapely long legs and well-rounded breasts. Since Emerson worked out, it also showed off her toned arms and shoulders. The dress was absolutely made for her body.

Emerson turned left and right, trying to see all sides of herself in the mirrors. "But is it appropriate for a dinner with the PC? Do I look like a hooker or call girl?"

"You do, but you're clearly not. You're a hot and sexy middle-aged woman on the prowl for some fun. Even if it is with the commish." Sydney nodded her approval. "Take it. It suits you. And you might get lucky with the poor guy."

Emerson looked over her shoulder at Sydney. "Why's he a poor guy?"

Sydney smirked. "'Cause one look at you and he'll be hard. And one kiss from you and you'll be fucking like randy teenagers. He won't know what hit him."

Snorting with laughter, Emerson covered her mouth, took one last look in the mirror, kicked up her leg behind her, whooped, and went to change.

After paying for the dress, they kept on shopping with Sydney telling Emerson all about Connor and their times together, the robbery next door, a few things about the idea she was working on, and mentoring Sean.

"How's that going? I know you had misgivings about it." Emerson sipped her after lunch coffee. "Anything you want me to tell Cormac tonight?"

"Won't you be too busy making out like randy teenagers to talk?" Sydney laughed and rested her cutlery on her plate. "So far, there's not much to tell and he's probably mentioned it to them at Sunday lunch."

"There haven't been any problems? You were worried."

"I was, and still am, just not to the degree I was," Sydney said. "He's under twenty-one, way too eager. He actually seems quite tame during our meetings, although we've only had two sessions." She shrugged a shoulder. "Maybe it won't be so bad after all. I hope he doesn't prove me wrong. It's a three month mentorship."

"So don't put the horse before the cart. Be on your toes, but don't let your guard down." Emerson paid the bill and gathered her bags. "Meanwhile, I want to get my hair done before tonight. I've booked in for three at my favourite salon. I'm getting my make-up done as well. You want to come?"

"It's not how I expected our day to go, so no. I'll get back to the brownstone and put my nose to the grindstone. Books don't write themselves, you know."

"Yours seem to." Emerson hailed a cab outside the restaurant. "How long does it take you to write one?"

"First draft, a month. Then another two months adding and researching if need be. I seem to do things backwards." Sydney climbed into the cab next to Emerson. "Most authors research for a book and then write it. But I write a first draft, usually rough as guts, and then spend a couple of months doing any research to make corrections, and I make it shine."

"Then you hand it in to CC?" Emerson asked.

"Nope. Gemma. Then we spend another month or so polishing it some more."

"And then CC gets it."

"And then the cover is done and yes, CC publishes it. That's why a book can come out every six months. But then I did have a catalogue when Pulsate took me on. I was already publishing e-books, but they paid for print and had multiple books to publish. But…I don't know…" Sydney rested her head in her hand, her elbow on the windowsill, her gaze directed at the view.

"No ideas, no books. You're slowing down." Emerson leaned toward the driver. "Pull over here, please."

The cab stopped and she gathered her bags. "I'll just be a few minutes and then we'll go to the salon. Please wait." She got out of the car and turned around. "You coming, Syd?"

"No, I'll wait till you get back. Don't be long."

Emerson entered her building and Sydney stared out the window. She realised she had been slowing down with her writing, and besides the issue in L.A., there was no other reason except she had no new ideas. The last book had got behind and was subsequently scrapped. The new book was happening quickly, but she'd still need some time to bring it into its full story. She was excited about it. It was new, and different, and inspired by New York. Maybe that was what had been missing. Excitement in her writing. It could be boring drudge work at times, sitting down for hours on end, putting pen to paper to write her mandatory twenty pages a day. Ten in the morning; ten in the afternoon. Sometimes she didn't come close to making it to twenty, and sometimes, she blasted past it and wrote another ten at night, or just kept writing all day. A sore wrist and hand was her only bedfellow in her semi-lonely writer's life.

It had been lonely since being here in New York, that was. L.A. had been magical for so long. A fantasy life in a fantasy town with fantasy people calling her friend. She'd partied often, stayed sober, and made notes of all she saw and heard. She'd been finally relishing in the kind of life she'd only ever dreamed about. But she had lived it for ten very long years while her books were made into movies. She dined with the rich, partied with the famous, and lived for the stories of the not so famous. She'd even managed to become fast friends with her favourite author, Jackie Collins, of the salacious bonkbuster Hollywood lifestyle novels. Jackie had taught her a thing or two about listening and watching and Sydney had made many a note in how to finagle even the most private stories out of people. And that lifestyle had given Sydney all kinds of ideas for stories and books. But…so much to write, so little time to write it.

The taxi door opened and she startled, ready to tell the person the cab was taken. "Jesus, Em, I thought it was someone trying to steal the cab." She watched Emerson shut the door.

"Ha! Not so lucky. *Marbella* salon, please." Emerson settled back and looked at Sydney. "You were far away. Thinking about hot Ryan number two?"

"Thinking about hot Ryan original?" Sydney teased. "You took a while."

"I had to freshen up. I'll be sitting in the salon for three hours."

"When's the date?"

"He picks me up at seven."

"From your place?"

"Of course."

"You'll have to call me tomorrow and tell me all about it."

"That's if I'm not busy tomorrow," Emerson eluded.

"Why wouldn't you…oh…" Sydney chuckled. "You naughty girl."

"I might just be. But what if you're a naughty girl tonight? Hot Ryan number two might come over."

"He might, but I won't hold my breath, and you shouldn't either. The family has lunch on Sundays unless you plan on going to that."

"If I stay the night I just might. We're here." She cut off what Sydney was about to say. "So, you don't want to come in and watch me get dolled up?"

"Considering all the shellac that will take, no thanks," Sydney quipped and watched her get out and turn around.

Emerson leaned into the car and frowned. "Oh, how nice of you, you cheeky sod. You'll just have to pay the cab fare, then."

"What! You bitch! Pay your own damn share," Sydney yelled.

"Nope. I paid for lunch and you insulted me. You pay it." Emerson slammed the door, waved her fingers, and strode into the salon, leaving Sydney spitting at paying for the cab fare.

Chapter 9

Sydney was busy writing when a banging pulled her attention away and downstairs. "Ah, and once again I have the pleasure of hot Ryan number two on this Saturday night. What brings you by?" She locked the doors behind him, turned off the front lights, and reset the alarm.

"It's my only night off all week and I wanted to spend it with my gal." Connor pulled her into his arms and landed an almighty smacking kiss on her lips.

Her arms slid around his neck and pulled him close, moving into the kiss like a hungry tiger that hadn't eaten in days. They were naked in moments and fucking against the wall, unable to stop long enough to make it to the couch in the living room, or the bed upstairs. It was hot, powerful, animalistic thrusting.

When satiated, Sydney pulled her pants on and asked if he wanted coffee.

"Got a beer? I need that more," Connor said as he zipped up his jeans. He didn't need to get his clothes off when fucking Sydney, but she needed to get naked from the waist down to accommodate him; something he liked the look and feel of very much. But this time, everything had come off.

"I might have something in the fridge." She led the way to the kitchen and flicked on the light. Finding four beers of a six pack left in the fridge, she pulled it out and dangled it by the plastic lining. "You can have these."

"Don't like that brand, but won't quibble." He grabbed the pack, ripped one from the plastic and cracked it open. He guzzled half down then set the can on the bench. "That'll do it. So…" He leaned against the bench and grabbed Sydney's hand. "What were you up to before I got here?"

"Deep into my writing." She held his hand to her chest and gazed into his eyes. "You interrupted me and unless you want something, I really need to get back to it."

"Oh, ho, ho. Is that the way it's gonna be," he joked, lifting up his captured hand to tweak her chin with his finger. "Ms Big Shot Writer's latest book is more important than me."

"*It* will make me money, *you* will not." She glanced away and played coy. "I'd charge you for it, but then that would make me a pro, which I'm not."

"Or it would make you the next Madam X," Connor replied, and sculled back another mouthful of beer.

Sydney's interest piqued. "That's actually not a bad idea for a book title. *The Next Madam X.* I am in her house after all."

"You do have her sex dungeon after all," Connor added. "Even if it's new. Imagine what would've been all over that equipment."

"Or *who* would've been all over that equipment.

Ugh." Sydney shuddered. "No, thanks. You have that in one of your warehouses somewhere as evidence, don't you? Bet you've all tried it out at some stage," she teased.

"Ha-ha." Connor finished off his beer and belched. "You know though, you kinda are picking up where she left off. You've already had one cop in the dungeon."

"It's not a dungeon! How many times do I have to say it before you stop calling it that," Sydney complained and held her forefinger up. "You're one cop. *One.* No politicians, no senators, lawyers, judges, or businessmen have passed through the door of this brownstone while I've been here. Just you, just one cop. *One.* So no." She noticed the twinkle in his eyes and the grin sliding across his lips. "I am not following in her footsteps, picking up where she left off, or becoming the next Madam X." She placed the empty can upside down in the sink to drain. "But then, you seemed to enjoy yourself down there."

"Fuck yeah, I did." Connor rested his right hand on his hip, and his left on the bench as he leant against it. "I've tried a few things in my time, been with a few women who had a few kinks, but never fucked a woman with a sex room."

"Hallelujah, he finally gets it." Sydney waved her hands to the heavens. "But had you ever been in one before?"

"Well…" he drawled and took her in his arms. "I'll never tell."

"Then you will never set foot in my dungeon again," Sydney quipped.

"Is that a euphemism?"

"Do you want it to be?"

"No." He shrugged. "Just want to fuck you."

"And which room would you like to do that in, detective?" Sydney nuzzled his neck.

"I don't care about which room we do it in; I just want to be in your dungeon."

She snorted with laughter. "My vagina is not a dungeon."

"I asked if it was a euphemism." He picked her up over his shoulder. "But since I'd like to be comfortable and spread out, your room it is." He strode out of the kitchen and upstairs, letting Sydney snap off the lights along the way.

*****

"Hey, sweetie, good to see you again."

"Honey. Good to see you're still alive and not making headlines in the paper." The man stood before her, hands in his hoodie pockets, the hood pulled low over his face, a thick coat over it to ward off the late autumn chill.

"Alive and kicking, baby." She slid her fingers up and down his jacket lapels. "You need some Honey tonight?"

"Yes, I do. And since I can rely on you to always be in the same spot, I can rely on our spot being free." He titled his head in the direction of the alley.

"Same as always?" Her hand hooked into his elbow and they strolled down the alley.

"Not quite." He glanced towards the street and pushed her between the bins that were their shield against the world. "I want to feel you. I want you to feel me. And I want you to show me how to pleasure you."

Her perfectly lined red lips went into an o. "Since when do men care about pleasing a woman, let alone a pro?"

"Practice makes perfect," he murmured. "Show me what you can do to me with your hands, and I'll return the favour."

"Oh, let me at it, big boy." Her hands expertly unzipped his pants and pulled him out. All of him. Both hands manipulated his ball sack. Kneading, rubbing, pulling, almost as if she were milking a cow.

Groaning, he placed his hands on the wall either side of her, his head falling, his eyes closed against the intense torture. "I'm coming. Fuck it, Honey." He thrust at her and she manipulated him to orgasm.

He collapsed against her, against the wall. "Where did you learn that?"

"Where do you think, sweetie?" Honey's hands kept up the torment, stroking his penis until it hardened in her hand. "Do you like it?"

"I want to know how a woman can please a man. I want to know how it feels to be in her hands, to have her around it, I want to know what pleasure I can get from it. What I'm supposed to get from it." He grunted, and ejaculated into Honey's hands.

She rubbed it over his penis and testicles, lubricating him. That's when he realised he was over her, her hands. His DNA was on her. He grabbed her hands.

"Now it's time for me. Show me how to pleasure you, Honey. Show me how to pleasure a woman." He removed his black leather gloves and put them in his coat pockets. He had white plastic gloves under them.

She took his hands and led them to her, under her

skirt. "You touch me here." While she manoeuvred his hands against her, he moved his fingers inside. Soft gasping cries came from her open mouth and her head fell back against the wall. She bucked to him, her lower body thrusting into his hand. The mound of his palm rubbed her clit; his finger rubbed her spot. And his hand was so perfect a size she came from both climaxes. A clit climax and a vag climax. It was rare that a john knew what to do. Rarer that they knew how to bring her to orgasm. But this one… *Oh God, fuck me*, she thought, panting for breath. *He knows all the moves.*

"Can I feel you? Can you feel me?" he asked, this thumb slowly rubbing her clit and it didn't take much to make her cry out. "Can you feel me?"

"Yes," she gasped, pushing his hand against her, pulsating to another climax. "Yes."

His fingers explored her, stroking, rubbing, pushing against each part of her. He stroked her inner thighs and ran his hands over her outer thighs and buttocks, squeezing them until she thrust against his penis. It went between her legs and she rubbed it against herself, making them both climax.

She didn't know she could have so many orgasms in one night, let alone at one time, but fuck this dude was good. "I've never been fucked like this before."

"Never?" His fingers moved inside her, sliding in and out in a slow sensual rhythm.

She groaned and thrust forward in time with his strokes.

He pulled out, lifted her up so she straddled him, and continued his torment.

Her legs hooked into the bin handles, her arms hooked

around his neck. She was wide open to him and the torment of his fingers inside her, and he brought her to the brink multiple times, always ending with her going over the edge.

He set her down, leaning them both against the wall. She was weak and weary, while he was ready for more. "Can I taste you?"

"What?" she murmured, exhausted and barely able to stand. "What do you mean?"

"Can I taste you?" He kneeled in front of her and grasped her hips. His mouth went to the soft flesh of her lower abdomen and kissed her.

She groaned and grasped his shoulders, knowing their rules were to never grab his hair or head. That his identity remains secret. Her hands gripped his coat and she thrust at his mouth. His lips tormented her just as his fingers had. His tongue flicked and licked and teased her. She came early, unable to hold on.

This was something he'd wanted to learn. He'd never tried with a woman before. While he enjoyed getting his dick sucked, he'd never gone down on a woman. And he didn't like it. The smell, the taste, the texture was repulsing him, but he had to learn to like it, or at least to tolerate it. He wondered if it was the same for them when his dick was in their mouth. Were women just as repulsed by the taste and texture of a man? Did they want to vomit like he did? He held his composure and his breath as his tongue slid inside her. Nope. Can't do it. He licked up to her clit and pulled away, spitting fluid from his mouth. God, he needed a drink. He got to his feet. "How was that?"

She sighed in delirium. "I don't know where you learned that from, but fuck me you learned it good." She watched him pull on his black gloves, and noted the manly fingers. "You're quite a big boy."

"So I've been told." He moved closer, his manhood still flying free. "There's just one more thing before I go."

"And what's that big boy?" she murmured, her fingers under his lapels. "You want to fuck for real?

"Yes." He turned her around and ground himself into her ass. "Get me hard, Honey. Get me hard."

She ground into him, pumping against him, feeling him harden. Just those motions alone made her horny as hell and close to the brink. "God, do it already," she cried. "Do it."

He didn't. He just held her hips and ground himself into her, toyed with her, played with her, pushing against her and then backed off. He bent her at the waist, her hands on the wall, and pushed the tip of his penis into her clit, into her opening, taking it in turns to tease and torment, push against one, then the other.

She bucked and gasped, and came multiple times, but he didn't relent; pushing in and out until they both came, and he kept pushing and kneading her ass, and touching her clit. He wanted to see if she would bleed. If she would scream in pain, beg him to stop, to not stop, to never come again.

She didn't because she wanted it, wanted the pain, the pleasure, the torment… She wanted him inside of her, wanted him outside of her, wanted him all over her, in her mouth, her body.

He pulled a pair of silk stockings from his pocket, and

wound it around both hands while he thrust her against the wall. He wrapped it around her neck and whispered in her ear. "Come for me, Honey. Come and don't stop."

*****

Sydney was back to writing on Sunday after Connor left, and when Emerson rang about her date.

"Have you seen it? We made the news and socials," she gabbled down the line.

"Seen what? I've been busy writing and you know I'm not on socials when I'm writing, or it's Sunday." Sydney laid her pen down and leaned back in her chair. "So? What am I supposed to have seen?"

"Well." Emerson cleared her throat. "The Police Commissioner, Cormac Ryan, and I, director, producer, writer, Emerson Lake, were photographed at the restaurant last night and made it to the gossip show this morning, and social media last night."

Sydney was impressed. "And how did he take that? He might've wanted a quiet dinner and no paps."

"He didn't seem overly fazed by it," she replied. "In fact. I wouldn't be surprised if he called them and said we'd be there."

"Is that something he'd do? Call the paps? He didn't seem like that type of guy to me." Sydney checked the clock. It was two in the afternoon. "Did you stay over?"

"Sydney!" Emerson exclaimed. "How dare you have such thoughts—"

"Did *he* stay over?" Sydney continued. "'Cause you would've had all of his entourage stay as well."

"Sydney Kingston, how dare you think I'm that type of woman, or that he's that type of man."

"I dare. Did you?"

"Of course I did." Emerson chuckled. "Why would I not? He's hot, and older than me."

"Which is surprising since you go for younger men," Sydney interrupted. "Did he have what all the young studs you bed have?"

"And then some," Emerson said. "He had the stamina of a bull, or a stallion, or whichever animal you want to use as an example. I think my dress got him excited and aroused and he hadn't been with anyone since his wife died."

"How long ago was that?" Sydney couldn't recall reading it anywhere and it hadn't come up at Sunday lunch. Or with Sean.

"Thirteen years ago. Can you imagine going without a lover or partner or a date in thirteen years?" Emerson shuddered. "Ugh. I certainly couldn't."

"Well, older folk like to cling to their partners after death. They take their time grieving and may not move on. Sometimes it's by choice, or because there's no one their age to move on to. How old is he again?"

"Seventy. Fifteen years older than me. Which is a fine age to date. Besides, he doesn't look seventy, whatever seventy is supposed to look like, and he can get it up fine without the little blue pill. So…"

"It had been so long between drinks that he got drunk with lust for a beautiful woman and fucked her madly all night." Sydney heard silence on the other end. "He did fuck you madly all night, didn't he?"

"Yes," Emerson murmured dreamily. "He certainly did."

"Oh." Sydney smacked her forehead with the palm of her hand. "You phased out there for a moment, thinking about last night. Do tell."

"Sydney…" A giggle burst out of Emerson. "He picked me up, but because I was wearing a long coat, he didn't get to see what I was wearing under it. He brought me a beautiful bouquet of red roses with baby's breath in it. And I put them in a vase before we went out. We had the escort and SUV because he's the commish, obviously, and we dined at *Spaldings*. That's the posh restaurant that has a three month waiting list just to get in."

"But you got in *because* he's the commish, right?"

"I guess, because he certainly didn't know me three months ago, so if he made the reservation a few days ago, he probably did." She paused. "Jesus, Syd, he gets special treatment at restaurants and probably dozens of other places. Is that wrong?"

"Celebs get special treatment all the time. Just look at everything you've got for free, or places you were able to walk into and get a table, or private room straight off the bat because who you are and what you do."

"True." Emerson nodded, but a frown slid over her face. "But he's the police commissioner. Isn't it illegal or something to do that?"

"Why do you care? Just get on with the rest of the story," Sydney pushed. "What did he think when he saw the dress?"

"Oh…" Another giggle. "We got to the restaurant and were escorted right in. We had a table with an amazing view of the city in a private area of the restaurant. And when the Maître d' showed us to the table and he took my coat, he saw the dress. So did the Maître d' and you should have seen the looks on their faces."

"You were poured into that thing and spilled over in all the right places."

"And so did his eyes out of his head," Emerson told her. "He was *very* appreciative."

"Bet he was," Sydney murmured, smiling. "How was the food? You did eat, didn't you?"

"Ha-ha," Emerson said. "Of course we did. But it was a struggle in that dress."

"Wasn't it stretchy?"

"Hell no! So, I just had small bites through the night. Not that he ate much either."

"Too busy checking you out," Sydney teased.

"Smarty pants. Yes, he was actually, but he did finish his steak which I suppose gave him his stamina later on."

"Three course, four course, five course meal? Did you have dessert?"

"We managed it before the flirting went way farther than mere flirting. I was rubbing his leg."

"Which one?"

"Oh, you! My foot was rubbing his calf, my hand was rubbing his thigh."

"Naughty!"

"I was. My fingers were rubbing his hand."

"Did *his* hand do anything?"

"Paid the bill, led me downstairs, and back to his place."

"Did he ask if you wanted to?"

"He did and I did. He's very attractive, and still in great shape."

"And he managed to get you out of that dress?"

"And my lingerie," Emerson quipped. "He's a very thoughtful lover. Asked if I wanted or liked certain things. I asked him if I could take the lead—"

"And lead you did. I've heard all about your exploits, Emerson Lake."

"You certainly have, just as I've heard all about yours, but—"

"Not all."

The silence was deafening.

"What!"

"I haven't told you all of my exploits." Sydney gazed at the clock counting the minutes ticking by. "I've kept a few things private. But if you took the lead in bed, then good for you. Did he enjoy it?"

"He did, which is why he had the stamina." Emerson frowned. "Sydney, why haven't you told me all of it?"

"Because, as I just said, I've kept some of it private. Have *you* told *me* all of yours?"

Emerson made a grumbling sound under her breath. "No…"

"So don't be upset then. Besides, the current situation needs to be kept private for many reasons."

"Why does you seeing Connor need to be kept private?"

"Considering he may have been seeing Laura, and now I'm mentoring her son, I'd like to keep it to myself. Anyway, you stayed the night?"

"Ah, yes, I did. We made passionate love a few times and fell asleep in each other's arms, waking up this morning the same way. It was nice."

"Good for you. Did you get out before the kids came?"

"Oh, God yes. I only had that dress and my coat; I didn't need them seeing me looking like that."

"Or their dad fucking someone wearing that dress. Although they do know who you are. Did the shows and socials get your name and occupation right?"

"What do you mean my…oh you." The realisation hit Emerson and she burst out laughing. "Yes, thank God. At least the ones I saw. Who knows, there could be a rumour that the commish is dating a hooker out later today on some website."

"Wearing that dress, if they don't know who you are, it's probably the next thing they think and then you'll sue their arse off. So, what are you doing today? Seeing Cormac again?"

"I'm having a relaxing day, and yes, he's already asked me out again."

"When?"

"He asked if we could have dinner every night this week. His house or mine. Just something quiet and peaceful."

"And one of you will stay over? What time does he have to get up?"

"Whatever time I make him, I suppose."

Sydney frowned. "You mean…" Her eyes widened. "Oh you. You're dirtier than the book I'm writing."

"Which you've barely mentioned," Emerson complained.

"That's because it's based on a sex room."

"The one in your basement?" Emerson's brows rose.

"That's the one. Bye, Em, see you next Saturday." Sydney ended the call and got back to work.

Chapter 10

Sydney entered CC's office on Wednesday afternoon. "CC, Gem." She paused. "Olivia, what are you doing here?"

"You called, darling. And I always come to their meetings because it's all about your career." Olivia flicked her hair over her shoulder, crossed her long legs, and straightened her bohemian style winter skirt over them. "Anything to do with a book."

"Ah, yeah. I guess. I've been too engrossed in the book. But I guess it's time to put a full proposal forward because there's some legalities needed."

CC sat straighter in her Chanel wingback chair. "And what legalities would they be, Sydney? We've never needed the lawyers before."

"No, but you'd better call him in because it concerns the next two books."

"Two?" CC perked up. "I'm all ears." Her ears were framed by her grey curls and pearl Chanel studs, and she was dressed in a Chanel pantsuit in pearl grey, with a soft pink pussy bow blouse under it. Rudimentary Chanel pearls were at her throat and a matching pearl brooch on her left lapel.

Sydney felt plain and boring next to CC. Her jeans, blue sweater, and funky earrings dangling to her shoulders seemed subpar. "Let's get the lawyer in for a chat first." She watched CC sigh and get up to make the call.

Once the call was made, CC popped a bottle of champagne and poured herself a glass. She held it to her lips, but paused. "Will I need the whole bottle for this?"

Sydney couldn't help laughing. "Probably not."

Eric Vember walked into the office. "CC, Gemma." He saw Sydney. "Sydney, to what do I owe this pleasure?"

"Close and lock the door," Sydney instructed and saw his puzzled frown.

He locked it and walked over to the couch and sat down. "Okay, it's serious. What's going on?"

Sydney proceeded through the proposal for the two books which she had merely mentioned previously. She kept their rapt attention until she finished and sat back. "Amy's helping with the information, and fact checking, but I guess we would need to fully ascertain whether it's all legal and the real deal."

"Jesus Christ," Olivia muttered, leaning back in her chair. "And you have all of the receipts and paperwork?"

Sydney nodded. "I do, and I've been very particular about it. My lawyer helped with everything that was required, and he's assured me it's all legal."

"And now you want to publish the books?" Gemma asked, unable to believe what she'd heard. "It's a hell of a story."

"It is," Sydney agreed. "But I perfectly understand if the novel never sees the light of day. The non-fic should.

It is about a real person, and thoroughly researched."

"And you own all the belongings?" Olivia asked.

"All of it. Everything that was left behind, I own outright and legally," Sydney replied.

"Then I don't really see the problem except when it comes to names," Eric said.

"And *that* would be our problem." Sydney sighed and rubbed her temple. "I've been putting different names in the novel. But the non-fic, that's a whole other ball game. And I know some of the people who are involved. It would be an absolute shit show of a court case if they fight it, unless, of course, we drop it with no warning and deal with the aftermath."

"Oh, no, no, no," CC and Eric said simultaneously. CC waved her hands back and forth. "I am not dealing with that legal shit show, to use your words. I don't know, Sydney." She leaned back and closed her eyes. "As much as I love the fact all of your books sell out in days, and soar past the million sales mark within a week, this would be a massive risk. We'd have to go over the novel thoroughly and the biography more so. I don't know." She rubbed her temple the way Sydney had.

"How about waiting until my final drafts are done and dusted?" Sydney suggested. "And then you can tell me whether we're publishing it or not. I can deny having any information other than what's public for the novel, but the biography is a different matter."

"And that would be a problem." Eric thought through the legalities that came to mind. "They could definitely take it to court to delay or cancel publishing. It may never be published."

"Even though it's all been annotated and authorised?" Sydney asked.

"You can't prove it's real, regardless. They could claim you made it up," he replied.

"Ah…bugger." Sydney deflated. "Look, I've been tearing though these two books and I'm about half way through the novel. And Amy's been digging up info for the bio. So let me finish them, and you can see what they're about before saying no. Besides, there are already dozens of books on them, so why would mine be different?"

CC reluctantly agreed. "Another month or two?"

"Probably. Unless I really get into them day and night." Sydney's phone alarm went off and she dug the phone out of her bag to turn it off. "I have the mentorship session with Sean now."

"How's that going? I remember you saying you weren't comfortable with it." Olivia said.

"And I'm still not. Although he hasn't tried anything yet," Sydney told her. "The two sessions we've had so far have been here and Victor took last week's to edit some of what he'd written. Victor says he's good and should get a YA deal out of it at the end."

"If his stories are as good as the example he sent in with the submission, he probably will be," CC said. "I remember showing it to Victor and he said it was excellent."

"He gave Sean some good tips, but then Sean turned around and told me he wants to try adult fiction," Sydney said.

"Why?" Gemma asked. "If he's good at YA."

"He is." Sydney shrugged. "But he's kinda right. He says he'll be an adult in a few years and why shouldn't he write for adults. I told him he needed experience because it helped with the storytelling. He's seventeen, and he doesn't have any."

"What genre does he want to write?" Gemma asked. She was one of the adult novel editors at the house, crossing several genres.

"He doesn't know. His family's full of cops and lawyers, and he said he should write crime but doesn't want to. Same with medical. So who knows, but I have to get to the session. I'll see you guys sometime next week." She unlocked the door and waved goodbye, walking down the hall to the boardroom to see Sean already there waiting. "Hey." She looked at her watch. "Sorry I'm late. I was having a meeting with the bigwigs."

He smiled brightly, admiring her sweater and earrings. "That's okay. But I thought if it was another ten minutes you might've forgotten and I'd have to go."

She set her bag on the table and sat down, pulling the chair closer to the table. "No, I said I'd do this so I'm doing it. So, what do you want to talk about this week?"

Sean pulled a stack of paper from his bag. "I wrote this over the weekend. It's not complete because I have no idea what it's going to be, so it's just a five page sample, but I wanted your thoughts on it to see if it's good enough." He handed it over.

"Good enough for what?" She took the stack and looked at the title. "Is this for adults?"

"Yep. My first go at it. I did as you suggested last week and came up with ideas, and when one made my eyes ache and my head explode then I went with it."

Sydney looked at him; saw his eager puppy dog expression in his blue eyes highlighted by the blue of his sweater, and wondered what he was up to.

"I want your opinion on it," he said. "If it's as good as my stories then I'll have another avenue to write in. I'll be able to go from one to the other when I become an adult." He pushed up his sleeves and leaned his arms on the table, seeing the frown on her face. "Don't be disappointed, or upset. I just want your opinion."

"I'm not upset. I just didn't think you'd have something ready a week on. We only discussed it last week."

"It's only five pages, a chapter, if you will," he said. "Go on, read it. I'll just read my book for school." He pulled out a calculus book and moved several seats down the table.

Unsure, Sydney shook her head, and settled in to read. The story was more of a scene in the life of two people, a man and a woman, and their failing marriage. The fights and arguments, the cheating, the scandal. It sucked her in until the final page when she sat back, staring at the paper. She took a few moments before speaking. "Sean."

"Yes?" He moved back to his seat.

"Is this about your parents?"

He shrugged a shoulder. "It could be any couple. It's not necessarily my parents."

"The man is cheating on his wife and she left work and became an alcoholic. Your mum left work and *is* an alcoholic. *Is* your father cheating on her?" She let out a long breath and stared at him. "Are they your parents?"

He sat unblinking, staring right back. "It could be any couple falling apart. But did you like it? How's my writing?"

"Ah…" Sydney shook her head. "Fucking hell…this is…" She waved a hand over it. "Just as good as your other stories."

A smile brightened his face. "Really? You really think so? So, I can write adult fiction as well as young adult? Yes!" He fist pumped. "That means I can go from writing YA in the next few years to writing for adults. I hope the transition is seamless. It will give me time to get some novels written so I can come out with a few of them."

"Ah, yeah, getting a stock up is a good idea. Release YA for the next couple of years, get your sea legs and perfect your adult while waiting. Good idea. Do you want me to pass this on to an editor to get ideas? Do you have anything else you've written or is this it?"

"Only that, so far. But if you think it will help, please send it on. I'd like to get an opinion now instead of in a few years so I can get a head start."

"Have you emailed Victor that list of questions you had?" She slid the papers across to him.

"I did and his answers were very helpful," he said. "He said I didn't really need creative writing in college or an MFA as I was already top level and it wouldn't teach me anything I couldn't learn here. Maybe I should do courses in other fields, or something completely different."

"Any idea what?" Sydney checked her watch and got up to get two bottles of water from the small fridge in the corner of the room. She placed one on the table in front of Sean, and cracked hers open and took a sip.

"There's so much I could do that could help with my writing. Law, psychology, art or drama. I don't know yet, I've been concentrating on the story all week." He opened his bottle and took a gulp.

"If you don't need to, then don't. Go through all of the classes and see what jumps out at you. Pick the ones that could go with your writing, then sit with it for a week or two. What gives you the tingles? But it would also come down to genres. What would you write in? What classes would help you with that? If you write in crime or thriller because of your family, then knowledge in the law would help, so a law or psychology degree would show readers you know what you're talking about." She took another sip of water.

"The way John Grisham was a lawyer, and Michael Crichton was a doctor," Sean said. "Yeah. I'll have a think about it and let you know next week."

"I can set up a session with an adult acquisition editor and send that to him today." Sydney motioned at the story. "I can leave a note with it or drop it off before we go."

"Oh, my God, can we?" Sean shot out of his seat. "It's nearly five, so can we do it now?"

Surprised, Sydney stuttered. "Ah, ah, yeah, I guess." She grabbed her bag and drink and led the way to Michael Cambridge's office and knocked.

He looked up from behind the pile of submissions on his desk and saw Sydney with a big boy behind her. "Hey, Syd, what's going on?"

"Hey, Michael, this is Sean." She stepped into the office and introduced him. Sean waved his fingers, too excited and scared to speak. "The mentee I have. He saw Victor last week because his submissions were YA, but he's written something pretty adult and wants to get your opinion on it. I was wondering if you could read it in the next week and meet with him next Wednesday at four to talk about adult genres and writing, as part of the mentorship."

"Ah, sure, just let me check my schedule." He flicked through his desk calendar. "Next Wednesday at four. Yep, I'm free. Let me write that in." He made the note. "And where are you meeting?"

"In the boardroom down the hall." Sydney motioned for Sean to hand over the story and he stepped forward to pass it to Michael.

"Okay, I'll have a look at this and make some notes for next week." Michael glanced briefly over the first few paragraphs. "Already I can see it's well-written. You seem to have a grasp on English and writing skills."

"Thank you. That's what Victor said." Sean nervously clenched his hands together. The stress of having another story read, and maybe published, was causing him more stress than the previous weeks combined.

"Victor's right. But I'll fit this in when I can and see you next week." He waved the papers and set them on his desk. "See you both next week. Bye, Syd, Sean."

"Michael." Sydney led the way to the bank of elevators and hit the down button. "So, not only have you had our top YA editor tell you you're a good writer, but now our top adult editor is telling you that you seem to be a good writer. That must feel good.”

“Yeah.” He gave a nervous nod. “But I’m not sure what I feel. Excited, nervous, scared.”

“Why scared?” The doors opened and they stepped in. “Why scared?” She watched him try and figure out how he was feeling.

“I don’t know,” he finally said. “Maybe because it’s the first adult thing I’ve written. Maybe because it’s being seen by an editor at a huge publishing house.”

“Maybe because you’re scared people will think it’s about you, your parents; your life?”

He stared at her. “No, it’s not about me.”

She noted the anger in his glare, furrowed brow, and pursed lips. The doors dinged open and his expression changed. But her heart didn’t stop racing in panic. It hadn’t been a friendly expression. She swallowed the lump in her throat and stepped into the foyer. “So, same time next week?”

“Absolutely.” He gently pulled her back. “Listen, Sydney, I just want to thank you for everything you’re doing for me. If this mentorship hadn’t happened, I don’t know where I’d be with my family. And I certainly wouldn’t be getting anywhere. Especially this far.”

Sydney shook her head. “It’s not me. It’s nothing about me. Your writing would’ve been picked up in submission because it’s that good.”

“Yeah, well, I say it’s all about you.” He stepped away. “I’ll see you next week, Sydney.”

Upstairs, Michael finished Sean’s story, leaned back in his seat, and let out a gush of pent-up air. “Fucking hell! If he can write like that now, nothing's going to stop him from being a best-selling author."

*****

The man silently jumped over the back fence in the alley and crept toward the back door of the brownstone. It was clear no one was home as no lights shone from any window.

He made his way to the back French doors, placed his hands either side of his face, and leant against the door, peering into the dark kitchen.

She wasn't home yet. But she would be soon. And he would be waiting. It was just a matter of where to wait. He stealthily walked along the porch and looked for the best place to hide.

He didn't want to be seen by her or anyone else, so it had to be dark and it had to be out of the way. But somewhere that still gave him a clear view of the windows *and* her.

He walked back along the porch and down to the yard. The garden was full of bushes and trees, but offered no real coverage. He continued to the garage and found a small pathway between the building and the fence which was high enough, and the few trees on the neighbour's side offered him cover and secrecy. He pulled his coat tighter around him to ward off the chill creeping around his neck. He wished he'd worn a scarf to stave off the wisps of air weaving their way down his back. The chill made him shudder. Or maybe it was the plan for tonight.

The household lights flared on. The hallway, the kitchen, the upstairs hall.

He watched her walk down the hallway into the kitchen with bags of takeaway Chinese. Watched her pour her food into bowls and watched as a man came in after her.

"Who the fuck are you?" he spat, on the lookout for any more people, as she and the man sat at the table with the bowls of food and gorged on it, feeding each other spring rolls and noodles. "Fucking hell. How am I supposed to get inside now? How am I supposed to do anything now?"

With a deeply furrowed brow, he stepped out of his hiding place and inched his way through the garden, using anything he came across as cover. He stopped at the side of the porch railing, hiding behind the huge pot plant holder and bush. He didn't know what type of bush it was, but there was only one bush he was there for and another man was in the way.

They finished off their meal and cleaned the table, putting leftovers in the fridge and cleaning down the surfaces. He watched the man grab her and kiss her. She responded and soon they were naked and fucking on the table.

His fists clenched by his side, his penis ached with erection as he watched the man pummel her insides just like he had wanted to. "And I will do it, Cassandra Kingsley. I can promise you that."

*****

Sydney and Connor spent the night exploring every item in the sex room.

"Are we trying out every contraption?" Connor picked up a spiked metal collar with chains dangling from it. "And what's this supposed to attach to?"

"The wall." Sydney picked up the chain and hooked it onto the metal loop on the wall. "You get chained up like a dog, blindfolded, or wearing a mask, hands tied behind your back, and get off on whatever happens."

Connor set it down and moved over to a giant wood wheel. "And this? It looks like the Wheel of Fortune wheel."

"Not quite." Sydney laughed. It's an enfettered wheel, although it does look similar. It's like the wheels that knife throwers use. They tie a person to the wheel, spin it, and then throw daggers at it. There is no knife throwing here, but you can tie two people to it and spin. You use the wheel's velocity to enter and exit the human body."

"Excuse me?" Connor cocked a brow. "It does what now?"

"A couple faces each other, naked, and as the wheel turns he slides in when they're upside down, and out when right side up."

"So, they fuck as they spin around?"

"Yep. And it's very intoxicating." Sydney's eyes became hooded with lust.

Connor turned from inspecting the wheel and slid a finger under her chin. "And you know this how?"

Sydney coyly looked up at him. "I've been told." She spun on her heel, pointed to the bed like contraption next to the wheel, and walked over to it. "Now, this is technically a stretching rack, but it's been altered to use as a whipping rack."

"And what's that?" Connor ran his fingers over the wood down one side.

"You're tied or chained to it, face up or down, and you're whipped for being a bad boy." Sydney pushed him onto it. "Care to try it out?"

Connor pulled her close, his arms sliding around her. "Can we fuck on it instead?"

"We could." She put her arms around his neck. "But it's mighty uncomfortable."

"And you know that how?" His hands slid over her ass.

Her left brow rose. "I've been told. There is a trapeze we could try out." She nodded in its direction. "Double hooked, extra strong chain, wide enough seat for two."

Connor looked over his shoulder at the trapeze. "Well, if we're going to give everything a go tonight, let's start with that."

"That's going to take all night," Sydney said. "We'd better get started."

Chapter 11

Sydney caught up with Emerson on Saturday for their usual girls' day out. "So, how's your love life been?" She put a forkful of Eggs Benedict into her mouth.

"Ah-maze-ing." Emerson blushed to the roots of her hair. "We've had dinner every night. He's made it because he picks me up on his way home. He's a very good cook."

"I don't care about the food, get to the good stuff," Sydney admonished. "Sex. Fucking. Love making."

Emerson's blush deepened and she glanced at the wandering gazes of the people at the nearby tables. "Keep your voice down, Syd. Everyone can hear."

"Who's everyone?" Sydney looked around the restaurant. There were maybe six or seven people nearby who would've heard her. "Just get on with the story. It's none of their business anyway."

Emerson sipped her coffee. "He made dinner every night, put on romantic music, we danced, we played the piano—"

"Made sweet music of your own." Sydney sniggered.

A bubbling laugh came from Emerson and she covered

her mouth. "Yes, yes we did."

"How many times?"

"Sydney!" Emerson exclaimed, and glanced around before answering. "Many. Each night."

"You in love?" Sydney asked around a mouthful of food.

Emerson's coffee cup paused at her mouth as she thought it through.

"Ah…" Sydney stopped eating and intently stared at her friend. "*Are* you in love? It would be hard not to be. He's very attractive."

"I don't know." Emerson took another sip and put the cup down. "I'm enjoying myself immensely. He's intelligent, smart, knowledgeable."

"A great kisser, a great fucker," Sydney added, and finished off her juice.

"Yes and yes, absolutely," Emerson agreed and shook her head. "I don't know if it's love. I know I enjoy his company, enjoy our time together—"

"Getting married?" Sydney asked, waving for the bill.

"You are incorrigible," Emerson complained. "Wedding bells aren't even on the radar, let alone in the near future." She drank the last of her coffee and pushed away from the table. "You want to talk about Connor?"

Sydney put her purse in her bag and slung it onto her shoulder before pushing her chair under the table and saying, "Not really. You know all there is to know."

They walked out of the restaurant and were instantly bathed in the golden rays of the autumn sun.

Sydney linked arms with Emerson and steered her along, pulling them to a stop outside of a sex shop where she stared at a huge blinking green neon arrow that had caught her attention. She couldn't remember why it seemed familiar, but it was definitely a nagging memory.

"Have the two of you used the sex room yet?" Emerson tucked a mass of curls behind her ear and moved them on, glancing around furtively. "Best not to stand outside a shop like that."

"Why?" Sydney looked around, but found normal people going about their normal Saturday routines. "Oh, you mean in case they catch you and claim you're getting something for the Police Commissioner of New York City." She couldn't help laughing.

"Sydney, it's not funny," Emerson complained. "It would look awful. Imagine the press. I'd be called a sex worker on top of everything else I do."

"Middle-aged sex worker who helps elderly men get their groove back." Sydney chortled.

"Oh, my God, would you stop." Emerson playfully slapped her on the arm. "Just stop. That's not even funny."

But Sydney's sniggering turned into laughter and Emerson couldn't help joining in.

"That's what the headlines will look like," Sydney said. "Thank God I keep my private life private."

"Would it matter if it got out?"

"Yes. After L.A. I decided to not be public with my private life. Oooh, a book shop. I want to see where my book is." Sydney pulled her in to see a huge stand of her books front and centre. She whipped out her phone and took pictures, then handed it to Emerson and stood by the display.

"Say cheese!" Emerson clicked away while Sydney posed. "I've done about twenty. That's enough." She handed the phone back and looked around the store. "This is nice. Good to see some physical book stores still exist."

"Yes, thank God. Otherwise, my books would be relegated to one teeny tiny spot on a shelf in a discount or department chain store." Sydney found a book she'd heard about and read the blurb. "Sounds interesting. Should I buy it?"

Emerson scanned the cover. "That's going to be turned into a movie; it's already been optioned."

"But is it any good?" Sydney frowned and considered her options. "I generally don't like buying books if I'm only going to read them once and put them on the shelf. That's a complete waste of money. I could borrow it from the library," she mused.

"It's not like you don't *have* money, but have you signed up to your neighbourhood library yet?"

"True. But again, waste of money and no, I haven't. Maybe I should. I don't know if I need *another* book to sit and do nothing. I don't even have time to read fiction, and generally don't read at all when I'm in writing mode. I have been reading some very interesting non-fiction books though. I bought them."

"What's the difference?" Emerson watched her friend put the book back on the shelf.

"The non-fics are for research. I'm writing a non-fic myself and need to know what the hell I'm talking about." Sydney moved on to the next shelf, scanning books with their colourful covers and cleverly crafted titles. "Always the same types of titles," she murmured. "So boring."

"Since when do you write non-fiction?" Emerson picked

up a book that had been marked down to half price.

"Since it has to do with the novel I've also been writing." Sydney arched her neck to look for the non-fiction section and headed towards it. She read every title on every spine and cover, but found none that had anything to do with her topic. "Oh, well."

"You still haven't told me what you're writing," Emerson said, following her from shelf to shelf. "I'm beginning to think it's imaginary."

Sydney snorted with laughter. "Oh, I can assure you it's very real and related in a very weird way to the Ryans." She looked at the closest shelves. "I can't find anything. You?"

"No, nothing for me." Emerson followed Sydney out the door. "Besides, I like to produce screenplays and not bring novels to life. It's been done already. *As a novel.*" They walked down the street.

"Hang on." Sydney stopped her and stepped to the side of the path. "You make *my* novels into movies."

Emerson grinned. "Yes, I know, but you and the few other authors I've made movies out of are the exception. Your books are actually good."

*****

Sydney spent Saturday night and all Sunday morning in bed with Connor, until he had to leave for family lunch and she got back to writing. With the ideas floating around her head, she wrote into the early hours of Monday, had four hours of sleep, and got up to write again all day.

Tuesday was the same. Page after page, chapter after chapter. Her hand ached, her arm ached, everything ached, but she didn't want to stop until it was all out of her head and on paper.

Wednesday morning was the same, until the time came for her appointment.

Eric had set her up with three antiques and ephemera experts to ascertain whether her artefacts were real, whether their provenance could be authenticated, and whether she could use any of it without being dragged into court.

She watched the men carefully go over the paperwork and books, magnifying glasses at the ready, white gloves on so fingerprints damaged nothing. After an hour, she finally said, "Well? Can I use the information in them?"

The men placed the items down and removed their gloves.

Martin Adair removed his spectacles and stared directly at her. "Ms Kingston, you seem to have the real thing. Where did you get them?"

"I bought them," Sydney replied, and glanced at Charles Gates and Graham Knight.

"We've studied the receipts and the detailed letter from your lawyer. All of that paperwork is in order and authentic," Graham said. "I say it's proof of ownership."

"But then the question is, if it's all authentic what happens if I use it, or word gets out that I have it and the names in the book don't want it coming out?"

"Then you will have a court case on your hands, Ms Kingston," Martin told her. He motioned at the documents. "While all of this may full well be the real deal, it doesn't mean you'd be allowed by law to release it to the public. If a case was brought against you, you'd have to give it all over as evidence and it could be lost to the world forever."

Sydney was puzzled. "Why would it be lost? I'm the owner."

"Because if it's taken to trial and you need to hand it over," Graham added, "you have no idea what will come of it. It could be lost, stolen, or just plain disappear."

Sydney's brows slowly rose as she realised what that meant. "Oh…I get it. Because of the men in the book, any one of them could order, no, blackmail someone into getting it for them, so they can blackmail anyone or everyone in the book." She glanced between each man. "That it?"

"That's one reason." Martin nodded. "But the main one would be that they would simply be destroyed."

"Damn!" Sydney rubbed her forehead and paced the room. "So, what do I do? Admit I have them? Keep names secret?"

"Keep it locked away and never mention any names." Martin picked up his briefcase. "Thank you for letting us see this." He gestured to the black leather bound notebook. "It could be an invaluable artefact if you wish to donate it and the other things to the museum."

"Even though it could be stolen from there, too?" Sydney escorted them to the door and opened both wide. "Thank you, gentlemen. Thank you for coming." She stood in the doorway watching them get into their cars and leave, then locked the doors and walked back into the living room. She packed up the items into their safety box and carried it upstairs to lock it away in the floor safe of her office. She'd just locked the safe door when banging sounded out downstairs. She went to the monitor beside the door and saw Connor. "Down in a minute," she buzzed, and hurried downstairs to let him in. "Hey."

"Hey, gorgeous." He pulled her into his arms and kissed her.

"Hey, yourself." Sydney wrapped her arms around his neck. "Didn't expect you now."

"Got some time; figured I'd come by and fuck my gal." He carried her inside, hearing the doors slam shut behind him. He put her down in the hallway and pulled his dick out. "Can't wait, Syd. Get your knickers off." His hands went to the band of her pants and found their way inside, pushing them both down. She was on him in seconds.

Sydney groaned in pleasure as she stumbled into the parlour and made it to the rug. Their mouths tasted, their hands groped, and they rode the hot fast waves to climax.

Gasping, Sydney opened her eyes and saw Connor above her, but a movement at the window drew her attention. "Oh, my God, there's someone out there." She shoved him off her and ran for her pants.

"What do you mean someone out there? Who did you see?" Connor zipped up and opened the doors, looking down to the basement window well and up and down the street. But there was no one. He closed the doors and found Sydney fully dressed. "What did you see?"

"I saw a movement at the window, the pane closest to the steps." Sydney pointed to it. "I didn't see a face, just a flash of white and brown."

"So, it could have been a bird." Connor stared out the window, looking at it from different angles to see if there were fingerprints or markings. "Yeah. I don't think it was a person. They would've had to lean over the stair railing."

"They could if they're tall," Sydney argued. "Leaning over wouldn't be a problem and I keep hearing on the news about stalkers, and prostitute killers, and peeping toms. Hell, the lady next door had her knickers stolen from the washing rack a couple of weeks back. The rack was on her back porch."

"It's New York." Connor shrugged a nonchalant shoulder. "There's stalkers everywhere."

"Yes." Sydney crossed her arms. "Why is that, considering you're a cop?"

He moved closer to her and put his hands up. "It ain't up to me, darlin'. I'm one man, there are over nine million people in this city thanks to the stupid mayors letting everyone in, and fewer than forty thousand cops to police it. We may be a little island, but it's a big population of stupid people doing stupid things."

"Because they can," Sydney said sarcastically, arms still crossed. "Well, maybe you'd better get back out there, detective, so you can catch a few. Did you catch my gift giver yet?"

"Your what?" His hands slid down her arms. "Oh…" It registered. "You meant the rat."

"Of course, I meant the rat. What did you bloody think I meant?" Sydney stormed down the hall to the kitchen and stood staring out the French doors. *Did the guy who jumped the neighbour's fence and steal her knickers jump mine too?* she thought. *Could he have been here and not made a sound, or shown his face? What if he's been in here? What if that was him in the window just now, the knicker thief.*

"Syd." Connor placed his hands on her shoulders, breathing in the apple scent of her shampoo as he always did. It tickled his nose. He loved smelling it every time they were together. It had become a comfort knowing she used the same shampoo and conditioner. "Syd." He gently turned her around. "I'm not saying there wasn't anything there. I didn't see any evidence that's all, and as far as your rat, have you looked into the previous owners and tenants? Hell, maybe it's someone fresh out of jail who thinks Madam X still resides here." He pushed her hair back on both sides, his fingers tangling themselves in it. "But what I do know is that I need to be back at the station by ten. So, we'd better get cracking on our fucking because I don't know if I'll see you on Saturday."

Because she felt like giving him a damn good thrashing, she led him downstairs to the sex room, stripped him naked, and tied him up.

*****

Connor left at nine-thirty. Rain was drizzling down, making the steps and sidewalk slick and wet. A fine mist enveloped the top of the trees, and lampposts cast an eerie glow down to the path and road.

Sydney watched him get in his car and shivered before locking herself away for the night. It was cold and dark, and she hated being alone. She set the alarm and went upstairs to the office. She needed to work to get her mind off things, but before she could sit down, banging came once again from downstairs.

She jumped. "Jesus! Who the hell is that now?" Checking the monitor, she saw Sean on her stoop banging on the door. "Down in a minute," she called through the monitor and hurried back downstairs, flicking on lights at every switch until she came to the front doors. She let him in. "Hey, how come you're here now? It's nearly ten."

His blue eyes glowered at her, his features grim. "Because we had a mentor session at four, Sydney, and you didn't turn up." He set his bag on the floor just inside the door. "You didn't turn up and I spoke to Michael for the hour. Which wasn't a bad thing. In fact, it was very productive, but that's not the point, is it now, Sydney?"

The heat from his glare was burning her face, the hands on hips and broad shouldered stance was meant to intimidate her, and it did, even though he was only seventeen.

"I sent my apologies to Michael to pass on to you. I had a series of appointments I had to deal with, and I knew I wouldn't make it, so I rang Michael. You don't actually need to see me every week. You can spend time with other people. It's part of your mentorship."

"But I wanted *you* to mentor me." His anger simmered underneath the surface, and he stepped closer. "That's why I applied for the mentorship—because you were doing it."

Sydney's brow furrowed in anger. "And the mentorship clearly says some weeks will be spent with editors, touring the printing facility, or publishing house. You even get to spend time with illustrators and cover designers, so no," she snapped. "You don't get to spend all twelve sessions with me. I'm sorry I couldn't make it this week; I rang Michael to take it. I'm assuming you got enough information out of him to help you decide what you're doing in the future. You didn't need me to be there."

"What was so important that you fobbed me off?" His hands waved in front of him. "I came to see you afterwards and saw three men leave. Who were they?"

Sydney's spidey senses tingled and her frown deepened, raging her anger to boiling point. "First of all, you had no need to come here." She stepped closer and returned his anger-filled stare. "Second, how the hell do you know where I live? And third, who those men are is none of your fucking business, Sean Ryan. *None* of this is any of your fucking business." She thrust her finger at him. "Do you understand me?"

"No, Sydney." His tone was low and threatening and he stepped right in front of her. He towered over her five eight frame and used it to his advantage. "You understand me. I signed up for the mentorship to be mentored by you. Every week for twelve weeks. And if you can't make it on Wednesday, then you damn well better call me and arrange for us to meet another day because that is the last time you stand me up." He lowered his head, so they were eye to eye. "Do you understand me, Sydney?"

Terror fled through her, her brain screamed at her to run, run out the back door and over the fence. To run upstairs and lock herself in her bedroom which was where the safe room was. To run down to the basement and out the back door even though it was triple bolted. Her brain screamed at her to run while she stood rooted to the spot unable to move, barely able to breathe. She stared into his eyes, willing herself to do something, crying to get out of harm's way, to get out of there before he became violent. "Fuck you, you little prick!"

His dinner plate sized hand slammed across her face, making her spin around in a full circle. Her legs twisted around themselves, and she tumbled against the stair railing. She clung to it while her feet righted themselves, and her left hand clung to the left side of her burning face.

He grabbed her left arm and then her right in the same vice grip. He pulled her against him and slammed his lips onto hers, trying to kiss her. His tongue tried forcing its way in, but she bit it and he tore back in screaming pain. "You bitch." He forced her back against the railing and kissed her again.

She managed to grab his crotch and squeeze, her heel went down his shin, and he stumbled back in pain, doubled over. She kicked and her boot landed right where her hand had just squeezed.

He fell to his knees, screaming in pain. "You slut. You fucking slut. You fuck my uncle, but you won't even let me kiss you." He bent so far over his head touched the floor.

Sydney panted for air, her hand on her lip. "How do you know that? How do you know that?" she screamed. "Are you stalking me, Sean? What the fuck would you know about that?"

With tears streaming down his face, he sat up and glared at her. "I saw you. When I came to see you. I saw those men leave and then started for your door. Then my uncle turned up and I saw him kiss you. I knew something was happening, so I walked up to your door and that's when I heard you. That's when I saw you fucking him on the floor," he yelled.

"That was you?" Sydney asked. "I thought I saw something. I was right. But when Connor checked outside he didn't see anyone."

"I hid from both of you. But I saw you. You fucked him, you whore. You're just a whore like my mother. He fucked her before he fucked you."

"What?" Sydney shook her head to clear her foggy brain. "Wait…Connor was fucking your mother before me?" She stared at his defeated expression. "Who knows that? She was cheating on your father with his brother? Why?" She was starting to get a very clear picture of how screwed up his family was, but then realised she'd already read about it. "The story. Your story *is* about them. You denied it."

"Of course, I denied it." He stumbled to his feet. "Of course, it's about my parents. My stupid fucking parents. My fucking father fucks prostitutes to get off on all of his kinks, and my mother leaves her work to spend more time with him and me, but ends up fucking my uncle and getting drunk." He wiped his face on the arm of his sweater.

"How long have you known about your mother and Connor?" Sydney moved slightly on the balls of her feet, trying to better position herself to run.

"Months." Sean sneered. "They didn't know I was home when he came over and they fucked in the kitchen multiple times." His face distorted into cruelty. "They didn't even know I was there. They didn't even know I filmed the whole thing. When they finished in the kitchen, they moved to the bedroom and fucked in my father's bed. Three times." He held up the three middle fingers of his right hand. "Three fucking times they fucked in my father's bed. Three. And I filmed it all."

Sydney knew there must be some type of mental crisis going on in his head. But that had nothing to do with her and she didn't want to be the one to deal with it. She was thinking about who to call when he stepped closer.

"Sydney, have you fucked Connor on the kitchen table?"

She swallowed the outpouring of saliva that suddenly formed in her mouth out of fear. "That's none of your business. I can call your grandfather to come and pick you up. We never need mention this ever again." She lightly moved from foot to foot.

"Except we are going to mention it, Sydney. Because I love you and I want you to stop fucking my uncle."

Astounded, she said, "What?"

He stepped closer and grasped her arms, noting she didn't pull away. "I love you, Sydney, don't you know that? I've loved you from the day you came to our house and took the time to come to my bedroom and talk to me. To read my stories to listen to my thoughts and dreams." One more step and there was barely an inch between them. "I've loved you since that day, Sydney, and my love has grown exponentially since, with every meeting, every week. I love you and I want to be with you. I want you to want and love me. And I want you to fuck me like you fuck my uncle." His expression hardened. So did his grip. "But you need to stop being a whore, Sydney. You need to stop being just like my mother and stop fucking my uncle because you're mine, Sydney. Not his. *Mine.*"

Sydney saw the craziness in his eyes and knew what had to be done. She hardened, and through gritted teeth she threatened, "Don't ever call me a whore or slut again, Sean Ryan. I am a grown woman who can *and will* fuck whoever I want, and if that's your uncle, then so be it. I'm not your issue; your father and mother are the issue. And you will not take your shit out on me. I don't love you; I don't want you, and my time as your mentor is over. Do you understand?" She stared into the craziness of his eyes. "I am no longer your mentor. You can be mentored by someone else. I'll call CC and tell her, but this is it, you won't come here, you won't see me ever again, and whether or not I see Connor, is *none* of your fucking business."

That enraged him and he pushed her against the wall, trying to shove his tongue into her mouth and his hand between her legs. His size held her in that position while his other hand found its way under her top to her breast.

She screamed against his lips and twisted her head sideways. "Get off me." She grabbed one of his hands, yanked his thumb back, and spun him around so his arm was behind his back. She used her whole body to push him towards the door and ran for the kitchen, grabbing a pan off the wall and hiding behind the doorway to the living room.

"Sydney," he roared, running into the kitchen. "You whore, where are you? Where are—"

Sydney cut him off with a frypan to his face.

He stumbled backward, turned, and bent over, his face to his hands. "You bitch, you fucking bitch." He stood up, but had no time to turn before everything went black.

Sydney gasped for air and sat on one of the bench stools, the pan still firmly in her hands. She needed to get him out of there and needed to make a call. But first, she needed Sean restrained before he woke up. She dug in the drawer for zip ties and pulled his hands together with one, his feet with another. With her breathing returning to normal, she looked for her phone, but it was upstairs and she and Sean were downstairs. While deciding what to do, she heard sirens and ran down the hallway and opened the doors to find Connor and two officers from the rat incident on her stoop. "Oh, God." She collapsed into Connor's arms and sobbed.

"Hey, hey." He led her inside. "I'm here now, what's happening?" Holding her at arm's-length, he studied her face. A red mark was changing colour.

Sydney looked from him to the officers and it finally registered. "I didn't call you. I didn't get to."

"The neighbours reported screams," Officer Velenksy said. "Female screams and a man shouting."

Sydney tried to clear her fogged mind. "Ah, yeah. But I was only going to call Connor. Can you two wait outside. I'll explain it to him."

Velenksy and Rotrain exchanged a look, but were

waved out by Connor.

"I'll deal with this. You guys just wait outside and cut the lights." He closed the door behind them and turned to Sydney. "What the hell happened?"

She walked into the kitchen and pointed to the body on the floor. "*He* happened."

"What the hell." Connor felt his nephew's pulse. "Still breathing. Did you hit him?"

"With a frypan. Twice."

"Did he hit you?" He nodded at her face.

She ignored the gesture. "Just get him out of here. No questions. Just say I thought someone had broken in. The stalker from next door or something and I hit him."

"That won't explain the screaming, and yelling of a male voice the neighbours heard."

"The neighbours can mind their own fucking business," Sydney spat. "His bag's by the door. I was going to call you, but you turned up anyway."

"Yeah. I was in the neighbourhood investigating a break-in, heard the call and sped on over." He pointed at Sean. "Guess we'd better get him untied. Gotta knife?"

"In the drawer," Sydney said and watched Connor cut the ties on Sean's wrists and ankles.

Sean groaned as Conner hauled him to his feet and grasped his head.

"You're pretty banged up," Connor told him, pulling Sean's left arm around his neck. He wrapped his right arm around Sean's waist to support him. "Let's get you home."

"You might want to take him to your place," Sydney suggested. "You two have some issues to sort out." She followed behind and picked up Sean's bag as Connor dragged Sean out the door. She saw Velenksy and Rotrain waiting on the sidewalk.

They stepped forward, but Connor shook his head. "Case of mistaken identity. Sydney thought she had an intruder, but it's just my nephew. Help me get him into my car."

They gave each other questioning looks, but helped get Sean into the backseat.

Connor shut the door and ran back up the stoop stairs to grab Sean's bag. "Sorry about this, Syd."

"You might be even sorrier when he's fully conscious," she said and kissed him. Her hand cupped his face. "Goodbye, Connor."

He gave her a puzzled look. "Goodbye? I'll see you again on Saturday."

"You probably won't." Sydney turned her back and walked inside. She closed both doors and leaned against the inside one. Sighing, she knew she needed to call CC about the mentorship so someone could take over.

And maybe I should call Em, but maybe I'll be seeing her on Saturday for our girls' day out. But then again, maybe not.

She walked into the kitchen, noticed the pan on the bench and put it away. She double checked the doors and windows and the security alarm. She also wondered if she should call Cormac and let him know. *They'll probably find out soon enough when Sean wakes up in Connor's house. If he goes at him, the fight could be worse than ours. Hell, Connor could kill him. What would Cormac do then?*

A sigh heaved her body and deflated it. It was time for bed. But first she needed paracetamol and a cold pack. *Then* bed.

Chapter 12

By Saturday, Sydney's face had a large, black and blue bruise on it from Sean's hand. She hadn't heard from him or Connor, or Cormac, or Emerson for that matter, so whatever had happened, it hadn't done the rounds of the family. But as she stood in front of the mirror looking at it, she debated calling off her day out with Emerson.

Exhaustion had driven her to bed earlier than normal Wednesday night, and every night since. She'd even napped during the day which was unusual for her when she was writing. It was pretty obvious the fight with Sean had taken it out of her mentally, and she'd barely written anything; didn't have the mental energy for it. Maybe a day out would kickstart her energy again.

Sydney carefully applied her make-up so you could barely see any discolouration. She brushed her hair over the left side of her face, and pinned it back on the right. When she was done, she went downstairs to wait for Emerson, pondering if she should tell her. She didn't get to ponder long because her phone rang. "Hey, Em, so where are we going?"

"Sorry, Syd, there's been change of plans. I should've called yesterday. We're in upstate New York for a couple of nights away. We'll be back tomorrow and I'm having lunch with the family."

Sydney tried to compute what she'd heard and realised she wouldn't be seeing her best friend that day. Everything in her drained out, leaving her empty. "You and Cormac have gone upstate for a mini holiday?"

"Yes. He asked me yesterday. It's two nights, two-ish days, just a mini break for both of us. It's very pretty with fall leaves, quiet and peaceful. No one prying or staring."

"And you're calling me now?" Sydney frowned at the resentment bubbling inside her. "After I put my make-up on and did my hair and got all dressed up?" she tried to joke. "What a waste of an hour and a tonne of make-up that was."

Emerson giggled, not even noticing the lack of humour in her best friend's voice. "Sorry, Syd. I can come and see you Monday to tell you all about it. I'll be staying over Sunday night."

"Yeah," Sydney muttered. "Might not be a fun lunch."

"We'll be telling the family we're dating. Although considering we had lunch a few months back, and they know me, I doubt it will be a surprise."

Not what I'm talking about, Sydney thought. "Well, have fun and I'll spend the day eating junk food and watching movies. All the writing I've been doing has run me ragged and I need to catch up on some sleep."

"Okay. Take care, Syd. They found another dead prostitute last night, so keep your doors locked. God, I'm so glad we're out of the city."

"And I'm glad I'm not a prostitute," Sydney quipped. "Bye, Em, see you next week. Have fun."

"Thanks, you too."

The call ended and Sydney turned off her phone as an empty lonely feeling clenched her stomach. She was losing her best friend—she just knew it.

*****

That night, Connor turned up on her doorstep, surprising her.

"I figured you might be dead, or you might never come back." She pulled the door back to let him in.

"Why wouldn't I be back, Syd?" He tweaked her chin as he passed into the hall. "Oh, what, you mean Sean? Yeah. That was ah…" He sighed and moved into the living room, falling onto one of the couches and putting his feet on the coffee table.

"That was ah what?" In the light of the TV, she saw the cuts and bruises on his face. "Oh, my God, did you two get into it?" She tucked her leg under her before sitting beside him. "You two got into it."

"We did." Connor took her hand and held it to his lips, staring up at her with his little boy expression. "He hurt me. But I hurt him more."

Sydney pulled her hand away. "What happened?"

"Ah, Syd," he groaned. "I don't really—"

"Tell me what happened," she demanded. "You're beat up; I take it he is too."

"Yeah, he is," Connor told her. "When he came to and was able to stand, he realised where he was and freaked out. I tried to calm him down, but copped a statue to the head." He touched the spot on his skull. "Little bastard hit me."

"And you hit him back," Sydney said, shifting positions. "Jesus, Connor. He's a seventeen-year-old kid."

"He's a fucking big kid and he's got a hell of a swing. He did some screaming about his parents and hit me a few times. I hit him a few times. We called it even."

Sydney pictured Sean's rage, the bloodthirsty vengeance in his eyes when he screamed about his uncle fucking his mother. "I somehow doubt that," she murmured. "So, what was it actually about?"

Connor briefly turned his head to glance at her. "Like I said. His parents. They've fucked the poor kid up and he needed someone to take it out on." He aimed his thumb at his chest. "And he chose me. It's over and done with and we won't be mentioning it at Sunday lunch."

"That's going to be some lunch," Sydney retorted, remembering that Emerson was going to be there.

"Not really."

Sydney cocked her head slightly. "Will you be telling them about Wednesday night?"

"What about Wednesday night?"

"You know full well what about it."

"Look, Syd." Connor grasped her hand again. "Whatever happened in this house on Wednesday night between you and Sean, is between you and Sean. It ain't any of my business, and it certainly ain't the family's business. Even though that bruise might be." He pointed to her face.

Sydney had forgotten she'd removed her make-up

that morning. "Guess it's a good thing I'm not coming to lunch then."

"Meanwhile, I've got the night off." Connor rolled towards her and put his arms around her. "What were we getting up to tonight?"

*****

Sunday came and went, and Sydney was surprised she didn't get a phone call from the family. Or Emerson.

But she did get a visit from Kieran and his girlfriend.

"Ah." Sydney stared at them in surprise. "Why are you here?"

"We came by—" Kieran started.

"On our way home," Sandy interrupted.

"To have a chat about Sean's mentorship with you and your publisher," Kieran finished. "He said at lunch that you had—"

"After moping around all day, we finally dragged it out of him," Sandy butted in.

"After moping around all day, he said you'd cancelled the mentorship and he couldn't do it anymore. We thought we'd stop by to see if there was anything to do to change your mind." Kieran's gaze moved to the bruise on Sydney's cheek.

Sydney's brows had furrowed the moment she'd seen them on the monitor, and now the pressure was giving her a headache. "I didn't cancel the mentorship; he still has that for another two months. I just can't be his mentor anymore. That's it."

Kieran exchanged a surprised look with Sandy.

"That's not the impression Sean gave. He seemed really depressed. Quiet, barely ate, which is unusual for him."

"He did seem angry at Connor, looked like he'd been in a fight, plus talked back to his mother and father," Sandy added.

"And copped a head slap for that," Kieran replied.

"From Declan?" Sydney asked dryly and got a nod in reply.

"But Dad shut them down," Kieran said. "Because your friend Emerson was there."

Sydney brightened. "And what do you all think of that?"

"We all think it's great that he's found someone to date," Kieran said. "And he seems really happy so nothing to complain about."

"Well." Sydney rubbed the spot between her brows. "As I said. He's probably pissed that I had to pull out, but the mentorship's still going, so he shouldn't have anything to complain about. He can still get help, and from the information he's been given, he will end up with a published book at the end of it. But if he throws it all away, then he won't have that and I hope he doesn't throw it away. So, keep encouraging him to go."

"Okay. Well, we'll go," Kieran said. "It's good to know it's not as dramatic as he made it out to be."

Sydney shook her head. "No, it certainly isn't. Nice to have seen you both." She was cut off by the arrival of Emerson in a cab. "Looks like I have another visitor. Hey," she called. "Not spending the night?"

Emerson closed the cab door and hurried up the stairs with her overnight bag and handbag. "That was the plan, but Cormac wanted to go and talk to Sean, bring him back to the house for the night to try and get out of him what was going on. Sean said you cancelled the mentorship."

Sydney rolled her eyes. "And as I just got through telling these two, I didn't cancel it, it's still ongoing. I just can't do it anymore."

"Oh." Emerson was confused. "That's not the impression he gave."

"So I've heard. Are you here for the night?"

"If you don't mind," Emerson said. "I'll catch a cab back to my place tomorrow as I don't have my car." She nodded at the Ryans. "Kieran, Sandy."

"Emerson. Ah, thanks for the explanation, Sydney, we'll get out of your hair." Kieran and Sandy bade them goodnight and left.

Sydney locked up and followed Emerson into the living room. "So now you can tell me about your two night get away with the commish."

Emerson faced her. "And you can tell me how the hell you got that massive bruise on your face and why you cancelled your mentorship."

Sydney breathed in slowly and blinked. "No. Want some popcorn? I can make some more."

"What do you mean, no." Emerson flung her arms up in exasperation and followed Sydney into the kitchen. "You have a hand sized bruise on your face *and* you cancelled on Sean. Does it have to do with him? Oh, my God." Her hands flew to her mouth and her eyes widened. "Oh, my God, Sydney, did he…"

"I'm not talking about it." Sydney pulled two cans of

Pepsi Max from the fridge and when the microwave dinged, grabbed the bag of popcorn and poured it into a movie theatre container.

"But, Sydney," Emerson argued.

"No!" Sydney's tone was sharp and to the point. "I'm not discussing it, or that family. Except for Cormac, who took you on a little get away and you didn't even tell me, so I got dressed up for nothing and missed our day out." She handed the popcorn container to Emerson and carried the cans of icy cola into the living room.

"And I would have been asking you about your bruise yesterday *in public.* Or did you cover it with all that fancy make-up of yours?" Emerson sat next to her and put two pieces of popcorn into her mouth. "*Was* it Sean? And why?"

"I'm not saying anything, on both counts." Sydney took a sip of her drink and the icy fluid drenched her parched throat. "It's not my business to be involved in."

"Fuck, Sydney!" Emerson munched on more popcorn, concern radiating from her body. "Are you okay, though? You're not hurt, other than the bruise?"

"I'm fine. But that's probably why I've slept a lot. Between writing two books and dealing with other stuff, it's caught up with me." She leaned back in her seat, propped her feet on the coffee table and grabbed some popcorn. "Now, tell me about this secret getaway."

She listened while Emerson told her all about it. The little inn they went to, the colour of the fall leaves, the walks they took. "You were there two nights and two-ish days; how many walks did you take?"

"Three on Saturday, one Sunday morning before

heading back. It was just a matter of being in the peace and quiet of nature. Out of the hustle and bustle of the city and God, was it quiet."

"Except for when you were fucking, right?" Sydney grinned. "Bring the house down with your screams?"

"Fun-nee." Emerson rolled her eyes. "We only did it like five times."

"Jesus, Em. You put some of us to shame."

"Yeah, right. I don't have a sex room in my basement. How many men have you had in there since you've been here?"

"Just the one and he went all night," Sydney bragged and changed the TV channel with the remote. She clicked through the channels until she found a couple having sex on a bed of fall leaves. "Hey, you and Cormac filmed your escapades and put them on TV."

"Sydney!" Emerson exclaimed. "Of course, we didn't, but don't think I *didn't* think about fucking in a bed of leaves. That *could* have been us."

They watched the scene until it ended, then Sydney changed to another channel. Images of Madam X flashed on the screen and Sydney stopped. "Ooh, let's watch this. When did it start?" She clicked on the information button and saw it had just started. They watched in rapt silence, but gasped when a picture of the brownstone flashed onto the screen.

"Fuck," Sydney dragged the word out, hoping the voice over person didn't reveal that she now lived there. She clung to every word and heaved a sigh and slumped onto the couch when the show went to an ad break. "Fuck. Now people are going to come around and gawp at the house. I hope they don't figure out I live here now."

"They probably will." Emerson finished the last of her drink. "I think records are pretty easy to find, and the house was well-known already, thanks to Madam X."

"Yep, it's even in one of the books about her." Sydney turned the volume down while the commercials were on. "Anyone who reads that book will see this house."

"A lot of houses in New York are famous *and* infamous. Crime bosses, mafia, murders, kidnappers."

"Madam X," Sydney cut in.

"And people who *went* to Madam X," Emerson added. "Many, many houses and places in this city are famous and have been for a long, long, time."

The show came back on and Sydney turned up the volume. They watched in silence until the show finished when Sydney sighed again. "No mention of me, thank God."

"Well, aren't you a lucky duck," Emerson mocked. "But it's been a long day for me. Is my bed ready?" She yawned and stretched her arms above her head.

"Why would it be? I didn't know you were coming," Sydney said. "But the spare room's always made up, so off you go, Sleeping Beauty. Go and get ready for bed and I'll clean up and be up in a few minutes." She gathered the cans and empty popcorn container and tidied the kitchen before checking the alarm system and turning off the TV. She found Emerson in the bathroom. "I will bid you goodnight. Everything is locked and loaded and should be all right. I'll see you in the morning when you're making breakfast."

Emerson snorted. "Good luck with that. The only

thing I make is toast, cereal, juice and coffee."

"Then I'll make eggs while you make everything else," Sydney said and went upstairs. She locked her door and deflated against it as a sigh left her and her hand went to her cheek. There was no way she was going to talk about what had happened. Not that she hadn't thought of calling Cormac, but this was one thing she didn't want getting out.

Chapter 13

After a leisurely breakfast with Emerson, Sydney was preparing to get back to writing when she received a call from CC.

"Darling, can you come in? It's important."

"How important? I'm just about to get into the book." Sydney stood at her desk sorting through her paperwork and the notebook she wrote in.

"It is," CC replied firmly. "It's about several things and they're all important."

Sydney sighed and closed her notebook. "I'll be there when I can." Ending the call, she locked her notebook and papers away and hurried to change before finding Amy working at the kitchen table. "CC needs to see me now. Doing anything important?"

"Just typing up your research." Amy typed away without looking up. "When exactly?"

"I told her when I can." Sydney picked up the pages already printed out. The research was thorough and had been helping nicely.

"And done with that page." Amy saved the document. "You know, it would be easier for you to take a taxi or

Uber. I could keep working." She looked up at her boss, hoping she'd agree.

"True, but you are my assistant, so driving me is part of your job, and another thing, you could go and do more research while I'm in there and I'll take a taxi home." Sydney set the papers on the table. "How's that? You get into the info about prison."

Amy glanced at the paperwork. "I got what I could find, but not the information from the prison. I need to chase that up today along with typing the rest of this up." She motioned to the notebook she was reading from. "So, you could take a taxi or Uber to go there and I could stay and work."

"Amy, it will take you ten minutes to get me there."

"More like thirty," Amy muttered.

"And then you can either come back and continue this, or go and do more research. Either way, I need to go now, so come on." Sydney headed for the front door and checked the system for open doors and windows. The doors were locked and only the bathroom windows were open on the fourth and fifth floors. She set the alarm and followed Amy out the door, locking both behind her.

Twenty minutes later, Sydney was dropped off and waving Amy goodbye. She glided up in the elevator, and five minutes later, strode into CC's office. "Okay." She dumped her bag on an easy chair. "What is it now? What's the need for me to come in?"

CC pointed at the chair for her to sit, and made herself comfortable in her personal easy chair. She waved at the door. "Come in and lock the door."

Sydney glanced over her shoulder to see Gemma and

Eric and swung her head back to CC. "What's going on? Is this about Sean? You're not cancelling the mentorship on him are you? Just because I'm not doing it anymore doesn't mean someone else can't." She finally sat in the chair, pushing her bag aside. "What's going on? Has his father called to complain? I had one of his uncles and his girlfriend on my doorstep last night asking why I'd cancelled. I told them I didn't."

"Part of it is about Sean, but no, no one has rung up and complained yet." CC smoothed her Chanel pants and pulled down the matching blazer. "I found it very unusual when you called and said you couldn't do it anymore. You wouldn't tell me why, although," she nodded at Sydney's face, "by the look of that bruise, I'd guess that he has something to do with it."

Fuck! Sydney mentally chided herself. She'd forgotten to put her make-up on and now wanted to slap herself for being so stupid as to not cover it. "I'm not discussing this."

"Either way, your suggestion of Victor or Michael was a good one and both have agreed to mentor Sean for the remainder of the mentorship. They'll take it in turns and work out a schedule of what to teach him. Even though both have said there's not a lot he needs being taught, they'll guide him to the end." CC smoothed her hair behind her ear. "Both have also said, we should publish his stories at the end of it."

"His YA stories, yes," Sydney agreed. "At least give him that. I have no idea how his adult fiction will work out, but Michael will help with that."

CC looked at Sydney's cheek. "Even though there's a

reason you quit, you still want him to have his work published. Isn't that rewarding bad behaviour?"

Sydney slowly breathed in, then let it out in a sigh. "He's potentially…" She paused, looking for the right words. "*Mindfucked* thanks to his parents and family and the way he's been treated. He did something wrong because he's very messed up, but he has talent, talent that needs nurturing and he can get that here."

CC sighed. "From what they both said, he is extremely talented, but legally…" She deferred to Eric. "If he's violent?"

"He's confused," Sydney jumped in. "And potentially mentally unwell. But with the right guidance at home, or with his grandfather, he should be okay."

"Can *you* guarantee that?" CC asked. "*Is* he with his grandfather? Does his grandfather know about that?" She pointed to Sydney's face. "Because unless he does, and Sean gets help, maybe we should cancel the mentorship."

"No!" Sydney exclaimed. "Don't do that. Look," she implored CC and Eric. "Wait until Wednesday and see if he comes in. If he does, continue, but on a strict warning. No more bullshit and he works hard." She sighed and her body fell back against the chair cushions. "Look. I thought about calling his grandfather, but I also called you and said don't cancel the program. He needs this. I think it's the only thing in his life that has meaning and is stable."

"And maybe you should tell his grandfather that," CC said. She glanced at Eric and nodded. "We'll keep it going, *against* better judgement, that is. But one wrong foot…" Her gaze darted to Sydney's face. "A *second* foot wrong, and he's out of here. Understood?"

Sydney smiled in relief. "Yes, CC, and thank you."

"It's not you who needs to thank me. It's Sean and his family." CC turned to Eric. "Maybe we should have a guard nearby when he's here."

"He won't do anything with Michael or Victor. They're men and not family." Sydney got up and selected a chilled bottle of water from the drinks fridge. "Is that it? Was there anything else you wanted me here on a Monday morning to discuss?" She drank a few mouthfuls before sitting down. The icy water danced on her tastebuds with the lemon fresh flavouring and slid down the waterslide of her throat. She drank some more, waiting for the silence to be broken. Finally, she said, "Well?"

"We've had some more letters, Sydney," Eric told her, and pulled them out of his briefcase. "We've had them looked over by a private company as we don't want the police involved. No fingerprints, no DNA, nothing to tie them to anyone except for the cut out magazine letters." He placed the letters on the coffee table and spread them out.

All white, one page, colourful magazine cut-out letters splashed across the pages.

Sydney picked one up. "*Die, you fucking bitch! When are you going to fucking die?*" She flicked it onto the coffee table. "So, that's like the last one you showed me. Pretty much says the same thing."

"All of them say the same thing as that one. But these are different." He pulled three pages from his briefcase and handed them to her.

"How are they different?" Sydney asked. "Isn't it all

fan mail?" She took them, glancing over each.

We're meant to be together.

We'll be together soon, my love.

I love you Cassandra, I can't wait for us to be married.

"They're for Cassandra Kingsley," Eric told her. "All addressed to Cassandra via Pulsate Publishing. Whoever sent them either—"

"Doesn't know my real name, or believes Cassandra is real," Sydney finished. "And so I have two whack-jobs stalking me." She put the letters on the table. "What are we doing about this? Are we ignoring it? Are we calling the police? Are we calling a private security firm who deals with stalkers of celebrities? What? What were we going to do about those?" She motioned at them. "Now that there's more, what are we doing?" Sitting back in the chair, Sydney rubbed her palms on the legs of her jeans. Stupid notes didn't normally make her nervous. The first ones had been laughable, when she was new to New York. Who had been on the ball fast enough to send her a letter within weeks of the move? But now that she'd been there a few months, they were different. Very different. Every day the news had talk about stalkers and peeping toms, and thank God she wasn't a prostitute or she'd rack up that cop tally. The last had been number eleven, and with the rat on her doorstep and the neighbour having her knickers stolen, clearly the Upper East Side wasn't as safe as she first thought.

"We, ah, I called that celebrity security firms. The one who tracks down stalkers and straightens out problems for actors, singers, etcetera," Eric said. "But their wait list is six months."

"Are they the ones who annihilate the problems and make them go away?" Sydney asked. "What's the name again? I think I've read a few stories of celebs using them to go to trial against stalkers."

"Landon Security," CC said. "We used them a few years ago with another stalker."

"Who was he stalking?" Sydney asked. "I never heard anything."

"It was before we acquired you," Gemma finally spoke up. "An author was being stalked by a severely ill mental patient and broke into her house. She writes under a pen name now and went quiet in her personal life. She even considered changing her name, it was so bad. He went to prison for twenty years. No parole."

"Jesus," Sydney muttered. "Are we on the waiting list?"

"We've been on the books since last time as clients, but unfortunately they can't take on any more cases at the moment." CC played with the three strands of pearls around her neck. "We're clients, but can't get help. How useless. How stupidly useless."

"Yeah." Sydney's stomach dropped. "What about the police? Oh, but Connor's not even doing anything about the rat, so why would he give a shit about the letters."

"Rat! What rat?" Eric asked, perking up in his seat.

"Ah…" Sydney stared at him dazedly. "Didn't I tell you about that?" Withering under his glare, Sydney quickly told him about her gift. "Don't worry, we called the cops and they took it as evidence."

"They can hardly keep a dead rat in the station or down at evidence," Eric scoffed. "They were probably told to throw it out and write it up. Was there a higher ranked officer or detective with them?"

"No. But Connor Ryan turned up and…" Sydney broke off and her gaze drifted up to the ceiling as her mind scrolled through the events.

"Sydney?" CC called. "Sydney."

"He wasn't the detective on scene. There was no detective on scene, just officers Velenksy and Vasquez. They took the rat. Connor took off. I don't think he did anything about it and I have no clue if Velenksy and Vasquez wrote up the report."

Eric sighed and rubbed his eyes. "I guess I'd better track that down and get some proof." He looked at Sydney. "Do you have proof?"

"We have it on camera and gave them a copy. Hopefully, Amy kept it for proof."

"Does it show who left it?" Gemma asked, disgusted by the whole thing.

"He's wearing a hooded coat and gloves. The cameras didn't get his face and the gift wouldn't have fingerprints. He may not even be the one who sent it. He could've just been the delivery boy."

"Is there a delivery van on the recording?" Eric asked hopefully.

"Not that I saw." Sydney shrugged. "Sorry."

"Okay, I'm going to need the details and that footage." Eric pulled a notebook from his case and clicked his pen on. "Give them to me."

Sydney told him everything she could remember and finished off her water which was now room temperature. It didn't have the same lemony taste.

"I'll get onto the officers and Detective Ryan." Eric

threw his notebook into his case. "As in the Police Commissioner's second son, Connor Ryan?"

Sydney's brows rose and she tried to hide her grin. "Yep."

"And how did he know where you lived, or what time to turn up?" CC asked.

Sydney told them the story. "He vaguely remembered the address. There was a doco on last night about Madam X. They showed a picture of the brownstone."

Eric winced. "That's not good. But there's also nothing you can do about it because it's well-known."

"That's what Emerson said when we saw it. She said there's thousands of famous and well-known homes for myriad reasons. Looks like I'll just have to suck it up and deal with it while waiting for Landon Security to give us the time of day." Another sigh left her and she checked her watch. "Was there anything else? I need to get back and keep writing."

"Considering what's going on, are these books a good idea?" CC rubbed her fingers over the three strand pearl bracelet on her left wrist. Smooth and cool to the touch, it was a habit she had when unnerved.

"Who knows. But I'm finishing them either way. Anything else?" Sydney stood and hauled her tote onto her shoulder. "Can I get a driver? Or do I need to call a cab?"

"Amy not picking you up?" CC rose from her chair and smoothed her suit. "I'd much prefer if she drove you."

"I told her to go back home or keep working."

"I'll drive you, but can you give me a few minutes?" Eric asked. "I'll go down to the station and speak to the officers if they're available. It might be easier." He packed his briefcase and slammed the lid shut.

"Sure. Are you taking the letters?" Sydney looked down at them, her gaze darting from one to the other.

"I'll leave them here as my focus is on the rat. I'll just be a few minutes."

"I'll wait by the elevators," Sydney told him and dragged her gaze away from the letters. "Keeping them safe, are we? We'll need them for evidence for Landon when they get around to calling us."

"I'll put them away," CC said. "You go and wait for Eric and lock yourself up when you get home. We wouldn't want anything like what happened to our last author happening to you."

Surprised, Sydney stared sharply at CC. "Something happened to her? Is that why he got twenty years no parole? What happened?"

"Nothing I'm going to tell you about." CC escorted her to the door. "It's private, as is your business. So go and wait for Eric and we'll see what we can get out of those two officers. I'll call to let you know."

"Okay." Sydney noticed their blank expressions and realised she wasn't going to get anything out of them. "Okay. I'll be at home all week writing. Call me. I'll have the phone on and plugged in."

"Stay safe, Sydney." CC closed the door on her.

Stunned, and feeling fobbed off, Sydney walked through the office to wait for Eric by the elevators. It gave her time to consider the change in mood after she'd asked about the other author. *Clearly they don't want to talk about it*, she thought. *Which I guess is understandable.*

I wouldn't want them blabbing to others about what's happening to me.

Eric rushed up to her and hit the button. "My car's in the basement—"

"I am not going down to a basement. I'll wait on the ground floor near the exit," Sydney blurted out. "No way am I going down to a basement under a high rise. *Especially* in *this* city."

Eric nodded as the door dinged open. "Fair enough. We'll stop on the ground floor and I'll take about ten minutes to get out. I have a blue Mazda."

"Okay, that's good. It's bad enough I can see Ground Zero from here." Her stomach lurched as the lift went down. "Ugh. I hate that. But seriously, why did Pulsate rent a space so close to *that* spot?"

"Because it has a great view and it's the business district." The door dinged open and he watched Sydney alight. "Give me ten. The garage is just down to the left." He pointed down the road as the door shut.

Feeling a little green around the gills, Sydney hurried outside and breathed in and out quickly. Once her stomach settled, she made her way to the garage opening for the building and waited for Eric, being watchful of anyone out to take advantage, or anyone who was nefarious looking. Not that she knew what nefarious looking people looked like, but considering the number of crime shows she'd watched over the years, it shouldn't be too hard. After keeping her eye out for a few minutes, a car horn beeped, dragging her attention from the street. Eric waved her over and she rushed to jump in and slam the door. "Quick, let's get out of here. There's too many nefarious looking people around."

He laughed and drove her home, waiting until she was inside and locked up before heading for the precinct.

"Amy," Sydney yelled after locking the doors. "You here?" She rushed for the bathroom under the stairs to freshen up, then walked into the kitchen for a cold drink and some food. She saw Amy hard at work typing up notes. "Jesus! How many pages are you doing? Has it taken you all this time?" She saw more piles of paper than this morning.

"It has, because I'm also typing up a transcript from the show you watched last night." She stopped typing and looked at Sydney. "After you mentioned it earlier, I tracked it down. I couldn't find a transcript online so I typed it out." She lifted up a stack of paper held together with a bulldog clip. "It's all done and printed. Quite a lot of information in it and it's all true. Or, at least, it doesn't deviate from all of the other information we've found. And no, they didn't give your address away, and only mentioned it once. Although..." She sighed. "People are gonna know where it is."

Sydney held up a can of Pepsi and saw Amy nod. "I know, but I'd like to keep the stalkers to a minimum." She cracked two cans into glasses.

"That's plural," Amy noted. "More than one now?" She watched the ice cubes being dropped into her drink and her mouth salivated. She'd forgotten to drink, or eat, since breakfast. That was the way it was when she worked, and now she was parched. She accepted the glass and sculled the lot. "Ah...that's good."

Sydney drank half of hers and sat at the table. "And

you haven't drunk since breakfast."

"Nope. So," Amy said to bring the conversation back on track, "more stalkers? You used plural."

Sydney grumbled under her breath and told her the story. "More letters; two stalkers at least. Plus, the rat, and the neighbour getting her knickers nicked, plus all of the stories on the radio and TV about peeping toms and people and prostitutes being attacked or killed."

"Prostitutes are people," Amy told her.

"I know, but what they do is making them separate to the rest of the people and they're getting killed *because* they're prostitutes."

Amy's brows furrowed. "You don't know that."

Sydney looked at her and tilted her head. "I'd say from the news stories that the profession is what's getting them killed. Wouldn't be the first time someone set out to kill pros."

Amy considered the comment. "That's true; I've come across it in my research. But still, is that the case now?"

"I'd say so. But I've got one, or two, or even four closer to home to deal with."

"Do we have a plan?" Amy's gaze never left Sydney.

"Did we have one before?" Sydney countered. "Just keep an eye out, stay as safe as possible, and if that doesn't work, use all the measures we can."

"Do we have the capacity to do that?" Amy sucked on an ice cube and crunched it between her teeth.

Sydney heard the bone cracking sound and took a deep, slow breath in. "We do, and I have no problem using it."

The doorbell rang throughout the house, startling

them both in the poignant silence.

"Do you want me to get it?" Amy rose from her chair.

"No, you get yourself another drink and I'll go and see." Sydney walked down the hall and checked the monitor. "That's interesting." She unlocked both doors and flung the vestibule open. "Alec, what are you doing here?"

"Hey, Sydney," the eldest Ryan brother said. "I came to talk to you about cancelling Sean's mentorship. I got the vibe on Sunday that something had gone down between the two of you, and with his face being bruised and battered, I thought we could have a chat."

Sydney's brows lowered to a deep v. "I heard he was bruised and battered, but then he did go home with Connor Wednesday night. They got into it over something."

Alec's jaw dropped. "What! What do you mean he went home with Connor? I'm here to talk to you about my nephew and the abuse you inflicted upon him. What the hell's going on?"

Sydney scoffed and crossed her arms. "What abuse! I couldn't make my meeting last week, so Sean showed up here around ten pissed off at me. We got into a fight and he slapped me, so I smacked him in the face with a frypan. The neighbours heard the yelling and called the cops. Connor turned up and I told him to take Sean home to his place. I cancelled *my* time with Sean, not the mentorship. If his face was bruised and battered, it ain't just from me. Try Connor, or better yet," she waved her finger in his face, "his abusive arsehole of a father. Either one of them could've done it."

Alec put his hands up in protest. "Wait just a minute. *You* fight with my nephew and you're going to pin the blame on my brother? *Two* of my brothers?"

"Why not! I haven't seen Sean since Connor took him home. Whatever happened between them is not on me. Try your brother before you come accusing me of any impropriety, especially since he's been screwing your sister-in-law." She noticed his shock as she stepped back and started closing the door, but Alec moved to block it.

"You had better be telling me the truth, Ms Kingston." His tone hardened and his blue eyes glared into hers. "Because if I find out there's been some inappropriate behaviour directed at my nephew, by you, then on behalf of the family, I will take action against you. Do you understand?"

All of the Ryans towered over her, but after L.A., Sydney didn't care to be threatened. "After the stunt Sean pulled on me Wednesday night, it's *your* family who will end up in the spotlight if the truth comes out." She stepped closer. "*All* of it. Now get out of my doorway. I have a book to write." Grabbing the door, she used it to push him out of the doorway and finally managed to close and lock it. "Fucking Ryans," she muttered, and locked the house door behind her.

Sydney moved into the parlour to watch Alec out the window. He slowly walked down the stoop stairs, glancing over his shoulder at the house every few steps. Puzzled, surprised, and a few other things, Sydney was sure. He slowly climbed into his car and sat behind the wheel for a few moments before starting the engine. With a long look at the brownstone, he finally drove off.

She sighed and wandered back to the kitchen.

"Wow," Amy said. "Is that how you got the bruise? Did Sean hit you?" She'd noticed it that morning, but Sydney's private life was none of her business, and not a part of her job requirement unless asked.

"Slapped with a very big, very open hand." Sydney picked up her drink and finished it off, holding it to her face to cool it down. "Sounds like Sean's been lying to everyone."

"Or, he lied and everyone picked up on something different. Didn't you say earlier that another brother turned up last night and told a similar story?"

"Yes," Sydney murmured. "But Kieran just picked up on the mentorship being cancelled, even though it hadn't. Alec's assuming Sean's bruises have to do with me. I haven't seen Sean since it happened on Wednesday, and he's seen Connor and or Declan since then, but Alec's linking it to me."

"And that bruise on your face." Amy nodded, pouring herself a third cola.

"Yeah." Sydney thought about Alec's words. "He either knows something or suspects something because he came here to talk about it. So, he either heard something at Sunday lunch…"

"Or he's assumed out of nothing." Amy sat at the table and watched Sydney. "What are you going to do? It sounded like he was threatening you."

"He was. But I'm not falling for it. I threatened him right back. Besides, from what Sean's told me, I doubt that family wants that business getting out. And IA would have a field day with it."

Amy frowned at the acronym. "IA?"

"Internal Affairs," Sydney said. "Isn't that who looks into cops?"

"I'm not sure—" Amy was cut off by the ringing of Sydney's phone.

"Hey, Eric. Talk to the two officers yet?" Sydney asked.

"I have and got a copy of the report. The box was down in evidence, but the rat was long gone, obviously. Not that you can't find them a dime a dozen in this city. But as I suspected, there wasn't much they could do. I've put in a request for it, so we can keep it preserved until Landon can take over if they're not going to be doing anything with it."

"Okay, you keep on with that and I'll keep writing, but…" She decided to mention the episode with Alec and told him the story. "Have you dealt with him before?"

"I've been in court with him and he's damn good at what he does. But I also know, like many other people in this town, that the Ryans aren't so clean. Douglas and Cormac might seem it, but some of those sons most definitely are not."

"Oh, interesting," Sydney murmured. "Okay, I'll keep you apprised if anything else happens with that family."

"Then you'd better tell me what happened with Sean."

Sydney breathed in. "No. Bye, Eric." She hung up and went to the fridge for another Pepsi. "So, what's for lunch?"

*****

Amy went home at five, and five minutes later Connor was banging on her door.

"What the bloody hell!" Sydney demanded when she opened the door to see a very pissed off Connor leaning against the door frame. "What's wrong with you?"

"What the fuck did you tell my brother?" he raged, taking two steps into the vestibule, his finger in her face, spit flying from his mouth. "What the fuck did you tell Alec about me and Sean?"

"How the fuck could I tell him anything when I don't even know what happened?" Sydney countered. "You came here Saturday night and refused to mention it. But apparently *you* smashed Sean's face up."

"I told you. We got into a fight because of you," he spat. "When he came to at my place, he went on the attack and smashed me in the face a few times before I could stop him. I smashed him back."

"Yeah, so nice of you, beating up a seventeen-year-old kid," Sydney sarcastically remarked and noticed the bruising on his face was now black. "Looks like he got you good."

"And I got him better," he regaled. "I told you, he blamed me for his parents' marriage falling apart. Told me to stop fucking you so you wouldn't be a whore like his mother. I asked him what was it to him and you know what he said?" He laughed maniacally. "He said he didn't want me, *me*, turning you into a whore. Are you fucking kidding me!"

Sydney stepped back and crossed her arms. He was the type of angry she didn't want to deal with. Just like Sean. Just like Declan. It clearly ran in the family, and

Eric's words floated through her mind. But then again, she'd been fucking Connor for weeks and he hadn't cared about Laura one iota. So why was he caring now. "Why are you here? *Now?*"

"Because you fucking told my brother about me and Laura and now he's pissed off."

"I know nothing about it. Alec made a stupid assumption that Sean's face was a result of our time together. He also noticed *my* face." She pointed to her bruise. "And made a wrong connection. I told him that I hadn't seen Sean since Wednesday and that he went home with you that night and probably would've seen his father since. So, he needed to talk to you two instead." Her anger bubbled over and her voice rose. "Maybe instead of fucking your sister-in-law and then beating up your nephew, you should be staying away from both of them, because, again, you didn't mention anything Saturday night which was *after* you beat him up. What did you do with him? Dump him on his daddy's doorstep so he could deal with him? And what about Sunday lunch at your father's? Everyone would've noticed all those cuts and bruises on you and Sean. How did you lie and get away with that?"

He sneered. "Neither of us said anything about it because I beat his pathetic little ass. That boy is a wimp and he knows it. Just like his pathetic wimp father."

"Who fucks prostitutes while his wife fucks his brother?"

The crack of Connor's hand across Sydney's face was as loud as a gunshot, and she spun around and into the open door. Stunned, with a ringing in her ear, she heard a faint, "Hey," and the ringing grew louder.

Sydney shook her head and cupped her cheek; the same one Sean had slapped, and looked down at Connor who was silent on the floor.

"You okay?" Amy asked, her phone recording everything in one hand, her stun gun crackling in the other.

"Huh?" The word sounded dull to Sydney's ears, and her vision was blurry.

"Yeah, glad I came back when I did. I forgot to leave the paperwork and took it with me. What are we going to do with him?" She motioned to Connor and kept the phone on him.

"Um..." Sydney swallowed the rising bile and breathed in. Her vision cleared. "Okay. We can call the cops or his father."

"Or roll him down the stairs and wait for him to wake up," Amy suggested. "We do need to get him out of the house. Here, hold the phone and keep recording." She shoved it into Sydney's hands, along with the stun gun, and picked up Connor's feet. She dragged him out of the house onto the stoop and rolled him down the stairs. Sydney filmed the whole thing and they stared down at him until he came to.

"What the fuck," he grumbled, rubbing the back of his head and rolling onto his side. He saw them standing on the stoop, Sydney with the camera, and Amy with the stun gun recharged and ready. "Did you two bitches do this to me?" he yelled, but ended in a coughing fit. "Fucking bitches. I'll have you arrested for this." He managed to push himself into a sitting position. "I'll have you fucking arrested."

"And I'll have you charged with assault," Sydney replied. "Amy filmed the whole thing. We have you slapping me on film. Whatever will your father think?"

Connor sent a scathing look her way. "You fucking bitch."

"You fucking arsehole," Sydney spat back. "You fuck me and then abuse me. Not on, Ryan. I know too much about you, just as I told Alec, and I really don't think any of you would want all of your dirty secrets getting out. Especially since you all think you run the fucking city. You don't. And one day, it will all come down around your ears. Now, you're going to leave and pretend this never happened. And you'll never set foot in this brownstone again, and never see me again. Do you understand?"

"Oh, I understand." Connor stumbled to his feet. "You're a fucking bitch and I never should have fucked you. Well, that was my big mistake." He held his arms out to the side for balance. "Big fucking mistake. Huge!"

"Yeah, it was," Sydney agreed. "The biggest mistake of my life. Getting involved with a Ryan, especially," she was yelling now, "a hot-headed arsehole who can't stop fucking women he shouldn't be fucking. I wish I'd never got involved with your family. It was the biggest mistake of my life and I never want to see any of you ever again." She gasped for breath. "The biggest mistake of my life!"

"Of *your* life? It was the biggest mistake of *mine*, you whore, so you can go fuck right off." He turned around to find a police car pulling up on the street. "And you two can fuck right off too." He thrust his finger at them and stumbled his way to his car. He managed to get it started and screeched off down the road.

Officer Velenksy alighted and walked up the stairs. "Everything okay? We received a call."

"No," Sydney said and handed the phone back to Amy. "But then I doubt Commissioner Ryan would want this getting out. I'll speak to him myself and the rest will be up to him."

Velenksy nodded and pointed to the phone. "I take it you have it all on camera."

"From before he slapped Sydney," Amy told her. "He was *very* angry."

Velensky's brows rose in shock. "Oh, my God. Ah, okay. Do you want to do anything about that?"

"Not this minute, no." Sydney shook her head, but a pinging sensation ripped through the back of her skull. She groaned and rubbed the spot. "I may need my chiropractor, though."

"I'll try to make an appointment for the morning," Amy said.

"That'd be great. In the meantime, is there any hope the two of you could do an occasional sweep of the street just in case he comes back?" Sydney asked. "Or the knicker-stealing stalker."

Amy snorted and burst into barely contained laughter.

"Don't laugh, Amy, it's not funny," Sydney playfully scolded. "It's very serious. Women's unmentionables are being stolen."

Amy ducked inside and they heard her laughter grow in decibels.

Velenksy couldn't help smiling. "I'll see what we can

do. In the meantime, I need to report something."

"Tell them it was a mouthy drunk who'd fallen down. He was shouting about the end of the world or something," Sydney suggested.

Velensky's smile grew. "I'll tell them it was a false alarm, but if this comes out…"

"Then I'm sure Commissioner Ryan will be grateful it was kept quiet for him to deal with. I'll see to that," Sydney promised and waved her off. She watched them slowly drive down the street and then called out, "Amy, you can come out now."

A respectful Amy passed her. "I left the papers on the hall table. I'll see you tomorrow."

"I'll wait until you're in your car and locked up tight," Sydney called and saw her hurry to her car three houses down. Once she was in, Sydney locked herself away, alarm set, and an ice pack, once again, on her face.

Chapter 14

On Tuesday morning, Sydney was able to get into her chiropractor thanks to Amy telling them she'd been assaulted twice and needed help. The practice quickly rearranged the schedule to fit her in.

They'd been back at the brownstone for an hour when banging came on the front door.

"God, who now?" Sydney moaned as the banging didn't let up.

"Which Ryan is left?" Amy queried.

Sydney paused, eyes wide. "Ah, fuck!"

"Who?" Amy whipped out her phone and stun gun.

"Declan!"

"Fucking hell." Amy checked her power gauge. "I'm fully charged, let's go."

They hurried down the hall and checked the monitor. It was indeed Declan Ryan and he wasn't letting up on the door.

Sydney took a deep breath and opened the inside door. They stepped into the vestibule, exchanged a glance, and Sydney opened the front door.

"About fucking time," Declan yelled. "You fucking

paedophile rapist. You raped my fucking son and think it's all right." His arms waved around with his words, fingers pointing, hands waving. "Who the fuck do you think you are?" He noticed Amy recording him and lunged for her, but Sydney lunged between them and pushed him back.

"Who the fuck are you to accuse me of such vile garbage?" she demanded. "Where the fuck do you get off standing on my stoop screaming such vile lies at the top of your lungs? You'd better watch it, Declan, or I'll have you for slander and defamation."

"Oh, slander and defamation," he mocked. "And I'll have you for statutory rape."

"I didn't rape anyone and if Sean's saying I did I'll sue him too. But considering the legal age of consent is seventeen and he's seventeen, then you can't stop him from having sex with anyone, but it sure as hell wasn't me. So, fuck off and get the fuck out of here before I call your father."

"Call my father? What are you, eight?" Declan declared. "What are you gonna call my father for? It's not like he's gonna spank me."

"No, but I can demote you, or strip you of your badge and gun entirely."

Declan froze, eyes wide, jaw hanging. He slowly turned to see his father standing on the sidewalk. "Dad. Ah, what are you doing here?"

"I came to see, Ms Kingston. You?" Cormac stood straight and tall, hands casually in his trench coat pockets.

"I…ah…" Declan stuttered, but didn't know how to finish the sentence.

"Came to accuse Sydney of having sex with Sean," Amy supplied. "Called her a rapist and paedophile. Lunged at me. Gotta say, Commish, he's just like Connor *and* Sean. Abusive assholes."

Cormac gave a nod. "Declan, go home. I will be by to talk to you later. And yes, you will be suspended from duty. This is not the way we treat civilians who have done nothing wrong."

"Nothing wrong," Declan yelled. "She raped my son. She coerced or forced or something him. How else did he end up a miserable dope who got himself beat up?"

"Try asking Connor that question. He did the most damage," Sydney called, making them both look up at her. "You two are so much alike," she told Declan. "Abusive arseholes who like beating people up."

"Where do you get off?" Declan lunged, finger pointing at her. "You raped my so—"

Cormac grabbed him by his coat and hauled him against his SUV, his left arm across his son's throat. "No one was raped. And no one did the raping. Sean is seventeen, and nothing happened between him and Sydney. Maybe you should get your facts straight before shouting your damn mouth off." He released Declan and pushed him towards his car and waved at his security detail to follow. "Go home. I want all of you at my house at eight and that's an order." He waited until Declan screeched off down the road before turning his attention to Sydney and Amy. With a heavy sigh, and even heavier tread, he walked up the stairs and stood in front of them. He gave a small smile and a nod, and said, "Sydney, I owe you an apology, and my eternal gratitude and thanks, but most definitely an apology."

Stunned, Sydney glanced at Amy. "Um…what for?"

Cormac pointed to her face. "Sean."

She lightly shrugged a shoulder. "Apple doesn't fall."

"And Connor," Amy added. "I'll leave you two alone."

"No, Ms Aldridge, I'd like to talk to you as well and offer an apology. May I come in?"

Intrigued, they glanced at each other and stepped aside, waving him in. Sydney shut the door and they followed him into the living room. "So, what's this about?" She and Amy stood in front of him waiting for an answer.

Another small smile. One of sorrow. "I know Emerson came here Sunday night, so she would have told you something about lunch, and that I wanted to talk to Sean. Maybe to get him to stay at my house for the night." He rocked slightly on his feet, his hands clenching in his pockets.

"She didn't mention much," Sydney replied. "Did you?"

"I did. And I got Sean's side of the story. But I'd like to hear yours."

"So, you can see if they're the same, or if one of us is lying?" Sydney noted that he seemed nervous. "Do you want to sit down?" she offered.

He cleared his throat. "No, thank you. Please, just tell me."

Sydney sighed, licked her lips, and gave him a quick rundown. "I couldn't make the appointment and called Michael, the editor he was seeing that day. But he turned up on my doorstep at ten and was really pissed. He'd seen the men I'd had an appointment with leave. Then saw Connor turn up and kiss me on the doorstep. We've been seeing each other since the lunch at your house." She noticed his expression didn't change, so he must've already known. "Sean looked in the window, saw us, and waited until he'd left. He called me a whore and a slut, and said that I was just like his mother because Connor had fucked her too." That didn't seem to surprise him either, but he closed his eyes and breathed in. "He grabbed me by the arms and forced himself on me. I bit his tongue, and pushed him away. He slapped me, and grabbed me again. I booted his shin and grabbed his testicles to get him off me, and ended up pushing him away, running into the kitchen and grabbing a frypan. I hid behind the living room door." She pointed to the spot on her left. "And when he came past I hit him in the face. He spun around, and when he stood up I smashed him over the head, tied him up, and heard the sirens. Conner was here and came in. I told him to take Sean to his house, which he did."

Cormac took another breath and stared down at the floor. "That's what he told me."

Relief flooded through Sydney. "At least he's not lying."

"No. Which is why I need to apologise to you, Ms Kingston. You were right in not wanting to mentor an impressionable teenage boy. Because he became very impressionable. You were right to be wary. I was wrong to force you into it. I'm sorry."

"What happened at Connor's? When he took him home?" she asked. "Connor came by last night yelling and screaming. He and Sean had beaten each other up."

"So Sean said. I took him to my place Sunday night. I

told Declan and Laura I'd be taking him for a few days. They didn't like it, neither did Sean, but I got it out of him. What had been happening in his family unit. He bawled like a baby on the floor."

"Was that the first you'd heard of Connor and Laura?" Sydney tried reading his expression, but his poker face was on.

"First time I heard. But not the first time I'd suspected." He looked around at the comfortable furnishings and décor. "He told me he was in love with you and went, in his words, ballistic when he found out you were seeing his uncle. That's when he told me. From what he said, and from what I can tell, the problems between his parents transferred to you. He admitted he shouldn't've taken out his anger on you. I think he's very confused and needs therapy."

"Absolutely," Sydney said. "And he needs to get the hell away from his parents."

Cormac agreed. "That's why Sean is staying with me for the remainder of his school year. I can keep an eye on him, along with Pop, and he'll be away from the fights and dramas. He'll have a stable home to come home to."

"Great idea," Sydney said. "And you can encourage him to continue with the mentorship."

Cormac looked at her in surprise. "Didn't you cancel that?"

She sighed. "For fuck's sake. I had Kieran and Sandy on my doorstep Sunday night asking the same thing, and then Alec on Monday, although he made some accusations, but still said the same thing. And between Connor and Declan, oi." Sydney rubbed her eyes. "Your sons need to be reined in, Cormac, because I have had abuse from three of them on top of Sean. No…" Her hands dropped. "I did not cancel the mentorship, I can't, it's with the publishing house. I just cancelled my involvement and suggested Victor and Michael, who he's already had sessions with, should take over. Jesus." She paced in front of him. "Why did he lie?"

Cormac frowned. "I don't think it was a lie per se, he said you couldn't do it anymore and I think we all just assumed you'd cancelled it."

"And Declan assumed a whole lot more which is suspicious." Sydney paused. "I wonder if Connor spoke to him. Or Alec. Unless he got something entirely different out of Sean."

"Highly possible, and I'll find out tonight," Cormac said. "I owe you an apology and if you think Sean is good enough—"

"He is. He could be a very successful author one day," Sydney told him. "He has a gift, and it needs to be nurtured. His parents won't and don't do that, but you and Douglas can. I think it's a very good idea for him to live with you and for the mentorship to continue. Apology accepted. We all live and learn and I will never mentor again."

Cormac breathed a sigh of relief. "Thank you, and now onto *my* thanks. I…looked into you after Sean unloaded his burden. I wanted to know more about you and found a redacted report out of L.A."

Sydney froze, unable to breathe, and she knew Amy was doing the same.

He looked at them apologetically. "I thought that

given Sean's story, that maybe something similar had happened there. I contacted an old friend of mine in the LAPD to find out what the report said. He told me, and sent me an un-redacted copy." He noticed Sydney's eyes close in pain. Both of them were deathly white, the blood having drained from their faces at the mention of L.A.

"Amy," he went on. "I am very sorry that happened to you. No woman should deal with, or go through, a sexual assault. I'm very sorry." He looked from her to Sydney who was now frowning at him. "And Sydney. I thank you, and owe you a great deal of gratitude and thanks for killing the bastard who did it."

Sydney inhaled sharply, her hands flying to her mouth. She stepped back. No one was supposed to know this secret beyond a select few. "Did Emerson…" she mumbled behind her hands.

"No." He shook his head. "She didn't tell me. I read it in the report. Does she know?"

Sydney nodded and looked at Amy. Her hands lowered. "He was in the house. I did what needed to be done. But why are you thanking me?" She turned her gaze to his.

"Because I saw the name of the assailant. He was a known stalker who raped and murdered his victims. We had no fingerprints, no DNA that we knew of, but we had a name of a suspect and identikit of a man seen in the same areas by other people. I saw on the report that his DNA was taken along with his fingerprints and all the reports are being gone through one by one to check against the evidence to see if they could find DNA after all. They've just finished that off this week and the families are being told. I got that report in at the same time and the match was conclusive. You killed a man that raped ten women."

"And you're thanking me?" Sydney said in confusion. "Why?"

"Because you and Amy were numbers eleven and twelve," he said carefully. "And my wife was number two."

Sydney and Amy stood in shock, eyes wide, mouths open.

"Fucking hell," Amy finally managed.

Sydney's eyes closed and she finally breathed. "Oh, my God. I'm so sorry. I'm so sorry."

"Thank you." Cormac gave a short nod. "I'll tell the family tonight before I read them the riot act over you and Sean. Their behaviour has been deplorable and vile, especially Connor's and Declan's. I am forever in your debt for what you did in L.A. and if there's anything I can do—"

"Keep your sons away from me," Sydney said. "And especially your grandson."

Another nod. "Agreed. Anything else?"

Sydney glanced at Amy, thinking it through. "You don't happen to know the guy who runs Landon Security, do you? I'm having trouble with some other stalkers, and we can't get looked into for six months because they're booked up."

"Holland Landon? He's an old friend of mine. I can absolutely give him a call for you. Does this have to do with the rat?"

"And a very big bunch of letters made from magazine

cut-outs." Sydney grimaced.

"I'll give Holland a call when I get home. I'll tell him to call you."

"No." Sydney shook her head. "Tell him to call CC or Eric at Pulsate Publishing. They used their services about ten or so years ago. They're on the client list; we just can't be seen for six months."

Cormac gave a sharp nod. "I'll do that; meanwhile, I'll take my leave and once again, apologies for not heeding your warning. And thank you for getting the killer off the streets." He made his way to the front door.

Sydney followed. "Does Emerson know about your wife? Will you tell her who the killer was?"

He paused, his hand on the knob, the door half opened. "Does she know everything about L.A.?"

"She does."

"Then I'll tell her. Are you seeing her again this week?"

"Not until Saturday, unless you whisk her away again," she lightly joked.

A soft grin lit up his face. "I might do that again one day soon. Goodbye, Ms Kingston, Ms Aldridge." He let go of the door and opened the second, stepping out onto the stoop. "Stay safe ladies, and protect yourselves."

"We will." They watched him deftly climb into the back of his SUV and take off down the road.

"Fucking hell," Amy murmured. "He knew."

"He does. And what a twist that was." Sydney locked the doors and went back to the kitchen. "What were we doing before he and Declan turned up?" She looked around, but couldn't for the life of her remember.

"I don't know, but I want to talk about it." Amy pulled her chair out and sat down.

"You sure?"

She nodded. "It's clearly time."

*****

The man watched them through the sliding doors. They'd talked well into the night. He watched the lights come on, watched them make and eat dinner. Watched them cry and hold each other. Watched them laugh and toast each other. He'd seen the commissioner turn up, but couldn't hear anything, just like now. He daren't get any closer. He didn't want to be seen. He knew that would be unwise and far too early for his plan.

He inched towards the house the darker it got, but he still couldn't hear them.

How he wished he was inside with them sharing whatever it was they were discussing.

"Don't worry, Cassandra, you and your assistant rejoice for now, but soon it will be us who are rejoicing. When we get married."

PART TWO

One year later

Chapter 15

"Ladies and gentlemen, welcome to *Rockefeller.* I'm your host, Rhett Rockefeller, and for the whole hour we have a very special guest, Sydney Kingston. She's the author who writes crime thrillers under the pen name, Cassandra Kingsley. So please, welcome our guest today, Sydney Kingston."

Rhett Rockefeller, no relation to the actual Rockefellers, flashed his huge pearly whites at the audience and the people at home. With movie star good looks, dark blond wavy hair, and crystal blue eyes, his smile could make women get their clothes off faster than Usain Bolt around a track. They all loved him while the men all hated his six-four, fit and healthy frame and trade mark smile. He was the highest earner on daytime TV for chat shows and earned every penny, nickel, dime, and cent. He walked to the stage and kissed Sydney hello when she strode out.

She waved to the crowd, walked up the two steps to the platform, and carefully sat in the chair next to Rhett's.

The studio was the biggest for daytime shows, fitting in five hundred audience members.

Coloured lights glared back at her, the adoring crowd applauded her, and the crew stood around the sound stage filming the whole thing.

Sydney crossed her ankles, adjusted her blazer, and looked at the host. Extremely good looking, he reminded her of the men from every novel by her friend and mentor, Jackie Collins.

The crowd finally calmed and Rhett leant over, touching his hand to her knee. "Sydney, darling, when we announced you would be coming on for a whole hour, the phones and website went haywire. Everyone wanted a ticket to come and see you." He waved the question cards he held in his hand at the crowd. "And as you can see, we're at capacity. All of these people are here for you."

The crowd cheered again, a few wolf whistles rang out, and Sydney blushed. This attention she was used to, but after L.A. it had become unwanted and made her uneasy. "That's nice," she said. "I hope you've all read my latest book and loved it." More cheers. She turned to Rhett. "And have you read it?"

"I've read the first…" He looked up at the ceiling to think about it. "Probably ten chapters. I only got the book two days ago and haven't had much time to get through it."

"At least you're honest," Sydney told him. "Many interviewers don't even bother reading the books they're interviewing for and then lie and say they read it and loved it."

"Very true." He nodded and held the hardcover of Sydney's latest thriller up for the camera. "*Twisted Affair,* by Cassandra Kingsley, which is the pen name for Sydney Kingston, is officially out tomorrow, but has already hit the New York Times and USA Today bestseller lists at number one. On both of them. And that's just the big charts, you've hit number one on a bunch of smaller charts as well." Acknowledging the audience, he stared down the barrel of the camera. "If you haven't got it, or ordered it, do so now. From what I've read so far, it's a thrill a minute like the rest of her stories."

He sat back in his seat, crossed his legs, and flipped the cover open. "It's a great cover, Sydney, your publisher has done it again, so let's launch into the questions." He held it up to the camera and audience. "Why a pen name?"

Sydney waved her hand at him. "Why a stage name?"

Caught off guard, he stumbled, "Well, it's because… it's showbiz."

"Exactly that," Sydney agreed. "Whether it's actors, presenters, musicians, or authors, anyone can use a nom de plume, a pen name, a stage name. Not everyone likes their name, and for some people, their names are hard to pronounce. So, they shorten it, or change it. It's nothing new. It also gives us a modicum of privacy for our private lives."

"But you're very public about the name." Rhett looked at the cover and the huge Cassandra Kingsley across the bottom. "How much privacy does it offer?"

"For me, not a lot anymore. But I also figured if I ever wrote in another genre, like middle-grade for example, then I'd pick another name, so my two radically different genres won't clash. It was for privacy to begin with, but then quickly became public once I moved to L.A., which is fine. But it's also caused problems."

"Which is something I want to get into later." Rhett flipped the book over and looked at the back cover. "Great picture of you, as always. Tell us about your book. What inspired it? Was it the one you were writing when you left L.A.?"

Sydney gave a soft laugh. "No, definitely not. The novel I started in L.A. was shelved when I got here. By the time I was here a month and had settled in, I went over all of my unfinished drafts and added that one to the pile. I had no emotion for it anymore, no need to even bother with it, so it was shelved." Sydney uncrossed and recrossed her legs into a more comfortable position. "I started writing a book not long after that, but that one I'll probably be publishing next year. There's a biography that goes with it, but we're waiting on lawyers to give us the go ahead." She pointed at the book. "And then this book came crashing into my brain not long after, so we went down to Florida for a warm sea breeze over winter frost and I finished it off. It came out pretty quickly, and then we geared up for release and here she is debuting September nineteenth."

"And what's it about?" Rhett held it up again for the camera. "You still haven't mentioned that."

"It's about a single woman who meets a family of very rich and powerful men. The affair she has is with one of them, and the affair one of them has with her is…in his mind." Sydney cast a mysterious smile at the audience who oohed and aahed.

"Wait, wait." Rhett held his hand up at the audience. "Just wait. She has an affair with one of them, but one of them has an affair with her *in his mind…* How does that happen?"

Sydney chuckled. "It sounds confusing, but isn't. He believes he's having an affair with her, but obviously, he's mentally unstable and it's all in his mind."

"Hence the title, *Twisted Affair*," Rhett said. "Was any of this based on real life? I see there's a stalker or two and something happens to the female lead's best friend."

"Not really," Sydney swiftly cut in. "I had a few things happen a year ago and I mixed them all up and had other things happen to the character. It was only vaguely inspired by real events."

"Who is the family of rich and powerful men based on?" Rhett uncrossed his legs and sat up straighter. "An L.A. family? A New York family? Mob, mafia, lawyers, businessmen, cops? What?"

Sydney cleared her throat. "You'll just have to form your own opinion. There are many, many rich powerful people in the world. It could be any of them, or it could be none of them and just figments of my imagination."

"Oh, right, your *imagination*," Rhett scoffed. "You live in Madam X's old brownstone. I'd bet a million dollars the book is based on that."

"And you'd lose because you'd be dead wrong," Sydney retorted with snark. "That's the next book. And thanks *so much* for revealing where I live."

More oohs and aahs from the audience and raised eyebrows from Rhett.

"Care to repeat that?" He leaned over to her. "The *next book* is based on Madam X?"

Changing tack, Sydney coyly shrugged a shoulder and

glanced at the audience. "Maybe."

"Holy cow, ladies and gentlemen, Sydney's next book sounds even better than this one. Can you tell us about it?"

"No," she playfully scolded. "Because I'm here to promote this one. *Twisted Affair*, out now in hardcover, and coming in paperback in March next year. It will also be out in e-book, audio, and foreign additions in the next six months."

Rhett got the audience applauding. "And you still own your digital rights, right?"

"Yes, the e-books and audio. Pulsate does my print and foreign print editions."

"You must make a motza with those. You started as an indie author, publishing yourself, and then did the deal with the publisher. That's clearly worked for you."

"It has. I also have no dates for when I have to produce a book. It's completely to my timetable."

"Which not many authors get," Rhett said. "For most it's a yearly production cycle."

"Or two years if some are lucky," Sydney added. "Many authors end up going years between getting their first and second books published, that's why indie, or self-publishing, is such a big business."

"But all self-published books are known to be crap." Rhett leaned back and swung his chair towards her. "It's well-known."

Sydney turned to the audience. "How many of you read my books when I published them?" Most of the audience put up a hand or cheered. "And who thought they were crap?" All hands went down. "So clearly, you all thought my books were good." She turned back to Rhett. "I am *really* sick and tired of hearing the same old crappy garbage from brain dead morons who read a few self-pubbed books and then declare that *all* self-pubbed books are crap. It's a lie. Because you haven't read every single self-pubbed book on the planet. It's like saying; *all* authors suffer from imposter syndrome, *all* writers suffer from writer's block, *all* authors are drunks and druggies, or *all* creatives are tortured souls. *None of it* is true. *All of it's* a lie, and there is no categorical evidence in this entire solar system *to prove* any of those lies. And the more you perpetuate the lies, the more of a liar you become. Why do you want to be an uneducated liar who refuses to see the truth?" Sydney asked, and looked at the audience in the studio and at home. "Just stop lying and making crap up that you can't back up. Because there *is no evidence* to back it up." She sighed and slid her hair over her shoulders. "It's so infuriating being labelled with something you don't suffer from by people who don't know you personally."

"You do make a good point, and it's not helpful for self-published authors," Rhett agreed. "People make claims about pretty much everything these days and they don't care if there's evidence or not. They just want to shoot their mouth off. But first we must go to a quick break. We'll see you right after this."

The stagehand counted them out to the break.

"Fantastic, Sydney." Rhett clasped his hands. "This is going fabulously. And if the next book's as good as your others, then I can't wait to see how you used Madam X to inspire a novel." He lifted his face for the make-up artist.

"Well, you'll have to wait, and hope it's out next year." Sydney took a sip of drink and had her face dabbed with powder and her lipstick topped up.

"And we're back in five…"

Sydney set her drink down and plastered a smile on her freshly coated lips.

"And welcome back to *Rockefeller*, I'm your host, Rhett Rockefeller, and my guest for the whole hour is author Sydney Kingston who you know better as Cassandra Kingsley. Now, Sydney, tell me, and our audience here in the studio, and those at home, why you disappeared for the last year? It's only recently come out in the press."

Sydney inwardly groaned, but outwardly sighed. "I didn't disappear, Rhett. It was getting chilly here in New York. My assistant and I headed for warmer weather so I could get the books finished. We were there for six months and then I treated myself to a European holiday for a few months before the book was due."

"It all sounds deliciously delectable," Rhett regaled. "You posted the holiday to your socials, as well as your progress, but I want to know about that delicious hot Italian stallion you posted about."

The blush rose up Sydney's throat to her cheeks. "*I didn't* post about him, *everyone else* did. I met him on holiday and was wined and dined. I had a good time."

"A good time," Rhett mocked. "From the looks of some of these photos…" He turned to the screen behind them that flashed the photos across. "I'd say you had a *very* good time."

"And all of this is *none* of your business," Sydney

retorted, embarrassed by the montage of pictures. She faced the audience and took a sip of water. "None of your business."

"Meow," came his catty reply and he looked at his cards. "Let's get into the real reason you escaped the city then. You had a stalker that was being dealt with."

Sydney froze, but hoped her expression was neutral.

"Landon Security did the job of catching your stalker and he's been brought before the court, charged, and sentenced. What can you tell us about the case? Will you write a book about it?"

Sydney considered her words before speaking. "I didn't leave the city *because* of the stalker. As I said, I left for warmer weather to write this book, so it was only *one* reason why I left. Yes, Landon Security was hired to find out who was sending me letters and a nasty little gift on my doorstep, and they found the guy. He was arrested and charged and now he's been sentenced to jail."

"He got two years, no parole," Rhett read from his card. "It hasn't been made public why he was doing those things, but what was the reason he gave?"

Again, Sydney considered her words. She didn't want to talk about it, but knew it was going to come up in every interview she did for the new book because it was currently news. "The usual. He was obsessed with me because of my books," she finally said. "I'm not going to say much more about it. It's over and done, behind me, in my past, I'm moving on."

"Will you put it in one of your books one day?" Rhett asked.

"Who said I haven't?" Sydney wiggled her brows at

the audience. She got a few cheers and claps for it.

"Well, I hope it's in next year's book about Madam X," Rhett told her. "I absolutely cannot wait for that. Now, I want to ask about the author community. Many authors are pretty supportive of each other, others are downright asses to each other, and many are neutral. We've seen some reviews of this book." He held up *Twisted Affair* for the camera to zoom in on. "And they're all pretty scathing of it. In fact, some authors seem to be scathing of all your books and your success. How do you deal with that? And what's your thought on it?"

A drip of sweat slowly made its way down Sydney's spine. She was starting to feel the heat under the studio lights in her turquoise sequinned blazer, plain turquoise pants, and matching top. She'd tried to dress cool, but hadn't dressed cool enough. She picked up her drink, took a sip, stared casually at the audience and said, "They're a bunch of whiny little pussies."

The crowd erupted into frenzied applause and Rhett laughed.

"Okay, okay." He calmed the audience and swung around in his chair so he could face Sydney. "I'm going to need you to explain that."

"No explanation needed," she replied. "The same authors have said pretty much the same thing about every book I've had success with. *The same thing,*" she dramatically repeated. "And yet when you compare my sales, book after book, to theirs, they come nowhere close to me. They're jealous little brats and whiny little pussies that need to grow up and sell their own books. If they put half as much energy into actually making their books better, *and* marketing them better than they do insulting me year after year, then they'd have better sales. *But they don't!*" Another hair flick for the dramatics and the camera, and she was done.

Rhett shook his head. He'd never had an author be so secretive and yet so out there on his stage before. "Whiny little pussies. You hear that, authors?" He looked straight down the barrel of the camera. "To all the authors who waste their bile on Sydney Kingston's books, she says you're whiny little pussies. And we'll be back after this break. Don't go anywhere."

The stagehand counted them out.

Rhett burst out laughing. "I can't believe you said that. That took guts, Sydney. It really did. Especially since you had a stalker a year ago. I'd say you may have set off another one with one of those authors. You'd better watch out." He tilted his head to have his nose powdered.

"Who said I had only one?" Sydney had a few sips of her refreshed drink. "*You* said that."

Rhett gazed at her quizzically. "You mean, you had more than one? But only one was caught by Landon—"

"Was it only one?"

"And we're back on in five…"

"If you say any of this on air I'll sue you. Keep your trap shut," she said as they came back on air. Her lips lifted into a smile.

"We're back for our last session with Sydney Kingston, you know her as Cassandra Kingsley, author of thrillers with spice and her latest is *Twisted Affair*, about a woman who gets involved with a rich and powerful family. Tell me, Sydney…" He turned towards her. "How many rich and powerful families have you met to gain inspiration for this book? And can you name them?"

A few audience members whooped.

"I met a few in Italy and throughout my European holiday," Sydney said. "Many were royal families who were fans of my books."

"That's right; you posted it to social media." Rhett crossed his legs and swung slightly from side to side, rubbing his hand provocatively up and down the spine of the book. "Royals who are so delicious," he murmured. "Who else? Any gangsters?"

Sydney chuckled. "I don't know if they were, but I met a few people who told me they were important somebodies. For all I know they were *un*important nobodies." That comment received a round of applause. "I have no idea if they were rich or not. Powerful or not. Mafia crime bosses or not. But I met a lot of people because they just couldn't leave me alone while I was on holiday."

"With your hot Italian lover?" Rhett quipped. "Come on, Sydney, do tell, for all of the single ladies in the audience and at home, did he have a name? Because you didn't tell us before."

Sydney tried to hide a smile, but failed. "His name's Gino, he's mid-thirties, and incredibly fucking hot."

The whole studio audience, crew, band alike, burst into wild applause and wolf whistles.

Sydney saw in the monitors that more photos were on the screen behind them. She glanced over her shoulder and went deep red. They were different from the ones before, of her and Gino making out on the beach in Capri. Gino's manhood stood out rather prominently in his tiny briefs.

"Jesus Christ," she muttered, wanting the earth to open up and swallow her whole. She spied Amy in the wings covering her mouth with uncontrollable laughter.

"Well, I mean…" Rhett glanced from the photos to Sydney. "I'd be making out with him too, looking like that. Was he good in bed? Did he have a big dick?"

"Oh, my God, Rhett," Sydney cried in shock and covered her face with her hands in embarrassment. "Bloody hell!"

"Okay, okay." Rhett grabbed a microphone from the stagehand and ran into the audience. "We have time or a few questions from our studio audience." He stopped by a young woman who looked to be mid-twenties. "What's your question for Sydney Kingston?"

The curly brunette with glasses stood up. "Hi, Ms Kingston. My name's Amber Wellchild and I'd love to write books like yours one day. Can you give me some advice?"

Sydney zeroed in on her. "Sure. If you haven't got an MFA or some other type of degree in writing, do a few courses in the genre you want to write in. Whether they're free or paid, you'll get a lot out of it and it'll get you on your way. And read as many books about writing as you can. I have a list of ones I've read on my website. Just write and keep writing to hone your craft. Also, join any local writers' groups."

"And we have another here." Rhett darted up the stairs

to a man and held the microphone in front of him. "What's your question, sir."

"Ms Kingston, I love your books and get every one of them signed when it comes out. You've done a few in a series; will there be any more of those, or are you just writing single books from now on?"

Sydney acknowledged him and his question with a nod. "I know the books you mean and they are a trilogy. There will be no more in that series. If I write another series though..." She shrugged. "Who knows. Thanks for your question. Next?"

Rhett landed next to a nervous looking young man with glasses and slicked down greasy hair. "And what do you have to ask, Ms Kingston?"

"Ah, yes, hello, Ms Kingston. Is the family in your novel, *Twisted Affair*, the Ryan family of New York?" He pushed his glasses up the bridge of his nose. "As in the Police Commissioner and his four law enforcement sons? You were involved with Connor Ryan, the second son, last year. Is that family the reason you left New York?"

Sydney's brows slid into a deep v. She tried not to panic and remained calm. "No. On all counts."

"Well, well, well." Rhett looked at Sydney in surprise. "Ms Kingston, have you been keeping secrets?

"No," came her sharp reply.

Rhett moved on, but the young man grabbed the microphone from him and hurried down the stairs towards her, yelling all the way. "You're lying, Ms Kingston. I know for a fact you were involved with Connor Ryan and his nephew Sean Ryan. I have it on ugh—" He was tackled to the floor by security and Rhett quickly picked up the microphone.

"Come now, that type of behaviour's not welcome here. Security, throw him out." He watched four burly guards carry the man by his arms and legs out of the studio and then turned to Sydney to see her deep frown and a worried, almost panicked, expression on her face. "Sydney, care to reply?"

Sydney looked from the camera to Rhett. "No, and both of you can fuck *right off.*"

Rhett said nothing for a few seconds and then turned to the camera. "And that's it for today, folks, please thank author, Sydney Kingston, and we'll be back tomorrow."

"Jesus fucking Christ!" Sydney snapped as the credits rolled over a blackened screen. She thrust up out of her seat and strode towards Amy. A member of the sound crew stopped her to remove her microphone, and she followed Amy to her dressing room, slamming the door when she entered. "Let's get out of here. I've had enough of this." Sydney grabbed her bag and turned to see Rhett in the doorway. "And what do you want?"

"Sydney, Sydney, Sydney," he murmured, his hands clasped prayer style in front of him. "You may not have answered that last question on stage, but your reply and your actions may have given it all away." He grasped her free hand. "We need to do another sit down."

Sydney yanked her hand from his and grimaced. "No, we don't. And no, my replies and my actions don't prove anything. What I'm sick and tired of are freaks and stalkers who think they know my life better than I do. They don't. And people like that last gentlemen, although that's way too nice of a word to use, they're the kind we need to be careful of because they're stalkers and they're the ones we need security firms to deal with because they can escalate to murder. And *you* did not protect me from it." She thrust a finger at his shocked, but unapologetic, face, and glanced at Amy who was waiting patiently. "It's time to go. We need lunch and I have another interview."

Amy nodded and waited for Sydney to pass before following to block Rhett.

But he was not to be deterred. "Sydney." He hurried up to her in the hallway as she kept walking. "I had a marvellous time interviewing you today. I hope to do it again next year when the new book comes out."

"And I will more than likely be back, but you had better up your game when it comes to the security of your guests." Sydney paused at the exit to the carpark, her hand resting on the handle of the door. "You're the biggest talk show in daytime. It would be stupid not to come on to promote myself."

"Any chance you could maybe come back in a couple of months to talk more about the book?" Rhett asked, his voice dripping in sugary sweetness. "Maybe I could get some of those whiny little pussy authors on and you can have it out on stage?"

"Oh, now I get your sugary sweetness. You want ratings. You want dramas. You want people fighting on stage." She pushed the door open, gave him a resounding no, and walked out into the crisp autumn air.

Once Sydney was in the chauffeur-driven car, she sighed. "God, I've had enough already."

"Most of that was pretty cool," Amy told her. "Some, a little hot, some, a little unnerving."

Sydney stared out the medium dark tinted window and touched the button to lower it a quarter. "That last guy was *definitely* unnerving."

"How did he know?" Amy mused. "Is he a neighbour? He didn't look familiar. Oh…" She remembered. "I took photos of him for Landon Security if we ever need them again. Both on monitor and when he was carried past me."

Sydney rubbed the back of her skull at the spot where it met her spine. It was starting to throb, which meant, if she wasn't careful, a migraine would ensue. "I think we should pass them on, anyway. They know I had more than one stalker; he could be one of them, or another one. And how the hell did he know so much unless he was, is, a neighbour and saw it all happen? Type up a report and send it off as soon as possible."

"Will do." Amy quickly made notes on her phone app so she could draft the email later.

They lunched in Manhattan before arriving at SXT for the radio interview. There would be many more in the next few weeks, along with countless more TV, magazine, print and website interviews. She also had list of podcasts lined up to do. The rest of September was jam-packed with wall-to-wall interviews.

"Hi, Ms Kingston." A bubbly young woman, who looked to be no more than twenty-one, introduced herself to Sydney and Amy. "I'm Rainbow Sky, the intern here at SXT. I'm to get you settled in the quiet room until you're ready to go on air. Please follow me." She led them down the hall to a nicely decorated waiting room. "Here you go. We have a drinks fridge and nibblies." She indicated to the side wall. "Plus, a tea and coffee bar if you so desire. Preston will see you in…" She checked her watch and then the schedule on her clipboard. "About fifteen minutes. I'll come and call you in ten. If you need the bathroom, it's down the hall. Okay, bye."

Sydney watched her walk out and muttered to Amy, "Rainbow Sky. She looks like a hippy straight from the '60s and '70s."

"But I do like her rainbow hued skirt," Amy said, perusing the drinks and nibblies. "I wonder where she got it from."

"It was nice," Sydney agreed, and sat down on one of four couches. "You could ask her when she comes back." Glancing around at the soft blue hues of the room, she admired the Greek village paintings on the wall. "I'd love to go to Greece, especially Mykonos."

"Then why didn't we when we were over there?" Amy sat beside her and pulled out her tablet. "We were just over the sea in Italy." She started whipping together the email.

"Yeah," Sydney murmured, then pulled her make-up purse out of her bag. "We could have and we should have, but I really just wanted to spend time exploring Italy."

"It is beautiful." Amy added the photos to the email. "Take a look." She handed the tablet over.

Sydney quickly read the email with a detailed description of the young man and what he'd said that Landon Security would receive. "CC Eric and CC at Pulsate so there's a record. Plus, me." She quickly refreshed her make-up and they spent the next few minutes talking before Rainbow came to collect them.

"Preston's ready for you now."

They followed her down the hall and around the corner. Both sides of the hall had multiple studios, and Preston Grant, the hottest man in radio, was in one of them talking into the microphone. They waited outside and asked who the other people were.

"Producer, and a couple of fans of yours," Rainbow told them. "Preston prefers to talk and not deal with buttons and ads and whatnot, so the producer's in there to do it."

Preston finished talking and saw the others in the room excitedly gesturing to the window. He spun around and saw Sydney. In an instant, the headphones were off and he was striding out the door. "Ms Kingston, it's a pleasure. I love your books, as you know, and it's great to have you back on the show."

"Thanks for inviting me back." Sydney smiled and shook his big meaty hand and took in his casual t-shirt and jeans outfit. "This is my third time."

"Is it?" Preston waved her and Amy into the room. "I've interviewed so many people it's hard to keep up. Everyone, meet Sydney Kingston, and her assistant, Amy."

Sydney shook hands with everyone, and pictures were quickly taken before they settled into chairs.

"Okay, Sydney, I watched *Rockefeller* before and I'll tell you now, I'll be touching on some of the points he did. Especially since your stalker's case hit the papers this week."

Sydney grimaced. "I was really hoping that wouldn't

come up at all this month. I just want to promote the new book."

"And I understand that," Preston said. "Just as you would've understood it was going to come up." He slid his headphones onto his bald head and adjusted the mic. "We're on in a minute. Let's get ready."

Sydney put on her headphones and cleared her throat. Amy nudged her and handed her a bottle of chilled water from the guest room. She took a few sips before Preston announced they were back on air.

"Ladies and gentlemen, we have a real treat for you today. Sydney Kingston is in the studio. Now some of you may be thinking *who*? But if you know the name Cassandra Kingsley and have read her books, then you know Sydney Kingston—author of those books behind the pen name. Welcome to the show again, Sydney. You were saying before it's your third time."

"Yes," Sydney replied. "Three years in a row now to promote a new book."

"And the new book is called *Twisted Affair* under your pen name of Cassandra Kingsley. Tell everyone why you chose a pen name."

Same old same old, Sydney thought. "When I started with self-publishing it was for privacy. But once I moved to L.A. and the books became movies, and I signed on with Pulsate for my print editions, it became common knowledge. By then, the name was a brand, so I kept it."

"A lot of authors do use pen names. I saw you and Rhett Rockefeller today on his show, and he asked the same question. We all know that Rhett Rockefeller is nowhere near being his name, but actors and stage people, and anyone in general, can use a different name. Pen names and stage names are nothing new, but many authors turn their names into brands, or become brands organically. Can you tell us how you turned the name Cassandra Kingsley into a brand?"

Impressed with the new line of conversation, Sydney launched into her answer. "It's simple, really, and not that hard for authors. There are three levels. One is a matter of genre. Are you sticking to the one genre? Two is, do you use the same font and size for your name across all of your books? Have you picked certain colours for your name on the cover and your website and any promotional product? We commonly think of brands, as MacDonald's, KFC, Walmart, Barnes & Noble, Amazon, Netflix. Their brand is, in part, the font for the name, the colour, the logo, and all of that's carried through to products and websites that become an author's brand. Genre, name style, website style. That is our forward facing brand that people see, and they recognise and instantly know. The third is how we behave, what we do, what we say, sometimes even what we wear can be a branding strategy for us. I'm always in sequins and sparkle, for example."

"And Cassandra Kingsley is a brand for you?" Preston asked. "Because it's an interesting concept. As you said, we're used to businesses being brands, but so are actors, singers, hosts, radio jocks, and dare I mention one of the things I hate most, influencers." He shuddered.

Sydney couldn't help chuckling. "I have the exact same reaction to influenzas, as I call them. But sadly, many have turned themselves into a brand. Name font, logo, colours. What they do, and sadly, how they behave—it's a brand, and quite frankly, quite sad. That people with no talent and nothing to back themselves up with, such as degrees, education, or knowledge can become millionaires within a year because they brand themselves into something that's actually nothing. All they do is flog product for cash."

"That's why most of the morons end up on OnlyFans," Preston said. "They're used to whoring themselves out. But let's move on." Sniggers went around the room. "I saw you on *Rockefeller*, and you talked about moving to Florida for warmer weather to write, but you also had a stalker. You said the reason you left was a bit of both. Can you tell us what happened, say, from deciding to move, or from one year ago. How you made your decision."

Sydney took a sip of water before speaking. "I was writing the other book, the one that will probably be out next year, and I had someone sending me letters via Pulsate, my publishing house. Landon Security took over the case. It was November, by that time, and I know I work better in warmer weather, so we decided to leave and let them deal with it, which they did. Meanwhile, I not only wrote this book, *Twisted Affair*, out now in hardcover at all good bookstores in real life and online, but I finished off the next book and its companion biography, plus wrote another novel. Well, more of a novella. I'll self-publish that as an e-book for Christmas for my fans and followers."

"Holy hell, talk about prolific," Preston said. "The warmer weather does seem to suit you. Will there be a print edition of that novella? And what's it about?"

"There will be in March next year to give the e-book time to sell, and *Twisted Affair* will roll out in e-book, audio, and paperback as well around the same time. So, lots of goodies to buy come next year. As for what it's about…" She paused to have a drink. "It's a dark romantic thriller reminiscent of my first three books. *Twisted Affair* is novel number eleven, and *The Perfect Man* is novella number six."

"Great title. So, it's a thriller about a woman finding the perfect man only for him to not be?" Preston asked. "The title's pretty obvious."

"Who said it's a woman finding the perfect man?" Sydney queried, a twinkle in her eye.

"Oh…" Preston was surprised. "So, it's a man who finds the perfect man?"

"Who said it's a man finding the perfect man?" Sydney shot back.

"Wait, you've confused me." Preston's hand went to his forehead as he thought about it. "But about a man or woman finding the perfect man?"

"Neither," Sydney lightly chastised. "*You* made an assumption about the plot."

"Okay, okay." Preston waved a hand in defeat. "Tell everyone what *The Perfect Man* is all about."

"Just that," Sydney said. "The man is perfect to all for everything. Whether he's the perfect business associate, worker, partner, lover, he is the jack of all trades that is perfect at everything, hence the perfect man. But as with all thrillers, there's a deep dark secret lying beneath the façade. What is it? What happens? Who's alive at the end of the book?" Sydney shrugged. "Who knows, but you'll just have to read it when it comes out on December fifteenth at Amazon and my website Cassandra Kingsley dot com."

Astounded, Preston could only gape. "Well, it sounds like you've done it again, Sydney Kingston. Another thriller from your pen name of Cassandra Kingsley. So, we have the novel *Twisted Affair* out now in hardcover, and a novella called *The Perfect Man* coming out on December fifteenth on Amazon and your website. Is it available on just those two places?"

"For now, yes." Sydney nodded in reply. "It's a novella for fans as an extra Chrissie pressie and exclusive to two websites. So, if you hate Amazon, buy it from me on my website and you'll get it via a download from the sale page."

"Everything sounds intriguing. Let's take a break and we'll be back in a few minutes with author Sydney Kingston."

The producer, a fifty something, skinny, brunet man called Hank Lowry, cut to the break.

"Okay, Sydney, when we get back, I want to talk some more about the book and who and what inspired it, then we'll take some calls and we'll be done." Preston took a swig from a black metal bottle. "We haven't gotten into it yet and it's what you're here to promote, so we'll get into it next."

Sydney nodded and took another sip of water, chatting with the others in the studio before being counted back in.

"We're on in three, two, one…"

"Welcome back to *The Preston Grant Show* with

your host Preston Grant. We have author Sydney Kingston in today talking about her new book *Twisted Affair* under her pen name of Cassandra Kingsley. So, Sydney…" He leaned back in his seat, pulled his microphone with him, cocked one leg on the other and stared up at the ceiling. "You mentioned on *Rockefeller*, and it's in the press release for the novel, that it's about a woman who gets involved with a rich and powerful family. She has an affair with one of them, and another has an affair with her, but in his mind. Can you elaborate on the book at all?"

"I can, a little." Sydney scratched her neck. "It's about a young woman, Myra Bently. She's thirty, attractive…a power hungry lawyer who meets this rich powerful family when her law firm is hired to defend them in court. She falls for one of them and they have an affair, while another member, who's not mentally well, believes they're having an affair with her. But it's in their mind."

"Interesting plot," Preston told her. "Are the characters based on anyone?"

"Anyone, everyone, and no one." Sydney laughed. "People always think characters have to be based on particular people, but they don't. They are amalgamations of every lawyer, every rich powerful family on the planet. A little bit mobster, a little bit law enforcement, a little bit fantasy, a little bit reality. There are many rich and powerful families in the world. From crime to law, royalty to tycoons. It could be any of them, it could be none of them. It could be all of them wrapped into one family."

"And is this Myra Bently based on anyone?"

"No. I've never worked with a female lawyer before, only men. So, I made sure I got the legalese from my experience, and consulted with Pulsate's lawyer, of course, and made her a woman."

"So, she gets involved with one of the family members. Son? Father?"

"Son of one brother. The family is headed by brothers, they both have a son each and she gets involved with one, while another is fantasising."

"And your thrillers always have a twist ending, does this one? Because I'm a quarter way through it and haven't finished yet." He picked up his hard cover copy and looked it over.

"Of course," Sydney said. "Because there are also daughters of the two men. They have one son and multiple daughters each and many of them are vying for a position in the male dominated family."

"Ah, so Myra might get involved with one of the daughters?" Hank said.

"Ah…" Sydney gave a soft chuckle. "I won't say, just to surprise everyone at the end."

"Now you've really got me intrigued." Preston flipped to the end of the book.

"Hey, no fair," Sydney cried in alarm. "Don't you dare read that out on air!"

Preston laughed and slammed the book shut. "I won't, but you've made *Twisted Affair* sound very intriguing, Sydney, and I'm going to have to speed through it just to see what happens."

"Good. Because the last few pages tell you nothing, they're about Myra. No one else."

"So, it's a full circle story?" Hank asked. "You start the book with Myra and end it on Myra."

"I do." Sydney nodded. "You see how she is at the beginning of the story and how it's changed her at the end." She took a sip of water.

"Now I *really* can't wait to finish it." Preston threw it on the desk. "But we will be right back after these messages to wrap up our interview with Sydney Kingston and take some calls."

Hank sent them to break and they all sighed. "We only have three minutes, don't get too comfy."

Sydney's attention was captured by Amy who handed her phone to her. She saw multiple messages from CC, Gemma, and Olivia, plus Emerson. They'd seen *Rockefeller* and were listening to Preston's show. They had all sent the thumbs up emoji in their texts.

A minute later they were back on the air to answer listener's calls.

"Hello, caller, you're on SXT listening to Preston Grant. That's me on my show. What's your name and what's your question for Sydney?"

"Ah, hi, my name's Raquel and I love all of your books, Ms Kingston. I've already read *Twisted Affair.* I stayed up all night reading it and that ending, oh, my God, it's incredible—"

"Don't give it away," Sydney jumped in.

"I won't, but my question is, do you plan out what's going to happen, or does it come to you as you write?"

"A bit of both," Sydney said. "My muse gives me an idea, sometimes vague, sometimes not. I'll let that idea percolate in my brain for a bit and then start writing down ideas of my own for it, and soon, a full idea forms. I'll make a brief outline. This needs to happen here, they need to meet there, this happens here, and whatnot, and then I start writing from page one chapter one all the way through. Sometimes I write prologues and the story develops itself as it goes. The endings also come into their own as the story unfolds. And sometimes, it ends up different to what I had planned. Other times they come out exactly *as* planned."

"And was the ending of *Twisted Affair* planned?" Raquel got in before Preston cut her off.

"It was about eighty percent," Sydney replied even though she was gone. "The rest added itself as I wrote the story."

"Great questions, Raquel," Preston said and pulled up the next caller. "Tell us your name and what's your question for Sydney?"

"Ah, hi, my name's Barry. I'm sixty-five and want to write a book. I want to know how Ms Kingston deals with writers' block, because I've got a bad case of it."

Sydney stopped herself from laughing. "Have you started writing yet, Barry?"

"No, I haven't, not yet."

"Then how can you have writers' block if you haven't written anything?" Sydney asked, her huge grin barely containing her laughter.

"Oh, well I guess I can't. So how do you deal with the dreaded block then?"

"By understanding, that in and of itself, it doesn't exist," Sydney replied. "The phrase, which is all it is, is not specific to the actual reason one can't write. You have to sit down and analyse the situation for that. Ask yourself, why can't I write? And see what pops into your mind. And after that, ask, why don't I want to? And your brain might just be honest enough to say, because I just don't bloody want to. It could also be because you're overworked in life, or have health issues or family dramas to deal with. Or that you haven't spent the time figuring out a story outline and character names and what they're going to do. I think people get so caught up in the excitement and fantasy of writing a book, they don't bother to actually figure out if it's for them or not. And maybe the story you want to tell isn't meant to be a book at all. Maybe it's just meant to be a short story, either on its own or in an anthology. Or maybe it's just meant to be told in a pamphlet or on a website. So, Barry…" Sydney took a breath and waved a hand to stop Preston cutting him off. "Sit down and figure out why, and name the actual problem, then you can solve it and move forward."

"Oh, thank you, Ms Kingston," Barry managed before being cut off.

"That's actually really good advice," Preston said. "The term writers' block isn't specific and the problem has an actual name, so figuring out the actual problem will be better for you *and* your problem."

"Exactly. There's this little thing called life that we all live and it gets in the way of doing what we want to do, like writing, because it actually takes precedence over everything else. So, when you figure out the *actual* problem, you will have a better time sailing through it than trying to figure out that non-existent idiot called writers' block."

"Okay, next caller. Name and question."

"Um hi, Ms Kingston, my name's Rebecca and my question is how long does it take you to write a book?"

"Good question, Rebecca," Sydney said. "And the answer is, it depends. When everything is flowing I can write ten pages in three hours or less, and I handwrite all of my books. I try and write in three to four blocks of time a day. Other days I get nothing out and that's because I've become stuck somewhere and need to figure it out. In total, a first draft of a novel can take a month or less if I'm very motivated, or up to three months if I'm not, or have other things to do at the same time. Editing then takes another few months to get it into shape for release."

"Then why does it take some authors a year?" Rebecca asked.

"Because they set daily word counts, and weekly work days, and that takes a while longer. It also depends on how long the book is and what they have going on in their lives or whether they need to research. I'm lucky to have an assistant who can read my handwriting, so she types up what I've written while I write the next part."

"Thanks for your call, Rebecca. It is true, isn't it, that all authors have their own schedule for writing and some will be faster than others," Preston said.

"It is. I just happen to have no life, so I can write all day," Sydney joked.

"Ha! That's hilarious," Preston played along. "Considering the hot Italian on your European vacation this year. No life my ass. Next caller, name and question."

"Hello, my name's Michael, and I wanted to ask Ms Kingston if she'd ever write a book with another author, or if she had considered branching out into screenwriting, or something, since her books have been turned into movies."

"Not yet, Michael, on both points. I don't know if I'd ever want to write with another author. I'm too protective of my work. As for screenplays, it's on the to-do list, but hasn't happened yet. However, I did work closely with the writers of the movies for the adaptions, so I learned a lot doing that and scored co-writer credits."

"Great question, Michael. And we have time for one last caller, but before we do I'll just say the title again, it's *Twisted Affair* by Cassandra Kingsley, Sydney Kingston's pen name. Sydney has been with us for the last hour, but the hour's nearly up, so we'll get to the last caller. Thanks for coming, Sydney; we hope it sells a million as always. Last caller, what's your name and your question for Sydney Kingston, aka, Cassandra Kingsley?"

"Yeah, my name's Bryan and I want to know how Ms Kingsley got involved with the Police Commissioner's grandson?"

Shaken, Sydney could only stare from Preston to Hank and back and saw both of them look from her to behind her. She turned to see Amy doing the hand across the neck motion for *cut this off now.*

Preston went into announcer mode. "Well, Bryan, I'm sure that would be a great answer, except both question and answer would be way too litigious for us here at SXT. We'll cut you off and thank Sydney Kingston, aka, Cassandra Kingsley, author of *Twisted*

Affair for coming in today. Can we get you back in December to talk about your novella? We'll book you in. Thanks for joining us folks, see you tomorrow. This had been Preston Grant for *The Preston Grant Show* here on SXT."

Hank hit a button and said, "We're done."

"Jesus fucking Christ," burst out of Amy.

Sydney removed her headphones and spun around to her. "Did he sound familiar?"

Amy studied her expression. "You mean…?"

"Could it have been him?"

Amy's eyes widened. "Ah…possibly. We'd better get you out of here. Stay home for the rest of the day."

Inhaling a shaky breath, Sydney gathered her drink and bag and turned to an inquisitive Preston Grant. "Thank you so much for having me on today; you and Rhett in one day, is a bit of a coup for the first day of promotion."

"All downhill from here, you mean," he joked, and walked around his desk to shake her hand. "Glad to have you back, Sydney, and I was serious about that novella of yours. Come back and promote it."

"I will. Let Pulsate know and we'll set something up for then." She nodded at the others. "Everyone, nice to have met you, but it's been a long day and it's time to go home."

"Thanks so much for coming, Sydney," Hank said. "*Loved* the book."

"Good to know." Sydney waved goodbye and she and Amy were escorted to the lift by Rainbow.

They were silent on the way down. Silent in the car.

Silent when they got to the brownstone and idled on the street.

"Was it him?" Sydney asked, fearing her life would soon be in upheaval again.

"I don't know. I can't remember what he sounds like," Amy replied.

"I don't, really, but the sound of that voice just…" Sydney looked out the window and sighed. That voice had triggered a memory, and not a very good one. She finally alighted, bade Amy goodnight, and went inside, hoping for a quiet night in front of the TV to get her mind off things. But quiet she was not met with.

"What do you mean you're dumping me? No, you bastard, I'm dumping you."

There was silence for a few moments and Sydney rolled her eyes.

"What do you mean I can't dump you? Of course I can. You're a cheating son of a bitch and I need to dump your sorry ass."

Sydney walked up to her room, dropped her bag in the walk-in closet, took off her jewellery, clothes, and shoes, and went into the bathroom for a long hot shower. While Nora, her house sitter, was on the phone to her boyfriend, this shower was the only place to get peace and quiet.

After a long hot scrub, and a change of clothes, Sydney made her way downstairs and into the kitchen for dinner, and Nora and her boyfriend were still going. She caught her eye and motioned for her to end the call.

"Look, I have to go, my boss is here, but I'm still dumping your sorry ass," Nora said, pacing the kitchen.

"What do you mean, no? I mean I'm dumping your sorry ass. You cheated on me you son of a bitch, end of story. Why should I put up with that?"

Sydney pulled out a pack of meat and frozen vegetables from the freezer and got the wok from the wall. She was done with the conversation and it was time Nora left. "End the call," she called sharply.

Nora glanced at her and nodded. "I gotta go, my boss is here and she needs to talk. What do you mean I can't talk to her? What do you mean I'm lying?"

"End the fucking call," Sydney demanded loudly enough for the boyfriend to hear.

"See," Nora told him. "You've pissed her off and I'm gonna cop it." She finally hung up and sighed. "He is *exhausting.*"

"So is listening to it." Sydney turned on the burner and placed the wok on it. She'd already put the meat in, and the veg was defrosting in a container in the microwave. "Aren't you exhausted by him?"

"Oh, I am," Nora complained, waving her long fingers. Her nails were painted bright colours to match her top. Her red curls were wrapped with rainbow ribbons and hung down her back. Skinny blue jeans and platform sandals finished her outfit. "We've been like this for a year now. Ever since he cheated on me." She sat down on a stool at the kitchen bench. "He cheated, so I dumped him. But then he promised he wouldn't do it again, so I took him back. But we've just had problems ever since. He thinks he can control me. I threaten to dump his sorry ass unless he stops, it's a love hate relationship." She twirled a curl around her finger.

"Sounds more like a hate-hate controlling relationship," Sydney said, shredding the lump of beef and adding the sachet of tomato sauce. The ragu would go perfectly with the vegetables, and she had double chocolate fudge ice cream for dessert. That's if Nora hadn't eaten it and put the container back in the freezer instead of the bin. "Why do you stay with him?"

Nora shrugged and blew a chewing gum bubble. "'Cause I love him."

"And how are you getting home tonight?" Sydney looked out the kitchen window to see dark clouds looming. "And when are you leaving?"

"When he picks me up."

Sydney's attention moved to Nora. "What? He's coming here to pick you up? You just told him you were dumping his sorry arse."

She giggled. "I know, but like I said. I love him."

A few minutes later, Sydney's ragu and vegetables were done and Nora's boyfriend, Lennie, was banging on the front door.

Nora hurried down the hall, grabbing her bag and coat from the rack. "I'm heading out, Ms K, do you need me tomorrow?" She opened the inside door, but paused.

"I do. I have more interviews." Sydney came up behind just as Lennie banged on the door again. She flung it open. "Stop banging on my fucking door, Leonard."

He jumped back and grasped his hands together in front of him, a sudden bundle of nerves at her angry face. "Ah, Ms Kingston. Sorry, Ms Kingston, I thought Nora was lying when she said you were home."

"No, she was not, and don't ever behave badly on my

stoop, at my door, or in my house, ever again."

"No, Ms Kingston." Riddled with shame, he looked from her to Nora. "You ready, babe?"

"Yeah, babe." Nora moved past Sydney and linked her arm in Lennie's. "Let's go. See you tomorrow, Ms K." She waved over her shoulder.

"Nine a.m.," Sydney told her. "We'll be out all day and most of the night. You can stay in the guest room so bring an overnight bag."

"Yes, Ms K," Nora called and climbed into Lennie's beat up old four wheel ute.

Lennie shut the door and hurried around to the driver's side. He started the truck and then took off, leaving Sydney shaking her head at the noise.

She locked both doors and checked the house system. All windows and doors were locked, so she set the alarm. Rushing back to the kitchen for her food, she pulled the window and French door curtains closed, served up her ragu on her vegetables, and settled into the living room for some mind-numbing TV.

*****

Outside, in the backyard, a man carefully came out from behind the garage.

He'd hidden between it and the fence, waiting for Sydney to come home. He'd heard the long drawn out and incredibly juvenile conversation the redhead had on the phone and wondered when she was going to shut the fuck up and leave. But when she had, Sydney had locked up the doors and closed the curtains, and now he couldn't see her at all.

He quietly made his way to the back steps, descended to the small alcove, and approached the basement door.

*****

Outside on the street, a man quietly made his way past the brownstones. Nonchalant and carefree, he was dressed in black from head to toe. He touched nothing, and kept his mouth closed. He walked past and moved on down the street before crossing over and walking back. He stopped across from the brownstone and took a small camera from his pocket, taking a few quick shots before putting it away.

He walked on down the road, crossed back over, and walked back to the brownstone. His gaze darted around to make sure no one was out, or watching from behind pulled aside curtains, and when he came to Sydney's home, he let himself down into the window well.

Chapter 16

Sydney arrived at the bookstore at ten forty-five for her book signing. Amy was with her, and Olivia met them there. They were waiting in the back room until it was time.

"The signing goes for two hours, from eleven until one. You have a book luncheon with industry insiders and a few competition winners at two until four. And then the book launch party tonight from seven-thirty."

Sydney deflated. "God, I feel tired and worn out already." She placed her bag on a table and crossed her arms. "I know every other year was full steam ahead for days on end, but I don't think I can do this anymore. I'm worn out from yesterday."

"Next year we'll space your events out one to two a day," Olivia said. "But this was your idea."

"Yeah, I know, but I've had a lot of other things going on." Sydney covered her yawn. "I also need oxygen, otherwise I'm just gonna yawn all day."

"Are we expecting a big crowd?" Amy asked. "Do we have security?"

The door opened and Sarah Concleif, the manager,

popped her head in. "We're all set, Ms Kingston, and so very excited to have you here. We stocked up on the book for those who wanted to buy it in line, and we're sold out already. The rep from the publisher is getting more sent over."

"That's great." Sydney smiled wanly. "Give me a few moments to freshen up and," she checked her watch, "we'll start right on time."

"Okay." Sarah closed the door, leaving them in a moment of silence.

"Okay," Sydney repeated with a sigh. "I need a drink, and my make-up."

Amy pulled the make-up purse from her oversized tote and quickly dabbed powder on Sydney's face.

Sydney drank a few mouthfuls of water before Amy reapplied her lipstick. "There, you are done."

"Multi-talented as always," Sydney said, checking her reflection in a compact mirror. "Okay, here we go."

Olivia opened the door and followed Sydney and Amy out of the room. They were escorted over to the cordoned off area where a long table had piles of Sydney's books, and banners strung up behind it and across the front of it.

Sydney took her seat at the table, tucked her handbag under her feet, and took a deep breath.

Amy stood behind her ready to take photos, and Olivia hovered nearby. A burly security guard stood either end of the roped off space.

The store had chosen to open at eleven, so no one was shopping when the signing started and Sarah and the staff opened the doors and welcomed everyone.

"Hello, everyone, and welcome to the book signing of Cassandra Kinsley's latest block buster, *Twisted Affair!*" Sarah excitedly exclaimed. "Please have your book ready for signing and your camera ready for taking a photo. Be respectful and no pushing. We have guards to watch you, so follow the roped section and let's get started." Sarah motioned to the walkway that had been outlined in red rope and under the watchful eye of the guards, the excited fans made their way down the side of the store to the back where Sydney was waiting.

For the next hour, she signed the half title pages of their books, leant across the table to have photos taken, and even signed posters of her books, the posters of their movie counterparts, and various pieces of memorabilia relating to them.

At the one hour mark, she had a seven minute break for food and water, and a make-up refresh, and started again.

Sydney had just signed a book and slid it to the right when another was placed before her. "And to whom do I make this out?" Her pen at the ready, she finally glanced up to see Douglas Ryan and beamed a smile when she noticed Emerson and Cormac beside him. "Well, hello strangers."

"Make it out to my favourite Commish Douglas Ryan," he joked. "How are you, Sydney?"

"Good," she said. "Em, long time no see." She saw her friend's arm linked through Cormac's. He was wearing a baseball cap, glasses, and casual clothes. "Still dating a year later are we? Going well?"

"You'd know that if you hadn't taken off to write

your steamy new thriller and then jet off to Italy for a steamy affair," Emerson joked. "Syd, been too long." They hugged across the table.

"You all here to get your books signed?" Sydney sat down and whipped a personalised message across Douglas's book page.

"We are, and I read it yesterday and loved it." Douglas picked up his book and read the message. "Nice. Another bestseller from the great Cassandra Kingsley for my bookshelf."

Sydney laughed and signed Emerson's and Cormac's books before Douglas slid another copy in front of her.

"For Sean."

Startled, Sydney glanced up. "What?" She looked between the two Ryan men. "Is that…"

"He's been good this last year," Cormac told her. "He stayed with us, excelled at school, and he's aced his first month of college. Plus, he had his young adult anthology published."

"I saw that. I'm glad he stayed with the mentorship. Everyone said he's exceeded their expectations. Initial sales did extremely well. But…" She looked down at the book. "Do I…personalise it, or just sign it?" Her insides were telling her to stay away from it all. To not write his name, or he'd see it as encouragement. "I don't want to—"

"He won't see it as encouragement," Douglas said. "He also wanted you to have this." He pulled out a gift wrapped parcel from his jacket pocket. "It's a signed copy of his book."

Surprised, Sydney accepted it and ripped open the

bright paper to reveal a paperback copy of Sean's anthology stories. She opened the cover and found the inscription on the half title page. *To Sydney, thank you for every ounce of encouragement you gave me, it meant the world. Sean.* And with that, Sydney put the book down, picked up her Paper Mate flair in turquoise, and wrote on the half title page of her book. *Sean, you've got a long way until you reach my bestseller status, but you're off to a good start. Glad you kept it up. Sydney.* She closed the cover and handed it to Douglas. "Em, you coming to the book launch tonight?"

"Of course, and I'm still trying to convince this guy here to come." She tugged on Cormac's arm.

"I don't want to turn up with an entourage and ruin the event," he said, as they moved along.

"You won't. I'll put all of you on the guest list, so bring another person or three." Sydney grabbed the next book that was slid in front of her. "Tonight, seven-thirty at *The Roxy.* Great views of New York. Be there." She dashed off her signature on the book and smiled up at the man. "Hello, enjoy the book?"

"Oh," the man gushed. "I haven't read it yet, but I started in line, and it's already so good. Can I get an ussie?" He turned round and took a photo of them with his phone. "Thanks."

Sydney kept signing for another hour before they packed up and left. They went to Pulsate to freshen up and rest for a while before heading for the luncheon at *Rembrandt.* The restaurant had amazing views of the city, as so many of them did.

Sydney was introduced by CC before speaking for a

few minutes. They sat down for lunch, and after Sydney freshened up, she sat on a small stage that had been set up to answer questions and chat.

Rhona Millgate, the publicist for Pulsate, asked the questions in a Q&A style chat for the fans and insiders who'd won the chance to be there. "Tell us how this book came about."

"Ooh," Sydney murmured. "Can't do that, it will give away some of my secrets." There were chuckles through the crowd. Sydney stared up at the ceiling. "I had moved into the brownstone and a lot of stuff just ended up happening. It gave me the inspiration for the book I started, which was not this one, and then a bunch of other stuff happened, and all of a sudden, other ideas came to me and pushed that book aside. And then, of course, other stuff happened, which has been in the papers, and I got away for a while. Then it just poured out."

"It's inspired by a lot of real life circumstances," Rhona said. "Which is understandable. Are the characters based on anyone?"

"Not really and sort of."

Rhona laughed and looked at the crowd. "That sounds confusing."

"And it can be," Sydney agreed. "When you choose to write about rich, powerful people, they could be based on millions of real life people, and so people have said, are they mafia, mobsters, cops, lawyers, is it this person, that family, it's…" Sydney shrugged. "Anyone and everyone and no one all at the same time. But fans and readers and critics will all go, oh, it's this person, it's that family. That's already happened."

"It has. I've seen the conspiracy theories online." Rhona glanced at the next question on her card. "Is that an issue for you? Are you worried someone might come up to you and say, hey, you wrote about me?"

"Worried?" Sydney thought about it. "Not really. Not with this book, or any of my previous ones. My Christmas novella, maybe. My next novel, if it's my next novel, absolutely."

"And your next novel's about Madam X?"

"It is. I guess it was hard not to write about it, considering I bought the brownstone for its history, and obviously I've read up on that history, and somewhere in the back of my mind I went, ooohhh that's an interesting idea, let's file that away."

"Do you reveal anything?"

"I don't know what I can reveal besides what's already been talked about on the news and printed in newspapers and books."

"Very true. Let's get back to *Twisted Affair.*" Rhona pointed to the banner behind them. "Great cover as always, thanks to Pulsate Publishing's cover designers. It's your eleventh published novel; how does it feel?"

Sydney glanced around the room while thinking through her answer. "It doesn't really feel anything. For me, it's what I do, it's nothing amazing, it's just a story I wrote."

"You're not excited every time you finish a book?" Rhona asked.

"Strangely, no. But my hand certainly is because it doesn't have to write for long hours at a time for a while, so it gets to take a break." Sydney gave a light laugh and the crowd chuckled.

"I heard you on, was it Rhett or Prestons's show yesterday, say that you'd also written your novella, and finished off the next book and its companion. The novella is coming out in December, but can you give us a hint about that other novel, Madam X?"

"Not on your life." Sydney shook her head and looked at the laughing crowd. "I'm not giving away *all* of my secrets."

"Okay, okay. Before we wrap this up and go to questions, as the publicist I can say that the e-book and audio will be out in time for Christmas, and the trade paperback in March. Foreign additions will roll out sometime across the next few months. Do you have questions for Sydney before she reads an excerpt from the book?"

A dozen plus hands flew up and Rhona hurried over to the closest person. "Hi, what's your question?"

"Hi, Ms Kingston. I heard about your novella on Preston Grant's show, can you give us a clue about that?"

"It's a forty thousand word novella which will be available on Amazon and my website from December fifteenth. The paperback and audio will come out in March. It's about the perfect man. Everyone thinks he's perfect, but is he, or was it just everyone's imagination?" Sydney watched the crowd's expressions and they seemed enthralled.

"Is that based on anyone?" Rhona asked and moved on to the next person.

"A couple of people, actually," Sydney told her, following

her short flaming red hairdo through the crowd.

"Ooohhh, do tell?" Rhona held the microphone in front of the next person.

Sydney shook her head. "Nope. Not on *my* life." She nodded at the lady. "Hello."

"Hello, Ms Kingston. I'm such a fan of your work. I have all of your books and all of them have been signed by you at some stage," the woman gabbled. "My question is, are any of your other books based on your life, or true events, or things that have happened to you or people you know?"

"This goes back to my answer before," Sydney told her. "I take ideas from everything and roll them up to come up with something else. I start the ball, the teeny tiny ball, and let my muse snowball that sucker until she's huge and done. It's a little bit of this and a little bit of that all mooshed together. Thanks for your question."

Rhona moved on and pushed up her bright pink glasses with her knuckle. "And all of those little bits make fabulous novels." She stopped beside a man. "Hello, what's your question?"

"Ah, hello, Ms Kingston, big fan, loved the book." The overweight man sweated through his busting-at-the-buttons shirt in the air-conditioned room. "I was wondering, if you've ever received hate mail and what do you do about it? I've seen some pretty awful stuff on socials about you and your books and it's just vile."

"It can be," Sydney agreed, keeping her racing heart in check. She took a sip of her drink and glanced at CC and Amy. "I've had some over the years. I think anyone in the spotlight does. My lawyer and publisher deal with it. And my assistant deals with anything online. We have layers of security in place, but luckily, not too many go through." She glanced at CC. "That I know of."

"Thanks for the question," Rhona told him and moved on. She stopped by five other people who asked their questions before wrapping the session up. "Okay, and now Sydney is going to read an excerpt from *Twisted Affair*, and then we have time for photos before we're done. Sydney over to you."

Sydney picked up her book and opened it to the page she'd bookmarked and read for the next three pages. Everyone was silent, enthralled by the story until she closed the book and they burst into a frenzied applause. Sydney thanked them and stepped off the stage. She spent the next twenty minutes taking photos and thanking everyone for coming before leaving with Amy, CC, and Olivia. Rhona was staying behind to corral everyone and hand out special promotional packages especially for the guests.

"Fucking hell, I can't wait to get home," Sydney groaned. "I need a nap, a shower, and food."

"A man," CC cut in dryly. "How come you didn't bring that hot Italian home with you?"

Sydney snorted with laughter. "Oh, how I wish."

They stepped out of the lift and went their separate ways.

Chapter 17

Sydney and Amy arrived home to find the brownstone broken into. The glass from the French doors in the kitchen lay shattered over the floor.

"What the fuck!" Sydney exploded. "Nora, Nora. Get your arse down here, or up here. Just get here now. Nora, Nora."

"I don't think she's in." Amy whipped out her phone and called the police. Her second call was to Landon Security, and her third was to Nora. "No answer." At the sound of sirens, she turned towards them and hurried to open the front doors. "In the kitchen, we haven't touched anything or gone anywhere else."

Officers Velenksy and Rotrain strode down the hall, quickly followed by a young man in jeans and a leather jacket.

"Hey, who are you?" Amy questioned as she followed him into the kitchen.

"Ms Kingston, good to see you again," Velenksy told her. "I *love* the new book."

Sydney managed a small laugh. "Thank you, but considering the circumstances, that's kind of funny." She spied the young man. "Ah, Ryan number five. Hello, Ethan."

"Hey, Sydney." He stood, hands on hips, surveying the scene. Now twenty-five, he was still a young version of his father, Connor. "Tell us what happened."

"We don't know. We came home from a book luncheon and found this mess." Sydney motioned to the glass and broken doors. "My house sitter, Nora, is nowhere to be seen, and Amy called you guys, Landon Security, and Nora. Nora's a no-show."

"Landon Security?" Ethan perked up. "You think this has to do with your stalker? I thought that was over. He's in for two years."

"Who said there was only one?" Sydney replied and saw the semi-shocked expression roll over his face. "Either way, they are my security service I've been using and your grandfather knows Holland from way back."

"Yeah, Grandpa and Pops said they were going to your book signing. Did you see them?" Ethan moved over to the door and inspected it for fingerprints.

"I did and signed their books. I've put them on the guest list for tonight and told them to bring an extra or three."

Ethan looked up. "Cool. I'll see if I can snag that invitation. I know my uncles Alec and Kieran have read the new one."

Sydney threw a line. "And your father?"

He took the bait. "Ha! I doubt it. He and Declan are just a little—" He shook his head and changed the subject. "We'll call in the CSIs for fingerprints," he told the officers. "Can you put out a bolo for Nora?" He turned to Sydney. "What's her last name?"

"Ah, Ramotti, I think she pronounced it. Not sure how to spell it," Sydney replied.

"Okay." He turned back to Velenksy and Rotrain. "Check multiple spellings and keep trying her number. Even go to her address."

"She could be out with Lennie, her boyfriend," Amy ventured.

"Or she could be dead in the house or yard," Sydney muttered. "We haven't checked it out."

All three officers withdrew their guns from their holsters and made a floor by floor sweep of the house. They found nothing.

"The bolted doors down in the basement, where do they lead?" Rotrain asked.

Sydney blushed, but kept a straight face. "One leads outside and has three metal bars and locks. The other leads to the entertainment room." She heard Amy snort behind her back.

"Could she be in there?" Rotrain asked.

Sydney barely considered it. "I keep the key hidden, and unless someone found it, unlocked the door, shoved her body in there, relocked it, and then put my key back, I doubt it. You haven't checked outside yet."

Ethan waved Rotrain and Velenksy outside and waited for them to leave. "That entertainment room wouldn't happen to be the famous sex room, would it?"

Sydney heard more garbled laughter behind her, tried to not laugh herself, and glanced over her shoulder to see Amy with her hands over her mouth, barely controlling herself. She turned back to Ethan. "Yes, it is. I was being…discreet."

Ethan grinned. "I'm gonna need to see it, just in case she's in there," he said seriously.

"She's not. Amy, keep trying her. Detective, I'll take you down."

Amy burst out laughing and hurried into the parlour.

"She finds so much humour in such banal things," Sydney said and noticed the officers come back in.

Ethan pointed to Rotrain. "Stand guard at this end, and you," he pointed to Velensky, "guard the front door and wait for the CSIs. I'm double checking the basement. Ms Kingston." He stepped aside and held out his arm.

Sydney sighed. "Hang on, I need the keys. Is it safe to go into my office?"

"It is, but make it quick."

She raced upstairs and retrieved the keys from her safe. They'd been in there for the last year, since she'd last used the room with Connor. She hurried downstairs and led Ethan down to the basement and unlocked the bolts and bars. Swinging open the door, she flicked on the lights.

No Nora.

She sighed in relief.

Ethan walked in, taking in the equipment. He picked up a whip with a red feather on the end, turned it in his hands, and laid it back. "You ever used any of this?" When he didn't receive a reply, he turned around and saw her leaning against the wall beside the door. "Well, Sydney Kingston, best-selling author." He slowly moved towards her, turned on by the atmosphere and the knowledge she'd fucked his father in that room.

She noticed the look in his eyes. "I have a feeling you

already know the answer to that."

He stopped in front of her and pushed the door closed, leaned against her, and taking her right hand placed it on his crotch and squeezed. "Yeah, I do." His lips were close to hers. "I heard him tell his friends all about it. He went on and on. How he fucked Sydney Kingston in the sex room of Madam X's brownstone."

Sydney massaged him, knowing she could have him under control in moments. He was a boy, nowhere near being the man his father was.

"You slept together." His lips lightly brushed her cheek.

"There was no sleeping." She squeezed and he shuddered.

"I don't want to sleep either," he whispered.

"But you're on duty." Sydney pushed him away and opened the door. "You have a crime to solve, detective, and I have a busy day."

Reluctantly, he walked out of the room and adjusted his jeans, waiting while Sydney locked and bolted the door.

They found the CSIs in the kitchen and Nora hysterical in the living room.

"Where the hell were you?" Sydney demanded. "Your job is to housesit."

"I was, Ms K. I just went to the corner shop for something, but I got talking to old Maria and before I knew it two hours was gone and I thought, I better hurry home, Ms K and Amy will be home soon." Tears streamed down her face. "I'm so sorry. Did they take anything?"

"We don't actually know because we haven't checked." Sydney turned to Ethan. "Can we go upstairs? I better check my bedroom and office."

"Sure, Velenksy, go with them."

Sydney dashed up to her bedroom with Amy and Velenksy following. They checked for missing jewellery, accessories and clothing. They checked the shower, toilet, and waste basket in case the intruder had left a message behind, and then flung the bed covers back. They found nothing.

Next, they searched the office and found all of Sydney's manuscripts intact. Nothing seemed out of place. Confused, they traipsed downstairs.

"Everything's in place," Sydney told Ethan. "At this stage, nothing's missing."

"Okay. Keep an eye out in case you find something is gone later." Ethan watched the CSIs leave. "They're done, so I'm done as well. I'll get back to the station and file a report and see you later tonight."

"Sure." Sydney followed him out the door to see Holland Landon walking up her stairs with his team behind him.

At sixty-seven he'd headed his own security company for twenty years after having to retire from the force, but he was as strong as an ox, still sharp minded, and fit and healthy.

"Holland." Ethan shook his hand. "Long time no see." He watched the team hurry into the house.

"Ethan!" Holland was shocked. "The last time I saw you…"

Ethan laughed. "Yeah, yeah. I was knee-high to a grasshopper."

Holland laughed along with him. "It was at your

graduation. How's your grandfather? Haven't seen him for a while."

"He's great. He'll be at Sydney's book launch tonight with Pops. I'm trying to finagle an invitation out of one of them."

"That's great. I'll be there as well. I can catch up with both him and Douglas. Meantime, I have a job to do. Can you send me a copy of your report and the findings?"

"Sure, Holland." Ethan shook hands again. "I'll see you tonight." He hurried down the stairs and to his car. He needed to talk to his grandfather or pops for that ticket.

"Sydney." Holland took her hand and was escorted through to the kitchen. "Anything stolen?"

"Not that we can find." Sydney sighed. "This is the first break-in, or whatever the hell this technically is." She heard Nora's quiet hiccoughing sobs coming from the living room. Amy was with her.

He watched his team go over everything with a fine-tooth comb, take photographs, scan for fingerprints, and set up lasers to scan the whole room. He pulled Sydney aside so they could do their job. "First time for everything."

"It means another stalker," Sydney murmured. "Fuck, we got one, but then one more?"

"We're considering the possibilities of someone being out for Madam X. This house is known as hers, and many people probably still think it is."

"So…what? They're after her books?" Sydney glanced at Nora and Amy, neither of whom was paying attention to them.

"Possibly," Holland replied. "We know the cops didn't find them. Did the new owners?"

"Wonder if they had issues," Sydney mused. "Maybe I should call them."

"Meanwhile, we'll do the job and let you get ready for tonight." Holland watched his team pack up. "Do you have a glazier coming?"

"Yes. But we also have the roller shutters. I had them put on last year."

"Then keep them locked at all times, even after the door's repaired." He squeezed her arm. "We'll take our leave." Holland followed his team out the front door and saw the glazier arrive. Noting they were women, he decided there was no need for him to stay.

An hour later, the glass was replaced, and the roller shutters firmly locked down tight. Sydney collapsed onto the couch and checked the time. "Damn! I was hoping for a nap. We have one hour before we have to leave and I need a shower and a change. And a complete overhaul."

"And some food." Amy groaned. "Got anything we can micro?"

"Probably." Sydney didn't move. "We did eat at the luncheon and there will be food at the launch."

"Including that cake you get every year." Amy laughed. "Always a book with a knife in it."

"Does it taste any good?" Nora asked from next to Amy.

"It does and we get to bring it home, so Nora…" Sydney moved her head forward to look past Amy. "Keep the alarm on and everything locked and no, Lennie's not invited."

"But what if he comes around?" She nibbled on a

chewed down fingernail.

"Tell him I said to fuck off. He's not welcome anytime he wants to come around. This is my house and you're doing a job. He's not welcome."

"He's not gonna like that." Nora started on another nail.

"I don't fucking care." Sydney hauled herself to her feet and raided the fridge and freezer.

They settled on microwave meals and ran around doing small jobs while they waited.

Once they'd finished, Sydney hurried up to her room to shower and change and Amy to the spare room she was using for the night.

They were both ready by the time the limo came to pick them up.

"Hope it goes well," Nora called from the front door. "And bring home the cake."

"Get inside and lock up," Sydney yelled. "And turn the damn alarm on." She saw Nora close the door and disappear inside, and then turn up in the parlour window waving madly.

Sydney and Amy settled back for the ride. "I hope she does as she's told."

"She's flighty, so she might not," Amy observed. She was dressed in a floor length black dress with diamantes sprinkled over it, her hair was piled into a topknot, and glittering stones dangled from her ears.

Sydney wore her usual sequinned pantsuit in blue and pink. She needed to feel happy, but calm for the night, and her favourite colours facilitated just that.

After being stuck in a traffic jam, they arrived at *The*

Roxy, a restaurant bar and grill, for the book launch, where they were met by Holland and his team out the front. CC and Olivia met them at the door and escorted Sydney in to her party.

Over a loud speaker came Rhona, "Ladies and gentlemen, the author of the hour, Sydney Kingston." She applauded madly along with the five hundred strong crowd.

Sydney waved to everyone and was escorted to the stage positioned to the right of the room, and took to the mic. "Hello, hello. Thank you all for coming and being here at the launch. The *official* launch of *Twisted Affair.*" She gazed across the crowd and saw Emerson waving madly. She was next to Cormac and Douglas. Ethan was beside him.

Sydney waved back. "I have just been told on the way here that it's already surpassed one million in sales and now the e-book and audio book will be out sooner than expected. Thank you all for helping make it another bestseller and I'll be coming around to schmooze with you all during the night. So eat, drink, and let's celebrate my latest book, and there will be a cake later." She waved a hand and left the stage.

"Fabulous job, Sydney." Rhona congratulated her from behind, giving Sydney's shoulders a squeeze. "Bookstores have ordered more. They're flying off the shelves."

"That's fantastic. I'm going to chat with Em for a bit and then circulate. Holland." She turned to him. "You caught up with Cormac and Douglas yet?"

"Not yet. I saw him arrive, so I'll escort you over." He led Sydney through the crowd of well-wishers until she ran into Emerson's arms.

"Syd."

"Em."

Emerson hugged her friend fiercely. "It's been too long and I've missed our Saturdays together." She pulled back and held Sydney at arm's length "I need to know all about your Italian toy boy and what you got up to in Capri."

Sydney's brows rose in amusement. "Oh, that's going to be a long story." She nodded at Cormac and Douglas. "Hello again."

"Hello, Sydney, thank you for including us," Cormac said. "It's been quite interesting seeing how one of these book launches plays out."

"And your security is in the background blending in, I take it," Sydney joked.

He grinned. "They are."

"Forget the interesting," Douglas cut in. "This is downright exciting. I've never been to a book launch before, let alone one of a close personal friend who's had lunch in our house." He smoothed the lapels of his navy suit jacket. "Are we too dressed up?" Both men were sharply dressed and looking good.

"Considering how your great-grandson dressed…" She pointed to Ethan in the same clothes he'd had on earlier. "The two of you are doing fine."

"Sydney," Ethan greeted her. "Got your French doors fixed?"

"I did, and the roller doors are firmly locked over them."

"Your French doors?" Douglas asked. "Did something happen? It must've for Ethan to know."

"My house sitter had to dash out and while she was gone the kitchen doors to the back yard were smashed in. We called the police and Landon Security." Sydney motioned at Landon. "Ethan and officers Velenksy and Rotrain beat them to it."

"Was anything missing? Oh, my God, Sydney, you could have been hurt." Emerson touched her arm gently. "I don't want to lose you. Your books are my gravy train."

Sydney's brows rose and she burst out laughing and Emerson joined in while the others looked at them strangely. Sydney stopped long enough to remind them Emerson had turned many of her books into movies. "But no," she said. "Ethan and the officers found no one in the house. We managed to track down my house sitter and she was fine. And so far…" She shrugged. "Nothing seems to be missing."

"Ethan?" Cormac turned to his grandson. "Your verdict?"

Ethan shrugged a shoulder. "I have no clue. The glass was smashed in, but nothing taken. No one was hurt, because no one was home. We're waiting on prints, but we got nothing."

"Holland, how about you? You're on the case?" Cormac turned to his old friend.

Holland nodded. "I am. We've been the security team for this since last year and we've run the fingerprints we did find, and found them to be Sydney's, Amy's and Nora's. There was nothing else. The intruder, if he intruded, didn't use a rock or brick to break the glass. They must have used a crow bar or bat. There was nothing."

"Mmm," Cormac muttered and felt Emerson tug on

his arm. "Ethan, make sure to run the details through the database to see if another crime matches. We might have a serial on our hands. Maybe this isn't the first and we could do something."

"Sure thing. I'll do it first thing in the morning and get reports from the officers. Meanwhile, I'm gonna head for the bar. Grandpa, Holland, Sydney, good to see you again." He left and two women moved closer.

"Hi." One waved. "I don't know if you remember me. I'm Sandy."

"Kieran's girlfriend." Sydney nodded. "We met at lunch and then when you came to my home. Of course, I see you got the invitation."

"I did," she gushed. "And, um, I'm the fiancée now." She held up her left hand to show off the sparkler on her ring finger.

Sydney's brows rose in surprise. "Congratulations. Set a date yet?"

"Next June." Sandy glowed with happiness. "We've already booked the month off from work, and rented the venue and reception hall."

"Those are the biggest things on the list. Good for you." Sydney glanced at the woman beside her. Dark, wavy, shoulder length hair, curvy but slim build, same height as Sandy, and wearing a mid-grey suit with a black blouse. "And you are? I don't think we've met."

"Hi, Ms Kingston. I'm Maria, Declan's partner." She thrust her hand forward. "His detective partner, that is. I'm a big fan of your books and managed to score the other invitation."

Sydney shook her hand. "Good to meet you, Maria.

Always good to meet a fan and God help you for having to work with Declan." That scored a small round of laughter. "Do you have a copy of *Twisted Affair*, or do you need one?" Sydney asked.

"Oh, I have my own." She fumbled in her bag for the book and a pen. "I hate to ask, but can I?" She held both out to Sydney.

"Sure." Sydney took the book and quickly signed it.

"Thank you so much. I couldn't get to the signing today." Maria glanced at the autograph and then tucked the book away.

"There'll be a few more over the coming weeks, as well as a few more events. Many are free; you just have to book in via the Pulsate website."

"Oh, I've already done that," Maria said. "They're next week. They booked out quickly."

"They did," Sydney said. "Pulsate's thinking of putting a few more on next month."

"I'll have to keep my eye out for those because I missed out," Sandy remarked. "But it all sounds so exciting."

"It can be, but after a few years of it, it can get repetitive."

"Speaking of repetition, I hate to be the one going on about not seeing you." Emerson linked arms with Sydney. "So, I'm going to whisk you away to the bar for a chat before you're swallowed by the rest of the crowd. Ladies, gents." Emerson nodded at them. "We're off to have a little chat." She escorted Sydney over to a quiet place at the bar. "God, how hectic."

"And you've been to the last few of these, so you know how they get." Sydney waved the bartender over. "You and Cormac are still going after a year?"

Emerson blushed to her roots. "Yes. We are and both very happy."

"Good." Sydney squeezed her arm. "I'm glad for you, Em."

"And you? Tell me about this hot Italian stud and why the hell you went to Florida?" Emerson scolded, thanking the bartender for her drink. She sipped at it.

Sydney took a sip of her drink and proceeded to give Emerson a bullet point list of what had happened in the last year, leaving out some minor details.

"Jesus, Syd. How many stalkers?" Emerson glared at her. "Are you okay?"

"I'm fine. But Landon thinks one's a peeping tom because of the neighbour's knickers, and one's because the house used to be Madam X's. All in all, the stalkers don't really have anything to do with me, except for the one who was sending those letters to me via Pulsate last year. The rat turned out to be the wrong address, can you believe it." Sydney laughed, but it didn't reach her eyes. The low music that filled the bar and grill was loud to her ears, and a throb was slowly getting worse on the left side of her head above her ear. She needed this day to be over.

"Oh, well, that's okay then." Emerson's comment dripped in sarcasm. She dunked her straw in her glass. "You know what, Syd? You could have told me."

"I did. The basics," Sydney reminded her. "You also came and said goodbye when we headed for Florida and I kept in touch on Saturdays so we could still talk instead of shop."

"All right. We managed to do that virtually while talking to each other via zoom." Emerson laughed.

"Yeah, we did keep in touch, but it just seems like more happened than what you told me."

"It kinda did. I needed to keep it secret while Landon did their job. I told you when it all came out." Sydney rubbed her throb and glanced around the bar.

Earthy tones, bricks and woods, low lights and low music. Not really her type of place, but a great bar and grill restaurant in the middle of Manhattan.

"And the Italian stud?" Emerson sipped her cocktail, her fingers still playing with the straw. "Anything you didn't tell me?"

"What, like a secret love child?" Sydney snorted. "He was a gigolo; I was a lonely rich old woman. He had a secret boyfriend. What?"

Emerson giggled and glanced over her shoulder. "No, silly. I mean like all of the details of the affair."

Sydney glanced over to Cormac, who was reminiscing with Holland. "Why? Need some hot steamy pointers?"

Emerson's laughter became uncontrollable. She put her glass on the bar and covered her mouth with both hands. "Oh, God no. No need for pointers."

"I should hope not knowing your sex life," Sydney quipped. "Viagra must be enough."

"Oh, my God, Sydney." Emerson's blush covered her entire face and neck.

"Get back to lover boy," Sydney told her and rested her hand on her friend's arm. "I need to mingle with my peeps." Hearing Emerson's snorting laughter behind her, Sydney set off around the room to do her meet and greet. One of Landon's security team was always nearby, as was Amy.

On her way around the room, Sydney came across Douglas. "Enjoying yourself?"

"I am." He held out his hand for hers and when he got it he went on. "I'm a little out of my league, but I've had a chat with your publisher, CC Charleston. Quite an exquisite woman."

Sydney stifled a grin, but her brows rose in reaction. "Is that so? Do I see another paring with one of my friends and colleagues?"

The grin spread across his face. "I don't know about that, but she asked me on a date this Saturday night."

"Wow!" Sydney's surprise continued. "The feisty old duck."

Douglas chuckled. "Her or me?"

Sydney grinned back. "Both. I see your future granddaughter-in-law and Declan's partner got the invitations along with Ethan."

"Yes." Douglas became thoughtful. "Ethan already knew and got in just because he'd seen you, and then Sandy and Maria found out next. So, we offered them the invitations. Although…" He drifted off and sighed.

"What?" she squeezed his hand.

"Although," he continued, "I offered it to Sean first."

Sydney pulled her hand away and leaned back in shock. "But—"

"I know." Douglas put his hands up to placate her. "I know. Cormac told me about last year. Connor, Sean, Declan. The whole mess made worse by Alec sticking his nose in. Cormac ripped into the family for that and demanded they all stay away from you."

"And yet Ethan turns up on my doorstep and now

my book launch," Sydney said, looking around the room, she spied the detective talking to a woman in the corner of the bar and felt a pang flare in her chest.

"I know. And for all his graces, Sean refused because he thought it would be inappropriate to come, and we congratulated him on his emotional growth." He paused and watched her brows furrow and lips purse. "He liked the book, by the way. And loved your inscription. He's glad that *you're* glad he continued with his mentorship and writing. He's become quite the celebrity in the family."

"Does Sierra still crap all over him the way she did?"

"No, she does not." He shook his head. "And after Cormac had a word in Declan's ear about his family, he leaves Sean alone too. Sean's been with us for the last year, and he's excelled. He's eighteen now."

"Yeah, I saw it all in the publicity for the book." Sydney gave a half-hearted smile and nodded. "I'm glad he chose not to come, because he wouldn't've made it past security."

"Yeah, I figured that. Sydney." He grasped her elbow. "I know what he and Connor did, and thank you for not doing anything. Pressing charges, taking them to court. Thank you for letting Cormac deal with it."

"Well, Holland had a hand in that, apparently." Sydney stepped closer. "He had a chat with Cormac."

"He did with both of us and we came up with a plan and followed through on it."

She was puzzled. "Which was?"

"Therapy for all. And suspension for Declan. He was on duty at the time he threatened you. Connor wasn't, but Cormac made them both pay restitution."

Sydney cocked her head. "Which was? Because I didn't receive anything in restitution."

Douglas blushed. "It was more for them to suffer the consequences for their actions."

"And yet I'm the one who had the black eye for months," Sydney scoffed. "And what about Sean? Did Cormac pay Sean's? Because again, I didn't get anything in restitution."

"Actually, Declan and Laura did that."

Surprised, Sydney looked back and stared into his eyes. "You're kidding? And what did they pay?"

"For Sean's therapy."

Sydney rolled her eyes. "Big whoop. I still didn't get anything for the assault. But he gets his drunk mummy and arsehole daddy to pay for *his* therapy." She paused a moment before adding, "How is she?"

"Still a drunk, but trying," Douglas muttered. "I shouldn't speak ill of my grandson's wife, or my great-grandson's mother, but she did try."

"Fell off the wagon?"

"She did. We're keeping an eye on her."

"And speaking of keeping an eye." Sydney sighed and saw Rhona approach them. "Time for work?"

"Time for greeting more guests and then we'll cut the cake." Rhona smiled her apologies to Douglas and led Sydney away.

They completed a circuit of the room, met all of the guests, and ended up behind the table with a ginormous book shaped cake with a dagger incoming out of it. The book was designed as the cover of *Twisted Affair.*

"Okay, ladies and gentlemen," Rhona called into the microphone. "Sydney's going to cut into her massive *Twisted Affair* book cake. You're all going to get a piece. We have a gift bag for all of you before you leave, and apparently, we need to be out at midnight and it's eleven now. How time has flown because we were all having fun. So, get yourselves a drink and we'll have waiters hand out cake. Take it away, Sydney." She turned to Sydney who was eating the knife part of the cake. "And she's already into it and went for the weapon, ladies and gentlemen."

The crowd cheered and Sydney shrugged. "It's good cake."

"Okay, everyone, cake is coming up."

The cake was cut and served and Sydney kept chatting to her guests. She managed to corner CC and ask her about seeing Douglas, spoke again with Maria and Sandy, and said goodnight to Emerson, Cormac, and Douglas on their way out.

Close to midnight, the night was finally wrapped up. It had been a long day and Sydney was sleeping in tomorrow. She handed out the gift bags as everyone left, and followed the last one out the door. Landon's team escorted her and Amy to their limo, and Amy was dropped off at her apartment. Sydney was then dropped off at her brownstone and the team waited for her to enter. They would wait to take Nora home, and for Sydney to lock up.

"Nora, I'm home. You can go now. The security team's waiting to take you home."

Nora came rushing in from the kitchen. "Did you get

the cake, Ms K?" She saw the big square box in Sydney's hands. "Can I have some?"

"I'll cut you a piece to take home, but the team's waiting outside. Get your coat and bag." She went to the kitchen to cut up the cake while Nora got ready to leave, and by the time Nora made it back to the kitchen Sydney had placed a large piece in a round container. "I want this container back and I gave you enough for Lennie if he drops by. Although why I'm feeding him, I don't know."

"Thanks, Ms K. When do you want me back?" Nora hungrily eyed the cake through the clear plastic.

"Not until next week when I have more interviews. So, you have some time off just like I do. Which is just as well because I'm exhausted." Sydney followed her to the front door and watched her hurry down the stairs to the car. "Monday at nine. Don't forget," she called.

"I got it in my phone, Ms K. See you then." Nora waved and climbed into the SUV.

The team waited for Sydney to lock up and set the alarm, then flash the front light twice to let them know she'd done it. They drove off to deliver Nora to her apartment.

Exhausted, Sydney checked the house system and hurried upstairs for a shower. She'd just dressed for bed and was pulling back the bed covers when the doorbell rang out, startling her and setting her heart off racing. She padded to the monitor on the wall next to the door to see who'd turned up.

Ethan!

Curious, she hurried down the stairs, tying her dressing

gown, and flicking on the lights as she went. Opening both doors, she said, "Why are you here?"

"Hey, Syd." He grinned. "Can I come in?"

"Ah, I guess." She moved the door to let him pass and then locked it, doing the same with the interior door.

He stood in the hallway, looking around. "Anyone else here?"

"Why? You planning on doing something? Your grandfather warned you all last year."

"Wow." He spun around in shock. "How do you know?"

"Douglas told me tonight. But Cormac told me last year when he saw me about Sean and the results of the murder kit on your grandmother."

"Yeah…" His brows furrowed. "Her murder was finally solved. And what about Sean?"

Sydney's brows rose in surprise. "Cormac banned the family from coming near me."

"Ah." Ethan thought back. "Not so much as banned, especially the rest of us, but definitely Alec, Declan, and my dad. Why, what did they do?"

"Never mind." Sydney shook her head, realising Cormac had never told them what Sean had done. "Why are you here?"

Ethan stepped closer and licked his lips in anticipation. "Well, after this afternoon, I thought I'd drop by to see you." He manoeuvred her against the stair railing. "We had a bit of fun down in the sex room."

The light bulb went off in Sydney's head. "Ah…and you thought you'd try and recreate what your father did."

He tilted his head and moved until his body touched

hers. "Or maybe you could show me what the two of you got up to and we could take it to a whole other level."

"Oh…" Sydney murmured against his lips that were hovering over hers. "You want to show me that you're better than your father." Her nipple hardened under his thumb.

"I'm younger, fitter, healthier." His lips brushed hers, and his hand massaged her breast.

She responded by unbuckling his belt, unzipping his fly, and pulling him out of his underwear.

He had her nightie up and her knickers down. She gripped the railing with one hand, and his rounded butt cheek with the other as he sucked on her breast. Her legs went around his waist as he thrust into her. When done, they came to a slow stop and Sydney put her legs down.

"Do you always find your way between a woman's legs?" Sydney panted and let go of the railing, but kept a hold of his ass.

"I do. It's like a homing pigeon. Always finds its way home." He ran his tongue across her lips, and his hands slid up her sides to both breasts.

"And how many homes has it been in?"

He huffed. "I'm only twenty-five and have been working non-stop, so not many at this point."

"Any as old as mine?" Sydney pushed his hands away and lowered her nightie.

"No. But no one as good as." Ethan put himself away. "I want to do that again. But better. I want to do to you what my old man did."

"Who said your father did anything?"

Ethan's brow rose. "You whipped him into submission."

"I certainly did."

"Care to try that with me?"

"Little boy, you're already submissive." She grabbed his jacket and pulled him downstairs. If his ass was anything like his father's it was going to be whipped into submission all night.

*****

The man stood staring at the brownstone. He'd been standing on the other side of the street, minding his own business, casing the place when the other guy pulled up and rang the bell.

He'd hidden, casually, behind the tree on the path, while he watched Sydney let him in. And then he'd moved a few steps left to try and see in the side glass windows, but couldn't make out anything. So, he'd casually crossed the street, climbed the stairs, and pretended to ring the bell. Glancing through the glass windows on the side, he'd seen two bodies in the hall, but nothing else. Pretending to ring the bell again, he waited a few moments and then left. After walking along the street to the guy's car, he leant down and slashed a gaping hole in both tyres.

He stood, looked around for any witnesses, and then walked around the car and slashed the other two tyres. He scraped the side and broke the side mirror before casually walking off down the street as if nothing had happened.

*****

The next morning, Ethan found his damaged car. "Jesus fucking Christ." He kicked a flat tyre. "What the fuck?"

"Don't you know we've had some moron wrecking cars?" Sydney called. "Why don't you call the cops? Oh wait…" She laughed and shut the door, leaving him to deal with his car by himself. She was having a lazy day at home and no one was going to ruin it. She flicked on the TV in the living room on the way through to the kitchen.

"And news just in, a woman was strangled to death on the Upper East Side. Her body found early this morning by a jogger. Police have no clues, so no suspects in custody, but are working the case. Next we have the weather…"

Sydney shivered, her hand hanging onto the open fridge door. The moment she heard Upper East Side, she'd frozen. She was in the Upper East Side, where she was right now. Standing in her Upper East Side brownstone, in her Upper East Side kitchen, hanging on to her Upper East Side fridge, and listening to her Upper East Side TV. "Fuck!" She closed the door and breathed in slowly. "Fuck, fuck, fuck!" Her breath came out in a whoosh. Was it time to run again? No, that was happening next month when she left for Europe and Australia to promote the book. Then what? Call Landon? Yes, call Landon.

She quickly made the call and spoke to Holland. He assured her he and his team would look into it, and to keep the doors and windows locked at all times.

"So, I'm a prisoner in my own home?" she complained.

"Have Amy come and stay. Or Emerson. Or go and stay in a hotel."

All the air in her body left her. "Thanks for nothing, if I'm murdered, I'll blame you."

"Keep your doors locked and you'll be fine," he said. "Meanwhile, I'll have a couple of shifts a day on your house."

"Thanks, Holland."

"No problem, Sydney. This is what Pulsate pays me for."

She hung up and wandered into the parlour to look out the window. Ethan had called a tow truck and his car was being hauled onto it. She waved at him and he rolled his eyes and shrugged.

*****

For the next few weeks, Sydney did countless interviews, TV, radio, magazines and newspapers, podcasts, and in person events. It was the same every year. She released a book and did six weeks of promotion. She'd be done by the end of October. Amy was with her every time, as were two Landon Security people, and Nora house sat during the day.

Nothing happened. No smashed French doors, no neighbourhood peeping tom, but then again, the fact that Ethan was spending every night there may have helped deter would-be stalkers.

Chapter 18

The first weeks of October flew by, and Sydney packed for her promotional tours of Europe and Australia. Europe was coming into winter, like New York, but Australia was coming into summer, and Sydney chose to pack one suitcase with warm clothes, and one with cool clothes. That way, she could cover both fall and spring, warm and cold weather. And if she packed properly, she might have room for more if she managed to find time to shop.

She was laying out her clothes on the bed to fold them into travel cubes when Nora came in.

"Hey, Ms K., Amy let me in. You're off again?" She slumped down in the easy chair by the bed. "How long for? Not that I mind, I like it here. And you have your food delivered."

Sydney rolled a top up and placed it in a medium sized cube. "And just remember. The order is the same week after week. If you need or want anything else, you'll have to get it yourself. Now…" She picked up another top. "You remember the rules?"

"Keep the doors locked twenty-four seven, but I can

open the windows, especially the kitchen, bathroom, and bedroom, but only during the day, and lock it up at night. Don't go in the basement, stay out of your room and the office, and keep the roller shutters down." She sighed and curled her red locks around her fingers.

"And," Sydney prompted.

"Lennie can come over and stay if he's good and if he's not I need to call Landon Security and they'll deal with him and anyone else that shouldn't be here."

"Correct." Sydney rolled a sweater and tucked it into the bottom of her winter case. "I don't mind him visiting, but if something's missing when I get home, I won't be happy."

"I'll make sure, Ms K. This is the coolest job I've had, I won't ruin it, or let Lennie, the big drongo." She rolled her eyes. "He's such a moron sometimes. So how long are you going for?"

Sydney suppressed a grin at the Aussie slang Nora had picked up from her. "I'll be back at the end of the month."

"In time for Halloween?" Nora asked excitedly. "Are you decorating?"

"I don't know if I'll be here, but I have some decorations in the basement storage room. You can put them up at the parlour windows and on the front door." Sydney finished with her sweaters and packed jeans on top of them. "If you're going to give out candy, make sure the Landon team are sitting out front in case something happens."

"Why would anything happen?" Nora wandered over to the bed and fingered a pretty kaftan top in multiple colours.

"We've had stalkers in the neighbourhood, Nora, *and* a smashed kitchen door. You need to be careful, and that's why Landon will be here on Halloween. Because it's the time weirdos come out more than any other time of the year."

"Besides, every single holiday, Christmas, New Year, Fourth of July," Nora said. "Is it okay if I go out during the day?"

"As long as the roller shutters are locked and the alarm's on." Sydney finished off two cubes and zipped them up. "I prefer that you're here from about five at night. It starts getting dark and you don't want crazies coming round. Make sure the house is locked up tightly at night."

"I will." Nora held up a kaftan top in front of her. "I like this. It's pretty."

"It is and I'm taking it with me. My room will be locked, so don't even think of getting in to try my clothes on."

Nora giggled. "No, Ms K. Tops like these aren't my thing." She looked down at her denim mini skirt and light rust orange tank top, paired with black ankle boots. Her matching denim jacket was downstairs.

Sydney finished packing another two cubes and organised them into her case. When she was happy, she zipped it up and set it on the floor. One more to go.

*****

Sydney and Amy flew first class to London for a week of promotion, then travelled to France and Italy. They shopped till they dropped on their days off, were treated like celebrities, and Sydney promoted the hell out of her book. After two weeks they flew to Sydney's homeland of Australia and travelled from state to state doing TV, magazine, radio and podcasts interviews, meet and greets and book lunches. It was all wildly successful, expensive, and extremely exhausting.

They flew back to New York, arriving on the thirtieth, and allowed Nora to do her trick or treat on Halloween. Everything had run smoothly while Sydney was away and she was pleased everything had gone well. She was going to stay home until December before the next onslaught for *The Perfect Man*, based on everything that had happened to her, was released. She just hoped and prayed no one figured it out…

*****

Sydney hibernated through November, with Ethan coming around to keep her company. Once Thanksgiving had been and gone, she decorated the house in a bright Christmas fashion. But once the calendar rolled over to December, she geared up for the release of her novella; the little something she'd written in Florida the year before. The idea had come to her while writing *Twisted Affair* and was a vague sequel, but still stand-alone enough to not be linked. And she hoped no one linked them…

*****

On the fifteenth, Sydney checked her Amazon dashboard while Amy checked the sales on the website. Both stores were evenly matched for sales, and by midday, both ticked over 250,000 sale mark each.

Emerson, CC, Gemma, and Olivia came over to celebrate, and keep an eye on sales, and by seven that night, sales had ticked over the 500,000 mark each. Sydney had now sold a million copies of *The Perfect Man*.

After a final glass of champagne, CC, Gemma, and Olivia left, Amy closed down the computer at eight and left with a Landon guard, and Sydney was left alone with Emerson.

"Now we can have a chat." Emerson pulled Sydney onto the couch. "You've sold another million books. Another bestseller on your hands." She dinged her glass against Sydney's and drank the last of her champagne that CC had brought over.

"We've chatted all day." Sydney let out a tired sigh and propped her feet on the coffee table. She tucked a cushion behind her head, and added, "So how goes the Commish Affair?"

Laughing, Emerson quickly put down her glass. "The Commish Affair? You really do think as a writer, don't you? Always coming up with titles and names, but, ah, it's not an affair. It developed into a relationship, which it did pretty quickly as you know. And it's going very well."

"Over a year now? He proposed yet?"

"Ha! No."

"Would you say yes if he did?"

The silence said a lot.

"Em?" Sydney watched her friend's face.

"I don't know," Emerson finally said. "I really don't know. I'm having fun, it's a great relationship, and we're seeing where things go." She cocked her leg onto her knee and massaged her ankle. "Would I say yes? I don't know. Would I say no? I don't know."

"Would you say yes one day?"

Emerson thought some more. "Maybe. I don't know. It would depend on how I felt about my life, how I felt about him, and having a life with him. I'd be a stepmother to four sons, and step-grandmother to four grandchildren."

"And however many Kieran and Sandy have," Sydney added. "But so? Here you are; mid-fifties, gorgeous, successful. A mega writer, director, producer, *multi* award winner for that work…please, the guy's lucky to have you *want* to date him."

Emerson giggled and blushed to her roots. "He's pretty special too, you know. But…" She lay back against the cushions. "After all the men, the relationships, and there have been a few, although I'm definitely not a whore who slept around, I have wondered if it was time to just be with one man. I mean, you saw what happened in L.A. I dated one guy a year because they all thought they could woo me and then take the fame that came with me. When I found that out, I dumped their sorry asses."

"You certainly did." Sydney nodded and checked the time. Ethan had said he'd drop by around ten or eleven. It was after nine. "I am happy for you." She sat up and checked her phone. "And if a relationship is the stability you want and need with a man older than you, then you go for it." She placed the phone back on the coffee table.

"Expecting someone?"

"Mmm, yeah, sort of."

"Is the hot Italian stud hiding out for Christmas?"

Laughter burst out of Sydney. "Hardly. I'm sure he's at home in the Riviera soaking up the adoration of a million women. I made him famous, after all."

"You certainly did." Emerson got to her feet and stretched. "Time for me to go then. My car's outside. You can watch me climb in."

"Landon's men are out there, too. Once I lock up, they'll go." She followed Emerson to the door and waited while she donned her coat.

"You know, Syd, you need to fall in love. It's quite a nice feeling." Emerson adjusted her collar and flung her cascading curls over it. She watched Sydney in the hall mirror.

"Yeah," Sydney murmured. "It might be nice...one day."

"But not today?"

Sydney shook her head sadly. "Not today. Maybe not ever. What then?"

"Don't you want to be in love, Syd?" Emerson turned to her friend, concerned by the sadness in Sydney's eyes.

Sydney shrugged a shoulder. "Maybe, maybe not. If no one's out there for me, then I'll have to deal with that, if not...so..." She changed the topic. "Can I be bridesmaid?"

"What?" It took a moment for Emerson to realise what she was talking about. "Oh, you." She lightly slapped her on the arm and opened the interior door. "Are we on for Saturday? I'm free."

"Sure." Sydney closed the door and held onto the front door. "You coming here first?"

"Ten a.m. for breakfast?" Emerson asked, kicking away some light snow on the stoop.

"Sure. You paying?"

"Considering you just sold a million books in one day, I'd say you have more than enough money to buy breakfast this week." Holding onto the concrete siding, she made her way downstairs and over to her car, two spaces down. "You're buying," she called, waving, and climbed into her car and started it to warm up.

Sydney watched her go, waiting until she was down the road. She turned and waved to the Landon security team, and locked the doors, retreating into the warmth. She set the alarm and texted the team. "All safe." She knew they would leave in a few minutes and be on call through the night. And she knew Ethan wouldn't come if they were there and she needed some male physical contact after having so much oestrogen in her house all day.

Tomorrow would be a rest day as she had Rhett Rockefeller and Preston Grant's shows to do, followed by a small handful of the biggest press. This time it was all limited, since it was just a novella, to the biggest TV, radio, magazine, newspaper, and podcast shows for interviews. And that was it.

A knock at the door sent her rushing to the monitor. Ethan. She quickly let him in, and he brushed off the snow on his jacket in the vestibule and kicked off his boots, leaving them as he strode into the living room. He rubbed his arms. "You got a fire going? It's freezing out there."

"No." Sydney set the alarm and followed him. "But the heating's been going all day."

"And I know another way to get warm." He pulled her into his arms, his lips finding hers, his tongue delving into her.

Sydney reciprocated. Her arms went around his neck, and her pelvis brushed against his. She was ready and willing for some sexy times. She finally pulled away, gasping for air. "Bed?"

"Sex room," he said, taking her hand and leading her downstairs.

*****

Two days later, Sydney was back on *Rockefeller* in front of a crowd of screaming fans.

"And we have Sydney Kingston who writes thrillers as Cassandra Kingsley back on the show today, but not for the whole hour," he told the audience who booed him. "Just for a segment to promote her Christmas novella, *The Perfect Man*." As he had no physical book to hold up, he held up a printed picture of the cover and it came up on screen behind him. "It's only out in e-book at the moment, came out two days ago, and has already sold a million and a half copies. Congratulations, Sydney."

"Thank you, Rhett, and it's definitely *not* a Christmas novella. It's just out for Christmas."

"Of course." He looked at the picture he was holding.

"Definitely not Christmas themed, people, but for those who haven't bought it yet, or don't know about it, it's available on Amazon and the Cassandra Kingsley website. Will you be selling it anywhere else?"

"Absolutely." Sydney crossed her legs and gently swung her foot. "I wanted to sell the e-book first, so in January, it will be sold on other sale sites and in March, the print and audio will be available. We've done a bit of a reverse this time. But, it's only a novella and smaller works are treated differently from main novels."

"And why's that?" Rhett sat back and crossed his legs in her direction.

"It's just the way my publishing deal is. I hold ownership of e-books and audio. Pulsate has print and foreign rights as I've stated previously. My main novels will come out in print first, but anything extra I want to write and sell is up to me. Whether it's short stories, poetry, essays, or novellas, I have the say over how they're published and Pulsate gets first dibs for print. And they wanted this one as well, so it's a Christmas present for my fans."

"Fantastic." Rhett addressed the audience. "How many have read it already?" At least half the crowd put their hand up. "And did you like it?" Rhett asked. Cheers and applause went through the audience. "So, Sydney, I think you mentioned it the last time you were here, but tell us what it's about."

"It's about a man that everyone thinks is perfect. He can do no wrong, butter wouldn't melt in his mouth, but you find out in the end that someone *is* wrong."

"And it's him?" Rhett asked.

"I didn't say that," Sydney replied. "If you haven't read it, Rhett, don't make assumptions."

"Now that's intrigued me," he said. "You said that someone is wrong. What does that mean? He's wrong? So not the perfect man after all. Or someone who thought he was perfect is wrong? What?"

"Can't say," she said. "I'm not giving away my storyline, Rhett. It's about a man everyone thinks is perfect, but everyone is not perfect either, and at the end, we all find out who's really not."

"Okay." He chuckled. "*The Perfect Man*, a novella from best-selling author Sydney Kingston, writing as Cassandra Kingsley, is out now for Christmas, but it's definitely not a Christmas story. Sydney, thanks for coming in today. We'll be right back after this, folks."

When the stagehand counted them out, Rhett turned to Sydney, holding out his hand to shake hers. "Great to have you back on the show, Sydney. Can't wait to see you for the next book."

"Thanks for having me, Rhett. See you next year." Sydney was escorted off stage and had her mic removed before going to the dressing room for her bag. Amy met her there and they left, the security team driving them to SXT for Preston Grant's show.

She was on air forty-five minutes later.

"And we have Sydney Kingston dropping by for a few minutes to talk about her latest work, *The Perfect Man*, a novella out in time for Christmas and available to buy on Cassandra Kingsley's website. Sydney how are you?"

"Great, Preston, you? Merry Christmas everyone."

"Merry Christmas to you, Sydney, which it would be.

A number one bestseller of Christmas."

"A very nice present indeed," she said. "Did you buy it?"

"I did and I've read it and that twist at the end, oh, my God." He made the hand motion for a chef's kiss. "My God, Sydney, you got me with that one."

"I got myself with that one. Muse came along right on cue and whipped it out."

"Is your muse important?" Rhett asked. "We've always heard authors mention the muse, and other artists and designers all say they have one, but how important is yours?"

"Very. I also think that she gives me the ideas and then makes sure I'm on the right path to get to the end. But sometimes, the end doesn't show itself until the story has played out, and then you might have thought I was heading in a particular direction, and then boom, she takes you to a twist and a conclusion you didn't see coming."

"And is it that way every time?" Hank asked.

"No, but most times. She just leads me there until I see it for myself and go, ah, that's where I was going."

"Did you outline this novella? Do you outline your novels? How did this one work?" Preston asked.

"I went off to Florida last year to write the new novel, and I finished off another plus a non-fiction, but this novella popped into my head because of writing *Twisted Affair* which came out in September. There was no plotline for *The Perfect Man*, just an idea that extended from what I was writing and I wrote it. It all came to me and all came out."

"So, it's a sequel to *Twisted Affair?*" Preston glanced at his e-reader. The cover of Sydney's book was clearly on display.

"No, but the story is of the same idea, theme, genre, and realm of men who think they're the be all and end all, and women who turn out to be tougher than first thought."

"Oh, that's a really good way of describing it," Hank said.

"Right." Sydney nodded in agreement. "It doesn't give too much away; it's not a sequel, but same genre, realm and story idea."

"Definitely." Preston swiped his screen and the blurb came up. He read it aloud for the audience. "I mean, I can just hear everyone at home or listening wherever they are going ooohhh."

Hank chuckled. "That's what I did when I read it."

"What do you mean? That's what *I* said when I read it," Sydney joked. "The girls in the cover design department did a good job with the cover and blurb."

"So, it's published by Pulsate then," Preston said.

"Just the print and foreign editions. But I get to use the cover for e-books and audio. It's part of our agreement for uniformity."

"Oh, that's a great idea, too," Preston said. "And a smart business move on your part."

"I thought so," she agreed.

"Okay." He looked at the clock on the wall. "We've been talking to Sydney Kingston, the author behind the Cassandra Kingsley thrillers. The latest is a novella and it's a Christmas present for her fans, and is available on her website at Cassandra Kingsley, and Amazon until next month when it goes wide and comes out in audio and print as well. If you haven't picked it up, do so. If you hate Amazon, buy it from the Cassandra Kingsley website. But do yourself a favour either way and buy it, especially if you're a fan of her books. Sydney Kingston thanks for dropping by and Merry Christmas."

"Merry Christmas, Preston, everyone. Enjoy the book." Sydney watched Hank countdown to break and removed her headphones. "Thanks for having me again."

"Thanks for coming in again, Sydney."

They shook hands and Sydney waved goodbye as she and Amy left. They were home within the hour.

Chapter 19

On Saturday, Emerson came to pick her up for their girl's day out, but because of the snow fall and freezing temperatures, Sydney told Emerson to stay and they sat on their computers all day shopping online in front of the toasty fire in the lounge room.

"Oh, this is so much better." Emerson sipped her wine. "Roaring fire, credit card in hand, PayPal at the ready, wine in my glass. What's for lunch?"

Sydney shrugged and clicked add to cart on a website. "Pizza?"

"Syd," Emerson complained. "It's five days before Christmas and you're eating pizza?"

"It's five days before Christmas; I can eat whatever I want."

"And what are you doing for Christmas?" Emerson clicked the buy now button on a white dress. The price tag was $2000.

"CC's having a party for all of us single members at Pulsate, so I'll probably go there." Sydney leaned back against the couch cushions. "You know, this is so much better shopping this way. What are you doing for dinner?

It's Saturday night."

"Cormac and I had planned something, but this weather is just, ugh…" She looked into the kitchen and out the expanse of windows and French doors. "Grey and gloomy."

"Have dinner here," Sydney suggested. "Call him up to come over."

"What?" Surprised, Emerson nearly spat out her wine. "You're offering dinner, here, tonight, with Cormac and me."

"Add Douglas if he's interested. It'll be a foursome." Sydney pressed the buy now button. Her resolve had not abstained.

"Huh." Emerson thought about it. "And what would you cook?"

"Roast chicken and veggies. There's plenty in the freezer. I can get it out now to defrost. Whack it in about five. Dinner at seven-thirty? Or do you want it earlier?"

"It's Saturday, so he's off work. I'll text." A few minutes of texts zoomed back and forth and it was agreed they'd arrive at six for a seven o'clock dinner.

Come casual, but rugged up, it's cold out, Emerson texted, signing off. She sat back. "Guess we'd better have lunch and get the chicken out."

"Right after I buy this handbag." Sydney hit the buy now button.

*****

Cormac and Douglas arrived at the brownstone at six, covered in snow and bearing bottles of alcohol.

Emerson helped them discard their coats and hung them in the vestibule to dry before escorting them into the living room and over to the fireplace to warm up.

"Another half hour or so they should be done." Sydney walked in from the kitchen to greet them and accept the wine. "Do I put it outside to chill? It's freezing out there."

"It would save on power," Douglas joked. "Let's crack one open now. I need to warm up."

He helped her by opening the bottle while she got the glasses, and a moment later the others were enjoying the red wine while she had a Pepsi. "Ah, good vintage," he said. "And from the smell of it, good food too."

"Roast chicken and vegetables with thick gooey gravy," Sydney said.

"My favourite kind of gravy," Douglas replied.

They chatted for the next hour until they sat at the table laden with dishes. The aromas wafted into the air, combining with each other to create a delectable feast for the senses.

"Can we talk about the ending of *The Perfect Man?*" Douglas asked.

"No," Sydney chastised. "No giving things away." She popped a forkful of chicken into her mouth and her taste buds exploded into gasms.

"It was superb and one I didn't see coming," he continued, unperturbed. "The same for *Twisted Affair.* The way your mind works is incredible."

"Well, thank you." Sydney was pleased with the praise.

"And dare I say it, even Sean was amazed."

"Pop, why bring him up?" Cormac asked. "After last year."

"And yet you thought it was okay to bring a spare book for Sydney to sign for him," Douglas argued. "We wouldn't know Sydney it if wasn't for Sean asking Laura to invite Emerson and Sydney over, and then to lunch. You two," he waved his knife between his son and Emerson, "wouldn't have met."

"And been getting jiggy with it for a year," Sydney murmured behind her Pepsi glass.

Emerson burst out laughing. "Oh, Syd." She hid behind her hands and wiped her tears away. "That's hilarious."

"But true," Douglas said and cut into a carrot.

"And how's the rest of the family?" Sydney changed the subject.

"The grandkids are in college or working, and the kids are doing well," Cormac said and speared a piece of roast potato before eating it.

"Good to hear. How does it feel being in Madam X's brownstone again?" Sydney popped a piece of carrot into her mouth, almost choking on her controlled laughter.

"I've been looking for the sex room, but that's in the basement, right?" Douglas didn't miss a beat.

Sydney burst out laughing. "Oh, come on, you all know where it is and what it looks like. You ransacked this house after you arrested her and took photos."

"I wish I *didn't* remember those photos." Cormac grimaced.

"Why?" Emerson asked, taking a sip of wine.

"Because I had to reprimand the majority of the officers who removed everything because of the idiotic behaviour they exhibited when doing so. That was a laugh a minute," he said dryly.

"Played with the equipment, did they?" Sydney exchanged a glance with Emerson and smirked.

"They did," Douglas supplied. "Oh, they did."

Sydney's brows rose and she tried to contain more laugher. "Could I see some of those pictures?"

"No," Cormac said firmly and scraped up the last of his meal. "They will stay hidden in the vault until the end of time."

"Pity." Sydney got her laughter under control. "Do you want to see the sex room?"

"No," Cormac repeated.

"Yes," Douglas replied at the same time, scoring a glare from his son.

"Boys, boys," Sydney placated. "You don't have to. I mean," she shrugged, "if you've seen the pictures, it's pretty much the same."

"That's right. You said you'd added everything back." Douglas remembered. "Why?"

"I was curious and thought, why not. This brownstone's famous, it'll add to completing it once again."

"Find anything left behind?" Cormac finished off his wine, and stared straight into her eyes.

Another shrug. "Why would I? I didn't rip the place apart or renovate it, but from all accounts, the previous owners didn't either." She gave him the same stare. "Why? Interested?"

"In the myth," Cormac replied coolly. "There were a lot of rumours at the time and I worried my men either hadn't found anything, or some of them had taken that which did not belong to them."

"Interesting," Sydney murmured. "But again, I didn't

renovate, the couple who did, though, did a fabulous job. Heating, including the underfloor variety, cooling, brand new appliances, large screen TV. The place is amazing with a library office upstairs, two floors of bedrooms, media room in the basement with laundry and a massive storage room. *Amazing* job."

"It certainly looks it," Douglas said. "But I do want to bring up something before we go."

"What's that?" Sydney asked.

"Sean."

"Ah," sighed out of her.

Cormac glared at his father. "Pop, give it a rest."

"No, no." Douglas waved his son away. "He had success with his first book this year, thanks to you, Sydney, for the mentoring and support, and he's working on a second and third which your publisher bought the rights to. He's become a bit of a celebrity in the family and he's happy and looking forward to the next few years of college and classes. He's really knuckled down and worked hard to better himself and I think that's because you convinced Cormac to still encourage him after you stepped away. Regardless of what he'd done, you still wanted him to work at it and not run away. And secondly," he saw her unease and squeezed her hand, "thank you for what you did with the murdering bastard in L.A. He took my son's wife away, and my grandchildren's mother away, and you finally stopped him. Thank you for that, and for still encouraging Sean. He's a lot better for it."

The silence was thick, and unfortunately there were plenty of knives to cut it with on the table which gave

Sydney ideas. Instead, she pushed back her chair and started clearing the dishes, blinking back the tears prickling her eyes.

Emerson got up to join her, and within minutes, the table had been cleared off and the leftovers put away.

"I guess I shouldn't have brought that up," Douglas said afterwards.

"No, probably not," Sydney told him when she set the tray of steaming coffee on the living room coffee table. Bowls of sweet biscuits and after-dinner mints accompanied them.

They spent the next hour chatting and watching TV before Cormac stood up to leave. "I think we need to be heading off now, Pop. Sydney." He shook her hand. "Thank you for dinner; it was just as good as that hotpot you made last year."

"Glad you enjoyed it," she said, watching Douglas reluctantly stand. "It's cold out, so rug up."

"Emerson, you coming?" Cormac watched her as he slid on his coat.

"No, I'm staying the night. But I'll see you tomorrow for lunch." She kissed him goodbye and she and Sydney watched them carefully tread down the snow covered stairs with the help of Cormac's escorts. They bundled into the car, waved, and drove off.

Emerson locked the doors and set the alarm, then followed Sydney into the living room and sat beside her on the couch. "You ignored Douglas when he thanked you. Do you want to talk about it?"

Sydney burst into tears and fell sideways into Emerson's arms.

*****

Sydney spent Christmas Eve and Day with CC, staying over at her luxurious penthouse for the night. Half of Pulsate's staff dropped in to celebrate, as did Amy, but Sydney was back in her home on the 26th to see Ethan waiting.

"Hey, waited long?" Sydney asked as he helped her up the stairs.

"About ten minutes. Long enough to call you to see when you were getting home. I have the week off and brought a bag of clothes so I don't have to leave."

They went inside, started a fire, and spent the rest of the week together.

*****

Sydney spent New Year's Eve and Day with CC. It was a repeat of Christmas with people coming and going so they had someone to celebrate with, and some*where* to celebrate. Emerson turned up for the fireworks with Cormac and Douglas.

"Wait, are you two seeing each other?" Sydney asked when she saw CC and Douglas canoodling. "Crikey!"

"Off and on since the book launch." CC preened, and gave a girlish giggle. "It's New Year."

"And *a* new year." Sydney sighed and wandered over to the floor-to-ceiling windows in CC's penthouse apartment that overlooked everything the city had to offer.

Another New Year's Eve and she was alone. Ethan was

325

working; half the family was. The rest were elsewhere, which is why Emerson, Cormac, and Douglas were there, and Amy was chatting to people. And as single as she was, something was nagging her. It usually did this time of year. Maybe it was because another year had come and gone and her life was still the same. Another book had been published and promoted and her life was still the same, except for the influx of cash into her bank account. But there was definitely something going on in her brain. She just needed to figure it out.

Midnight came and they oohed and aahed over the fireworks. This was Sydney's first in New York as she'd celebrated in Florida last year, and after a long New Year's Day, she finally made it home for a shower and a notepad. It was time for the plan. The new plan for a new year, and what she wanted to do and achieve. But first, she needed to figure out what was going on.

Chapter 20

On January fifteenth, the print and audio versions of *The Perfect Man* went up for sale online and in store. The print sold out within twenty-four hours.

Sydney celebrated with CC, Gemma, Olivia, Amy, and Emerson at Pulsate. The TV was playing softly in the background. Sydney had just cheered to herself when she glanced at the screen and saw a photo of Laura pop up. "What the hell?" She quickly found the remote and turned it up. "Shoosh everyone."

"Doctor Laura Ackerman, the wife of Detective Declan Ryan of the NYPD, and daughter-in-law of Police Commissioner Cormac Ryan, was found dead in her home by her son Sean. He called his grandfather who sent paramedics around, but it was too late. Dr Ryan was a decorated surgeon with a successful career. She leaves behind her husband and son."

"Jesus fucking Christ." Sydney spun around to see Emerson drained of colour. Her hands were over her mouth. "Jesus, Em." She quickly put the remote and her glass down to comfort her. "I'm sorry."

"For what?" Emerson waved her off. "Laura rarely came

to family lunch anymore, so I haven't seen her in months. And we were only college roommates thirty something years ago."

"Go, go to Cormac. You need each other." Sydney gathered Emerson's bag and coat and ushered her from the room and over to the elevators. "Will he be at home? Do you need a lift? A taxi?" The doors opened and she helped her in. They whooshed down and Sydney escorted Emerson out into a cab. "Em, call me." She saw her dazed expression. "Em, snap out of it. You need to go to Cormac. Call me when you're with it and give them my condolences." She gave the cab driver Cormac's address and shut the door, watching the cab drive away. Sydney decided to let the family know, and hurried back upstairs.

"Oh, Douglas, we're so sorry," CC cried into the phone. "We've just seen it on TV. How awful for the family."

Sydney indicated for the phone, and after a moment, CC handed it to her. "Douglas, Sydney. Are you at home?"

"I'm home. Cormac's at Declan's and Laura's."

"I've just sent Emerson to you in a taxi. She's in shock, as we all are. My condolences."

"Thank you, Sydney, we'll look out for Emerson."

"Thank you." She handed the phone back to CC and sat down, deflating into the cushions. "Poor Sean, like he needed this after getting his shit together."

*****

A week later, on a rainy, thunderous afternoon, Sydney

noticed photos of Laura's funeral starting to appear on social media. "What the fuck..." she muttered, looking at the hashtags. #ripryanwhore was the most common one, and stupidly, she clicked on it.

At least a hundred plus photos and videos had been posted; mostly by some person who was clearly at the cemetery recording the whole thing in the distance so no one would see them. They zoomed in on the family standing in the downpour.

Sydney homed in on Sean. He was tall, slimmer than a year ago, his brows furrowed so deeply it made him look exactly like his father. She sighed, and looked for Emerson, huddled under one of the huge umbrellas with Cormac's arm around her.

Douglas stood nearby with CC under another, and that surprised Sydney. They were so close after a few months that she was invited to the funeral. The rest of the family, and people she didn't know, were crying, wiping away their tears that mixed with the rain, huddled under large black umbrellas, wearing their black clothing and looking morose. Her gaze darted back to Sean. That is not going to make him happy.

After hours of scrolling on social media, Sydney took a break to make an early dinner, having forgotten lunch. She stirred the hotpot on the stove top and gave it a few more minutes. Glancing out the window, she saw it was dark and yet only five in the afternoon, with the lights already on in the brownstone, and the neighbouring homes.

Wandering over to the window, she saw outside was forbidding and cold. A shiver slid down her back. She rubbed her arms to ward off the chill, and grabbed the tablet monitor. After she tapped a few buttons, the roller shutters started descending.

The doorbell rang out through the house and she checked the tablet for the front door camera. "Oh, my God." Shocked, she turned off the stove and went to the front door, opening it on a dark, cold, and freezing evening, and an even more freezing Sean Ryan. "What are you…"

"I didn't know where else to go," he murmured, his blue eyes full of water. Tears or rain, or probably both. "But I just…" His head shook. "Walked."

"All the way from the cemetery?" Sydney didn't know whether to let him in. It was pouring and he would be soaked through. "The cemetery's in Brooklyn."

"Yeah." He frowned. "How did you know?"

"Someone put it on social media. They're not being kind." His sad sorrowful face deflated her, and she opened the door to let him in. "I shouldn't be doing this," she said softly as he stepped into the vestibule and she closed the door behind him. "But I know you buried your mother today." She helped him out of his sopping coat and blazer and he kicked off his shoes.

"The fire's going, go and get warm. I'll get you a towel." She locked the doors and hurried to the hallway storage closet for something to dry him with, and handed him a large fluffy green bath towel.

He pushed it over his head with both hands, soaking up the rain, and then wiped himself down before sitting on the easy chair to the side of the fireplace.

"Um…" Sydney took a few steps away. "Do you…

need food? Coffee?"

He thrust up and she stumbled back. "What I need is to apologise."

"What!" Stunned, she stopped moving. "What?"

He took a step towards her, his eyes pleading. "I'm so sorry for everything I did. I didn't know where I was going. I just walked here. I didn't even think about it." His hands were in front of him, pleading. "I'm sorry for being an asshole last year. I'm sorry for hitting you. That was the last thing I wanted to ever do. I don't know why I did it; I was stupid and screwed up and young. My mom was fucking my uncle; my dad was fucking prostitutes. Mom was unhappy, Dad was crazy, and I was falling apart in my brain so much it hurt."

He breathed out and ran his hands through his hair. "I was a fucked up kid who was being screwed over by the people who should've been taking care of me and I fucked up and took it out on you when I found out about you and Connor. And I'm so sorry, Sydney. I am truly so sorry, and nothing I ever do will make it up to you, will make you forgive me for hitting you, or kissing you, or hurting you."

His hands fell to his sides and he sighed. "When Grandpa took me in I started seeing a psychiatrist and he did some tests and found out that I have mild ADHD and I'm on the autism spectrum. And while the diagnosis helped me understand why my brain is the way it is and I did what I did, it doesn't make up for what I did to you and I am so sorry, Sydney. You were my mentor, my cheerleader, my supporter, my biggest supporter even ahead of Grandpa and Pops. And I…" His head shook in despair before bowing it. "I have felt a massive rock of guilt ever since. I've felt horrible and nothing will ever make up for it."

Taking a deep breath, Sydney let it out slowly, contemplating her words. "I tend to not forgive, and I certainly don't forget. But I can move on, which is what I did. That is what I suggested to your grandfather, and I'm glad you did as well, and I'm glad he got you out of your parents' house because that was really toxic. I'm glad he kept on at you to keep up with the mentoring, and I'm glad you were published. But I will not forgive or forget what you, Connor, and Declan did."

He barely nodded. "I understand." Looking around, he added, "Can I stay here awhile? It's nice and warm and I just want to talk about it if you don't mind. But I can go if you don't want me here."

She considered the moment and sighed. "You hungry?"

"Starving."

"Sit down and get warm. I'll get you a bowl of food." She scooped up a big bowl of hotpot and put it on a tray. "I'm going to have to call your grandfather. They'll be worried about you." She set the tray on his legs, and her hand brushed his. She snatched it away and rubbed the spot, frowning at him and his big blue eyes.

"I'm eighteen. An adult. It doesn't matter if I'm out. They can't stop me. Besides..." He shrugged and scooped up a spoonful of beef balls. "Considering what I've been through, I really don't want to see any of them right now. Especially Connor and my old man."

"Why?" Sydney asked, knowing full well why. "They're your family."

Sean glared up at her. "Because they killed my mother."

Stunned, Sydney could only sink into the easy chair opposite him as he told the story. "So, you think the affair did this?"

"I think my father did this."

"Not the alcohol or the depression?"

"He drove her to that. She wouldn't've done it, otherwise."

"Do you have proof?"

"I might have. But I'd need to check it out first."

"Then what will you do?" Sydney's fear level surpassed its peak. There was an insanity in Sean's eyes. But, also clarity and determination.

Sean stared at her, unblinking. "Make him pay."

*****

In the morning, Sydney rang Douglas who came with Cormac to collect Sean.

Cormac stood on her doorstep as she opened the door and waved him in. "He's in the parlour. Slept all night."

Cormac walked past her into the room and saw his grandson sleeping on a couch. He gently shook his shoulder. "Sean, it's time to go home."

"What?" Sean lurched awake and yawned. "Yeah. I guess so." He threw back the blanket and stood. "Thanks for listening, Sydney, and again, I apologise for everything I put you through last year." He looked at Cormac. "Grandpa. I'll just get dressed."

Cormac pulled Sydney aside when Sean went for his shoes. "How was he?"

"Depressed, disillusioned, a scared little boy who'd lost his mother. He turned up sopping wet, so I fed him, got him dry and warm and he flaked out on the couch. Figured I'd wait until now to call."

"You could have sent a text, or called last night." He apprised her with his truth telling skills.

"And as he reminded me, he's an adult and can be out on his own," Sydney replied. "Besides, I didn't want a replay of Declan and Connor on my doorstep, and he needed time to grieve away from the family and talk to someone who's neutral. The funeral ended up on social media, you know. Someone was there filming it and taking photos."

Cormac sighed with a nod. "I know; it turned up in the damn papers this morning. I've read the riot act to the editors." He saw Sean pop back into the hallway fully dressed.

"Ready to go?"

"I am." He smiled at his grandson. "And you look better than you did yesterday, so let's get you home. Pop's waiting in the car, and Emerson's at home."

"I see CC was there for Douglas." Sydney followed him to the door. "Just as Em was there for you."

"She was." Cormac paused at the vestibule door. "Thank you for helping him. You didn't have to."

"I know, but he's still a kid and now he'll need help again. He found his mother dead in their house. He's going to need lots of help."

"And we'll make sure he gets it." Cormac waved Sean on, but Sean held his arm out and they walked down the stairs together.

Sydney watched Cormac get into the car, waved to Douglas, and saw Sean glance over his shoulder.

His eyes were dead and bored into hers. He nodded and climbed into the car.

Sydney quickly locked the doors and reset the alarm. She shuddered. There was evil in Sean, and after what he'd said last night, she knew he was serious about making his father and uncle pay.

PART THREE

Eight months later

Chapter 21

"Welcome to *Rockefeller.* Our special guest today is Sydney Kingston, author of the Cassandra Kingsley novels, and we have her for the whole hour, so let's get to it," Rhett Rockefeller yelled at his screaming audience before taking his seat on stage as the opening credits rolled and they watched the producer countdown to air time. "And we're back with Sydney Kingston and her latest thriller, *The Shape of You,* under the pen name Cassandra Kingsley. Sydney, Sydney, Sydney." Rhett leaned back in his seat and crossed his legs. "I've read this book, completely, and it is not about Madam X. You told us last year we'd be getting a novel about Madam X."

"And I didn't realise how many legalities there would be concerning it," Sydney told him. She wore a blue sequinned blazer with plain matching pants, and her top was a cool print with subtle sequins for extra sparkle. Her hair was clipped up into a twist with a diamante barrette.

"She was one of New York's most famous *and* infamous madams," Rhett said. "If not *the* most famous. I guess her client list would be one for the history books."

"It certainly is," Sydney said. "Which is why my lawyer keeps suggesting we put it off. Mind you," she added as she turned to the audience, "my novel's a completely made up piece of fiction based on her story. I don't actually *name* people in the book, but my lawyer says if I mention any type of high powered job, such as, oh, I don't know, the *mayor, lawyers, judges, mob bosses,* and so on, I could be in serious trouble because people would figure it out." She shrugged. "That's not my fault. I didn't make all those men visit a madam to get their ass spanked."

The crowd whooped and cheered and Rhett laughed and waved at them to quiet down. "Do you know names, Sydney?"

"Why would I, Rhett?" she replied innocently. "If I mention a job, then people will connect the dots. Although I seriously don't know why men would be so embarrassed about going to a madam; they have no problem embarrassing themselves in public every day." More cheers as she nodded at the crowd. "Right, ladies?"

"I completely get it." Rhett rested Sydney's latest hardcover on his knee. "Something like that could damage a career—"

"Why?" Sydney butted in. "Is getting your ass spanked with a whip illegal in this country?"

Rhett blushed and shushed the rambunctious crowd. "Technically no."

"So, women provide the service, and men have no problem with that, or using that service, but *they* made it illegal and then freak out when it's been found out that they've been using it. Isn't it all rather hypocritical and contradictory?" Sydney turned to the crowd. "Men use women, but make us pay for it by making the service illegal. No wonder women get treated like shit in this country."

"Okay, okay, we've strayed way too far off track, so let's get back onto it." Rhett held up Sydney's book to the camera. "Cassandra Kingsley, *The Shape of You*, the new psychological thriller out now in all bookstores. It's already hit number one on the bestseller charts. Tell us what it's about, Sydney, because the cover clearly shows a hand sliding over a body even though the picture's frosted or faded in the background."

Sydney breathed in. "Well, it's about a woman falling for a guy after refusing to have feelings for him. It's about the emotions she feels along the way, and finally when she's with him for the first time, the shape of him is imprinted on her. Body, mind, soul."

"And obviously there's twists and turns along the way. It wouldn't be a thriller without them, but what struck me most was there were no ages mentioned. Not that it matters, I automatically thought they were adults, but some suggested the characters are teenagers. What can you tell us about that?"

Sydney frowned. "It's whatever you want it to be. As with every book we read we form the story in our mind. If teenagers or young people identify with the characters and think that, then fine. If older people think they're older characters, that's fine. What's the big deal? It's whatever you make it, and before you ask, yes, I left the ages out on purpose."

Rhett nodded. "I was going to ask that next. So really,

it's up to us, the reader, to get what we perceive out of it."

"You do you, Rhett, and everyone else can do them. As long as you buy the book and give it a good review, I don't care how old you think the characters are."

"Okay. So, it's about love between a man and a woman, or male and female couple of the same age, and how they learn to love and be intimate mentally, emotionally, and physically, not just with each other, but with themselves. Because I'll tell you, some people cannot stand being with themselves. But tell us, where did the idea come from? How did you come up with it? And you went back to Florida to spend time writing it. What's Florida got that we don't?"

Sydney laughed. "Warmer weather. Plain and simple. If I'd known how cold New York was going to be in winter, I may not have come here. But now it seems to be a bit of a good luck thing. We head down there; I write like crazy, get multiple books written, go off on holiday, and then come back and publish. It's a great life."

"And where did you come up with the idea?" Rhett held the book up for the camera. "This book's got some spice to it, I'll tell you, ladies and gentlemen, there are some sex scenes that will, woo, blow your toupee off, gentlemen." He fanned himself with his hand. "How come you added the spice?"

Amused, Sydney said, "No idea. It just came to me, probably as a result of the things that happened in New York the last time I was here."

"But you did make time for a holiday and this year it was Greece, Athens, and the beautiful Greek islands. Mykonos, Santorini, Naxos, and the rest. I'm so jealous, and, of course, the paps managed to find you and invade your privacy and get photos of you with a hot Greek. What's his name?"

Photos of the two of them popped up on the screen behind them and the crowd whooped in delight.

"Spiros, and he is hot," she agreed.

"Any plans for Spiros to come to New York, or is he left in your dust like Gino?"

Sydney chuckled along with the audience. "Holiday romances, that's all they are. If I end up over there again next year, I'll have another one."

"You heard it here first, ladies and gentlemen. We'll be back shortly."

The producer counted them out and they had three minutes.

"I gotta say, Sydney, I got turned on by this book." Rhett tilted his face for a fresh coat of powder. "After last year's interview, I finished reading *Twisted Affair* and it was amazing. I read *The Perfect Man*, it was amazing. But this one, ooh." He shivered. "It has something a little different, a lot of sex, not just doing it, but thinking about it, it's spicy."

"And we're back on in three, two, one…"

"Welcome back to *Rockefeller.* We're with Sydney Kingston, author of the novels under the name Cassandra Kinsley. The latest is *The Shape of You.* It's sexy, it's different from her other books. Now Sydney." Rhett turned to her. "We were saying before the break about how you went back to Florida, and how you didn't release the novel about Madam X. Landon Security brought another stalker to court this year; it's getting to be a habit with you. A stalker a year, just like a book a year. Can you tell us about it?" He leaned back in his chair and settled in.

"Nothing to tell, Rhett; not my stalker. He was found to be a peeping tom from a number of neighbourhoods up my way and had been doing it awhile. He'd also been stealing ladies' undergarments when he could. So, a bit of a pervert as well."

"So I read in the papers. What I find about New York is it may only be a rough thirteen miles by two miles, but with over eight million people on this island, there are a hell of a lot of perverts, rapists, murderers, and criminals in general. We're like sardines in a submarine, all tightly packed and too many rotten ones stinking up the joint. Don't you agree?"

"It's a good analogy, and sadly, a true one," Sydney said. "New York is an amazing city, but human beings can be the scum of the Earth, no matter where they are."

"Very true," Rhett agreed. "And you write some pretty scummy characters in your books. Is that planned?"

"To a degree. You know if you're going to write in a particular genre such as crime or thriller, you're going to need a scummy villain who gets it in the end; whether it's male or female. You don't get a James Bond movie without a scummy villain. If we did, there'd be an uproar that it wasn't a real James Bond movie."

"Yes, yes." Rhett nodded excitedly. "Completely agree with that because it's true. Now, before we run out of time, are you *having* a book launch, *had* a book launch?"

"The book launch is tonight and I'll do promotion for the next few weeks."

"And do you have anything coming out for Christmas like last year for your fans?" Rhett held the book up one last time for the camera.

"You'll have to wait and see. I may have, I may not have," she teased.

"You'll have to stay tuned, ladies and gentlemen, but Sydney's crime thriller, *The Shape of You*, is available now in hardcover, and coming soon to every other format. We'll see you next year, Sydney."

"Same bat time, same bat channel," she quipped, getting a laugh out of the audience.

The camera zoomed in on Rhett. "Fantastic. Thanks, Sydney. Back to say goodbye in a few minutes, folks."

Sydney waited for the break to roll and shook Rhett's hand. "And we're done for another year. Good to know you actually read the whole book this time."

"I did and I loved every page of it." He smiled as an assistant took a photo of them. "And I can't wait for your next one because I've devoured every single one."

"Then you'd better stay tuned because there might be a few things coming," she said, and waved her fingers goodbye as she walked away. She met up with Amy in the dressing room and they headed back to the brownstone where they spent a few hours before changing and going to the book launch atop the *Belljar* restaurant in Manhattan. With gorgeous sun soaked views in every direction, it was the perfect afternoon for a five hundred person party to celebrate another book.

"Thank you so much for coming," Sydney said into the microphone. "It just seems like yesterday I launched the last one and here we are again." She received cheers and applause. "I hope you all read it, I hope you all loved it, and I hope you all keep it instead of passing it on or throwing it out. Meanwhile, let's party." She left the stage and merged into the crowd.

"Syd." Emerson rushed up to her best friend and enveloped her in a huge bear hug. "It's been too long."

"I know, but we kept in contact every Saturday, just like last year. And this year you came down for a couple of weeks." Sydney pulled back and stared at her. "I know you moved to New York to be with me, and I keep pissing off, so I am sorry."

Puzzled, Emerson shook her head. "What? No. I mean, yeah, I moved here because of the shit in L.A., and wanted to be near my BFF, but we've both settled into lives here, just as we had in L.A., so it's fine. As you said, we still had our online shopping extravaganzas on Saturdays, and I came down for a holiday, you were only there four months and *then* pissed off to Greece and met *another* hot Mediterranean stud. How do you do it?"

Sydney laughed. "Who knows. It might be a Spaniard next year."

"Olé!" Emerson said in a sexy tone. "Mind if I come?"

"I certainly do."

Emerson turned around to see Cormac and slid her arm through the crook of his. "I meant for a holiday. I managed to fly into Italy last year, and Greece this year, but only for a week each. I need a larger holiday and Spain next year sounds good."

"Then I might come along," he suggested. "Sydney, how are you?"

Sydney bristled slightly at the interruption. "Cormac.

Good, you? Or should I even ask since you're still dating Em."

"I'm doing fantastic, as is the new book, I see." He looked around the crowd and spotted a few people he knew of, but didn't know personally. "Even the mayor's here."

"Yeah." Sydney spun around in his direction to watch the mayor. "Maybe he thought this book was the one about Madam X and decided to see what's what."

"What happened to that book?" Emerson asked. "Did you even write it?"

Sydney turned back to them. "I did, and it's edited, formatted, and printed with a cover and proofs. We wanted a hard version of it to see what it would be like. Same with the bio of her I wrote. They exist; it's just a matter of *when* do we put them out."

"A lot of men would be worried about that book," Cormac said calmly, his hands in his pockets. "A lot of powerful men would be in it."

Sydney gave a shake of her head. "Not in either one of them. But in her client list, sure." She stared him square in the eye. "As I said on *Rockefeller* today, why are they so scared of people knowing they get their asses spanked? It's just foreplay."

Cormac's eyes narrowed and stared unblinkingly at Sydney.

She stared unblinking back, only to be interrupted by the mayor.

"Sydney Kingston, it is a pleasure. Nick Mananos." He encaged Sydney's hand within both of his large ones and pumped it up and down. "It's such a pleasure to finally meet you. I had to make a donation to your favourite charity to get onto the guest list."

Sydney frowned and yanked her hand from his. "No need to be so handsy, mayor. There was no need to bribe your way into the party you weren't invited to."

His dazzling smile froze. "What?"

"I know who's on the guest list. You weren't invited, and you've just told me you bribed your way in. Why?" She cocked her head to the side and took in his devastating good looks. He had dark, slicked back hair, hazel eyes, tanned skin, and shiny white teeth. "Scared this book was about Madam X, as I mentioned last year? Scared that I may have mentioned a mayor of New York City in the book? Scared people might think it was you?" She smiled sweetly and motioned to Cormac then Emerson. "You know Cormac, obviously, but this is my best friend, writer, director, producer, Emerson Lake. So far, she's turned five of my books into movies."

"And another two are on the way," Emerson said excitedly. "*Twisted Affair* and *The Perfect Man* are in pre-production as we speak."

"Oh, that's so nice." Nick smiled a sickening saccharine smile and nodded. "Emerson, pleasure to meet you. Cormac."

"Nick," was all Cormac said as he tried hiding a grin.

"Ah, Sydney." Nick saw her left brow rise and felt the beads of sweat slide down his back. "Ah, Ms Kingston, why would I be scared about any of that?"

"Because Madam X had a client list," Sydney said. "It's common knowledge and I cover it in the biography I wrote as the companion to the novel."

He licked his lips and swallowed his nerves. "But no one knows where that list is, or if it even existed in the first place."

"Oh, it exists," Sydney told him. "The girls who worked for her all mentioned it. Her lawyer mentioned it, and other reporters have mentioned it. But for some reason…" She lightly shrugged. "No one knows where it is. Who knows, it may surface one day, but again, why is everyone so worried about people finding out they had their ass spanked? Men get away with everything anyway, isn't that right, Mr Mayor?" She raised her brow again.

He breathed in. "I have no idea what you mean, Ms Kingston. It was a pleasure meeting you. Excuse me, I must leave early." He nodded at all of them. "Cormac, Ms Lake." He strode away, his flunkies either side.

"And exactly what *do* you know, Syd?" Emerson asked curiously.

"A lot." Sydney wiggled her brows. "Amy did my research, and we found a lot. But, alas, I need to mingle and I see another Ryan coming this way."

Cormac turned around to see his father and stepped aside.

"Sydney," Douglas greeted her warmly. "How are you, my dear? Another smash bestseller."

"It is, and I've been pretty good, thank you. You're looking fit and healthy."

"I'm spry as a rabbit and ready for the winter hibernation." He patted his still flat stomach. "And the doctor says I'm fit as a fiddle."

"Good to know." She smiled. "How'd you like the book?"

"Well, this one's a whole lot spicier than your previous books. But I didn't mind one bit. And I certainly don't think Cormac minded after Emerson read the book."

"Oh, my God." Sydney's brows rose rapidly and her jaw dropped in shock.

"Douglas, how could you?" Emerson went bright red and covered her face.

"Pop, seriously. There's no need for that," Cormac complained.

"Okay." Sydney looked away in embarrassment. "Ah, I'm off to mingle." She left them arguing over a lack of decorum and made her way through the crowd, coming across Maria, Declan's detective partner.

"Hey, you," she said, giving Sydney a hug. "Good to see you again. Haven't seen you since you got back to town."

They'd been friendly since meeting at the launch for *Twisted Affair.*

"In all fairness, I only got back at the end of August," Sydney said, picking a drink from the tray a waiter was holding. "It's been non-stop book talk since getting ready for the next few weeks."

"I saw the photos of you and the hunky Greek." Maria sipped her cocktail. "I'm jealous. You should have invited me, I'm single and like Mediterranean men."

"Who doesn't? I told Em I might head for Spain next year. She invited herself along."

"Oh, my God, can I invite myself along?" Maria asked. "I love Spain."

"I don't know if I'm actually going yet. I probably won't know until next year."

"Are you heading back to Florida to write?"

"I don't know that, either. But it seems to make me more productive, so…" She shrugged and looked around the restaurant, spying CC canoodling with Douglas. "Man, that's weird."

"What?" Maria craned her neck in the direction Sydney was looking.

"I move here and my best friend meets Cormac and starts dating him. And then my publisher starts dating his father. Who's next? My editor, agent, assistant? Are they going to start dating the Ryan boys?"

"I heard that," Amy said from behind them. "Maria, Syd. Some singer wants to meet you."

"Who? I don't remember a singer on the guest list."

"Don't know, but they want to meet you, so let's get you over there so we can get home."

They left Maria to go and chat to the singer in question. It was some up-and-coming Australian who was a huge fan.

The afternoon turned into evening, and the sun setting over the bay made for a magnificent dusk and photo opportunity before everyone departed.

As everyone left, Sydney thanked them and said goodbye.

When Emerson, Cormac and Douglas departed she said, "I forgot to ask before how the family are. I know Em's told me through the year when we talked, but I didn't get to say it when it happened. I'm sorry about Laura. I know that hit Sean hard, but it must've hit the rest of the family hard as well."

Cormac breathed deeply and gave a nod. "It did.

Especially Sean, though, as he was just starting to have a better relationship with her."

"Declan, on the other hand," Douglas muttered.

"We're not getting into that, Pop," Cormac warned. "Some members didn't take it well. I'll leave it at that. And thank you."

Curious, Sydney glanced between him and Douglas, and made the decision to call Douglas in a couple of days to see if he'd be interested in a chat. "Thank you all for coming. I have a few weeks' worth of promotion to go if anyone wants to pop along to any of it."

"I might, since I don't have much else to do these days. Although knowing you, Sydney, has made me popular at my bridge club," Douglas said. "I'm getting more attention that I ever did."

"And I'll keep in touch about the movies," Emerson promised. "They'll be filmed next year."

"Great, can't wait." Sydney watched them leave and said goodbye to the rest of the guests before heading home, exhausted, with Amy.

Chapter 22

The next day, Sydney was on *The Preston Grant Show*.

"Sydney Kingston you've done it again," he said into the mic. "Another number one best-selling novel under your author name of Cassandra Kingsley. With a spicier than normal title, *The Shape of You*. I don't know how you do it, Sydney."

"Neither do I." She laughed. "But, like many other authors, I write a great book and have enough fans to buy it the day it comes out making it number one."

"According to Nielsen Book Scan that we checked, it surpassed one million today. That's extraordinary. Tell us about the book, the latest thriller, *The Shape of You*."

"It's about a man and a woman trying to find themselves while trying to find their way to each other and then together."

"I don't know whether that's cryptic, or just vague," Preston joked and everyone laughed.

"And I understand that, but I don't like giving the story away. The best way is to read the blurb."

Preston read it out on air and turned the book over in his hands. "It's an amazing cover, yet not very thrillery, like your previous ones. Although if I remember, the cover of *The Perfect Man* wasn't a thriller cover either. It was just a guy."

"Oh, good memory," Sydney said. "It was called *The Perfect Man* so it needed a man on the cover."

"But he's holding a rose," Preston complained.

"Did you see the back of the paperback?" Sydney asked. "You needed to, the internet went berserk."

"No, I didn't." Preston adjusted his mic. "Why? What's different about the back cover?

"It shows his back," Sydney started, and saw the tablet Amy was holding over her shoulder. "Here, here's the whole cover." She handed it to Preston.

"Oh, my God, yeah, now I get it. On the cover, the front cover, the guy is holding the rose in front of him, but on the back cover of the paperback, ladies and gentlemen, he's holding a knife up behind his back. So not so much the perfect man after all, but it's only on the print cover." He handed the tablet back.

"Also, on my website and the image has been added to the Amazon sale page so people have seen it since it was published."

"And how many copies of the paperback did you sell?" Hank asked.

"It's just ticked over two mill," Sydney told him.

"Jesus Christ!" Preston exclaimed. "And *Twisted Affair* has gone three or four mill now, I saw."

"It has," Sydney noted. "And *The Shape of You* is coming up behind, but have you actually looked closely at the cover of the book?"

Preston picked up the hard cover. "It's hands and

body curves."

"What's the body in?" Sydney asked.

"Ah…" He peered closer. "Oh, wait…is that water or some kind of fabric?"

"It's whatever you think it is, but it's to give the impression that something's happened."

"So wait…" Preston held it up so she could see the cover. "Is it water or fabric?"

"It's a sheet."

"Because they fuck in the book." Preston turned it around for another look. "A lot."

Sydney shook off the shock of him saying fuck on live radio. "Don't give too much away."

"I think everyone knows by now that the book has more sex in it than your others. So even though there's the thriller aspect, the couple also fucks, which isn't normal stuff for Cassandra Kingsley. How come?"

Sydney shrugged nonchalantly. "It's the story that came to me. That's what I wrote, regardless."

"And where's the Madam X book you said was coming?" Preston asked.

"Still on hold, unfortunately. It's written, done, proofs were published to see how it looked, but legalities keep getting in the way," Sydney informed him.

"Any of the men in Madam X's client list trying to sue you to keep it from being published?" Preston asked. "Because we all know there is one."

"A few have very quietly asked that it not be published, but the cold hard fact is, I don't mention names in either the novel or the biography. I mention specific jobs and job titles, so yeah; it would be easy to pick who the person was. As Jackie Collins says, I've changed the names of the not so innocent."

"So, no real names, all made up, but real job titles, yeah?" Preston leaned forward, intrigued by it all.

"No real names, all made up, but real job titles, yeah," Sydney repeated. "Which is why they're scared. And the particular people who quietly inquired wanted copies of the book before it went to print."

"Did they get it?"

"Fuck no!" Sydney exclaimed. "Their shit was eye roll inducing, let me tell you. They went to a madam and then had her arrested and thrown in jail, so what did they expect was going to happen to her files and notebooks? Of course, people know who her clients were, they're just morons. Are they going to kill off everyone that worked for her and might know the truth? I'm surprised they haven't already. Just goes to show they have no problem outing themselves."

"Will it ever be published?" Preston pushed the book away and leaned back, pulling the mic with him.

"Who knows at this rate? We've spoken to higher-ups, but they're all worried they're in it. We keep telling them, no names. Jesus, boys!" Sydney rolled her eyes. "This is what happens when you get your ass spanked. It comes back to bite you in the ass instead."

Preston laughed and applauded her. "Well done, Sydney Kingston. I hope that book is published one day because I really want to read it. But you're here for *The Shape of You*, your latest thriller which is going gangbusters as usual. I haven't read it yet; only the blurb and the online synopsis, but I will get to it this weekend.

It's my weekend reading. What will you be doing this weekend?"

"Who said it's a what?" Sydney cheekily said. "But I'll be wondering if you'll want to get your ass spanked when you've finished."

The boys in the room couldn't contain their laughter.

"We'll be right back, folks," Preston told the audience.

Hank had to roll to ad through his tears.

Everyone removed their headphones and shook hands.

"That was hilarious, Sydney, and now I can't wait to read it." Preston wiped his face. "But seriously, I'd love to read that Madam X novel. Could you sneak me a copy?"

"Why don't you stay tuned for Christmas instead," she said cryptically and walked out the door before he could say anything else.

*****

Sydney and Amy went home to rest and change for a book signing that afternoon.

"Hey," Nora called from the kitchen when they entered. "Just getting myself a snack. Want anything?"

"We've ordered pizza," Amy said. "It should be here any—" She was interrupted the doorbell. "Minute," she finished, and went to pay for it. She came back with a half meat lovers half chicken barbecue pizza the size of a car tyre sizzling in the box. She placed it on the table and flipped the lid open. The scent of meat and vegetables quickly filled the room.

"Ooohhh, that smells good." Nora nibbled on her bottom lip and looked down at her vegan crackers and cheese.

"You're welcome to have some." Sydney handed Amy a plate and then slid two slices of each onto her own.

Amy hesitated, and then grabbed a slice of each.

"No, it's okay." Nora watched Sydney get up and grab a pizza cutter from the drawer.

"We'll cut a couple of pieces in half, so we have more. Then you can have a slice of each." Sydney deftly sliced one piece of each in half and shared it with Amy. Having one and a half pieces of each variety wasn't a problem.

"Actually." Nora quickly settled at the table, plate in front of her, her crackers and cheese long forgotten. "If you don't mind."

Sydney served her and picked up her half slice of chicken, devouring it in four mouthfuls. She hadn't eaten since breakfast and it was almost three.

"Mmm, this is good," Nora mumbled around her slice. "So long since I've had pizza." She swallowed and took a swig of cola. "The last time I had pizza was with Lennie before I dumped his sorry ass."

"For good this time?" Sydney was used to the histrionics between her and her boyfriend. She'd heard them since last year.

"So far. He got so controlling, Ms K. When you went off to Florida again, he thought he could come round here and be king of the castle. I kept telling him, it's not his house and certainly not mine, so he couldn't do as he liked." She bit another piece off the slice. "But did he listen to me?" she mumbled. "No. He thought he could stay in your room. I said no and banished him. He thought he could get into your office. I said no and banished him. He thought we could try out the sex room. I said most definitely not, and if he didn't stop hunting for treasure and going where he liked, then he wouldn't be allowed in anymore."

Sydney had stopped eating to listen, surprised at the turn of events. She raised a brow at Amy who looked shocked. "And when was that, Nora?"

"While you were in Florida." She swallowed the last bite of her first piece and started on the second, completely unaware of her boss's gaze. "I kicked him out and told him to go home or I'd call the cops and Landon Security to get rid of him. I told him Landon checks in every night. He didn't like that either."

Sydney took a breath and exchanged another glance with Amy. "What about after I came back, and then headed off to Greece?"

Nora shrugged. "He did the same. But when you called and said you were coming home, I told him to get out. He'd been knocking on walls and floors. I didn't know why, and then I caught him doing it and asked. He said he was looking for Madam X's diary and any money she may have left behind. I told him, for like, the millionth time, to not be stupid because the couple renovated it and found nothing. So why would Ms K find anything. Why would there be anything left and that he needed to go. He wanted to get a hammer and smash a wall in. I told him I'd call the cops." She finished half her second slice and stopped to finish off her drink. "That's how I got this shiner." She pointed to her face. "He went digging for a hammer and stuff in the tool box and tried to smash a wall, but I jumped in front of him and stopped him. So, he hit me instead. It was an accident; I was in the way, on purpose, of course, trying to stop him. I told him if he did damage to your house he'd be arrested and I wasn't going to date someone who was willing to smash up someone else's home. Besides, I'd called Landon before I jumped in front and they have a key, so they came in and stopped him. It really scared him, Ms K. You should have seen his face. White as a ghost when those two big beefy security guards hauled him out. I told him I wasn't going to date him anymore and this was it. He could have jeopardised my job here and I'd be gone. So, no more."

"And when was that?" Amy asked.

"A couple of days after Ms K called that she was coming home. So, um…" Nora looked up at the ceiling as she thought. "Mid-August."

Amy nodded and looked at Sydney. Landon had told them all about it. But now they were hearing how much worse it was.

"Lennie had no right trying to get into my room or my office. It isn't his house. From now on, he's not invited. *And* he *will* be arrested for trespassing. Even if you get back with him, which I hope you don't." Sydney drank the remains of her Pepsi and pushed her chair back. "I hope it's well and truly over between you because he also has no right to damage my house." She cleared the plates while Amy cleared the glasses and took the pizza box out to the bin.

"I know, Ms K. That's why I stepped between him and the wall." Nora touched her fingers to her still yellow cheek.

"And thank you, Nora. You were brave, but you

could've let him do it and then I would've had him arrested and made him pay for repairs. That would've taught him a lesson. You didn't need to get hurt in the process."

"I know, Ms K." Nora sat on a stool and leaned on the island bench. "But I also used it as an excuse to break up with him. He's been controlling for some time now and I'm just sick of it. Now I have a shiner for it."

"And I wish it hadn't happened." Sydney wiped her hands on the tea towel and hung it on the stove handle. "We're off to rest and get ready for later. We're being picked up at five, and won't be back until probably close to midnight."

"That's okay. I'll watch TV or Netflix or something," Nora said. "Are you getting a cake tonight?"

"For the book? No, that came home from the launch the other day." Sydney checked her watch. "Shit. No time for a rest, Amy; better get changed. It's already after four."

They hurried upstairs and were ready to leave when the car turned up, arriving at the book talk and fan signing at five-thirty.

Sydney greeted her fans, waving and smiling as she made her way to the stage. She would be doing the talk before signing books.

"Well, hello everyone," Rhona said to the hundred strong crowd. "You are here to see Ms Sydney Kingston for an intimate book talk. She'll read an excerpt, answer questions, and then we're heading over to the side and opening up for the signing. We understand there's already a long line of people waiting for that. But let's get this started now, with Ms Sydney Kingston." She sat on the chair beside Sydney while the audience cheered. "Sydney, welcome."

"Rhona, audience." Sydney nodded her acknowledgment. "Pleasure to be here. Look at all of you lucky ducks here for the talk."

It had been a competition for the best 25 words or less as to why they wanted to come to the book talk for Sydney and her new book.

"Let's get into the book, Sydney. As publicist for Pulsate Publishing, the company that prints all of your books, every year I am blown away by what you come out with. And every year I have to come up with a campaign to get your books out there, but I have to say…" She looked around the audience. "At this rate, I don't have to do anything because the Cassandra Kingsley novels sell themselves. They really do. We're starting off with a reading from *The Shape of You.*" She picked up the book to show off before handing it to Sydney. "That way, we can get a feel of what the book is like. I've picked the best pages to read, not sex, but definitely spice. So, take it away, Sydney."

Sydney opened the book at the book mark and saw what Rhona had chosen. "Ah, this bit. You're going to love this," she told the audience.

They sat in rapt silence while Sydney spoke, reading two pages from the book. When she was finished, she closed the book and handed it back to Rhona. "Well, they were a couple of hot and spicy pages." A few titters went through the crowd.

"Let's get into talking about this book. Who's it about?" Rhona leaned towards Sydney. "Anyone hot in your life? Is it about the hot Italian from last year?"

Sydney laughed. "Oh, God no, and I will never reveal my sources or my influences. I don't know, Rhona." She sighed and waved her hands around her head. "Muse is here somewhere. She gives me all the ideas. She forms them and formulates the plan and plot of it all. I'm just the one she writes her stories through. But I will say this, oftentimes, it's based on something and then completely changed, so the not so innocent can't identify themselves."

"And your muse is responsible for all of your ideas?"

"Of course."

"When did you get the idea?"

"Early New Year. January, and it started forming from then. Once Valentine's Day was over, I went to Florida for the warmer weather and, as I seem to do, wrote non-stop, almost, until I'd finished it in April."

"And that was your first draft, which are always clean," Rhona said. "And from there you had edits, the cover, and blurb done. Do you come up with the cover yourself, or is it all Pulsate?"

"I'll let the design team know what's in my head, tell them a few scenes from the book and if I can find a similar style cover from another author I'll suggest that for inspiration. This cover was inspired by a French novel. The image was a body blurred in linen, hands all over. In my case, two bodies."

"Yes, I did see that and had to look closely when I first saw the cover. Did you notice that folks?" Rhona held the book up for them. "If you look closely, it's two bodies, wrapped in a satin sheet, hands touching, all blurred to look out of focus and dreamy. Definitely a different style for you, Syd. Veering off from the normal thriller style covers."

"There's more romance and sex in it and that's the image I got while writing it, so that's what we came up with."

"And it follows up the very successful *Twisted Affair* from last year and the novella you released at Christmas, *The Perfect Man*. You always write more than one book a year, and oftentimes release novellas and short stories on your own. Is there anything coming for Christmas this year?"

"There may be, I don't know yet. *Twisted Affair* got the juices flowing and *The Perfect Man* was a carry on from that. Who knows what I've got coming out next."

She went on to answer questions from the audience, sign their books, and take photos with them. When finished, she walked towards the other side of the store for the signing, with Amy, Rhona, and Landon Security in tow.

A sound started up in the store and caught their attention. A kerfuffle followed and their gaze turned to see. A man hurried up to Sydney and threw a tin of white paint at her. It splashed onto her torso and up to her face before falling down her body to drip down her jeans and pool on her boots. The stench of solvent wafted over her, invading her sinuses.

Stunned into silence, Sydney could only watch Landon's guards slam the man to the ground and cuff his hands behind his back. One of them called the police. The other called Holland Landon.

"Oh, my God, Sydney," Rhona shrieked.

"Oh, Ms Kingston." Melissa Burnell, the manager, came rushing over, her jaw hanging in shock as she looked from Sydney to the books on the nearby shelves. "Oh, my God. My store, my books, oh."

Amy snapped to attention. "We need to get Sydney to a backroom to clean up. Get rags, get towels, get whatever you have," she told her and they rushed Sydney to the storeroom. They wiped her down the best they could, but that wasn't good enough. Her clothes were ruined.

She'd been able to save most of her jewellery and had taken it off. "Amy, is there a store nearby? Go and buy me some jeans, a top or t-shirt, and some shoes so I can change."

"Are you still going ahead with the signing?" Melissa asked. "But you're covered in paint."

"I won't be when I change," Sydney said, watching Amy hurry out the door and Detective Ryan and his partner walk in.

"Oh, my God, Sydney," Maria cried. "Are you okay?" She took in the destroyed outfit and Sydney's pissed off expression.

"Do I look okay?" Sydney asked, raising a brow. "I have paint all over me. Toxic fumes up my nose, and my clothes are probably destroyed."

"So, what happened?" Declan asked, a little unnerved seeing Sydney for the first time in two years. The last time had been when he reamed her out over grooming Sean.

"What does it look like, Declan?" Sydney snapped. "Some wanker threw paint over me and now I have to wait for Amy to buy me some clothes so I can change and continue with the signing."

"You're going ahead with it?" he said in a cocky tone. "Why would you…" He waved his hand at her. "Bother now?"

"Because it's the job," Sydney replied. "Just as getting spat on and called a pig is part of yours."

Declan sneered at her. "Yeah, it's in every brochure welcoming us to the academy. We've arrested the asshole and I'll take him and charge him with assault, criminal damage to the store, and whatnot. You'll need to give your statement as will you." He pointed to the manager. "And you can put in a damage report. We have our team taking photos to show the damage as we'll need photos of you, Ms Kingston."

"Make sure Landon Security gets a report so I can file personal damages against the thug," Sydney told them as Amy rushed in.

"I only got jeans, a t-shirt, and sneakers." Amy dropped the bags onto the desk. "Do you need Sydney's clothes?' she asked. "Because you'll need to get out for her to change."

"Not at this time," Declan said. "We'll get the tech guys in to take photos. Maria." He left the room with Maria following. She waved goodbye.

The techs came in and photographed and videoed Sydney from every angle before allowing her to change.

She quickly slid into the jeans and blue t-shirt, and laced up matching sneakers. "How'd you manage to get them in matching colours?" She stood up and adjusted the t-shirt. "Wonder Woman. Really?"

Amy shrugged. "Thought it was suitable, considering

the situation." There was a knock at the door and she opened it to Declan. "Detective, you're back."

He looked a little sheepish, and said, "Ah, yeah, hey, ah, can I talk to Sydney for a second?"

Amy opened the door to let him in and closed it after him. "I'm staying." She crossed her arms and stood sentry at the door.

He looked from Amy to Sydney. "Yeah, I ah, I ah, need to apologise for what happened a couple a years ago."

"Because your father demoted you, reamed you out, and banned you from seeing me, not because you realised you were wrong and should apologise?" Sydney asked.

He had trouble answering and looked everywhere but at Sydney. "Ah, yeah. But look, ah, after what you did in L.A., you got balls, you know. And you got my mother's killer. So, thank you for that. And ah, I'm…sorry for what I did with Sean. Turns out, I ballsed that up myself."

"No shit, Sherlock! You did, and I hope you still feel bad about it." Sydney arched her brow.

He had the decency to go bright red and embarrassment overcame him. "Yeah, yeah, you're right. After all of that, ah, I'm sorry for my behaviour and ah…" He started backing away. "I ah, need to go. So, again, sorry." He turned and saw Amy had opened the door. "Ah, thanks. I'll get on this right away. Sorry 'bout your outfit."

Amy closed the door after him. "What the actual fuck?" she asked in amazement.

"You can say that again," Sydney replied.

An hour after the incident, Sydney took her place behind the desk and the signing proceeded. She stayed an extra hour to make up the time, took photos, chatted, and explained the situation with anyone who asked. It wasn't the first time someone had been an arsehole to her, but it was the first time she'd had paint thrown at her. When her hand tired, she flexed it and slid on her wrist strap to keep going, and by eleven, had finished signing everyone's book.

At midnight, she entered the brownstone under the watchful eye of Landon Security and headed up to bed as they took Nora home.

*****

He turned away as the security team drove off. He'd followed Sydney home from the signing, having been lucky enough to win a ticket to the book talk, and had donned a disguise so she wouldn't recognise him. He didn't want that. Didn't want her to know who he was. To recognise him.

He quickly made his way down the road, turned right at the corner, and hurried to the back lane that would lead him to Sydney's back yard. He hurried, silently, and jumped the fence when he arrived. Quiet as a feline. No sound to be heard.

He walked across the yard, staring up at her bedroom window. The light was barely discernible behind heavy curtains. But he knew she was in there. She'd be in the shower washing off the paint. Scrubbing her delicate flesh clean of the stain. He salivated, licked his lips in anticipation, and made his way down to the basement door.

*****

The next morning, the incident turned up on social media and in the news; mainly gossip sites who stole pictures from those who were there and posted about it.

Amy scrolled on. "Not too many saw it, just a few who were already in the store waiting, and someone was arrested by the cops. They were with the dickhead who threw the paint from the look of it."

"Great, that's all I need. Pictures of me with paint from head to toe in the press. Fucking hell."

"Don't think you can stop it, unfortunately, so I suppose it'll come up tomorrow during your interviews. You'd better have something prepped."

Groaning, Sydney was about to say something when her phone rang. "Hey, Em."

"Oh, my God, Sydney, are you okay? You got painted last night."

"Technically," Sydney replied. "A few paint fumes, my clothes wrecked, my jewellery survived, luckily, nothing other than that."

"That's good to know. And good for you for changing clothes and getting on with it."

"That's the job. Problem was, Ryan number three turned up with Maria."

"Declan? Jesus! How'd that go?"

"Awkwardly," Sydney said. "He apologised, well, tried to apologise for two years ago. Told him too little, too late."

"That's going to be a great Sunday lunch," Emerson said sarcastically. "Considering Sean's still living with

Cormac and Douglas half the time."

"Only half? Is he on campus?"

"Monday through Thursday. Friday to Sunday he's at home. Busy little beaver he is too. Always writing, locking himself away in his room, or out in the backyard looking at the city."

"I haven't heard from him since the funeral, so at least he's abided by Cormac's rule."

"Can't say the same for Declan, though." Emerson chucked. "But at least it's been two years."

"And it can be another two years for all I care." Sydney yawned. "We on for Saturday?"

"Of course. You working?"

"Nope. Everything's Monday through Thursday. Friday, Saturday and Sunday are free."

"Great. I'll come and pick you up. See you then. Bye, Syd."

"Bye, Em."

Chapter 23

On Thursday, Sydney had radio interviews all morning and magazine interviews all afternoon. She and Amy found time for lunch and dinner, and in between it all they stopped for a spot of shopping before heading home around eight.

Laughing and giggling about all they'd bought and done, they alighted from the limo that dropped them off five houses down, and walked the rest of the way to the brownstone.

As they approached, Sydney saw that the parlour curtains were wide open with the interior lights shining through, and the door looked to be at an odd angle. "Is the door shut? It doesn't look it."

They arrived at the bottom of the stairs to find the door was open and the body of Nora lying upside down on the stoop, her torso draping the stairs, blood seeping out of her and crawling down the concrete steps. It pooled at Sydney's feet.

"Oh, my God." Sydney's bags fell from her hands. "No," came out in a scream and she moved up the stairs, arms out, towards Nora. "No, no, no, no." She felt for a pulse and found one. "Help me get her flat. She's still alive. Call the ambulance. Somebody help," she screamed and they half dragged, half carried Nora back to the stoop to lay her flat.

While Amy called 911, Sydney took off her coat and covered the wounds. "Put the phone on speaker, hold it to her body. Nora." She leaned close. "Nora, can you hear me? Hang on, sweetie. The ambulance is on its way. Hang on, Nora." She helped Amy hold the coat to the wounds with more force, constantly looking in Nora's eyes. "You're not alone, Nora. We're here. We're here, hang on, sweet girl, just hang on." She checked Nora's neck. No pulse. She started chest compressions. "Come on, Nora, don't leave. You deserve more out of life than this. Come on, baby, come back." She stopped to breathe into Nora's mouth then resumed pumping. "Come back, Nora. Come back. Come on, baby." She stopped and breathed into her mouth. "Come on, Nora, sweet girl, come back. You have to watch the house next year, come on." She resumed chest compressions and didn't even realise the paramedics had arrived, the cops had arrived, and three Ryans were on her stairs staring at her.

Declan moved up to the stoop and leant down to feel Nora's pulse. He shook his head. "Sydney…Sydney… Sydney!" He grabbed her hands and she looked up sharply at him. "She's gone," he said softly. "She's gone." He watched her and Amy take a moment to comprehend his comment and the situation and then burst into tears. He took a step back before turning to his brother and nephew who watched them in shock. "Ethan, control the crowd." He pointed at the sticky beaks across the road. "Connor, get the scene processed."

"And why are you in charge?" Connor demanded. "I'm older."

"Not now, Connor. I got here first; it's my crime scene, I take lead, now go." Declan waved him off and carefully avoided Nora's blood on the way down the stairs. He spoke to the paramedics. "She's gone, but do your thing. I'll get crime scene in." He looked around and saw the toppled shopping and handbags on the path and picked them up.

The paramedics moved up the stairs slowly, avoiding any evidence. They knelt beside a crying Sydney and Amy, checked for a heartbeat, checked her pupils, and blood pressure. Exchanging a glance, they shook their heads and called the coroner.

Declan moved back up to the stoop. "Amy, Sydney, let's get you inside. They need to take care of the body." He gently grasped Sydney by the arms and pulled her back, and once she was leaning against him, lifted her up so she was standing. "Amy." He grasped her arm and pulled her up, then led them both into the brownstone, sitting them side by side on the couch in the living room. He looked around. If the door was open, maybe there'd been a robbery. Stealthily moving into the kitchen, he saw the doors shut and the shutters down. He moved upstairs and turned the knob on the library door. It was locked. Up to the next floor, he checked the bedrooms, and on the top floor, the master was also locked. He rushed down to the basement and found the back door triple bolted. He hurried back upstairs and looked above the front door.

"She had surveillance," Connor told him.

Declan eyed his older brother. "And you know this how?"

"She got a dead rat two years ago, I'm assuming they're still working, as they have Landon Security on the side." Connor pointed at one with his pen. "State of the art."

"And speaking of Landon." Declan looked up and down the street. "I don't see any of them here. Wouldn't they have seen it happen?"

"Probably," Connor drawled, watching Nora's body be zipped into a body bag. "Poor girl. So young. Doesn't deserve that."

"Did you know her?" Declan asked, his stomach churning with memories of Laura's body being carried away the year before in the same manner. He pushed the memories down and swallowed the lump in his throat.

"No, never met her," Connor replied, walking around the pool of blood on the stoop. "Guess we'd better talk to Syd and get that recording."

"Syd?" Declan raised a brow. "You're close enough to call her that?"

"I was," Connor returned. "Once."

Ethan came bounding up the stairs. "Hey, Grandpa's coming. It must've got out that this is Sydney's house."

"Ah, damn. The whole goddamn family's gonna be here in a minute," Declan complained as all three watched the cavalcade of SUVs pull up behind his car. Cormac, Douglas and Emerson climbed out with Emerson running ahead.

"Sydney? Is it Sydney?" she screeched, running for the

stairs, only to be stopped by Ethan.

"No, no, stop, watch the crime scene," Declan yelled, his hand flying out to stop her. "Go up the side, stick to the rail, so you don't step in the blood. It's not her, Emerson. She's inside. Sydney's inside." He waited for his father and grandfather to ascend the stairs and look over the crime scene before they gathered in Sydney's living room.

"Sydney." Emerson flew to her friend, hugging her as she sat statue still. She looked at her face and wiped the tears away. "Syd. Amy. You okay?"

"Alive," Amy managed.

Emerson sat beside Sydney, seeing their bloodstained hands. "Oh, my God. Who?"

"The house sitter," Declan said, looking down at the three of them.

"Nora?" Emerson glanced from him to Sydney. "Oh, my God. That sweet girl. Who would do this to her?"

At those words, Sydney and Amy looked at each other and said one name in unison. "Lennie."

"Who's Lennie?" Declan asked, pulling out his notebook.

"Her boyfriend. He's been harassing her for over a year. They fight, break up, get back together. She dumped him, she said for good, in August. He was about to demolish my basement wall looking for Madam X's diary or money." Sydney noticed several Ryans flinch. "She stepped between him and the wall and copped a hammer to the face. Landon got him out and had charges laid."

"He should be on file then," Connor said. "You got a last name?"

Sydney sighed and shook her head. "No, but I think he's a mechanic. He wears an overall onesie with his name on it across the left breast. No idea where he lives."

"We'll track him down, don't worry," Declan said. "Anyone else you can think of? You got Landon Security. We'll need those files."

"I'll get you a copy." Amy looked at her hands and got to her feet. "You'd think I'd be used to this." She hurried away to wash.

"She never talked about anyone else," Sydney murmured, staring at her hands. The blood wasn't quite dry. "They were on again, off again. All the goddamn time."

"And your stalkers?" Declan pushed on. "You've had a couple."

"And so far, not violent, *unlike* members of *your* family," Sydney replied, sending a scathing glare at Declan and Connor, before that fell away and she looked at Cormac and Douglas. "She said this was the best job she'd ever had and didn't want to lose it even for Lennie. She was only in her twenties." The tears poured forth. "She had so much to still live for and do." She broke down, her head falling into her stained hands.

Emerson rubbed her back and said to Cormac. "I'm going to stay."

He nodded. "Of course. Pop and I will go. Sydney, we're so very sorry for your loss, and if there's anything we can do, let us know." He turned to his sons. "Boys, no need for all of you. Start clearing up the crime scene and get this street back to normal. The residents deserve that." He left with Douglas following.

"Ethan," Connor said. "Let's go."

Ethan glanced at his father and then longingly looked at Sydney. They'd broken up just after New Year, more specifically after his aunt Laura's death. She'd told him his family was too fucking complicated. He'd agreed, but wanted to continue seeing her; he was falling in love with her. She'd told him he was a sweet kid and she was too old for him, she didn't want a relationship, just fun. Time to move on. He hadn't seen her since. With a last longing look, he left with his father.

Amy came into the living room. "The last 24 hours surveillance. Landon would have the same."

"Was there meant to be a car out there standing guard?" Declan pocketed the disc.

"No." Sydney wearily shook her head. "Only if there were threats of some kind. There hadn't been except for the dude who threw paint on me and he's being monitored."

"Okay, we'll check the footage and this dude who threw paint again. Meantime…" He paused, trying to find the words. "I'm sorry about your house sitter. You obviously liked her a lot and this sucks." He hurried out the door.

"What do we do now?" Sydney asked. "What do we do?"

"Let the police do their job," Emerson said, rubbing her back. "Oh, Syd, I'm so sorry."

"So am I," Sydney replied. "She didn't deserve it, so I need to do something."

"Like what?" Amy rubbed at the remnants of the blood that wouldn't come off after washing.

"Like paying for her funeral, with the family's blessing. Casket, headstone, service, anything she would've wanted." Sydney absentmindedly rubbed her hand the way Amy was doing. "I need to do something to make it up to her. Even if it's killing the cunt who did this."

*****

Rhona and Pulsate cancelled all promotion forthwith when Emerson called them with the news. CC told her to tell Sydney not worry about anything and take all the time she needed.

Sydney spoke to Eric about a lawyer and he hooked her up with one. She needed to know what she was in for legally, and needed someone to approach the family. Her lawyer did, and Sydney met with them on the weekend. Coming to an arrangement, crying and reminiscing with memories, Sydney offered to pay for the funeral and service.

Only the best for Nora.

*****

The funeral was held a week later. Nora was buried in a white coffin with gold details. An angel headstone had been picked, and doves were released. It was a beautiful service, and even though Sydney sensed hatred towards her, she held up under the strain. Nora deserved this, so she bore it.

*****

Lennie was arrested for the crime, even though the footage didn't show the man's face. He pleaded innocent, but considering he'd run after the stabbing and the cops found him in upstate New York, it didn't bode well for Lennie Cuzco.

He was charged with first degree murder and sent to Rikers Island to await trial.

*****

Finally, in December, Sydney emerged from her self-imposed hibernation of grief and met with CC at Pulsate. Olivia, Gemma, Amy, and Emerson attended.

"I'm thinking of leaving New York," Sydney told them. "Permanently."

"What!" Emerson cried. "But where would you go? Back to Australia? I wouldn't see you!"

"I know," Sydney said morosely. "But after everything, this just feels..." She threw her hands up in resignation and sighed. "Cursed. The brownstone is cursed. New York is cursed. I'm cursed."

"Don't be ridiculous," Emerson chastised. "Of course you're not. Maybe you just need a priest or something to come in and cleanse the place."

"Nora was killed there, Emerson," Sydney snapped. "You don't cleanse that away."

"Do the police know if she was the target?" CC caught the hurt look Emerson flashed Sydney. "Maybe it was you they were after."

"God, can you imagine?" Sydney said, and rubbed her tired eyes. "But Nora looked nothing like me. She had long red hair and pale skin and was skinnier than me. Plus, the lights were on. There was no reason to mistake her for me, or me for her. If she'd been stalked, he'd know what she looked like. If I was being stalked, he'd know what I looked like. So why would he make a mistake? It had to be Lennie."

"You don't know that," CC told her. "It could have been someone she knew, but wasn't Lennie. He's declared he's innocent. What if he is?"

"It'd be one hell of a joke if he was," Sydney said. "One of us was the target. One of us ended up dead after standing on the stoop under bright lights. There was no mistake. He was after Nora."

"What if it was a woman?" Amy inquired. "What if a woman who hates Nora dressed up like a man and went after her? Or, for that matter, what if a woman was after you and dressed up like a man to get to you? But she may not have known what you looked like and assumed Nora was you because she was there."

"Who would do that?" Sydney asked. "Why would a woman be after me?"

"A sick psycho fan," Olivia considered. "Maybe she thinks you took her boyfriend."

Sydney thought about all the men she'd been with since moving into the brownstone. Declan Ryan was the latest, and that had come as a complete surprise to both of them. He'd stopped by every few days to see how she was and to update her on the case, to sympathise with the death of a loved one. And one night, while crying and drinking, a lethal combination that really should never happen, Sydney and Declan had started kissing and one thing led to another and they fucked on the kitchen table. That was November and he'd been a regular visitor ever since, even getting to use the sex room which he liked more than most should.

"I don't think so," she finally said. "I've only had a couple of gentleman callers since being here. I've spent most of my time in Florida or Europe, so really, what's the point in me staying here?"

"How about moving?" Gemma asked. "Just move to a more secure location. An apartment, a hotel suite?"

"Invasive, intrusive," Sydney replied. "I need privacy, quiet."

"Otherwise, you can't have gentlemen callers." Olivia sniggered.

"It's coming up to Christmas in a few weeks," Emerson said quietly. "What will you do? Where will you go?"

Sydney gave a half-hearted shrug. "Don't know, Em. Maybe I'll keep hibernating and let Christmas and New Year bypass me altogether."

"You can't spend it alone." Emerson was shocked. "Come spend it with us."

"Why not? Why can't I spend it alone?" Sydney asked her. "I spent it with CC last year, and I most certainly can't spend it with the Ryans."

"Ah…" Emerson realised. "Sean."

"Two years ago, Cormac said he'd tell his family to stay away from me. So far, half of them haven't. But Sean has, except for after his mother's funeral, and I won't jeopardise his mental health. He's too young. Maybe I'll do something for Nora's family, or work at a soup kitchen or something." Sydney got to her feet and meandered over to the window overlooking the city. She shivered as she looked at the Freedom Tower, and knew her issues didn't even come close to what those who went through that day experienced. But what was she going to do? Move to another house? Another state? Another country?

"Sydney, dear." CC stood beside her and smoothed her Chanel jacket. "Whatever you decide to do will be up to you. We'll still have our relationship, of course, as we can do that via Zoom and emails."

"I know. I just…" Sydney shrugged. "I'm at a loss. This has me shaken up and the last time someone died at my house we packed up everything and ran away. So, what do I do now?"

"Celebrate Nora, keep on with your life, and make sure her killer is put behind bars," CC suggested. "You can't stop living because others don't."

Sydney stared at the Freedom Tower. "So many others don't."

"I know, and one day, I won't and you won't. One day, every single person in this room will be gone and it will be empty and we'll all be in the great beyond. Don't stop living, Sydney. You need to keep moving on. Moving forward."

Sydney thought about all of the plans she had. The plans she had to execute before her time was done. She breathed in, her body shifting upwards with the intake. "You're right, CC I need to keep living. I have plans to execute and they need to be done sooner, rather than later. I had a five year plan when I moved here. We're two years in and I have books to write and release." She turned to face everyone. "It's Christmas in a few weeks. I won't be getting you presents, same as always, and I'll continue in exile until the week of it, but CC, if you're having a party like last year, then I'm in."

"Oh, darling, I don't know if I will. Douglas has invited me to spend Christmas and New Year with him and the family, so I'm not sure if I'll have the party. Unless I have it earlier. It is for the company after all."

Surprised, Sydney could only breathe. All words failed her. She'd lost Emerson to the Ryan family, now she'd lost CC. She found her voice. "Whatever you plan to do is up to you. But if it's a party, I'm in. Amy? What are you doing?"

"Not sure. My family's on holiday this year, so who knows. Maybe we can party together?"

"Maybe," Sydney murmured and crossed her arms and sat down. "Maybe it's time to let go and once New Year rolls around set next year's plan in motion. I have one every year, so I'll set my mind on that and think about the future come January. I'll either move or just get on with it. But for now, I suck it up and finish grieving."

And there was only one plan Sydney had in mind that needed to be executed soon.

PART FOUR

Nine months later

Chapter 24

"Coming up today on *Rockefeller*, Sydney Kingston with her new novel."

The opening credits rolled and Rhett took the seat next to Sydney. He was counted in and said, "Hello, and welcome to *Rockefeller*. I'm your host, Rhett Rockefeller, and today we talk the latest novel by Sydney Kingston under her pen name of Cassandra Kingsley. Welcome to the show for another year, Sydney."

"Thanks for having me back, Rhett. I've been on every year for years, even before I moved here. You seem to be the first stop on the promo tour every time I release." Though she had a new book to promote, Sydney didn't want to be there. The book, and the idea behind it, were still too fresh.

"We're back to the thriller covers we know and love from Cassandra Kingsley, the pen name you write under. *Her Last Words* is the name of the book, folks, and yes, it's a little macabre looking. Does it have anything to do with last September, Sydney? You don't have to talk about it."

"Her family got a chance to read it," Sydney said

quietly. "I wrote it, showed them, and they said she'd be excited about being the inspiration for a Cassandra Kingsley novel. She told them she loved working for her favourite author and they wanted me to publish it, in her honour. That's why it's dedicated to her."

Rhett nodded, and gave the moment silence before moving on. "For those who don't know, last year in September, a year ago, just a week after releasing her last book, *The Shape of You*, Sydney's house sitter, Nora Ramotti, was brutally murdered on the steps of Sydney's brownstone. Sydney, and her assistant Amy, found her and tried to save her. But they were too late. She died." Rhett cleared his throat and breathed in. "Sydney not only paid for Nora's funeral, but wrote the book in her honour. Now, Sydney." He swivelled in his chair to look at her and gently placed a hand on her arm. "This must've been hard? Tell us how you did it."

Sydney breathed slowly. She'd known this was going happen, and had prepared for it. But under the hot blaring studio lights, her stomach churned and sweat dripped down her spine. "I hibernated until January. Grieved in private. Didn't finish promoting the last book, but I didn't really need to, the publicity over Nora escalated sales. For some reason, people thought it had to do with Madam X, but I don't believe it did." She breathed in. "I believe someone mistook her for me, or knew it was her and took her life because they wanted to. When January came, I got myself in gear with my usual business plan, but all I could think of was Nora and finding her body." Her eyes watered and a tear spilled over and down her cheek. "And suddenly the idea sprang to mind. Almost as if Nora was telling me what happened and I wrote it all down. This is her story as told by her from the plane she's on. She hadn't crossed over yet. I believed she was still around to get her story out."

"Oh, Sydney." Rhett quickly swiped at his cheek so no one saw the tear. "Many people listening or even watching, won't or don't believe in ghosts."

"I don't care!" Sydney cut in. "This isn't about them and their beliefs, this is about a sweet young girl who wouldn't hurt a fly being stabbed on my stoop on the Upper East Side for fuck's sake." Sydney turned to glare into the camera. "And if you did it, I'm going to use every last cent I have hunting you down so I can kill you myself. You got that you motherfucking cunt!"

"Okay, we'll take a break now, back after these messages." Rhett smiled until the monitor went black, then let out, "Fuck, Sydney, you can't swear on my show."

"Just did," Sydney retorted. "What are you gonna do about it? I'm here to promote my book about the death of a young girl. Of course, this interview was going to get heated. You knew it would. You expected it."

"And we're back in three, two, one..."

"Welcome back to *Rockefeller*, where I can't promise there will be no more swearing," Rhett joked. "But in all seriousness, the topic of your book, Sydney, is an incredibly hot one. Still, after a year…how much closer are they to finding young Nora's killer?"

"They're not," Sydney said. "And they let the only suspect they did have go because there wasn't enough evidence against him."

"That would be Lennie Cuzco, Nora's ex-boyfriend," Rhett told the audience. "He's been silent since getting out of prison after the trial. Which was way too fast in my opinion. So, this book has been dedicated to Nora and you said her spirit gave you the story. How did that work?" He leaned back in his chair, looking at the cover of the book.

"Just like my muse, and maybe it was and not Nora, I was given the initial idea and the rest flooded in like tidal waves. I couldn't write fast enough, so I started dictating the book instead, and it poured out of me. When Amy, my assistant, was typing it up, she swears she heard Nora's voice on the recordings." She shuddered. "I listened back to them and Amy pointed out which parts, and I gotta say, it kinda did sound like her. I was either channelling her, or her spirit was coming through. It was quite eerie, but she obviously wanted her story told, and I told it."

"The novel doesn't actually solve *her* homicide, and things are a little twisty at the end in the book, and I won't say too much about it, but did she tell you who it was?" Rhett asked.

"I really don't know," Sydney said in all honesty. "I received what I think I was meant to receive, and as long as I heard her voice, she was telling her story. She may or may not have remembered who killed her, but then again, maybe there's a clue in there somewhere that someone can find, because I still think it was Lennie."

"And she and her boyfriend had had fights and broken up just weeks prior to her death," Rhett mentioned. "It was all over the news for months and has now stirred back up thanks to this book. Your new book, *Her Last Words*. All I can say is I hope they find the son of a bitch because too many women and children suffer at the hands of asshole men, not just in this country, but around the world. Asshole men are arrogant and entitled enough to do what they like and use their religion, or their colour, their race, their culture, their ethnicity, or even their financial status as an excuse to get away with it. And it needs to stop. It's time it stopped," Rhett declared and the audience cheered wildly.

"In fact." He stood up and faced the audience. "It *is* time to make it stop, and as the host of America's most popular daytime TV show, I vow right here, right now, to do more to get this insanity into the spotlight. To get more stories of the women and children whose lives are taken by animal asshole men." The audience got to their feet, applauding as loud as they could. "As a man, *I* need to do more to help. To bring light to the dark, bring publicity to the forgotten. I don't care what race, colour, creed, ethnicity, nationality, sex, age, religion, blood group or star sign you are, if you rape you're a rapist, if you kill you're a murderer, if you molest you're a paedophile. If you are the victim of any asshole of a man, you will be promoted on this show."

He walked back and forth addressing the crowd like a preacher high on adrenaline. "Once a month, hell, once a fortnight, we will do a show on missing people, dead people, victims of crime, crimes against women and children, and I will do what I can to help bring justice to the families of the victims. Even if it's as simple as showing their picture and telling you their name here on

Rockefeller. My promise is to help the families of victims of the most heinous crimes of all. And," he thrust a thick forefinger at the camera, "we will get results. We'll be right back, ladies and gentlemen." He spun around and walked back to his seat.

Sydney appraised him with a scornful raised eyebrow, her legs crossed. She was playing with a ring on her left hand. "Really, Rhett? You're going to solve crimes and help families by giving them what? Five minutes of your time once a fortnight?"

"I'm going to do more than that, Sydney, you've got me inspired now." He drank half of his water and it was quickly refilled. "I used to be a reporter, remember, back in my early days. And back then I was always looking for a juicy story to sink my teeth into, but I never had the chance. Now I do. I have the money to hire detectives, I have the status to draw attention, and I have the highest ratings in daytime TV to broadcast to the world."

Sydney eyed him ruefully. "I wish you luck, Rhett, and hope nothing happens to you. There's a lot of arseholes out there, so I hope none of them kills you to keep you quiet and their secret kept safely in the dark."

"And we're back in three, two, one…"

"Welcome back to *Rockefeller.* Just before the break I went on a bit of a rant about victims and the assholes committing the crimes. I meant every word. It's all inspired by Sydney Kingston's latest novel, *Her Last Words,* written for, and about, her young house sitter who was brutally murdered on her doorstep. But…" Rhett relaxed into his chair. "Let's talk about everything else you've done in the last year, Sydney. Normally, or for the last few years, you've disappeared down to Florida to write, and then taken a European vacation where you've canoodled with a hot new lover." He glanced at the crowd and waited for them to titter. Only a few did. "But this year, you didn't. Care to share what you did, because there was nothing much on your socials explaining your absence."

She gave a light shrug. "Besides choosing to *not* celebrate my fiftieth birthday this year, and dealing with the release of the movies for *Twisted Affair* and *The Perfect Man*, I had a quiet Christmas and New Year, hibernating until January when I started writing the book. I didn't go to Florida this time because Nora's not there. She's here, at the brownstone, and I wrote the book in January. Amy typed it up in February, it was edited and type set in March, cover in April."

"But only released now. Why the wait?"

"September is my release date. But I was also writing other things, including opinion pieces for websites and magazines. I worked this case with Landon Security, and with help from the detective on the case. Like you, I got an instinct to look into victims and there are thousands, and I wasn't done writing about it *or* them. I felt Nora was urging me on, pushing me to write more and more as if I'd come to a conclusion eventually. I spent time at refuges and shelters, donated goods and supplies, convinced some businesses to get involved by donating their leftover daily food, spare tins, fruit and veg, linen and bedding. I went to scratch and dent sales and scored white goods for the shelters if they needed them. I worked my arse off this summer helping out in all five boroughs of New York, donating my time, money, *and* mouth to helping victims of crime and the pursuit of the arsehole cunts committing them. Quite frankly…"

She paused for the applause to die down before continuing. "It's time the death penalty was overhauled in most western countries, my own included, and brought back for rape, murder, and paedophilia. Criminals need to be pushed through faster, got rid of faster, and for the love of fucking God, stop your stupid fucking brain dead love affair with guns."

The crowd stood as one, cheering, and screaming wildly.

Rhett calmed them down. "And that, ladies and gentlemen, is why Sydney Kingston didn't go to Florida this year, because she was too busy bringing crimes into the light and helping people in need. Go out and buy Sydney's latest book, inspired by the real life murder of her house sitter. *Her Last Words*, out now in hard cover at all good bookstores."

"And in audio, e-book, and paperback," Sydney added. "*All* formats are out now and *all* royalties will go to Nora's favourite animal shelters where she volunteered."

"Fantastic. Go and buy it now, folks. Sydney, thanks for stopping by and I might just get you to come on and help with my shows on crime. We'll be back tomorrow, same time, same channel. See you tomorrow, folks." He waved at the audience and turned to Sydney, pretending to engage in conversation until the show was off air.

"And we're out."

"Sydney, I was serious. Work with me on this project and we'll see how many victims we can help." He held her right hand between his. "And I want to know about all of the refuges and shelters you helped and we can highlight them and the work they do for victims of crime. Shine a light on all of it."

"Impressive, Rhett." She shook his hand. "We'll just have to wait and see if you come through with the goods, but for now, I need to leave."

"Of course. Let me walk you back to your dressing room." He held one hand to her back as they walked out of the studio and down the hall.

Amy was waiting for them and thanked Rhett for his determination to help before he left them alone and she closed the door.

Sydney fell straight down onto the sofa and burst into tears.

Chapter 25

That afternoon she appeared on another regular show on her press list. *The Book Show* with Richard Walker. With ten million regular viewers, it was a show she never missed doing. Except for last year.

"Sydney Kingston, we have you back for the first time in two years. Unfortunately, we didn't get to see you last year due to the death of your young house sitter. You cancelled all promotion after that."

"My publishing house did," Sydney corrected. "I was in no frame of mind to talk about a book after that happened."

"Of course. But you've come back with a novel based on the tragic death of young Nora Ramotti. She was your house sitter who was stabbed to death on your stoop and left to die. Because I don't want to get too macabre for our audience at home, many authors write fictional retellings of true crime, real life experiences, so this is no different and you obviously drew inspiration from it. I saw you on *Rockefeller* earlier and you claimed Nora spoke to you. Can you tell us more about that?"

Sydney pushed down the queasiness in her stomach

and breathed slowly. "I believe in spirits. I don't believe a spirit always passes straight over to wherever it is we go. I believe some stick around. I feel that Nora stuck around because she might have been confused as to what happened to her. Maybe she didn't understand she needed to pass over, or maybe she couldn't until her murder was solved, and she used me as her conduit."

"Very interesting," Richard murmured. "Very interesting. And, of course, many cultures have their own beliefs about the dead and death in general, including many non-religious people. Because it's not always about religion and what one is taught, but about what traditions and beliefs one's culture hands down from generation to generation. Let's get onto something a little lighter. You live in Madam X's old brownstone. You said a couple of year ago that you'd written a novel based on that, but we're yet to see it. Do you think that all of the stalkers you've experienced, and now your young house sitter's death, has to do with that? Madam X died in jail. Maybe she's haunting the brownstone, or someone's out to get whatever they think they're owed by her and they hounded you and killed Nora to get revenge."

"A little far-fetched, but entirely possible," Sydney said. "And it could have just been Nora's ex-boyfriend, Lennie Cuzco."

"And it could have been one for your ex-boyfriends," Richard countered.

"I don't have any," Sydney replied.

"At all?" Richard was surprised. "Not the Italian or Greek?"

"I've had lovers, not boyfriends," Sydney said. "There

is a difference."

"So, it could have been one of your ex-lovers then?"

"No. Next subject."

"Okay, then. Ms Kingston wants to move on," Richard snarked. "Let's turn to other authors. A couple of years ago, you were being a smart alec about the authors who complained about you and no one's said anything since. But now, we have a few authors getting in digs about how you're not coming up with anything original. You have to take what's happened to you and write about it. What do you say to that?"

Sydney rolled her eyes and sighed. "I don't know how much more original I can get than to write about my own experiences, and I *still* outsell those twats a hundred thousand to one, so they can take a hike. Petty bullshit born out of jealousy doesn't interest me."

"Does the debut novel by author Bryan Jamison interest you?"

Sydney took a deep breath, her brows furrowing. "Who?"

"Bryan Jamison. The hot new author with the hot new thriller, *Illicit Things*. It debuted this week at number two on all the charts, right behind you. You have competition in your genre, Sydney. What do you say to that?"

"Never heard of him, don't know what he looks like, where he came from, or what his book looks like. We'll see if he can cut it with his sophomore book shall we? Beginner's luck, master fluke…how long will it last on the charts under me. Can't wait to see how fast he drops. What's it like?"

Richard handed her the hardcover.

Sydney stared at it, well aware the camera was on her. "It's a cover." She looked at the publisher mark. "Viceroy Publishing. Well, what would you expect? Viceroy has always been number two to my publisher Pulsate, so their books are number two to any Pulsate author." She checked the back cover. "No author photo." Not that she always had one. Upon reading the blurb, she laughed. "Crappy blurb like the crappy cover. Viceroy will never best Pulsate. Have you read it?" Handing it back, she picked up her glass and took a sip of water.

"I have, and I have to say it's good. Just as good as yours, Sydney. All of yours."

Her heart sped up. "*All* of mine? Have you met the guy? Has he done interviews?"

"No, but we've contacted Viceroy for an interview and they're keeping him quiet for now."

"Wonder why." Sydney shifted in her seat. "Hiding a hot new author is *not* the done thing. Hell, even I do promo after keeping to myself."

"And you got even more promo after *Twisted Affair* and *The Perfect Man* were made into movies this year," Richard said. "Will *The Shape of You* and *Her Last Words* be turned into moves as well?"

"Absolutely. Emerson Lake, writer, director, producer extraordinaire, and my best friend, brought them to life as she did the five before them. They hit the screens this year and were a runaway success. She's already bought the rights to *The Shape of You* and *Her Last Words*. She's also been hard at work on a documentary about the victims of crime and it's being made in conjunction with the movie. We're hoping it will be released in the first half of next year." Sydney took another sip of water. "Bet Byron what's-its will never get his books turned into movies."

"It's Bryan, and actually he is," Richard told her. "The rights have been bought by Netflix for three million. It was a bidding war with Amazon and Apple."

Sydney took a long sip and eyed Richard. "Really? Good for him."

"Do I detect a hint of sarcasm?" Richard knew he was getting TV gold.

"Not at all, Richard. Considering how tough the publishing business is, it's very rare these days for a debut author, or debut novel, to get picked up by a film company. Of course, getting optioned doesn't mean much—"

"They're already casting."

Sydney seethed inside. After the struggle she'd had, how dare some upstart pip squeak come out of the gate and get it all? "Are they? Congrats to him." This time, her words were dripping in sarcasm.

*****

"Who the fucking hell is Bryan Jamison?" Sydney demanded when she stalked into CC's office. She dumped her bag on the couch and thrust her hands onto her hips.

"Who's who?" CC inquired from behind her desk, calmly setting down her delicate Chanel teacup.

"Bryan Jamison. Apparently, he's the hot new thriller author from Viceroy. Number two on the charts behind me. Richard Walker asked me about him on *The Book Show* this afternoon."

"Mmm, never heard of him." CC picked up her phone and tapped in the number. "Rhona, dear," she said when Rhona answered. "Have you heard of a Bryan Jamison at Viceroy? Sydney's been asked about him and I've never heard of him." Pause. "You have? Good, can you come to my office?"

Sydney paced while CC continued drinking her tea, and a few moments later, Rhona came through the door in a burst of orange and pink. "What did you say about Bryan?"

"That I'd never heard of him and he wasn't going to rate since Viceroy authors always ran second to Pulsate authors," Sydney said, eyeing off Rhona's colourful artist smock that clashed with her hair and glasses.

"Well, he certainly is. Number two that is," Rhona said. "His debut novel scorched the competition to land at that position because you beat him out. I've heard a few other authors aren't happy about it, especially Viceroy authors. There's mumbling that he's getting more publicity and marketing than them and he's not even showing his face. No one's seen him, knows who he is, or what he looks like."

"Except Viceroy," Sydney replied. "They'd have to in order to give him a deal and then plan his launch. Wait…did he have a launch?"

"There was a launch for his book, but I don't recall seeing him or his name in the publicity or the gossip rags. Lots of other celebrities and authors, though," Rhona said.

"A book launch without the author," CC murmured.

"That's a new one."

"I thought so." Rhona sat in the chair opposite CC. "They lauded it as a new technique, trying to drum up publicity for the book, not the author."

"Interesting concept." Sydney rested her hands on the back of the chair beside Rhona. "But without the author, I'm suspecting it's someone who writes already, wanted to use a pen name, and didn't want anyone to know it was them. It's probably not a male at all."

"Entirely possible." Rhona looked up at Sydney. "I haven't read the book, but the general consensus is that it's good. Even better than the reigning queen's."

Sydney snorted in disgust. "That's what Richard Walker said to me today on *The Book Show*. That it was better than *all* of mine. The pompous prick. Probably just wanted to get a rise out of me."

"He probably did," Rhona replied. "But no interviewer should ever pit people against each other. What's the point in pitting authors against one another? There isn't one. Every author writes the way they write. Writes the stories they write. No one's better or worse than another. It's just tacky in my opinion."

"Can you find out more about this Byron what's-it?" Sydney asked. "I saw the book and Amy googled him on the way over, but there's very little out there."

"Almost as if he doesn't actually exist," Rhona said. "Which may be the point. Keep himself about of the spotlight and off Google until the book does well. If it bombed, no one would care."

"Either way, see what you can find out and I'll speak to some people I know." CC poured herself another cup of tea. "I think we should keep ahead of the hottest new author in thrillers, so we can market and publicise Sydney's books to combat his."

"Maybe I need to put out two novels a year, instead of one, and the stories and novellas I've been putting out as e-books." Sydney nibbled on her lip as she paced. "Publish regularly every three to four months. Keep my name out there, in the press."

"Do you have enough to do that?" CC asked. "And what if people get sick and tired of you putting out books for money?"

"I wonder how many weeks *Madam X* would be in the charts?" Sydney murmured. "Maybe it's time to release it."

"Weren't you going to do that in secret last December?" CC tried to remember back.

"I was, three days before Christmas, but Nora..." Sydney left the sentence hanging and took a deep breath in to quell her queasy insides.

"Have we sorted the legals?" Rhona asked. "If we have, we could release it."

"We've had no queries since Sydney first mentioned it," CC said. "After the first year, and then not releasing it, they all dropped off with their threats."

"As of now, I'm still number one." Sydney paced the room in thought. "He's only number two and I hope he stays there. But what if there's no follow up? Does he have a second book deal in the works? Does he have three or four or five?"

"I can find out," Rhona told them. "I have a friend who works at Viceroy and I'll see what I can get out of her."

"Can you do it now?" Sydney asked. "I don't have any

more interviews and I can wait awhile."

"Sure." Rhona nodded and quickly left the room.

Sydney sighed and let herself fall onto the couch. "I have my own book launch tomorrow. He hasn't been invited, has he?"

"Why would he if he's with Viceroy?" CC asked. "You'll have a few of our authors though, especially new ones so they can get a feel for launches."

"Have they released yet, or just signed and are still working on it?" Sydney asked.

"Working on it, yet to be published. Next year will be their time and obviously not at the same time as you. We know your date; we know the schedule to market and publicise you."

They chatted for another ten minutes before Rhona came rushing in.

"You will not believe it. He's contracted for a three book deal, and Jillian, my friend, said everyone at the house was so excited to get an author that could compete with Sydney on her expertise level, they signed him straight away for three books. Apparently the next two are ready to go and will be released six months apart. He'd already written them before submitting."

"Fucking hell!" Shock settled over Sydney. "A novel every six months. I did that at the beginning, got a stock up, but then when Pulsate came along I reduced it to one novel and short stories, or novellas. If he's got three novels ready to go and they've bought three, I wonder if he's got even more stocked up."

"Probably has considering they bought them all," Rhona suggested. "Jillian said they're really excited and hope he overtakes Sydney as the thriller master. No one else really comes close. I need to read his book to find out for myself."

"Looks as if we all need to." CC pulled out her desk drawer and rummaged in the petty cash tin. "Rhona, can you run down to the bookshop and get us some copies? We need to see what we're up against."

"No need. Jillian's going to bring me some copies after work and meet me here. I'll get them to you," Rhona said. "Do you want yours tonight or tomorrow, CC? I can leave it on your desk."

"I want it today so I can read it tonight. I'll stay with you." CC carried her teapot and cup to her drinks bar and deftly cleaned them out in the sink. "We need to know what we're up against. Now."

Sydney checked her watch. "It's only another hour or so. Mind if we wait for a copy?"

"Not at all. I can go over some publicity ideas to keep you at number one," Rhona told her. "I'll just go and get my notepad and phone."

At five-twenty, Rhona got a text and rushed for the lift. She was back fifteen minutes later with a shopping bag. "Jillian and I are meeting for dinner later to discuss the books. Meanwhile, she's given me five copies." She handed them out and they all stood staring at the cover of *Illicit Things*. "It's an interesting cover," she murmured, her fingers sliding over the jacket. She turned it over and saw no author photo. "Nothing on the back. Not good." The blurb was on the inside cover flap. "Interesting blurb." She read the bio on the back cover flap. "Still no photo and a fairly plain bio. Doesn't say an age, where he's from, no social media, and no website."

"It's like he doesn't exist," Sydney muttered. "Pen name for sure."

"Not that that's a bad thing," CC said. "You use a pen name."

"But I have socials in that pen name," Sydney replied. "Once my books became movies, my photo was everywhere. And we also say it's a pen name."

"Now, but not at first," Rhona said, reading the first page of the book. "Wowza. Listen to this. *When I first saw her I hated her. When I first met her I was excited by her. When I first kissed her I knew I not only loved her, but I wanted to fuck her. The problem was, she was thirty years older than me. It didn't stop me loving her, wanting her, needing her. It just made me grow up faster and put my plans on hold. For a while.* Wow, no wonder it's number two on the chart."

"Jesus," Sydney muttered. "Sounds like *Twisted Affair.* Maybe he copied me."

"Regardless, it's nearly six, so why don't we all go home and read the book. Just out of curiosity, Rhona, why don't you get a copy to Eric so he can check it for any plagiarism and make a note if there is."

"I'll make notes as well. It sounds interesting," Rhona said. "I'll see you tomorrow, CC Sydney, Amy. See you at your launch tomorrow afternoon." She hurried out of the room.

"We'll go as well." Sydney shouldered her bag. "I have a feeling I'll be up all night reading this."

They gathered their things and made their way downstairs, going in separate directions just so they could get to reading the book.

Sydney arrived home and locked herself away. She showered and changed, had a quick bite to eat, then sat in a comfortable chair in the parlour with a light over her shoulder. From the very first page she was enthralled and didn't stop until the last page was read long after midnight. Her heart was pounding in time with the thoughts in her mind. *Why do I know this story? Why do I know this writing?*

It was indeed similar in vein to *Twisted Affair*; love that starts off unrequited turns obsessive and eventually becomes the one thing that can no longer hold back. The affair was twisted in his book, illicit, and very similar in nature.

Have I been ripped off? Sydney thought, stretching out her legs and back. *Did he take Twisted Affair and just rewrite it from a male's point of view?* Something nagged her. Had she read the book before? Met the author before? She didn't know, but she absolutely knew *something* was happening.

Chapter 26

Sydney and Amy arrived at the book launch at two in the afternoon. It was a glorious autumn day, still warm, and the rooftop restaurant was the perfect place with the perfect views.

"Thank you all so much for coming again every year just like clockwork." Sydney smiled at the audience, seeing familiar faces and some not so familiar faces. "We are here for the launch of my amazing new novel, *Her Last Words*." Tears prickled her eyes and she took a breath. "I hope you've enjoyed it, if you've read it. And I hope you will if you haven't. All royalties for this book are going to Nora's favourite animal shelters and her family is here today if anyone wants a chat. I'm coming down to mingle; I'll see everyone at some point."

Emerson was the first person she came to when she walked off stage and into her arms. "Em."

"Syd. I haven't seen you in a couple of weeks." Emerson held her hands and squeezed. "You okay with all of this promotion?"

"I'm fine, just been busy prepping for it as I do every year. You know it takes me awhile to get my wardrobe sorted, and shows slotted in."

"But you've brought Nora into today. You okay?"

Sydney saw the concern on her face. "I'm fine, Em. Especially about this. Meanwhile, I'm pissed about that new author's book, that Byron Jamson and *Illicit Things*. Rhona got us copies yesterday and I read it last night. Have you read it yet?"

"No, but I've seen it. Why?"

"I can swear it's familiar. Not just the story, though it's very similar to *Twisted Affair*. But the writing is familiar as well."

"Do you know Bryan Jamison?"

"No, but as we realised yesterday, with no website or social, it could just be a pen name, and according to Rhona's friend, Jillian, who works at Viceroy, the publisher of Byron's book, they paid for three books that he had stocked up. He got a three book deal." Sydney's gaze wandered away and came to rest on a man on the other side of the rooftop. In the afternoon glow and reflective light, she saw him. Brown wavy hair, silver rimmed aviators, a beard. He appeared tall and familiar. Dread washed over her. "Is that…"

Emerson looked over her shoulder. "Who? Where?"

A woman moved in front of him and when she moved on, he was gone.

Sydney blinked in the odd light. "I thought I saw…" Another naggy feeling hit her. She craned her neck to look around the rooftop garden, but didn't see him. "Guess it doesn't matter. I'll come across him. Either way." She breathed in and let it out in a whoosh. "I'm glad you're here. Cormac and Douglas with you?"

"No. Cormac's at work and Douglas has been unwell."

"Is he okay? Nothing serious, I hope."

"Unfortunately, it is. Really bad pneumonia. He's been on bed rest after a hospital stint, but he wishes he could have come. He has read the book, though, and thanks you for the autographed copy I passed on."

"Which was only a couple of weeks ago when you didn't tell me he was sick." Sydney saw Rhona motion for her to move on and nodded.

"I know." Emerson gave a slight shrug. "They wanted to keep it quiet. He became ill after Sandy and Kieran's wedding."

"Made the news. I saw it in the local gossip columns."

"Yes, in June. He got sick soon after. I'd better let you get to your other guests." Emerson hugged her again. "Congrats, as always, and the movies are selling nicely."

"So are Byron Jamson's apparently," Sydney sniped. "His first book's in movie production."

"Not necessarily." Emerson gave her a big wink. "I'll see you later."

Sydney watched her walk away and knew something was up. She did an internal happy dance and moved on to meet and greet the rest of her guests. She eventually came across a small group consisting of other publishing house authors. "Don't worry, I know you're only here because your publishers made you."

Mariah Richmond smirked. She was a romance author with Bellbow House, made good sales figures, but didn't come close to Sydney's. She dunked her straw into her drink. "I wouldn't be here, otherwise."

"How sad that your publisher made you come to

another author's book launch," Sydney remarked. "Especially one you're so jealous of." She arched her brow and stared at the others. "Don't know why you bothered, really. You'll never beat me in sales, no matter how hard you try." Her gaze landed on a balding, middle-aged man in a green knitted sweater and bland grey pants. "Dick, how's the crime novel going? Have you actually finished it yet?"

Dick screwed up his face. "My name is Richard, Sydney, as you full well know. You just like being a bitch for the enjoyment and entertainment of it." He glanced at the others who chuckled behind their glasses.

"I know it's Richard, but since you act like a dick, that's what I'll call you, and no, I'm not a bitch, *Dick*, I just don't like you. In fact…" She looked from one to another. "I don't like any of you because you're arseholes who spread shit about me years ago and I pulled you up about it on a TV show. I don't have the patience, time, or energy for snotnosed authors like you, and the only reason your publishers sent you was because they know that. So, you lot can fuck right off because no matter what you say or do you'll never outsell me and if I'm right, none of you has ever cracked the top one hundred on any bestseller list. Toodles." She waved her fingers at their sour faces and walked off.

Sydney searched the crowd for the person she'd seen earlier, but she couldn't find him. There was something so familiar, but she couldn't put her finger on it. She came across CC and Rhona chatting away. "Did you two read the book last night? I was up after midnight, but I can swear it's along the same line as *Twisted Affair*."

"It did seem a little like that." Rhona nodded and her glasses slid down her nose. She pushed them up. "Similar story about illicit love."

"I only read a few chapters before falling asleep," CC said, holding her champagne glass with both hands. "I'd been on the phone with Douglas for a couple of hours talking about *Her Last Words*, and this new one, by this new author."

"Em told me he's been sick. Have you seen him?"

"I have. I'll be seeing him this weekend. He loves your new book, by the way. But he hasn't read *Illicit Things* yet."

"You know, there's something familiar about the writing. This Byron Jamson—"

"*Bryan Jamison*," Rhona corrected.

"Is it?" Sydney shrugged. "The writing is familiar, as if I've read it somewhere; it's similar to another book. If it's a pen name, it could be a well-known author writing under it."

"Like J.K. Rowling," CC suggested.

"Or Stephen King," Sydney added. "Exactly. How differently is a person going to write regardless of how many names they write under?"

"It would depend," Rhona said. "You all have a style, a voice, certain words you use, phrasing, etcetera. Maybe it's one of our old authors? Someone who wasn't selling well and we let go. Or someone that's been mentored by us."

A bell dinged loudly in Sydney's head and thoughts sprang into her mind. The writing. Where she'd seen it. The person from before and why he'd been so familiar. The wind was knocked out of her. Her jaw dropped in shock as she saw him across the rooftop. "Oh, my God. Oh, my God…"

"Sydney." CC put a concerned hand on her arm.

Catching her breath, Sydney blinked and looked from him to CC. "I'm fine."

A few minutes later, as she rushed through the crowd, he stepped in front of her, bringing her to a stop. Her gaze travelled up until it reached his eyes. His sapphire blue eyes and his wavy brown hair… She breathed in, almost suffocated on the emotions, and raced off into the restaurant. She left without saying a word.

Chapter 27

"Welcome back to SXT with Preston Grant. We have Sydney Kingston in the studio today, talking about her latest Cassandra Kingsley novel, *Her Last Words*, written for, and dedicated to, her house sitter, Nora Ramotti, who was fatefully stabbed on her stoop. All royalties from the book will go to Nora's favourite animal shelters. But you know all of that; so let's get into more exciting things. Sydney Kingston, you volunteered at shelters and refuges this past year. Why?"

Stumped by his question, all Sydney could say was, "Ah, why not?"

"Well, I guess it's a good thing to give back and volunteer. You certainly did that. But why did *you* do it?"

"As a way of giving back," Sydney told him. "I've earned good money from my book sales and after Nora…" She paused a moment to breathe and squash down the sudden lump in her throat. "I thought I should put it to good use and give back. Help out. So, I did."

"Admirable thing to do. You also wrote many opinion pieces for magazines and websites. Were they something you'd wanted to do?"

"I'd done a couple over the years here and there, but this year I had more to say."

"And say it you did," Preston said. "And you backed up your words with money and time, which a lot of people do not do, or refuse to do. Tell us about the animal shelter the royalties go to."

Sydney cleared her throat. "Nora volunteered at an animal shelter in Brooklyn, and one over in Queens, in her spare time. It's the same business, they just have shelters in each borough, so the money will be divided up between all five. They would take in cats and dogs, spay and neuter them, nurse them back to health if they needed to and try and rehome them. Sadly, sometimes they had to put some down. Nora would often say how much she wished she could take them all. She'd persuaded all of her family and friends to take as many animals as they could."

"Very noble of her," Preston replied with a slight nod. "You've said in recent interviews her family read the book first. They gave their blessing."

"They did. I wrote and dictated it, Amy typed it up and I gave it an edit. And then a voice, my muse, or maybe Nora herself, said to pass it on to them so they could read it. Her mom and dad felt it needed to be published and I agreed."

"Do they believe her ex-boyfriend did it?"

Sydney shrugged a shoulder. "We've talked about it and Lennie was arrested early on. I can't think of anyone else who'd want to do it. Neither can her family. But due to not having enough evidence, he was freed. Which pisses me off."

"Detective Declan Ryan of the NYPD, the Police Commissioner's son, was the lead detective. Do you think he did all he could to find the person who did this, or was Lennie the most convenient target? I mean, this isn't an episode of *Blue Bloods* where a murder is wrapped up in forty minutes."

"He did what he could, as all cops and detectives do," Sydney replied evenly. "They can only go by the evidence collected, the information given, the suspects at hand."

"And Lennie Cuzco was a suspect from the start because he was the easiest—"

"He did try and demolish my house and hit Nora with a hammer when she tried to stop him. He harassed her at my home multiple times, and I had to tell him to stop or I'd ban him. He didn't treat her well, and she told me as much every time we discussed her on again off again relationship with him."

"Okay, fair enough. But let's stay on the Ryans. The royalty of the New York police force. The Kennedys of cops. There are photos of Declan going into your house at night, and leaving even later. Was something happening between the two of you? Was it purely professional?"

"You mean those incredibly dark and grainy photos where you can't tell *who's* entering my home?" Sydney retorted. "Really, Preston? You know better than to gossip. Detective Ryan would stop by every few days to catch me up, or to ask if I remembered anything else. If you're going to make my grieving into some R-rated movie for gossip, forget it, not fucking interested. I'm here to promote my latest novel."

"Of course, it's just that years ago, Declan's brother, Connor Ryan, was on your doorstep—"

"And! Your point is? That I've had stalkers? Sure. I had stalkers when I moved into the brownstone. A dead rat was left on my doorstep. Connor was the detective who attended for a few months. I didn't see any of them again until Nora's…" Sydney paused and breathed evenly, giving him the evil eye. "I'm here about the book, Preston. Let's stick to my writing, or I'll leave and never do your show again."

"Of course," he said smoothly. "You've had a couple of stalkers over the last few years, have they all been taken care of?"

"I had three, and one was a neighbourhood peeping tom, nothing personal. And yes, they've all been taken care of. But then again, this is New York, we never know who's out there watching, following, stalking. How many stalkers have you had, Preston?"

"A few actually, over the last thirty years. I've had vile letters, death threats, bomb threats, and had someone break into my house."

"Well, there you go then," Sydney said. "Mentally sick individuals abound."

"They certainly do. A quick change of subject before we go. Have you read *Illicit Things* by Bryan Jamison yet? He's still sitting at number two on the bestseller lists behind you. Are you threatened by the new kid on the block?"

Sydney snorted. "Hardly! A debut author needs to prove themselves many times over before they're a threat. They need to show they have what it takes to have hit after hit. It's no different for actors or singers. One hit means nothing if you have nothing to back it up with. That's why we have so many one hit wonders. They have nothing to back it up with. When his second and third come out next year, we'll see how he goes. Besides, no one's heard of him."

"That's true, and the publisher is keeping him close to the chest. No website, socials—"

"Photos," Sydney cut in. "The publisher barely has a bio for him."

"Yeah, I saw that. All very mysterious, don't you think? But have you read the book?"

"I did. Last night. It seemed *very* familiar."

"A little along the lines of *Twisted Affair* from two years ago," Preston said. "Yeah, same storyline, but with a twist. It's almost as if he took your book and wrote his own version. Which there's nothing wrong with."

"I have to disagree with that," Sydney said. "Stop using someone else's story or book or movie to make your own. Come up with your own idea."

"Just as you do. We're talking to Sydney Kingston, author of the Cassandra Kingsley novels. The latest smash thriller is *Her Last Words* which is out now in all formats. The royalties are going to Nora Ramotti's favourite animal shelters around the city. Nora was the house sitter of Sydney's who sadly lost her life last year. This time last year, in fact, when Sydney was promoting her last novel, *The Shape of You.* She lost her life in a stabbing, but at least she wasn't alone. Sydney and her assistant arrived home to find her, but were too late. Even though they tried to revive her, their attempts were futile. Sadly. Nora's killer is still out there and Sydney, and now Rhett Rockefeller, won't stop until they find him, so go and buy Sydney's novel, *Her Last Words*, and support the animal shelter in Nora's name. You can even adopt a cat or dog while you're at it. Sydney, these have been trying times for you, no doubt, but if there is anything we can do here at SXT and *The Preston Grant Show*, let us know and we'll help out."

Sydney was impressed, but talk was cheap. "Thanks, Preston, will do. Bye, everyone."

"Bye, Sydney. That was Sydney Kingston, author of *Her Last Words*, out now folks."

Chapter 28

He followed the man home from work, waiting in the cold, dark alley, watching him for most of the afternoon. He had watched him most days these last months, since finding him. Lennie Cuzco had been hiding in plain sight at his parents' house in upstate New York, working at his father's garage as a mechanic.

Lennie had a routine. Lock up at five, but stay an hour to finish off paperwork, or a car he'd worked on, then leave and walk the back streets to his local bar where he had a drink or two, before walking home a mile away and across the field to his parents' house. They lived just outside of town, with other houses dotted around. It was a small town, ten or so thousand people. Quiet and leafy, with the leaves turning golden brown or rust red, covering the streets and yards in a soft, but crunchy mattress of flora.

Because Lennie had the same routine, it wasn't hard to figure out the best place to deal with him. Quiet, no people, no one to see.

He checked his watch. Nearly six. Just a few minutes more.

It hadn't taken long to find him. His parents' house was always the go-to for where he'd end up hiding out, but it had taken two months to track his behaviour, and now, on the anniversary, he would finally understand what justice was.

Lennie locked up and walked down the side alley to the next street, turned right, and walked two blocks to the bar.

The man followed slowly. The hood of his black jacket was over his head, black beanie pulled down low, and black scarf wrapped around his neck. Black gloves protected his hands from the cold. And from leaving fingerprints. He sat in the side alley across from the bar, waiting.

An hour later, Lennie appeared at the bar's door, pulled up his coat collar against the cold, and quietly set upon his way home. He cut down the side alley and took the street past his father's garage and kept on going.

He watched Lennie from a distance, from the other side of the road. Knew Lennie had to cross over to cut across the field of his parents' farm. He bided his time.

Lennie finally checked the road and crossed over, jumping the fence into the field, partly wheat, partly corn, and a whole lot of weeds one could easily hide in. Or be lost in.

He jumped the fence and quickly made his way around the field so he could get ahead of Lennie. He'd staked it out previously, even set his drone above it to find the best way in and around it. He was ahead of Lennie and prepared, so he ducked down, hid just inside the field, and pulled out the knife.

It was the same knife Lennie had killed Nora with.

When searching the field with the drone, he'd found

a few anomalies and followed them up. And lo and behold, there it was in a plastic zip up bag, along with the overalls, with Nora's blood all over it. He'd taken photos and samples and had it analysed. Definitely Nora's blood.

He glanced at the house, knew the parents would be in the lounge room out the back with their TV dinners, and waited. A moment later, Lennie loomed into view and he attacked, stabbing him three times in the stomach in quick, quiet succession. He put a hand over a stunned Lennie's mouth, and lowered him to the ground.

He pulled out his phone and hit the video record button. "Why did you kill your girlfriend Nora? And don't deny it, because I found the knife and just stabbed you with it. Tell me, Lennie, or I'll let you die. Why did you kill her?" He pressed his free hand across Lennie's neck. "Tell me."

Struggling, not just for air, but to get the hand off the neck, Lennie gurgled, "I didn't."

"I just told you, Lennie." The man leaned in closer. "I found the knife you did it with and stabbed you with it." He pressed harder on his neck. "Tell me why you did it."

"Because." Lennie gasped, clawing at the arm. "She left me."

"That can't be the only pathetic reason," the man said. "You killed your ex-girlfriend because she left you. Why, Lennie?" He pushed on his neck.

"I'm telling you," Lennie gurgled. "I told her I'd do it. If she left me. I told her I'd kill myself too."

"Yet you didn't." The man leaned his knee into Lennie's stomach and saw the blood ooze out.

"Coz I was arrested and put in prison." Lennie's grasp

weakened and his brain became hazy. "Am I dying?"

"Just like you left Nora to die on the stairs of the house she was watching. You're a guilty piece of shit, Lennie Cuzco." He pushed his hand into Lennie's neck and his knee into his stomach. "And now you're going to die the same way, the same way poor Nora died one year ago today. Happy anniversary, Lennie." He pushed until the life of Lennie Cuzco was gone. Until the last breath was exhaled and his death rattle sounded. He took photos before unzipping his jacket and pulling out the plastic zip bag from a bag strapped to his chest. It was the one he'd found the knife in. He returned the bloody knife to the bag and zipped it up. He also had the uniform Lennie was wearing in a bag. He quickly pulled out a small kit from a pocket of his jacket and snapped an SD card in the phone connector and downloaded a copy of the video to the card. He placed the card into a small Ziploc bag. It was evidence he was going to give the police. Just not in person.

He packed away his phone, zipped up his pockets and jacket, and quickly looked to see if the house was still in darkness. He knew there were no outside night lights to come on and no dog to worry about.

Hauling Lennie up under the armpits, he quickly pulled him backwards towards the house and set him at the bottom of the stairs. He pulled out the three zip bags, containing the mechanic's uniform, the knife, and the SD card, and laid them on the porch stairs. Then he carefully pulled Lennie up to the porch, turned him around, and laid him backwards, his body cascading down the stairs as Nora's had done, over the bags of evidence. He didn't want the parents finding them before the police.

When all was set, he rushed back to the field and called 911. "Hello, can I be put through to Detective Declan Ryan of the NYPD?" His voice was mechanised by the attachment and within a moment he was through.

"Detective Ryan."

"Hello, detective. I've found Lennie Cuzco. He's confessed to the murder of Nora Ramotti. I have it on video. I also have the weapon, and the overalls that he buried on his parents' farm. They're under his body. Get here as fast as you can, detective, you'll want to see how he died the same death as sweet young Nora. And on the anniversary," he mocked and ended the call.

Waiting until he heard sirens, which was a good fifteen minutes, he rushed into the field and disappeared.

The local police pulled into the Cuzco farm, their headlights highlighting the body of Lennie draped over the stairs. The sheriff sat in his car staring at him. He'd received a call from an NYPD detective about a dead body and he'd been told to deal with the crime scene carefully and to photograph everything. He hadn't taken it seriously until now. They didn't have murders in their town; had been lucky in avoiding that. But here was a suspected killer all laid out for him.

He opened his door just as the Cuzco's opened their front door and noticed their son.

Lennie's mother screamed and opened the screen door to get to her son, but the sheriff raced up the stairs to stop her. This was now a crime scene; he informed them, so they must please wait inside. He'd take care of it.

An hour later, after the crime scene had been carefully examined and the body and evidence photographed, Declan turned up in time to see Lennie's body being placed into the body bag. He scratched his head and looked skyward. Someone had delivered Lennie to him on a plate.

*****

Sydney was preparing to head out for more interviews when she opened her door to find three Ryans on her doorstep. "Again, all three of you on my stoop. What now?"

"You might want to sit down, Syd," Connor said. "We have some news."

"And I have interviews," Sydney informed them. "I don't have time."

Ethan, eager to get in first, said, "We found Lennie, Nora's boyfriend. Someone killed him the way he killed her." Despite not having seen her in over a year, he still had feelings for her and had a buzz in his crotch just being in her presence. He was also ignoring the glares from his father and uncle.

"Jesus, Ethan," Declan sniped. "I'm in charge here." He turned to Sydney, noting the serious, disbelieving expression. His voice softened. "Syd, he's telling the truth."

"Syd?" Connor raised a brow at his brother. "Since when are you close enough to call her that?"

"Can the crap," Sydney snapped at them. "What do you mean you found Lennie's body and why the hell are all three of you on my doorstep telling me?"

"*They* shouldn't be here," Declan snarked at his

brother and nephew. "It's my case. I got a call last night telling me where Lennie was and that the evidence of Nora's murder would be under him. It was."

Stunned silence blasted Sydney's eardrums, although it was anything but silent. It was a high pitched alarm system squealing though her head. "Evidence?"

"The knife used to kill her, the uniform he was wearing covered in blood, and an SD card of the murderer doing the murdering. He got a confession before Lennie died."

"And why did he…" Sydney's insides shook. Nerves? Fear? Anger? All three? She didn't know.

"Because she left him and he'd said he'd kill her and himself," Declan said. "Syd?" He took a step closer and put his hand on her elbow. "You wanna go back inside and sit for a minute?" He glanced at Amy to see her stark white face. "Amy. Let's get you both inside." He escorted them both in and sat them on the living room couch with Connor and Ethan on either side. Just like a year ago.

"Who knows?" Sydney asked.

"I've spoken to her family. They know. They know he admitted it. That we have the evidence. They know a hundred percent he did it," Declan said.

Sydney nodded slowly, unable to fully comprehend the situation. "How? After a year? He disappeared after his release."

"Yeah, well, we had no evidence so the judge let him free. I figured he did it, panicked, and fled to his parents' farm where he buried the evidence in secret. Then he got back to New York where we picked him up. It took me just over an hour to get there, so he could have easily managed it."

"And he did it because she broke up with him?" Amy asked. "What a gutless piece of shit. A fucking gutless piece of shit cunt of a male. I won't say man because he's clearly not one."

"He's dead." Sydney frowned. "In the same way?"

"Stabbed three times with the same knife, in the same spots, almost." Declan's brows furrowed. It had been bugging him all night. The killer knew where he was, had found the buried items, and then killed Lennie the same way.

"On the anniversary," Sydney murmured. "Last night. The anniversary."

"Yeah, look, Syd." Declan sat on the coffee table in front of her. "I know you've had your share of stalkers, but Lennie killed Nora. So, it wasn't anyone after you and got her by surprise, it was her ex after her. This isn't your fault."

"All of that is cold comfort, Declan," she said and looked at her watch. "If that's all you have to tell me, I need to pull myself together so I can get through the day. I'll wait until tonight before I fall apart. Anything else?" She stared expectantly at all three.

"No." Declan stood and stepped aside. "We'll let you deal with this and if you have any questions, just call me and I'll tell you what I can." His heart broke for her and Nora, even though he hadn't met or known her. An ex being a selfish piece of garbage human wasn't a good enough excuse to take a life and ruin countless others. And even though he hadn't been involved with Sydney since the beginning of the year, he still remembered their time fondly. "We'll leave you to it." He ushered Connor and Ethan out the door and closed it firmly behind them.

"You didn't answer me before," Connor said.

"About what?"

"About how close are the two of you in order to call her Syd," Connor replied.

Declan sent a scathing glare his way and headed back to his car, leaving Connor frowning at his back, and Ethan wondering if his uncle would be back to fuck Sydney that night. Or if this was his chance to get back together with her.

Sydney sat thinking about Lennie and the few times she'd had to deal with him. He'd rubbed her the wrong way, and after finding out he'd tried to smash down her wall and hit Nora instead, she'd taken out a restraining order against him and encouraged Nora to do the same. But all of that had come too little too late. Nora was dead, and Lennie had been caught then let go, and now finally someone had taken justice into their own hands. She had no sympathy for him or his family, and wished she could see the crime scene photos. She wanted to see his body. The same stab marks. The same type of position splayed on the stairs of his parents' house. If this wasn't telling her something she didn't know what would.

So far, the stalkers had been dealt with by Landon. Lennie had finally been taken care of, but there were others out there. Others who were being monitored and never mentioned unless necessary. Once the promotion for this book was over, she was going to reveal all. The time had come. Come New Year, she was no longer playing their game. She was playing hers.

A new day would be dawning. For everyone.

PART FIVE

One year later

Chapter 29

"Bryan Jamison, oh, my God. We finally have you in person," Rhett Rockefeller told the man on his stage. "Three smash hit thrillers on your hands and you've scored your first number one, having been pipped at the post the last two times by reigning queen, Sydney Kingston. But you've beaten her out of the sales gate by releasing your book before hers. How does it feel to finally be number one?"

"It feels pretty good, Rhett," the author said. "We scheduled the release for the first of September to get ahead of her and we did it. But I know it won't last long. Pulsate are already advertising Sydney's next book which will release on the nineteenth. I only have three weeks to celebrate before she takes over."

"You know, Bryan, I have to say, the fact I finally have you on my stage after being incognito behind the curtains is exciting. This is the first time you've done an in person interview. How come you waited so long? Or should I say, how come *you* kept us all waiting so long?"

The author crossed his legs and settled his hands in his lap. His long brown hair was neatly tied back into a low ponytail, his beard thick and neatly trimmed. His silver wire rimmed circular glasses framed his brown eyes, which stared inquisitively at Rhett who was standing in the audience. "It was all part of the publicity. A build up to get people interested in my books. Think of it as the TV show, *The Voice*, for authors. You get to read the books without knowing what I look like, so you don't get any preconceived notion about it or me."

Rhett nodded and glanced around the audience. "Great concept; it certainly worked. Three massive bestsellers all released six months apart. Most authors release a novel a year, or every two. Were they already completed before you were picked up, or did you just finish them off after you signed?"

"They were already written, Rhett, plus another three novels had been written at the time of signing. I've written six more since."

"Jesus, talk about prolific," Rhett said to the audience. "So, you had six books written at the time of signing, and the deal was for three. Do you have another deal in place?"

"I do. I have another three book deal and those three will come out in the next three years."

"And you've written *another* six since the original signing?"

"Yes. My novels are about a hundred thousand words, and it takes me three months apiece. I signed a year and a half ago, so I'm right on track to keep writing."

"Your publisher must love you. They can keep getting thrillers out of you for years to come. Are they all thrillers?"

"Yes, mainly. Obviously, there is some romance, a

little action, a little adventure. Gotta keep the action moving in the stories to keep people interested."

"You're definitely competing with Sydney Kingston, then. She's well into double digits. If she releases a novel a month, she'll be into the fifties if you add up all of the novellas and novels she's released. Not to mention all of the opinion pieces she's written in the last few years. Do you see it as a competition? Have you read Sydney's work?"

"I have read all of Ms Kingston's work and it's amazing. Some of it inspired me with my ideas and they evolved into what I've written. But no, it's not a competition, Rhett. Sydney's an amazing woman, I'm a man, we both write equally good thriller novels. There's more than enough room for both of us at the top." He gently pushed his glasses up and rested his hand back in his lap.

Rhett observed the soft spoken author on stage. "I have to say, Bryan, you are nothing like I imagined you were."

Bryan's eyes twinkled. "And what was that, Rhett?"

"I…" Rhett shook his head. "I have no idea. Probably someone like Grisham, Patterson, or Childs. That age and ilk and looks."

"I'll take that as a compliment," Bryan said with a nod. "They're great writers and there's much to respect about their time in publishing."

"Absolutely." Rhett looked at the card in his hands. "Now, let's get to talking about your smash hit number one thriller, *Creeper.* It's your latest release, so tell us what it's about."

"It's about a guy who creeps around doing things he shouldn't," Bryan replied. "He's a stalker, stalking the number one romance author in the world, terrorizing her in the dark, making her believe she's going crazy."

"And where did you get the inspiration for that?" Rhett asked. "Was that from one of Sydney Kingston's books, or from all of the court cases involving her?"

"Well." Bryan gave a soft smirk. "I haven't read that many involving her, just the one from a few years ago. But the news is definitely a place to seek inspiration."

"Have you met Sydney, yet? She is your competition."

"No, not yet, but I did ask my publisher to invite her to my book launch tomorrow. I'd like to meet her."

"Has she accepted the invitation?"

"I have no idea. I hope so."

"Okay, so you completed this book deal with *Illicit Things, Sinister Motives* and now *Creeper.* Can you tell us about the next three books?"

"It's a trilogy. Each book is titled with a single word. *She. Is. Mine.* My publisher wants to change the titles, they told me I can't name a book *Is.*" He shrugged. "I said why not. It will look good on the spines when all three are released."

"Interesting concept," Rhett said. "And they're thrillers, obviously."

"Absolutely. It's my field now."

Rhett's interest perked up. "Now?"

"I was writing other genres while learning the ins and outs of writing. I finally found my niche with thrillers."

"Will any of that early work see the light of day?"

"Maybe," Bryan said. "Maybe not."

"Okay, we're going to take some questions from the audience. Yes, you, ma'am." He thrust the microphone into the face of a twenty-something woman.

She stood up and went beet red. "Um, yeah, hi, Bryan. I just wanted to ask of you are married or single."

A few wolf whistles went through the crowd, making Bryan blush.

"Not married, no."

"Okay, and you, sir." Rhett stepped beside a middle-aged gentleman. "What's your question for Bryan Jamison, hottest new thriller author on the planet."

"Hello, Bryan, my name's Dean, I just wondered how you went about getting a publisher. Like a lot of people, I want to write a book, but just reading about all the rejections authors get is exhausting. What qualifications do you have?"

"Hello, Dean, I've been writing since school, like most people, and I was lucky enough to have mentors in my English teachers, and then an actual mentorship. I went on to do writing and English at college and made many contacts. I perfected my writing and submitted to the appropriate people. So, if you can, study writing at a college, or writing school, for a semester or a year and really hone your craft. It will help you in the long run."

"Great, thank you," Dean said and sat down.

"We have time for one more." Rhett raced across the floor and came to a puffing stop beside another woman. "And what would you like to ask Bryan?"

The woman stood up and tugged down her skirt. "Hi, Bryan, I just wanted to know if you wear boxers or briefs to bed." The crowd cheered and the woman turned bright red. "I was dared by my friend to ask." She pulled on the top of the woman beside her who was covering her face in embarrassment.

"Well, that's a rather personal question that objectifies men," Rhett said. "Bryan?"

"Neither," was all Bryan said to more catcalls.

"And that's where we'll end our show today ladies and gentlemen. Thank our guest, Bryan Jamison, the hottest thriller author behind Sydney Kingston. His new book, *Creeper*, is out now at all good bookstores. We'll be back after this break."

The stage director counted them out to break and Rhett hurried to the stage. "Thank you so much for coming, Bryan, it's good to finally put a face to the name." He held out his to shake Bryan's.

"Rhett, thank you for having me. It's been quite a debut. Can't wait to come back next year." Bryan was escorted off stage and over to the wings.

"Absolutely loved having you here and thank you for letting me be the first to have you. I have to get back on stage for the next guest. I'll see you next time, Bryan." Another hand shake and Rhett was running back to the stage.

Bryan sighed, gave a curt nod, and headed for the door, glad it was over.

*****

"So that's the little fucker trying to take my crown." Sydney leaned back in her seat in CC's office. Everyone was there; Olivia, Gemma, Eric, Rhona, Amy, and

Emerson. "That's the little fucker. And because Viceroy knows I publish in September, they released his book *before* mine instead of at the same time like last year, that little fucker gets the top spot for three weeks before me. Fucking hell!"

Rhona turned off the TV. "Considering what your next book is, it's going to blow everyone's socks off for the next year, and Bryan Jamison will be long gone."

"Maybe." Sydney rubbed her tired eyes and sighed. She'd been writing non-stop since January, and had released a novella just before Bryan's second book in March to outsmart him and scored the top spot for four weeks. But now... While she had a decent stock of stories she could release over the next few years, it had exhausted her...so had her extra-curricular activities.

She'd attended the premieres of her movies, and the release of Emerson's documentary based on the novel, *Her Last Words*. She'd worked with assault groups and victims of crime, as well as helped Rhett out with his crime shows.

"We could use that to our advantage." Rhona tapped her chin thoughtfully. "I could whip up some promo posters or fliers, saying how your new book will rip his from the top of the charts and blow everyone away."

"Don't they already say that?" CC asked. "We've had this campaign planned for the last year. The only problem is, we're not advertising the book until the day it's released, so we can't get interest in it, the same as always."

"Sydney will do that via her socials," Rhona said. "The secret frosty cover drums up interest, keeping the title secret until release day and then boom!" She slapped her hands together creating a loud clap making everyone jump. "They all find out exactly what Sydney's releasing."

"What are you releasing, Sydney?" Emerson asked.

"Something very special and long awaited," Sydney told her. "It's going to create a buzz like no one's ever seen and I hope it will be my biggest seller to date."

"Any ideas? A clue?" Emerson tugged her friend's sleeve. "Even for me?" she wheedled.

Sydney chuckled. "Sorry, Em, very few people know. It's best kept that way until release day."

"Will I get an advance copy? Or do I wait for the launch?" Emerson asked. "And I don't think Douglas will be able to make it. He's pretty much been homebound since his pneumonia last year. It took the energy right out of him."

"I'll get copies to you all," CC told her. "I'll bring them myself on release day." She glanced at Sydney. They'd had a conversation about the contents of the book and whether it would reflect on the Ryans. Sydney believed not, and refused to change a thing.

"So, what do we do about that pissant?" Sydney asked.

"I don't think you have anything to worry about," Rhona said. "He's had three good books, and you've had…what? Fifteen or something. He has a long way to catch up."

Sydney crossed her legs and started swinging her foot. Was Bryan Jamison to be worried over? It was his first outing in public and he wasn't that flash a person. But as for his writing, he was good. His books were good. But then again, so were hers and she had a long track record no one could beat. Even him. "I suppose we'll see a lot more of him on TV and radio; on all the outlets I see every year."

"We will. But don't worry, they'll want you when your book releases," Rhona said. "They'll be clambering over each other to get you."

*****

"Welcome to *The Preston Grant Show*, Bryan Jamison."

The crew in the studio applauded wildly and Bryan nodded shyly.

"*The Preston Grant Show* is your first radio promotional stop. Thank you for gracing us with your presence, Bryan. We finally get to see you in the flesh, in person, after three smash hit thrillers. Welcome to the show."

"Thank you for having me, Preston. It's good to be here, finally." Bryan carefully observed everyone in the studio with him.

"Why has it taken so long for you to do any promotional work? Your books have been massive bestsellers, but we haven't seen you until now. Why not?"

"It was purely to get publicity," Bryan replied. "Let the books speak for themselves."

"And you've obviously been around the traps awhile," Preston went on. "You said on *Rockefeller* that you did your training in college in English and writing and you've put in the hard yards because these books are fabulous." Preston looked at the hard cover of *Creeper* in his hand. "The cover is amazing and it's your first number one hit because Sydney Kingston's latest Cassandra Kingsley thriller isn't out yet. It must be great to be number one."

Bryan gazed at Preston. "It is. Very great. To know that my books have been instant hits, that all of the hard work I put in for so many years paid off. It's incredible."

"And how many years have you put in?" Preston pushed on. "You're what? Late thirties, early forties? How long have you been at this if you did English and writing at college?"

"Quite a few years," Bryan said, swinging lightly in his chair. "It seemed like forever at certain points, certain stages in my life. I worked hard at it and it finally paid off."

"It certainly did. I'd like to talk about your book deal, if you don't mind. It's been mentioned that you had a three book deal, which is rare these days, especially for new authors, and now you've signed another three book deal. Can you tell us what a three book deal is worth these days? We've heard six figures, seven figures, even eight figures."

"I was very lucky to get a healthy deal," Bryan told him. "I won't say how much. It was for three books, remember, and they knew the books would be stiff competition for Sydney's books, which is why the price was high. It came to a healthy seven figure deal per book. So much so, I bought my own place outright and paid off outstanding debts I had in full. Those deals have been very helpful to me in doing that."

"You paid off a new place outright? What was it? A condo, apartment, house?"

"It's an apartment in a very nice part of the town. And I've furnished it as well."

"The money must have been good if you've paid for all of that. And the second deal?"

"Exactly the same as the first," Bryan said.

"So let me get this straight. You've gone from what? Broke wannabe author to mega millionaire almost overnight. Even I know authors don't get an advance in full straight up. Have you earned royalties yet? How did the payments work?"

"Because I already had the books, and they required limited editing, I was paid in full. Normally you get a payment as incentive to write, then the next upon release of the finished product. But all three were done, so I was paid in full up front. Same again this time. And I've just started receiving royalties for *Sinister Motives*."

"Six months after its release, so that's pretty good. A mega millionaire, twice over, and now earning royalties for your second book that only came out six months ago," Preston said. "You pay your taxes?"

"Why are you asking him that?" Hank asked. "It's not something that's everyone's business."

"I know, but if he made seven figures straight up, then I'm just wondering what the tax situation's like." Preston looked from Hank to Bryan. "I know it's personal, but I've never met an author whose advance was one payment and seven figures. How does the tax work on that? Did you buy your apartment first? Put away half for your taxes? What?"

Bryan cleared his throat and took a sip of water. "Well, Preston, Hank is right. My taxes are no one's business. But, since I made seven figures straight up, I set half aside for taxes and put the other half into two bank accounts; one for living and one for savings. When I did my taxes, I had the money to pay it. Then I went and bought my apartment and furnishings. I also bought two cars; a normal around town car, and a Porche Spyder. It's my dream car. The rest I live on for a weekly wage and to pay my regular household bills."

"Okay, there you go." Preston motioned towards him. "Bryan Jamison, ladies and gentlemen, on *The Preston Grant Show*. He's the hot-to-trot author of *Illicit Things*, *Sinister Motives*, and the latest release, *Creeper*, that has debuted at number one on the bestseller charts beating out Sydney Kingston who writes as Cassandra Kingsley. Sydney's latest book isn't due out for another seventeen days. Have you met Sydney yet? What do you think of her? What does she think of you?"

"I haven't met Sydney yet," Bryan responded. "I don't know if she's read *Creeper* yet, or what she thinks of me or it, but I think a lot of her. She's an amazing writer who'll be remembered amongst the greatest thriller writers of all time. I think she's beating out other women in her genre. I'd love to meet her and hope I do one day. She's invited to my book launch this evening."

"Think she'll turn up?"

"I hope she does. I see her as a peer and would love to chat to her about our writing process, see if we're similar or different."

"Is that what you authors discuss when you get together?" Hank asked. "Your writing process."

"Well, I've only met a few other authors at this time,"

Bryan replied. "Besides our books, and what other authors we've met, we talk shop and how to write our bestsellers."

"Or the money you do or don't make," Preston added. "Have you had any issues with other authors hating on you for getting seven figures?"

"It didn't come up until recently, and I never mentioned it until today. This is my second interview and it's come up. I was given a three book deal, the money's for all three books, and it's a gamble that's more than paid off for my publisher, Viceroy Publishing. If other authors have an issue with how much it's been reported that I earn, they can take it up with their publisher."

"Good point," Preston conceded. "So, tell the listeners about the book before we wrap up the show."

"It's about a man who stalks the most famous romance author in the world and makes her think she's crazy. He creeps, hence the title, *Creeper.*"

"And is it based on any real life author? Danielle Steele is probably the reigning queen of romances."

Bryan softly laughed. "No, it's not about any author in particular. I just picked a genre of books, chose romance, picked a genre of creeps, and it was a stalker. It's not based on anyone in particular."

"Well, Bryan Jamison, thank you for stopping by for the first time on *The Preston Grant Show.* Go out and get his three novels, *Illicit Things, Sinister Motives,* and *Creeper.* He's finally showing us his face and we get to see what he looks like. He's currently number one on the bestseller chart and has another three book deal for the next three years. Thanks for coming, Bryan."

"Thanks for having me, Preston."

Sydney snapped off the radio and huffed around the living room. She'd been listening to the show for the last hour to hear what the upstart said, and she didn't like what she heard. "He wants to meet me and talk about writing process," she spat. "That's laughable, who the fuck does this guy think he is?"

Her phone rang out and she picked it up. "Hey, Rhona, did you hear—"

"Oh, I heard all right. Seven figures for three books. That's anywhere from one mill to a cent off ten mill. And he hopes to meet you at his book launch. Were you even invited?"

"Not that I know of. Who do invitations normally go to? You?"

"Me or CC and I do *not* recall receiving one from Viceroy inviting you to his book launch."

"Then why keep saying it unless they told him they did but actually didn't."

"Entirely possible. I'll ask CC if she's heard anything, and text you. Meantime, get ready to launch your next book with those videos made for socials. Everything's ready to go, we just have to push the button and get copies out to everyone the night before."

"Okay. And can you check with Landon as well? Maybe the email or personal invitation or whatever they were supposed to send went to them; if not, they're lying."

"Will do. Meanwhile, don't worry, Sydney, we have the promo out, you'll have your videos out, and bang, it'll be out. The biggest story since…um…"

"My last one?" Sydney chuckled. "Don't worry about it, Rhona, just let me know if you find that imaginary invitation." Sydney ended the call and put her phone on the coffee table. She wasn't worried about Byron Jamson's book sales, or his three book deal, or his prolific nature. What she was worried about, was the fact he sounded vaguely familiar.

*****

"Welcome to *The Book Show*. I'm your host, Richard Walker. Today on the show we have reclusive author, Bryan Jamison who scored three top bestsellers within a year, and for the first time, he's promoting them. Welcome to the show, Bryan Jamison."

Bryan had frowned at the word reclusive. "Thank you, Richard, but let's clear up one thing right out of the gate, I'm not reclusive."

"What would you call it then? Your first bestseller was this time last year, you've had two more since, but have only now come out of the woodwork."

"Hardly, Richard. It was a good promotional strategy. I was never reclusive. And I'll thank you kindly to stop saying it."

Richard stared in disbelief. He rarely came up against authors on the offensive, but then again, Bryan had a point. "Let's talk about the promotional strategy. It's clearly worked."

"It certainly did. By me staying out of it, it garnered interest like never before. The publisher wanted attention on my books, not me."

"But now you're out in public, we can put a face to the books. How does that feel? Is it freeing?"

"No, definitely not." Bryan adjusted his glasses. The brown check pattern of his shirt made his eyes look darker, and with the combination of a biscuit coloured corduroy blazer with brown elbow patches, and his long brown ponytail, he knew he came off as someone older. "It's definitely not freeing; now there's pressure. Pressure to do promotion, TV, radio. As I said at the beginning, I'm not reclusive, but promotion is not my forte. I'm just a private, quiet person who knows how to write and can take time to hide away and produce work that is good enough to sell well. I'm not the type of person to go looking for publicity. I'd rather you just read my books and not worry about me or what I look like, or heaven forbid, if I'm single or what I wear to bed."

Richard chuckled. "I did see that on *Rockefeller* the other day. Those questions must've been offensive."

"If I was a woman, they most certainly would've been called that. But because I'm a man, apparently it's okay. It's not. It's inappropriate to either sex."

"Good point." Richard eyed the man before him and wondered if he was a professor. "What was your job before writer? I'm just looking at your outfit and wondering if you taught writing somewhere, or if you're a scientist."

"My outfit makes you think I'm a professor of some sort?" Bryan arched a brow. "I've been told that because of my check shirts, corduroy jackets, and knit vests. Some think I'm a hippy because of my long hair, but I'm not. I did work in a publishing house years back, started from the bottom up to learn the craft. I wanted to learn what goes into a good book that a publisher would want to buy and sell. It was an interesting education."

"And are you published by that publisher?"

"No, I'm not. But it taught me a lot."

"Let's get into your books. Three books, a three book deal, all three out within a year, *and* you have another three book deal for your next books. What is *your* writing process like? You seem to be prolific."

"If writing book after book makes me prolific, I suppose I am." Bryan smiled shyly. "I take three months to write a book from idea to edit. For the first two weeks I come up with an idea, figure out the plotline, characters, scenes, beats, etcetera. Then for the next eight weeks I write all day, most days, and all night, most nights. Sometimes I can be at my desk for twenty four hours straight, but it means I'm finished in eight weeks, no matter the daily word count. In the last two weeks, I edit. Four times only, every few days, doing other things inbetween. The first is a spelling edit, the second is a structure and beat edit, the third is to finish off anything else I want to add or move or change, and the last, the fourth is a printout edit. I print out and slash with a red pen if necessary, which it usually isn't. By then, there's not much to be fixed and I, and the book, are done."

"And all of that's twelve weeks? No wonder you can write four books a year." Richard crossed his legs and held up the book. "Where did the idea for *Creeper* come from? Do you get ideas long before you sit down and start the process, or did you come up with it the first two weeks?"

"It had been a very small idea in the back of my mind since I started *Illicit Things*. I knew the three books would have the same vibe because that's the vibe I was in when coming up with the ideas. I have a small notebook by my bed, and another that I carry around with me, like most authors. I write down ideas and had written down a little vague idea for it. Once *Illicit Things* was finished, along came *Sinister Motives*, and by the time that was finished, *Creeper* had fully formed in my mind, so I immediately wrote out the plotline and characters, and out it came."

"So, you don't always come up with ideas in the first two weeks?"

"Not fully formed ideas, no. Just little snippets of what could be."

"And has your family been amazed by your success? Are you amazed by your success?"

"I'm most definitely amazed by my success. I think everyone who writes a book wants it to succeed. Wants it to be a bestseller, wants to be successful out of it, and I'm no different. It's nice to have no debt and my own home. It's nice to be able to pay the bills and have food in the fridge, and it's all because I worked hard to learn the craft of writing a book, and have made a career out of it."

"Are you currently writing a book, or is that on hold for promotion?"

"I'm currently in information gathering mode. I finished a book last month and knew this month would be busy with promo, so I'm on the lookout for new ideas."

"Is that something you always do? Be on the lookout for ideas when you're out and about?"

"Whether it's the news, the newspaper, a gossip site, you'd be amazed where you can get ideas. I'm always on the lookout."

"And as we wrap up the show, tell us how your book launch went last night. We have some footage." Richard pointed to the monitor and the video of the launch played.

"It was good. Technically my first," Bryan said as he watched it. "Some fans won a spot to come along and celebrate. I did a reading from *Creeper*, as well as from my others, and did a Q&A. It was great."

"Did Sydney Kingston turn up? I heard she was invited."

"Unfortunately, no. That's disappointing as I really wanted to meet her and see if she'd read the book. I'd love to get her opinion on my work."

"And why is that?"

"She's my peer, not just as an author, but in the genre, and she's amazing at what she does."

"You can always turn up at her next book launch."

"If I'm invited. But I would like to get her next book and have it autographed."

"Well, you only have fifteen days left before Sydney's release date. I can't wait to see what her book's going to be about. The ads for it are very secretive."

"They are, but it adds to the excitement," Bryan said. "It's very intriguing."

"It certainly is and we'll be having her on in a couple of weeks. Meanwhile, Bryan Jamison, thank you for coming on *The Book Show*." Richard shook his hand and turned to the camera as it zoomed in on him.

"Thanks for tuning in this week, folks, we'll see you next time when we have Noroto Ting, the author of *The Wind.* I'll see you next week."

Sydney turned down the volume and watched Richard and Bryan chat as the credits rolled over them. They hadn't found this so-called invitation and they'd looked in all three levels of Pulsate, getting every employee to check their desks, inboxes, and emails, and even if they had she didn't know if she would've gone. What she did know, was that her brain was nagging at her. His voice was familiar. The way he spoke was not.

She knew she'd never met him, had never met anyone looking like that, but knew there was something. The way he looked, the way he spoke, the words he used. Bryan Jamison *had* to be a pseudonym for someone she knew.

Chapter 30

On the ninth of September, Sydney posted a picture of a Times New Roman X to her socials. The caption read, *Ten days to go until you receive two new surprises. Stay tuned for the trip of a lifetime. XXX. Especially those who know. XXX.*

By the end of the day, the image had over a million likes and over eight hundred thousand comments. Everyone was excited and trying to figure out what the new book would be about. Sydney weighed in with, *While I cannot read all of your comments, those I have read are wrong. You don't even come close. XXX.*

She spent the next week getting ready for the onslaught of media that would come in not only the next few weeks, but probably for the rest of the year, and on September eighteenth, she posted another X picture with the caption, *One day to go, everyone. The surprise will go live tomorrow, will be on shelves tomorrow, will shock everyone tomorrow. Stay tuned for the book tour. I'm looking forward to it. XXX.*

Selected bookstores around the city were getting their deliveries at nine that night so the books could be on display first thing in the morning. They were updating the image on sales sites the moment it went live, or hitting publish on the sites they were holding back on. Sydney was set to update the book page on her website just after midnight. It was all happening at midnight, the books were releasing at midnight, the onslaught would happen at midnight.

They all sat in CC's office and prepared for the onslaught.

*****

"Madam X by Cassandra Kingsley is the latest release from Sydney Kingston and is accompanied by the biography Sydney's written on the infamous madam."

"Cassandra Kingsley's new novel, bombshell Madam X, has the companion biography titled Madam X, New York's Madam to the Rich and Famous, both written by Sydney Kingston."

"Sydney Kingston has done it again. She's released her new bestseller Madam X, a novel about New York's madam with its sidekick biography also written by Sydney. I'm sure the rich and powerful of New York will go nuts when they find out about this…"

"Oh, I'm sure they will." Sydney flicked to another station on CC's TV, trying to find another breakfast show to see what they were saying. "Guaranteed number one bestseller, right?"

"Of course, darling." CC downed a painkiller with her tea. After dropping off copies to Emerson, Cormac, and Douglas, and warning them to be prepared, she'd stayed up all night with everyone else in the office to watch the city fall apart.

They'd sent copies to all breakfast and morning show hosts, daytime and nighttime hosts, plus radio shows; especially the ones Sydney would be doing interviews on. It had all been very secretive, the parcels being delivered in person, where possible to the hosts at home, or on their way home from work yesterday.

A hundred bookstores around the city had the stock and had already set up window displays and posted to social media to get the interest up.

Sydney had released another video to social media, introducing her latest novel and its companion biography. Her website had crashed from people viewing the book's page. Her Amazon stats showed she'd already sold over one million e-books, while her socials went crazy with comments. All physical stock would arrive at Amazon and other stores during the day.

Pulsate Publishing had taken the potentially unwise move of printing three million copies of each book, hoping whoever bought the novel would buy the biography and vice versa. Their promotion was going hardcore across the board now they could reveal the titles and covers. They were determined to sell through and hoped to go into a second print run. They were all in on these books and knew that lawsuits could happen.

Eric hurried into the office. "I've had phone calls from lawyers so far threatening to sue. I told them to actually read the damn thing and educate themselves before threatening us."

"How'd they take that?" Sydney asked.

"Silently," he replied. "And then they hung up."

Sydney snorted and flicked though the stations again. "Chickenshit lawyers."

"I've been scanning socials, websites, ours, theirs, to watch sales. I've released the audio books as well, so three current formats. It's selling well." Rhona stood up from leaning over CC's desk and cracked her back. "I think it's time for breakfast."

"There's a Maccas down the road," Sydney said. "I'll have the brekkie wraps and hotcakes."

"There's a what?" Rhona asked.

"A Maccas." Sydney glanced at her and saw her puzzled face. "That's what we call MacDonald's. Do you do brekkie wraps? Hell, I'll just have one of everything. My treat."

"In that case, so will I," Rhona said. "Let's write up the order."

A half hour later, they were eating their way through a room full of steamy hot food, watching the breakfast shows change to morning shows, change to daytime shows, change to nighttime shows, and every single one had mentioned Sydney's new books. The publicity was priceless.

"I don't know how much we've eaten today, but I am stuffed and need to go home." Sydney checked the time. "It's been twenty-four hours since I got here and I'm going to sleep for another twenty-four." She stood up and stretched and yawned at the same time.

"I stopped answering calls at five," Eric said, wearily getting to his feet. "All lawyers are threatening lawsuits. God, how stupid does it look to threaten a lawsuit before you've even read the damn book you want to sue over. I'm going. See you tomorrow."

"Just before you do." Rhona walked into the office. "Both books were sold out by six and stores reordered, or more stores ordered in the hundreds with the next print run which I've already organised of another three million of each. You'll be the highest selling author in Pulsate's history, Sydney."

"You've ordered another three million of each book?" CC got to her feet. "Can we afford that?'

"Considering we sold six million books in one day," Rhona said. "Yes. Because Europe, Australia, Asia, all want it. It was only available to America for print. And we certainly didn't expect to sell out, or, well, we did, but not in the first day. Sydney normally sells one to two million a book, not three. So, I've ordered another three of each. We'll contact the stores and they'll start coming in batches in two days."

"Fucking hell!" Sydney exclaimed. "How many lawyers are in New York?"

"Why?" Eric asked.

"Clearly they're the ones who bought the books," she joked. "No wonder I sold out."

"Possibly," Eric said. "Night all. See you tomorrow when I field another rash of calls." He left and Rhona handed the papers to CC.

"I'm off too. Anyone else?"

They all agreed to leave and take the day off because come two days' time, the public onslaught of interviews would start and there would be no stopping it.

*****

The book launch for *Madam X* and its companion biography was a huge affair. Over one thousand people had been invited, promotional banners and posters hung from walls and across doorways, and Sydney's book cake was a huge X. Anyone who was anyone in the media and book world was invited. And all of them wanted to talk to Sydney.

"Well, hello." Sydney stood on the stage staring at the crowd. "Welcome to the book launch of *Madam X*, my latest novel and number one bestseller, plus, its companion *Madam X: New York's Madam to the Rich and Powerful*, that's also a number one bestseller. It seems that whoever buys the novel buys the biography as well, so thank you very much. Although most of you received yours free, so yours don't count to the bestsellers chart… I'm up here to let you know I won't be answering questions. Leave that for TV and radio shows when I'm on them. Tonight is all about the book and celebrating its, make that, *their* debut. I will be doing a reading from both later and yes, I have my facts triple checked, so the biography is based on everything that was reported. But for now, enjoy the launch of *Madam X*."

Sydney left the stage to thunderous applause and multiple flashes going off. Every last detail was being recorded, as always, but on a bigger scale. This book was huge, so the launch had to be too.

Emerson came rushing up to her. "Oh, my God, Syd, no wonder you didn't want to tell me what the book was about. Holy Jesus." She hugged her tightly. "It gave Douglas heart palpitations and he had to check into the hospital. We thought he was having a stroke." She pulled back. "You didn't release this on purpose, did you?"

Sydney chuckled and took in her best friend's appearance; a sexy red dress that had her cleavage on show, and curls piled high on her head showing off the big red earrings dangling from her ears. "No, I didn't, but I wouldn't be surprised if you gave the guy a heart attack in that dress. Va va voom."

"Oh, Syd." Emerson giggled and hid behind her hand. "I think I nearly gave Cormac one when he saw me in this dress."

"Is he here?" Sydney scanned the room. She didn't see him anywhere and could hardly hear over the racket of the attendees.

"No. He decided to stay home with Douglas. He didn't have a heart attack, so he's back home for the night."

"Did they enjoy the books?" Sydney saw Rhona standing nearby watching her.

"Well…" Emerson paused. "They enjoyed the novel, but were a little worried you were going to name names in the biography."

Sydney shook her head. "That was the one thing I wasn't allowed to do, legally. I would've copped lawsuits left, right, and centre, even if it was true. But I don't see why he'd worry. He's a good American catholic boy, isn't he? If he hasn't done anything wrong, he'd have nothing to worry about."

Emerson raised an inquisitive brow at her. "If he hasn't

done anything wrong? What does that mean?"

"It means, if he has nothing to hide why did he have a panic attack over the book? The book wouldn't've sent him to the hospital." Sydney acknowledged Rhona's wave. "I gotta go and promote the book. Enjoy the night. I'll try and catch you before you leave, or I leave. And we'll have a catch-up after the hubbub dies down, which should be soon." She hugged her again. "Or by Christmas anyway. You know what you're doing for the holidays?"

"Having it with Cormac and the family. But I'd also like us to do something if we can fit it in."

"Dinner at my place?" Sydney suggested. "Or a weekday dinner at Cormac's when the family's not there. Or CC's if she's not doing it again this year."

"Not sure, but I'll start checking with everyone and see what we can fit in." Emerson squeezed her hand and went to look for CC.

Rhona led Sydney through the crowd, and she stopped to talk to everyone. They had a million questions, but Sydney had only one answer. "Leave them until I'm on your show."

Three hours later, she was back on stage giving a reading from each book. She'd picked the sauciest passage from the novel, and a daring one from the biography. Both received thunderous applause.

"And as someone who's had to deal with stalkers since coming to New York," Sydney said. "It probably wasn't a good idea to buy an infamous madam's former brownstone. But at least it gave me these books." She held them up and laughed. "Half the time I didn't know if the stalkers were for me or Madam X, so it's been quite a year, as usual. I've been here in New York for four years and so much more has happened here than in L.A. and it's made me think. Think about the people who've been hurt, the people we've lost. The people we wish would get lost."

She chuckled and then sobered. "It's been a rough four years in an infamous madam's brownstone. I had a dead rat in a gift box on my doorstep, stalkers, a dear sweet girl murdered on my stoop, and then a year later her killer, her ex-boyfriend was murdered in the same fashion. A lot has happened, folks."

She gazed across the inquisitive, but sombre faces in the crowd. "And so, I decided to go out with a bang. Next year is fresh and new, and I'm taking a break. I'm going home to Australia for a while to enjoy a stalker-free vacation. I won't be writing, I won't be publishing. I'm just taking a break because I need it. So, here's to a new book, raise your glasses, and let's celebrate my biggest novel ever. *Madam X*. She may be dead, but she has driven me out of the brownstone for a quieter life back home. Thank you for being here."

Sydney applauded and stepped away from the microphone, making her way down from the stage to find Emerson, Amy, CC, Rhona, Gemma, and Olivia waiting.

"What the hell do you mean you're going home?" they all demanded at once.

A sigh heaved Sydney's body and she deflated, putting her hands up in surrender. "I need a break. A break from New York, America, the stalkers. I just want to go home for a while and do other stuff. It's been years since I lived there. I miss the old girl."

"So, it's just a holiday?" CC fretted, playing with a string of pearls. "You will be back?"

With a limp shrug of a shoulder, Sydney replied, "I don't know, CC, I don't know how long I want to be gone. To be there. It could be six months, a year, forever. I don't know. But what are you worried about? You'll still publish my books. I'll still come back to promote, if I can. I have a massive stockpile, even though I just said I probably wasn't publishing."

"Why now?" Emerson slid her arm through Sydney's. "Is something wrong?"

"Besides my stalkers and Nora being killed on my doorstep?" Sydney replied and shook her head. "I can't deal with it anymore. I might even sell it. It's jinxed. When I was walking through the crowd all of the thoughts I'd been having this last year just kind of cemented in my head. It's time to go home for a while. To get away from here to just… Argh," she growled and waved a hand. "I can't do this anymore. Not for a while, I need a break and shouldn't have to keep explaining myself."

"Understandable," Amy said. "What about me?"

"You can still be my assistant. Still type up my messy handwriting. Damn, I'll have to dictate it and send it via email, but hey." Sydney rubbed her arm. "You'll be able to work for others and set up your own business the way you've talked about."

"Can I come with you?" Amy asked hopefully.

That shocked Sydney. "Ah…would you want to?"

"Possibly," Amy replied. "I haven't lived in Australia. Only visited."

"Well, I don't know what you'd do for me there. All of my current books are typed up." A light bulb went off above Sydney's head and she snapped her fingers. "I know, you can work at Pulsate as CC's assistant, and she can deal with me via you. How about that?" They both looked at CC who seemed surprised.

"Oh, I don't know if I need an assistant."

"You do," Gemma and Rhona said in unison.

CC glanced at them. "Well, yes, I suppose with my age it would be good to deal with Sydney when she's gone. You could be our go-between. Yes. I think I could fit you in as an assistant."

Sydney nodded encouragingly at Amy who brightened.

"I guess I could. But I'm so used to working for you," Amy told Sydney.

"I know." Sydney consoled her. "But I don't know how long I'll be gone, or if I'll be back. And your family's here, so you can be my U.S. assistant and still help out with research and information, and everything else you do. I just won't be doing a lot for a while. I won't be doing much in Aus to need an assistant, but I'll still need one here. I just need to get out of here for a while. Out of America. We can still work together."

"I think that would be perfectly reasonable," Emerson told Amy. "You'll still work for Sydney via CC."

Amy looked at CC who smiled.

"We'll think of something," CC said. "Sydney, when are you planning on leaving?"

"January, new year new start. Free time to sit on a

sunny beach and do sweet FA."

"Wish I could join you." Emerson sighed. "It sounds heavenly."

"Why don't you? You can help me pick a house," Sydney suggested. "It's summer at that time in Aus. We'll book a hotel suite, sit under palm trees, sip cocktails."

"And buy houses," Emerson added.

"Not like we can't afford them!" Sydney exclaimed and turned to Amy. "Come for a holiday before heading back to work for CC. See Australia."

Amy could barely contain her excitement. "Seriously? Yes!"

"Okay, then." Sydney looked at the rest of them. "In the meantime, I have a couple of books to promote."

Chapter 31

Two days later, Sydney was back on *Rockefeller.*

"Sydney Kingston you've finally done it. You finally released the long awaited novel, *Madam X* and its companion biography. Oh, my God." He dramatically collapsed back in his seat. "Both are incredible. I read them the night I got them. You told us about this what…three years ago now, but legalities were holding you back. And then of course, you released an absolute plethora of novels since, but here we are. Sydney Kingston, *Madam X,* your biggest seller to date."

"That was the plan," Sydney said.

"Tell us about it, Sydney." Rhett held both books up for the camera. "You only write novels, but you wrote a biography as well."

"That's what happens when you do research on a known person, you unearth all sorts of things and write down details, and next thing you know you have enough for a book."

"You did the research on Madam X before writing the novel?"

"No. I started writing scenes for the novel beforehand.

I knew who owned the brownstone, I had the basics. I wrote the scenes and kept going while my assistant did the research. We scored quite a bit."

"Such as?" Rhett asked. "Did you speak to her lawyer?"

"Her lawyers, her bank, her estate manager, some of the girls who worked for her, so many people spoke to us about her. It was incredible."

"And you and your assistant collected all of this and you wrote the biography." Rhett flicked through the pages. "Had you finished the novel yet?"

"Once the new information came in, the plot changed a little. I was able to add more to it and finish developing the storyline into what it is now. I then worked on putting the bio together."

"Did you have lawyers breathing down your neck?"

"Not while writing it, but afterwards, yes. Everything had to be legal; everything had to be safe and publishable."

"Otherwise, you'd be sued?"

"Otherwise, I'd be sued. I still could be even though we've dotted every i and crossed every t. We know rich and powerful men can be litigious."

"They certainly can be." Rhett flicked through the pages and came to the photos in the middle. "You obviously obtained permission to use these photographs. We have Madam X herself, Josephine Pompadour, several of her growing up, and here in New York. We have photos of ledgers and papers and her, I can't believe you got a picture of this…have a look at this, ladies and gentlemen." He turned the book around to face the camera. "Can you zoom in on this photo down the bottom?" His fingers tapped the picture. "This one. It's

Madam X's client list. A little black, it looks to be leather, book, and on the inside page it says *The Client List of Madam X.*" Rhett righted the book and looked at the photo. "Is this real?"

"It is." Sydney's heart beat faster.

"Did you see it yourself?"

"I did." Her heart thundered in her chest and she was worried the mic would pick it up.

Surprised, Rhett looked at her sharply. "You've seen the client list of Madam X?"

"I've seen the book, yes. It's very real."

"Wait…" He put his hand up, leaned back in his chair, crossed his legs and took a deep breath. "The client list of Madam X exists? All of the rumours of ledgers, paperwork, diaries. The infamous list is real. They all exist?"

"They do." She nodded, a secretive smile on her lips. "I've seen them with my own two eyes. I watched while they were being photographed for the biography."

"And who owns them now? Her lawyers? The museum?"

"Can't say. That was part of the deal. But they do exist and are very real, and I've read them. They all came in very handy for the novel. It helped round out some of the characters."

"You know who her clients were?" Rhett swiped his hand over his mouth and looked at his audience. "Wow, ladies and gentlemen. I am in shock. Sydney you know who her clients were."

"So did her lawyer, so do all of the ladies who worked for her. And so do all of the people who visited her."

"And that means what?" Rhett took a breath as he tried to figure it all out. "The cops didn't find the books."

"No."

"The cops don't have the books?"

"No."

"And they weren't buried with her body which was one of my thoughts."

"No."

"Which means someone had them. Who? Her lawyer? One of the ladies?"

"No and no."

"So, who has them?" he asked, coming up blank. "How did you find those books?"

"I didn't. But I know who did, and I know who currently has them. They're being kept under lock and key until the owner figures out what to do with them."

"That's a lot of names who could come after you, or the owner, to find them. Imagine the mob bosses and crime lords, cops, lawyers, judges, rich and powerful billionaires who went to her, as we said a few years ago, to get their asses spanked, who would do anything to stop that information from coming out."

"And I recall saying, they only got their assess spanked, and no one cares considering everything else going on in the world. A rich guy having a fetish for ass spanking doesn't actually matter in the grand scheme of things these days."

The audience clapped and cheered.

"Very true." Rhett stared at the photo of the little black book. "There would be a lot of powerful men in that book. High ranking, high rolling. Are you worried something will happen?"

"I don't have the book. I don't have any of it. And considering I haven't named names in either book, and my biography isn't the first one, I really don't know what all the fuss has been about. We had lawyers ringing up to sue me before they'd even read the book. That's how pathetic they are."

"Or how scared." Rhett closed the book. "You're right, no names are mentioned, but you didn't answer my question. Are you worried something will happen? You know names."

"So do do a couple of hundred other people. And considering what's happened to me in the last four years here, and in the ten years in L.A., I'll defend myself if I have to and I've proved that. There's nothing to fear from me. I won't name names. I haven't done. I just wrote a novel about an infamous madam, and wrote, I think it's the thirteenth biography which may be unlucky." She grinned. "So, if anyone's watching that's worried about your name coming out, don't be. I won't be telling. Besides, none of you are interesting enough to talk about in the first place. Your fetishes are; you are not."

"Holy, Jesus, she detailed their fetishes?" Rhett's mouth dropped. "Oh, my God."

"Name, job description, physical description, fetishes. That's how they're all listed in the book." Sydney knew she was taking a big gamble talking about it, giving the details she was, but she wanted to go out with a bang.

"You're kidding?" Rhett again turned to the audience. "Ladies and gentlemen I need to see this little black book."

He swung his chair back to Sydney. "How many names—"

"A thousand."

Rhett's jaw dropped again. "You counted them?"

"A certain number per page, a certain number of pages in the book, and it's the only one we know of."

"She had a thousand clients, people, my God. And she had about twenty girls."

"A hundred at one time. They came in via the basement door. Now you see how much information I had for the book, the novel, that is. But everything I've said today is in the biography."

"It is, but it's still shocking to hear and I must've missed a few details when I was in such a rush to read them both. And how many have you sold?"

"Sold out three mill of each on day one. Ordered three mill each more, and sold another two and a half of each. There's still a million to sell, folks and we're only five days in."

"That's five and a half million copies of each book in just five days. Is that a new record for fastest selling novel or biography, ladies and gentlemen?"

The crowd applauded.

"It is for Pulsate, and for me," Sydney said.

"You heard it here, folks. If you haven't already bought *Madam X,* or *Madam X: New York's Madam to the Rich and Powerful* by Cassandra Kingsley, Sydney Kingston's pen name, do so. There's a half a million copies of each left before it goes into another print run. I was at the book launch the other night and picked up on some things you were saying, Sydney. You said you're leaving New York."

"Yes. For a very long, extended holiday. I want to get back to Aus and have a nice break before the next novel's released. It's been a busy year, Rhett, as you know. I've helped you with your crime series, released the movies for *The Shape of You* and *Her Last Words*, along with the documentary of the same name in Nora's honour, and worked with victims of crime. It's time for a long holiday."

"It has been a busy year for you. Will you release this time next year?"

"I don't know."

"With everything that's happened, I suppose you wouldn't. Well, it's great to have you back on the show. Sydney Kingston, folks."

*****

The next few days were filled with interviews. The Today Show, multiple times, NBC Today, Kelly and Mark, Kelly Clarkson, The Late Show. The whole week was filled with TV shows, both in America and abroad.

In the second week of publicity Sydney started on the radio interviews with Preston Grant being top of that list.

Preston leant into his mic. "You were promised the book years ago, ladies and gentlemen, and now it's here with its companion biography. Welcome to the show, Sydney Kingston."

Sydney nodded at everyone in the studio as they applauded and whistled. "Thanks for having me back."

"How could we not? Let's get into it. Tell us about the novel, *Madam X*, and how the inspiration, the idea, all came about." Preston leant back in his chair and crossed his arms over his white *Choose Life* t-shirt.

Sydney flashed back to the day in Cormac's house when Sean had mentioned how it would make a great idea for a novel. "Ah…it was four years ago, not long after I'd moved here and I was having lunch with some people and one of them suggested it would make a great idea for a novel. When I got home I started writing a scene that had popped into my head, and every couple of days I'd write some more down. By the time we started researching her and the house, all of that information gave me more ideas, and when I went to Florida, I finished off both."

"And you've actually managed to see the client list," Preston asked. "The infamous little black book of Josephine Pompadour who became Madam X. It actually does exist?"

Sydney nodded. "It does and I've seen it and it's hidden away under lock and key."

"Under your lock and key?" Hank asked.

"God no, not mine. I don't have it," Sydney told him. "But I'll say this again, most of the men in the book are dead. I've said it on many TV shows this week, now I'll say it on radio. At least three quarters of the men in the book are dead. I don't know why so many people are worried about it."

"So, if it's a thousand names long, then at least seven hundred and fifty are dead," Preston said. "And only two hundred and fifty are still alive to sue you. Do you in, mob style."

"Don't give them any ideas," Sydney interjected.

"I really don't see why they'd bother suing you. You've mentioned no names, and if they sued you, they would out themselves."

"Exactly. Which is why they'd want to keep it secret. I've already said I won't tell. They don't need to worry."

Preston went on. "Someone who does need to worry, though, is Bryan Jamison. He's been number one for three weeks and God help anyone who had, or has, a book released this month because you've blown everyone out of the water. You've topped both the fiction and non-fiction charts simultaneously. Does every other author on the planet need to worry?" He shifted in his gas lift chair.

"Hardly," she scoffed. "America's not the only country with author or book charts, and eventually another book will come out and knock mine off the top of the list as I do to others."

"When do you think that will happen?" Preston asked. "If it's over five and a half million in sales, you're gonna be there awhile."

"Probably not until you release a book again, and then you'll knock yourself off," Hank said.

Sydney laughed. "I hope so. At least until the new year. Then I'll give everyone else a go."

"Do you think…" Preston sat back, stared up at the wall, and cocked one leg on the other. "Do you think, that this type of subject is a no brainer? As in, it's your best-selling book, it's also about a madam spanking asses. There's sex in it, for obvious reasons, but most of your books have limited sex. *The Shape of You* had sex, because of its plot, and obviously so does this one. But doesn't it say sex sells to Sydney Kingston?"

"Not necessarily," she replied with a head tilt. "I've looked back at all of my books, paperbacks sell more than hardcovers, e-books sell more than paperback, but across the board, my books tend to sell around the same number. A million hard, a million plus for paper, anywhere past that for e-books, and audio varies. Foreign is a little different. *The Shape of You* sold a little more because of the circumstances of the time. But *Madam X* has blown all of my books out of the water and I think it's simply because of the subject matter."

"New York's infamous Madam X," Preston interjected. "She's well-known, her clients are well-known; it's a well-known story."

"Exactly." Sydney resumed speaking. "It was going to be released years ago, and was mentioned, so it was known that I had written it. And with everything that's happened in the last two years, right on my doorstep, and the subsequent novel and movie and documentary about it, plus Rhett Rockefeller having me help him with his victim of crime series, I think everything just built it up. I'm living in her brownstone; it couldn't be helped. I see, on average, two to three people taking photographs of the building per week when I'm there. At least I hope they're taking photos of the building and the history and not because they're stalking me. I've had enough of them."

"Do you think stalkers are the result of you living in that brownstone?"

"It's possible. The previous tenants often complained of it. It's on record with the police, and I've spoken to them myself. They often had gawkers taking photos or getting their companions to take photos of them outside. They even had people knock on the door or buzz them to see the sex room. The tenants had had enough so they left. Then the owners put her on the market and that was when I was looking to buy."

"And you think your stalkers were just after Madam X?" Preston asked, his fingers lightly tapping the desk.

"Well, the peeping tom wasn't. He was a neighbourhood guy. The first stalker admitted to thinking Madam X still lived there, so." She shrugged. "Who knows. Famous people have stalkers all the time. We've discussed this before."

"That's true, they do. I've had a few idiots harass me." Preston adjusted the position of his mic. "We had Bryan Jamison on a few weeks ago. Yes, we're moving on. He said you'd been invited to his book launch but didn't turn up. Was he at yours?"

"I wasn't invited to his launch, so I'd say he lied or Viceroy lied to him." Sydney paused to take a sip of water. "We looked high and low for that supposed invitation and there wasn't one. So no, I wasn't invited and neither was he. You were though, as were many celebrities and media people."

"And it was a great launch," Preston said. "You really didn't get an invitation after he told everyone you had one."

Sydney shook her head. "Nope. We checked emails in case it was electronic. We checked the mail room, we checked every office on every floor and there was no invitation."

"Wow. How unusual is that?" Hank asked.

"As in, said one was sent but it wasn't?" Sydney asked. "Don't know. But it's bloody rude, either way."

"You haven't met Bryan Jamison yet?" Preston moved on. "I'd love to get you both in here on the show together, so we can have duelling authors."

"Like duelling banjos?" Hank laughed and quickly found a clip of the sound.

"Like duelling banjos," Preston repeated, listening to the song. "Duelling authors on the same genre, duking it out for the top spot."

"From what I saw, I'd eat him alive, he's such a weed," Sydney joked.

"When did you see him? What show?" Preston asked.

"*Rockefeller* and *The Book Show*, and then I heard him here."

"You know what he looks like, at least, like the rest of us. I thought he was a professor or something in that corduroy jacket. The guy must be in his forties." Preston laughed. "Either way, he's written three damn good books, so he knows his stuff. I'd love to get the both of you in here together before you head off on your sojourn to Australia, Sydney."

"Or you could wait until this time next year when I release another blockbuster," she quipped. "It will give me a year to prepare for eating him alive."

"Didn't you say you won't be publishing next year, though?" Preston asked. "You mentioned it at the launch, I think."

"Ah, yeah." She sighed. "But old habits and all that. I'll probably publish something anyway."

"Okay, folks, it's time to go. We've had Sydney Kingston,

aka, Cassandra Kingsley, in today talking about both of her new books. *Madam X* and the companion biography, *Madam X: New York's Madam to the Rich and Powerful.* Sydney, always a pleasure."

"Preston. Same time next time."

"It's a date. And we'll have Bryan Jamison on as well. Bye, folks."

Chapter 32

Sydney's press tour continued into October, with multiple interviews each day. She was busy from sun up to sun down, and sometimes midnight depending on what show she was on. And it wasn't just America that wanted to talk to her. It was many European and Asian countries as well as Australia. Magazine and newspaper interviews were done on days between radio and TV. Some were done on the run to the next appointment.

Sydney was wrapping up a magazine shoot when she heard her phone ringing. "Amy, can you grab that?" She pulled off the jacket she was wearing, handed it back to the stylist, and moved behind the dressing screen to change.

Amy checked the phone and frowned. "Hey, Em, Syd's just changing."

"Oh, God, Amy, can you get Sydney out to Cormac's house? Douglas wants to see her. He's nearing his last moments and wants to see her. Cormac will send an escort. Where are you?"

Amy told her the address and promised they'd get there as soon as possible. "Sydney," she yelled. "Hurry up, we gotta go. It's an emergency."

"What is?" Sydney pulled on her shoes and checked her outfit, making sure she had everything before stepping out from the dressing area. "What is?"

"You need to get to Cormac's. Douglas is on his deathbed and wants to talk to you. Cormac's sending a squad car for an escort."

"What!" Sydney frowned, puzzled by the whole ordeal. "Why would he want to see me? Wait, did you say he was on his deathbed? Shit!" After a stunned pause, she took a breath and added, "Let's get our stuff and hurry downstairs. We have a driver, though, Landon Security. Not that it matters, I guess." She turned to the interviewer and thanked her and the crew for the shoot. "I hope you have everything you need, but we must dash off. Thank you so much." They grabbed their coats and bags, double checked that they had everything, and hurried for the elevator. After a ten minute wait, they exited the building to be met personally by Cormac's lieutenant.

"Ms Kingston, we need to get you to the Commissioner's. Do you have a car?"

"We do. Landon Security is driving us." Sydney pointed to her driver who was waiting outside the car.

"Tell them to follow us." The lieutenant waved him over. "We need to get Sydney to Commissioner Ryan's house; it's an emergency. Can you follow us?"

The driver nodded and hurried back to his car.

Sydney and Amy climbed into the SUV and he got in behind them. With sirens blaring and lights flashing, they raced through the city across to Brooklyn, and screeched to a halt in front of Cormac's house. The lieutenant alighted and helped Sydney down, and she rushed off as he helped Amy.

Sydney dashed to the door and it was opened by Ethan.

"Syd, you look amazing," he managed before she breezed past him.

"So why am I here? It's been four years since I was here last." She turned to the living room, saw Sean, did a double take, and stumbled to her right.

"Easy," Ethan said gently, grasping her arms from behind and steadying her.

"Why am I here?" she asked all the questioning Ryan faces of every family member.

"Syd." Emerson appeared from the hallway. "Come with me." She held her arms out and Sydney moved into them.

"What's going on?" Sydney asked as she was led down the hall to the back of the house.

"Douglas wants to talk to you. We think he's at his end." Emerson stopped at the door and knocked gently.

It was opened a few moments later by Cormac. "Sydney, glad you could make it," he said softly. "My father would like to talk to you."

Sydney was surprised by his haggard and worn out appearance. "Cormac." She stepped into the room and saw the patient supine in his bed. "Douglas."

He looked over at her. "Sydney. I need to talk to you, please." He tried to gesture to the bed beside him, but could barely raise his hand. "Cormac, close the door."

Sydney moved over to the bed and sat as Cormac closed the door. "Now, what did you rush me out of a photo shoot for," she joked.

He barely managed to hold out his hand for her to take. "I need to confess my sins before I go and I don't have long."

"You have a family priest for that." Sydney gently squeezed his hand.

"But I can't tell a priest this. Sydney." He paused to breathe a couple of times. "The book, Josephine's book. You saw it. It was in your book on her."

"The little black book containing her client list? Yes, I saw it. Why?"

"Did you read it?"

She gazed into his glassy eyes, saw the fervoured, but weak fear they contained. She took a breath. "Yes."

"You know what's in it?"

Her left brow rose. "Yes, Douglas. I do."

"You," another breath, "said on Preston's show that at least three quarters are dead."

"Yes. We counted exactly seven hundred and fifty from that list are gone."

"You know the names on that list."

"Yes, Douglas, I do. Is this what you can't tell the priest?"

"Yes." His hand fell to the bed. "You know I can't tell him. And I know you won't tell either." His eyes never left hers. "Please don't tell anyone, Sydney. I want to take this to my grave. But I needed to cleanse my soul of sin before I died."

"And you want me to say what, Douglas? Say ten hail Marys, I forgive you, your family forgives you? God forgives you?"

"It was after Marion had died. I wasn't coping well, and for some reason I sank low enough to do it. I sank low enough to drink too much and see a madam."

"Your secret's safe with me, Douglas." She smiled. "I would never tell anyone. I will never tell anyone anyway. Because I have a secret of my own to keep." She leaned closer. "I've not only seen the book, the ledgers, the paperwork, but I *own* them." She sat back and gauged his reaction. It was puzzled and disbelieving. "When the former owners bought the brownstone, and slowly renovated it, they ran out of money and were having problems because of former associates of Josephine's. The brownstone was ransacked multiple times. Leftover items were stolen, and, considering the slash and burn job you lot did on the house, there was a lot of damage to fix. I approached the owners after they had quietly approached a broker to see what they had found. I bought it, for a lot. And that enabled them to complete the renovations."

"The owners found the book? Where?" Douglas frowned at the thoughts rushing back.

"The one room you didn't demolish. The basement toilet. It was hidden in the false wall Josephine had the toilet attached to. She was smart."

"Does that mean the owners read the books?"

"Probably did. But unless they can read shorthand, I doubt they had any idea."

"Shorthand." His breath became shallow. "I'll be damned. But that doesn't stop the fact, there are two hundred and fifty names left on that list who are alive."

"And you'll soon be the seven hundred and fifty-first who isn't," Sydney said. "Don't worry, Douglas, my lips are sealed. But that leaves two hundred and forty-nine names and some of them are very well-known, especially in this family…" She leaned closer and hardened with hatred. "And now, let me tell you a secret I hope makes you rot in hell."

Five minutes later, Sydney opened the door and motioned for Cormac to go in. "He's struggling and nearly gone. I'll leave you." She closed the door behind him and saw Ethan and Sean standing down the hallway watching her. She shuddered and turned to Emerson. "That was something."

"What did he want?" Emerson asked. "He wouldn't tell us."

"And I promised I wouldn't either. He just needed…" She paused to find the right word. "Redemption."

"He couldn't get that from the priest?"

Sydney shrugged. "I don't know. It was his choice." She cast a glance down the hall. Ethan leaned, lovestruck, against the stair railing staring at her. Sean stood tall, muscular, hands in pockets, his brown hair short at the back, wavy at the front. His blue eyes stood out even behind the silver wire framed glasses he wore. She inhaled deeply to calm her racing heart. "It's been four years since I was here last."

"Come on." Emerson linked her arm through Sydney's, saw the boys, and waved them away, before leading her back to the living room. "Can I get you anything?"

Sydney noticed a weary, but suspicious Amy sitting in a chair close to the living room hall door that lead to the front door. "No. We'll be out of here in a few minutes."

"So, what did our grandfather want to talk to you

about?" Alec asked, moving over to her from his spot by the cold unlit fireplace. "It's unusual that he'd want to talk to you."

"Probably wanted to know the plotline of her next ten books," Connor joked. "So, he wouldn't miss out on them."

Sydney cracked a small smile. "No. It wasn't that."

"Then what?" Alec demanded. "What did he want to talk to you about, Sydney?"

Giving him an arched brow, she replied, "The answer to that is none of your goddamn business, Alec."

"Oh, come on," Alec barked. "The old man's on his deathbed and he wants to talk to you?"

"Take it easy, Alec," Declan warned.

"What do you mean, take it easy, Declan?" Alec pounced on him. "I'm surprised you're not going off at her considering you're the family hothead."

"Ties with Connor, doesn't he?" slid out of Sydney's mouth before she could think about it. She got small grins from both Connor and Declan before Alec turned back to her.

"What did our grandfather want to say to you, Sydney?"

Sydney's anger riled up. "What he wanted to tell me is none of *your* fucking business. It was a private conversation and I'm keeping it private."

"She's right, Alec. Just stop." Cormac, morose and hands in pockets, sighed behind them.

Sydney's gaze darted from Cormac to Sean and back. Both had the same stance and looked very much alike.

Cormac looked around at his family. "He's gone. He's at peace."

Silence settled over the room, but it felt suffocating

and smothering to Sydney. "My condolences. It's time I took my leave. Cormac." She nodded and looked at the family. "Everyone."

"I'll escort you and Amy out." Emerson led the way to the front door.

Once it was closed and they were back outside, Sydney breathed deeply. "That was suffocating."

"Alec did get a little intense," Emerson said, and pulled them to a stop three quarters of the way down the front path. "Syd, you were in there quite a while."

"As I said, he needed to get something off his chest. You staying here, Em?"

"I am." Emerson gazed at the house and tucked a strand of hair away. "I basically live here now, as you know."

"Four years you guys have dated, and you basically moved in when? Just admit you've been ensconced here for at least two years. Still have your loft apartment?"

"Renting it out. It's good income, not that I need it." Emerson gave a soft smile.

"When are you two going to get married?"

Emerson shrugged. "We've considered it. He doesn't want to retire until he's 75 and suggested we go on a world tour and basically holiday for the rest of our lives."

"So, when's he proposing?"

Emerson slowly shook her head. "No idea. But if we do, I want you as my maid of honour."

"Nothing honourable about me," Sydney quipped.

"Speaking of, I hope whatever it was Douglas needed to unburden himself to you has left him in peace," Emerson continued.

"I think it has. We had a good chat. He invited me to

the funeral, but I declined."

"Oh, we haven't even thought of that. But from what he's said, he has it all planned out." Emerson shivered in the early October air. "He wanted to make it as easy as possible."

"Which we should all do, and it's why I have a very detailed will." Sydney zipped up her coat. "You get back inside, and warm up. Cormac needs you."

"And sometimes, I just need my best friend, but she's off gallivanting around the world or hiding herself away to work," Emerson replied.

"Then let me know when you're free and we'll have our girls' day at my house. I have Sundays off, but I'm free this Saturday."

"It's a date," Emerson said and hugged Sydney and Amy. "Thanks for coming."

"Bye, Em, get back inside." Sydney watched her friend hurry up the path and inside, then saw the curtain move and noticed Sean watching her.

An icy chill shuddered down her spine and she turned away, climbed into the Landon Security SUV and left the Ryan house behind.

*****

The funeral of Commissioner Douglas Ryan was a grand affair. So grand it made it into most New York newspapers. Sydney read one article and closed the paper. She knew CC had attended out of respect. They'd dated since meeting. Her heart broke for the family, but knew they would rally as a unit. That's what law enforcement families did.

Chapter 33

Two weeks later, exhausted from promotion that wouldn't stop, Sydney turned up to the book launch of fellow author, Carlie Hansen's latest romance novel, *In The Wind*. They'd known each other for almost ten years, but only saw each other on the odd occasion, and at author functions. And even though Carlie was with another publisher, Sydney was always invited.

The launch was at *The Romeo*, a restaurant set in a hotel ballroom with a fantastic view of the city that was one of New York's primary locations for romance movies. The publishing house spared no expense as Carlie was their biggest romance author.

"Sydney!"

Sydney stopped gazing around the lavish party long enough to see Carlie coming towards her. "Hey, Carlie, long time no see." They embraced and took a few moments to chat.

"Thank you so much for coming," Carlie said. "I wasn't sure you'd make it, considering the wildly successful book tour for *Madam X* is still going."

"Considering I got the invitation early I was able to

slot it in. I see quite a few of us authors were invited. I'll say hello as I cruise the party."

"Absolutely, a lot of you were on the list. Not only KL Publishing authors, but many that I know personally. And you're always top of the list because you've been so super supportive over my time in publishing."

"Well, some of us have to stay together," Sydney said, and glanced around the room. "Love what they did with the place. Romance galore." The ballroom was strewn with red and white. Balloons, streamers, banners. Even the heart shaped cakes and cookies were coloured with red and white icing and little heart decorations. The cocktails were red, the lighting red. Everywhere you looked was a sea of red.

Sydney suffocated in the bloodiness of it all, and her heart pounded in her chest while the music pounded in her ears even though it wasn't that loud. She needed a drink. "Congrats, Carlie. I'm going to mingle. Anyone I should be on the lookout for?"

"The same author everyone else is on the lookout for," Carlie said slyly and looked in his direction. "The man of the hour, even though it's *my* book launch."

Sydney looked across the room to the gaggle of females all gathered around a tall, lean man with a brown ponytail and glasses. His tan corduroy jacket was being dusted off by one of the women. "Ugh, Byron Jamson. God, why is he here?"

Carlie giggled. "It's Bryan, Sydney. And he's here because he's the biggest thriller author behind you, *and* your competition. My publisher also thought he'd be a drawcard."

"But he's with *Viceroy.*"

"I know, but it got more people here." Carlie shrugged. "Have you met him yet? I managed to have a quick chat with him when he got here and before he was eaten alive by all of his current admirers."

"What's he like? I haven't met him yet, I only saw him on TV and heard him on Preston Grant's radio show." Sydney studied him. He seemed quiet, shy. He would pull back slightly if someone touched him, and he kept his hands on his drink glass or in front of him.

"He seems nice enough. Quiet, intelligent." Carlie sipped her blood red cocktail. "Pretty much what we saw on TV."

"Did he reiterate why it took him so long to come out?" Sydney craned her neck and stepped to the side for a better view.

"He's gay?" Carlie was surprised. "I hadn't heard."

Sydney laughed. "I meant, come out in the open as the author. He's talked about it during a few interviews, just wondered if he'd mentioned it again. And how the hell would I know if he's gay?"

"Oh." Carlie blushed to her roots and took a quick sip of her drink. "No, he didn't. But as he said on TV, they wanted the books to speak for themselves, before revealing who'd written them."

"Does he seem familiar to you?" Sydney asked. "I've got this weird feeling. His book *Illicit Things* was a rip-off of my book *Twisted Affair*, and his writing seemed familiar, but I just can't…" She slowly shook her head. "I just can't recall where, or why."

"Maybe it will come to you when you finally meet."

Sydney huffed. "Yeah right. I have no interest in meeting him."

"Then why have you been staring at him the whole time?" Carlie asked and glanced from Sydney to Bryan. "And look, now he's staring at you and wow, does he look interested."

"Nope." Sydney grasped Carlie's arm. "Congrats on the book. I'm going to mingle." As she took off she heard Carlie say, "Go mingle in his direction."

Nope, not happening, Sydney thought and headed for the bar that was full of alcohol bottles in the shape of hearts. "Wow, where did all of these come from?"

"Our Valentine's party," the barman said. "We keep them packed up for the rest of the year so we don't have to buy more. What'll you have?"

"Some sort of citrusy tang mocktail, thanks. I don't drink alcohol anymore."

"Anymore?"

Sydney blushed to her roots. "Bad decisions come from drinking."

He laughed and got to work. "Coming right up."

Sydney watched him whip up her drink and shake it into the glass.

He presented it to her with a flourish. "Madam."

"Thank you." She took a sip, let the taste tingle in her mouth and dance on her tastebuds, and gave him a nod. "Very nice, and just the right amount of tang."

He gave her a smile and went to serve another guest.

"Sydney Kingston, the one and only. Or do I call you Cassandra Kingsley? My biggest rival."

Sydney spun around to come face to face with Bryan

Jamison. He was a good half a head taller than her at over six feet. Lean, with a swimmer's body which somehow looked out of place in the checked shirt under a knitted sweater and his corduroy jacket. "Oh, my God, it even has patches on the elbows. Where'd you get that? From a thrift store?" burst out of her mouth before she could stop it. Not that she didn't mean it. It did look like something from a thrift shop.

"A recycle boutique, actually," Bryan said. "Not that there's anything wrong with thrift shops. I quite like scrounging around them for bargains. You never know what you'll find. But I guess from the look of your outfit, you've never been in one. Just expensive Rodeo Drive boutiques for you, huh?"

Sydney's brows rose in scorn. "I never shopped on Rodeo Drive the whole time I was in L.A. so no. Smaller boutiques, however, I did frequent; especially those who had different clothing from the norm. Or, I had a lot made. And yes, I've been in thrift stores, went to them all the time in Australia, and L.A. and here. I go at least once a month, not that you'd know, you pompous prick. You dress like a forty-something college professor."

"How do you know I'm not?" Bryan stepped closer. The pounding in his ears grew louder and it wasn't from the music. It was from his heart racing in his chest.

Sydney's eyes narrowed. "I don't, but you certainly dress like one." She changed tack. "What's the real reason you didn't show your face until now? What was wrong with last year, or back in March? Your publishing house released all three of your books in one year and apparently paid you well enough for it. Two million per book, I've been told. So why the hold back?" She studied his brown eyes whose stare unnerved her. His silver round wire frame glasses seemed familiar. So did his lips, even though they were half-hidden by a thick brown beard. She stared at it, and noticed it didn't seem quite right.

"I've mentioned that several times in my interviews," he said. "It was purely for publicity. We wanted the books to sell on their own. To see if they could. It was an experiment of sorts."

"And book number two? It wasn't publicised long before it came out?"

"And you beat me to that, too," Bryan retorted. "You still managed to release a novella and hit the number one spot on the bestseller charts ahead of me. How do you do that, Sydney Kingston?"

Sydney watched the sly smile lift the corners of his lips. "I watch my competition, Byron Jamson, and because I have a stack of stories ready to go, I can release at a moment's notice. And yes, I still beat you."

The sly smile turned upside down. "It's Bryan. Bryan Jamison. Which you full well know."

"Do I?" Sydney sipped her drink. "Do I *really?* Mr I came out of nowhere with a book that's smashed the charts even though no one's ever heard of me and I won't even bother doing press or promo for it. Do I? Do I really?"

"Yes, Sydney. You do."

Stunned by the change in his voice, Sydney stared hard at him. She'd heard it before. But where? "What did you say?"

"I said, yes, Sydney, you do. Why? Are you okay? You

don't look so good. Are you ill?"

His voice was back to normal.

Sydney took a deep breath and stepped back. "No, Byron, I'm not, but it's time for me to mingle." She turned on her heel and headed for the exit.

*****

October turned to November. The promotion trail was slowing down, and things were easing off. Sydney spent more time with Emerson, having girls' days in, or shopping for Thanksgiving and Christmas.

Emerson asked Sydney to join them for Thanksgiving. Sydney said it probably wasn't a good idea considering she'd slept with multiple members of the family.

Shocked, Emerson demanded to know how many, but Sydney only admitted to two.

Instead, Sydney invited CC, Amy, and the rest of Pulsate Publishing over for the festivities, as well as Nora's family. They'd kept in touch that last two years and were happy with the book and documentary helping keep her spirit alive. And Rhett Rockefeller's show on the crime had helped as well, especially as it had reported upon Lennie's subsequent murder and then proceeded to do an entirely new show on both murders. Lennie's killer, for all anyone knew, was still out there.

*****

After Thanksgiving, Sydney was invited to another book launch. This time it was for Melanie Sotherby, a middle-grade author who had started at Pulsate.

Melanie had been a winner of the mentorship program and had her first three books published by Pulsate. The first had sold well, but the subsequent books hadn't. She was let go and published her next two books herself, then Viceroy approached her and gave her a deal. Something that everyone at Pulsate was still pissed about.

"Sydney." Melanie ran up and hugged her old friend. "I haven't seen you in so long." She held Sydney at arm's length. "Ms I can never have a bad book and they'll all go to number one. I've missed you."

"Well, you shouldn't have gone to Viceroy," Sydney joked. "Good to see you, Melanie. It's been a few years."

"About two years, when you released *Her Last Words* and then the movie and documentary. I wanted to stand behind that and support it because I'd lost an old school friend the same way."

"Yes." Sydney remembered. "And what a shocking story that was. Rhett Rockefeller did a show on it."

"He did and they actually found her killer after all these years. But let's not dwell on the macabre, hey, it's good to see you. There are a few other Pulsate authors here, along with my mentor and editor, plus some Viceroy authors, including man of the hour, Bryan Jamison."

"You're the second author I know who's called him that," Sydney said. "He's not that great. In fact, he's not great at all."

Melanie's brows rose. "Is someone jealous?"

"Of what?" Sydney protested. "I smashed his book out of the park. I've smashed all of his books out of the park. What have I got to be jealous of?"

"Good point," Melanie agreed. "But you clearly don't like him."

"There's something about him I just don't like," Sydney said. "But we're not here to talk about him. We're here for you. Congrats Melanie. You've got another smash hit on your hands and it's all thanks to Pulsate."

Melanie laughed at the dig. "It certainly is, so enjoy yourself, I'm off to party."

They parted ways and Sydney mingled, chatting with other authors and some editors. She was even waylaid by a Viceroy acquisitions editor who tried to convince her to move to their author stables.

"I'm happy where I am," she told them. "Besides, you've got Byron Jamson. You don't need me." She playfully slapped him on the arm and moved on, coming across Erica Montare, a Pulsate author who'd been Melanie's mentor. They chatted for a few minutes before getting drinks at the bar.

"Anyone here you don't like?" Erica asked, knocking back a shot.

"Byron Jamson."

"It's Bryan Jamison."

"Is it?"

Erica laughed. "Like that, is it? You know I'm on your side because I'm still at Pulsate. So, if that little bitch is your arch enemy, he's *our* arch enemy and *we* hate him."

Sydney's laughter slowed down. "Little bitch he is, and yes we do."

Erica held up another shot. "Cheers to little bitches we hate." They clinked glasses and downed their drinks.

Sydney moved on after refreshing her drink, and found herself in front of the band that was playing in a corner of the room. She swayed left to right in syncopated beats with the song, but a few songs later, became aware of someone standing behind her and quickly turned to find Bryan. "What do you want?" she snapped in a moment of quiet between songs. She walked over to the side of the room away from the band and sat on one of the stools set up around the room.

"Just wanted to say hello." He stood in front of her and rested his glass on the table. "Hello, Sydney Kingston."

"Byron Jamson."

He breathed in sharply and shook his head. "You just can't help yourself. Sydney, Sydney, Sydney. You know full well what my name is."

"And I don't care." She sipped her drink while looking off to her left.

He moved closer until he was breathing on her, and in her ear, he said, "You *will care*, Sydney. One day, very soon, you will care *a lot*."

Scared, Sydney could only watch as he walked away and disappeared into the crowd. What the hell had he meant by that? Was it a threat? Was it a precursor to what was to come? Did she have to get Landon Security to look into him? Maybe she should anyway. Who the hell was Byron Jamson actually? Pen name? Real name? Jesus, what if he was actually one of her stalkers? What if he was a new stalker? What if he just wanted to fuck her?

Wait what! Where the hell did that come from?

What if he was just attracted to her and was awkwardly coming onto her?

No, that's ridiculous. Don't be stupid.

Was she attracted to him?

No…not really…no. But there's something about him I can't put my finger on. But it definitely isn't attraction.

You sure about that?

Yes, absolutely. I'm not attracted to him whatsoever, but he is hiding something and I plan on finding out.

By fucking him?

What! Oh, my God, stop that!

It's a suggestion worthy of investigating.

No, it isn't. Just stop it.

Sydney mingled for another half an hour. She didn't see Bryan, so said her goodbyes and left.

*****

November turned into a chilly December first as the crunchy snow thickened on sidewalks, roads, and lawns.

Emerson, Amy, and those closest to Sydney at Pulsate came over to deck the tree and fill the house with decorations. Not that any of it mattered. She would be alone at Christmas as she was most Christmases unless one of the Ryans came over, but she'd put them behind her. Except for every now and then.

"I'm having my Christmas and New Year parties again," CC declared. "Douglas wanted me to, and I want to keep doing it for my people while I'm alive. Which won't be for much longer."

"You're only seventy-five, CC. You'll outlive all of us." Gemma hung a ball on the tree. It was set up in the parlour window so it could be seen from outside.

"Hardly, my young girl, but thank you for saying so. So, to those who will be free, single, or alone for both periods, please come over to my penthouse and we'll deck the halls with plenty of food and wine."

"Count me in. I hate being alone this time of year and I've missed your parties." Sydney hung a Chanel double C ornament on the tree; a present from CC.

"Yes, I did too. Although I had them a day earlier, I wanted to spend those times with Douglas. He told me to get back to them and help others find their true love." She patted her hair into place and picked up her champagne glass.

"Find their true love? At your Christmas and New Year parties? Since when?" Sydney asked.

"Well, we did. And he thought others would," CC said.

"The two of you found true love?" Sydney was astounded. "With each other?"

"Of course, darling." CC carefully sat on one of the parlour chairs. "We had a few good years together. It was nice for someone our age."

"Again, CC, you're only seventy-five," Gemma reminded her.

"Oh, posh." CC waved a hand. "Do stop that. I may not have many years left, but it's always nice to find love again at any age."

Sydney exchanged a look with Emerson and wondered about her. "So…" She kept her voice low. "Has Cormac proposed yet? And is he *your* true love?"

Emerson snorted. "No, and I don't know."

"Wait, what?" Sydney was stunned. "He's not your true love?"

"I love him, don't get me wrong, I do," Emerson quickly said, and finished setting up the sleigh ornament on the fireplace mantel. "I love him enough to marry him. But I know what CC's saying. I'm nearly sixty, he's nearly seventy-five, and he plans to retire the day he turns seventy-five and we'll travel a lot after that. As for true love." She shrugged. "I don't know. I've changed a lot in the last four years. In L.A. I was bonking young men left, right, and centre, dating older men, whenever I wanted where I wanted. It was great, it was freeing, and then I met Cormac and that changed. I only wanted to be with him and I have been since. I'd absolutely say yes if he asked, and he will, but I don't know if he's my true love. I love him and want no one else. Does that equate to a true love?"

"Yes, it does," CC called out. "I've seen the two of you when I've been over. You're most definitely well connected to each other. And I say he's your true love."

"He had a wife," Emerson reminded her. "What about her?"

"What about her?" CC asked. "She was his first wife, who gave him four sons. She did her job, but sadly, she was taken from this world like poor young Nora. And like Sydney and Amy almost were." She saw the shocked looks on their faces and waved a hand at them. "Oh, stop. You know full well what I'm talking about. His wife is long gone. If she wasn't, would they still be together? Sure. Just like Douglas and Marion would have been. But they passed away and then Cormac met you, Emerson. He's found love again, and you've found love for what? The hundredth time? Thousandth time?"

"Ooohhh, them's fightin' words," Sydney joked.

"Actually, CC, I've never been in love. Not mature adult love." Emerson picked up the bottle of champagne and swigged it back. "I had teenage love, an early twenties love, but, when you get to this age, you realise they weren't true love. I had lust and lots of it. That's what I wanted at the time while I was busy making TV and films. But now..." She shrugged. "I don't know. I guess I was just waiting for the right guy to come along to fall in love with. And I have, so yeah, when he proposes I'll say yes."

"When will that be?" Amy asked as she wrapped up everything to be stored away until the new year.

"I'm thinking it will be at Christmas." Emerson drank another mouthful. "We've discussed... *He's* discussed," she corrected. "Getting married again. His first wife, their marriage, he said he'd like to do it again, and how did I feel about it. We left it up to him to pick the time and place."

"And I get to be bridesmaid, huh." Sydney finished off the tree and stepped back. "Merry Christmas to me. I'll have to catch the bouquet, otherwise there's no other way I'm getting married. I'm already an old spinster."

"Hardly! How many of the Ryan boys have you slept with?" Emerson retorted. "You can still get the men."

Everyone in the room catcalled Sydney and she waved at them to stop. "Too many to mention," she joked. "But then again, who knows what's going to happen this Christmas New Year period? And who knows what will happen once I head back to Aus? I might find myself an Aussie guy on the beach."

"And then I get to be maid of honour at *your* wedding," Emerson said, raising the bottle in cheers. "Three cheers to Sydney getting married."

*****

On December fifteenth, Sydney turned up at Rhett Rockefeller's Christmas party. Ever since they'd worked together on his victim of crime shows, she'd been invited to all of his parties and launches. But she also noticed she wasn't the only one invited. "Ah, Jesus." She turned away as Bryan came up to her.

"Sydney."

"Byron."

"That joke's gone beyond old." He nudged his glasses up the bridge of his nose with his knuckle. "In fact, it's now mouldy."

"Who said it's a joke?" She sipped her drink, refusing to look at him, and gazed across the crowd of A-list celebrities, TV show hosts, and movie stars. There were some influencers she couldn't stand, and an author she couldn't tolerate, and he was right beside her.

"You can't seriously think my name's Byron when you know full well it's Bryan. And it's also beyond disrespectful at this point."

She eyed him up and down. "It was also disrespectful of you to keep saying I'd been invited to your book launch when I hadn't been. Either you lied, or Viceroy lied to you, because we couldn't find an invitation anywhere. Not in our emails, not in our mail. No one at Pulsate had this so-called invitation. So where was it?"

His brows furrowed. "You should've had it. My publicist made sure to send you one and I saw it myself because I'm the one who said to invite you."

"You!" she mocked. "Why would you want to invite me to your book launch?"

"Because you're an incredible author and I wanted to personally thank you for inspiring me to write. Your books are amazing and gave me so many ideas for novels. *You* have given me so many ideas for novels. I wanted to thank you for it. For all of the years of inspiration."

Sydney could only stare at him. It was a strange statement to make. "Have we met before?"

He laughed. "Of course we have. Twice before at other authors' book launches."

"No. I mean before that. You come off as vaguely familiar, but I can't place you."

"Well, I'd like to come off with you, Sydney Kingston." He leaned closer and said in her ear, "Don't you feel it, Sydney? You can deny it all you like, but there's an attraction between us that's been building since we met. I certainly don't deny it. And I'll admit it right now. I'm very attracted to you, Sydney, and I know you're attracted to me."

Sydney pulled away. "You know no such thing, you arrogant prick." She stared into his face, studying the lines and ridges. There was something so familiar about him, but the eye colour, the hair, and even the beard was wrong. "If we've met before, just say it. Stop the lies. You lied about the invitation to your launch and you're lying now. What are you doing? Trying to get me into bed as some sort of joke? Some sort of con or dare or bet?" She stepped away from him. "How dare you try and humiliate me, Byron Jamson, you son of a bitch. How dare you." She strode off, leaving him stunned and bemused.

Oh, this game's, good, he thought, and finished off his drink. He followed, staying within hearing distance, catching her eye here and there, chatting to celebrities and A-listers who'd read his book. He was promised a lot of things. *I'll get you into my next movie, my next movie's based on your book, I want to turn your books into movies.*

But all the while, his gaze kept wandering to Sydney. He'd raise a brow at her and smile, and she'd hurry off. He'd follow, grab her attention again, watch her hurry off again.

He spoke to Rhett, who introduced him to some bigwig producer, spoke to Preston Grant who wanted to get him back on air in the new year, and spoke to someone who carried on as if they knew him personally, but he'd never met them and had no clue who they were. He looked around for Sydney and spied her at the bar. Excusing himself, he made his way through the crowd to her side.

"A beer," he told the bartender and turned to Sydney. "It's hard to keep up with you. You keep running away." He nodded at the barman as he placed his beer in front of him and swigged half back, but managed to grab hold of Sydney's arm as she tried to run off. "Stop running, Sydney."

She shook him off and hurried for the exit, blood racing, heart freaking out in her chest. What the hell was going on? Was she attracted to him? Hell no!

"Sydney." He grabbed her arm and spun her around. "Stop running away from me."

She shook herself free. "Why can't you just leave me alone?"

"Because I'm attracted to you and I'm trying to tell you that, but it's clearly not working well. I like you, Sydney, a lot. I'm attracted to you. Do you want to get a drink sometime?"

Sydney's jaw dropped slowly open and two words came out of her mouth. "Fuck no!"

*****

Christmas Eve was celebrated at CC's where Emerson and Cormac turned up around ten and Emerson presented the square cut diamond engagement ring on her finger.

"Congrats." Sydney hugged her tightly, tears springing to her eyes. She was losing her best friend and didn't like it one bit. Although…hadn't she been losing her for four years already, and now this was the final nail in the coffin?

Emerson rubbed Sydney's back. "It's okay, Syd, you okay?" She pulled back and looked into her best friend's watery eyes. "Aw, Syd, it's okay."

"I know," Sydney said tearfully. "I know, it's just so much has happened in four years and now this. I really do need to get away for a while." Emerson wiped at her tears and she grabbed her hand to examine the ring, turning her hand this way and that. "It's okay, I guess. I take it you said yes."

Emerson giggled. "Of course I did. I told you I would. I know you don't like diamonds, but I do and it's perfect."

"Yeah." The misery in Sydney's tone evident. "Not for me."

"Aw, Syd." Emerson embraced her again. "Are you feeling left out?"

"A little. Like every New Year. It's getting harder. This time of year. Especially since Nora."

"I guess it would. Where are you spending tomorrow? Here?"

"Yeah," Sydney repeated, pulling back to wipe her face. "I must look a mess. But at least CC and Amy will be here and others will drop by. We'll do different things through the day to fill in time and then have a nice lunch."

"That's better than nothing." Emerson helped wipe the tears away. "We spent some time with the kids and grandkids before coming here. We'll spend more time with the others tomorrow. Maybe we can stop by again." She glanced over her shoulder at Cormac who nodded.

"Once the family's gone after lunch, we can come back for dinner," he said, his smile accommodating Emerson, but it didn't reach his eyes and Sydney noticed.

She narrowed her eyes at him before moving her gaze to Emerson. "Don't go out of your way just to please me, Em. I'm a big girl, it's just been a really sucky two years, that's all."

"Biggest selling novel and biography at the same time really sucks," CC said as she passed them with a platter of food and set it on the coffee table in the living area before coming back to them. "Darling, are you sure you don't want to stay?"

"I'm only going back to Aus, CC. It's a holiday. Just like going to Florida to write and then onto Europe for a vacay. I need to get away and give my brain a break, and my soul, the brownstone, and everything that's happened has killed my spirits and I need a change of lifestyle. It's just a holiday, CC, a nice long holiday."

"Well, then, we'll see you this time next year," she said, and went off to entertain.

Emerson caught Sydney's expression. "We will see you again, won't we, Syd?"

Sydney breathed in. "Maybe I'll be here to promote the next book, so I might stay through January, unless I convince you to come to Aus for a warm and sunny Christmas."

"That does sound good, but we kinda had that in L.A.," Emerson said.

"It wasn't *warm* warm," Sydney said. "It was cold most years, especially by Australian standards."

"Well then, we'd better plan for Christmas in Australia," Emerson agreed, slipping her arms through Cormac's. "Maybe we can make it part of the honeymoon."

"Getting married next year?" Sydney asked in surprise.

"Year after," Emerson said. "In the end, we decided to do it the day Cormac retires. Which will also be his seventy-fifth."

"Oh." Sydney's brows rose. "Why wait so long? You'll also be sixty, Em, having a party?"

"Are you coming back for it?" Emerson asked. "Otherwise, I might come to you."

"I'd have no problem if you did. Just tell me the time and place and I'll be there."

"I haven't sorted that out yet, but I'll let you know when I do."

They mingled with the other guests and sang carols, watching them on TV until it was past midnight and all those who weren't staying went home.

*****

Christmas Day was much the same, with at least twenty people coming back to spend the day with people they knew. Cormac and Emerson turned up for dinner. Once the day was over, it was back to normal, with Sydney doing last minute shopping before her holiday. She was leaving mid-January and was considering a few things that might shock some people. Emerson and Sydney enjoyed days of after-Christmas shopping at the sales, and then New Year's Eve and Day were much the same as Christmas as they counted down the seconds and counted in the year.

Chapter 34

Sydney turned up to the first party of the new year. A party for Rhett Rockefeller. *Rockefeller* blasted its way into another year, which also happened to be its record breaking twentieth year. And just like his Christmas party, this party was filled with A-grade celebrities; many personal friends of Rhett's. Authors, singers, musicians, actors, hosts, the list went on. All for bragging rights.

"Sydney." Rhett came over, his arms wide, and gave her a Hollywood kiss. "So good of you to come. You're one of my closest friends and guests. Thank you so much for your help the last few years with getting the crime show up and going. Starting it off with Nora's death really helped and then we not only found the killer, but his murder ended up on the show as well."

Sydney quelled the rising anxiety in her stomach. "Glad to be of service, Rhett. Thanks for having me on all these years and helping to make my books bestsellers."

"Oh, Sydney. They were already bestsellers when you came on. You did that all on your own. You didn't need me for that."

"No, I didn't," she agreed with a wicked grin. "Congrats

on the show. I'm off to mingle." She chatted to a few actresses she knew. One had been in the movie for *Twisted Affair*, and another was in *The Perfect Man*. They told her how her movies had helped their careers. She thanked them for the fantastic jobs they did bringing her characters to life, and moved on to speak to a favourite singer, a band whose latest single she loved, and a couple of TV and radio hosts.

She stopped off at the bar for a drink and found herself next to Bryan Jamison. "Oh, for fuck's sake." She picked up her drink and turned to go, but he stepped in front of her.

"Sydney," he said, lightly touching her elbow. "It's time you stopped running from me."

Sydney knocked back her drink and slammed the glass onto the bar, thanking God it didn't smash. "I'm not running from you, Byron, I'm just not interested in speaking to you or being around you. Why can't you take a hint?"

"Because the hint I'm getting is that underneath that hostile exterior you're displaying you're actually interested in me."

Sydney burst out laughing, drawing the attention of those nearby. "You *are* kidding, right? Me? Attracted to you?" she cried, laughter still leaking around her words. "Oh, my God, what an arrogant son of a bitch you are, Byron! To think that I'd be attracted to the likes of you." She glanced at him up and down. "A forty-something professor who thinks he can write novels better than mine? Ha!" She spun around and stalked off for the exit, waving goodbye as she went.

A Landon Security driver picked her up and took her home.

Who in the goddamn hell does he think he is? She boiled inside, watching the lights of the city pass by as they headed home. *Arrogant piece of shit!*

When they arrived at the brownstone, the car waited until she was safely inside before driving away.

Sydney stomped her way up the stairs to each floor and into her bedroom. Her suitcases were in the closet packed and ready to go; she just had her cabin bag open for that night's clothing and her travel attire and toiletries.

She quickly undressed and hung her clothes up to air before showering and sliding into a silky robe. As she flung the covers on her bed back, she heard the doorbell ring out.

"Who the hell could that be at this time of night?" Sydney checked the monitor on the wall and saw Bryan Jamison on her stoop. She hit the intercom. "What the fucking hell do you want and how the fucking hell do you know where I live?"

"I had a cab follow your car, but I had to work up the courage to actually ring your bell."

"Oh, so you're a stalker now," she declared.

"I'm not stalking you, Sydney. I just want to fuck you."

Her hand fell from the button in shock. What the fucking hell!

Thinking it preposterous, Sydney stormed downstairs and flung open both doors. "Who in the goddamn hell do you think you are saying that? Why would you, of all people, want to fuck me—"

"Because you're gorgeous—"

"And why would you stalk me all these months and lie about me—"

"Because I've fallen in love with you—"

"And tell the world I was invited when I wasn't and now you tell me at Rhett's' party that you're attracted to me. What a load of baloney. You bullshitting piece of…" She finally stopped to take a breath. "What did you say?"

He'd been so quiet she'd barely heard him, but then she'd just steamrolled over him with her words. Stunned, she could only stare at him.

"I said, because you're gorgeous and I've fallen in love with you." His usually soft voice was firm and clear. "What I said at Rhett's Christmas party was also true, Sydney. I *am* attracted to you, and now I've found myself falling in love with you because you're gorgeous and amazing and talented and brilliant and so many other things I could go on forever." He licked his lips and moved closer. "I want to be with you, Sydney. Even if it's just for one night. I want you, Sydney."

Sydney couldn't move. The only two parts of her that *were* moving was her blood and her brain. Not even her mouth, which hung open. Nothing else.

"Sydney." Bryan took another step closer, this one bringing him right to the front door step. "Sydney, I've fallen in love with you and want one night with you. And if you can see it in your heart to give me more time than that, I'll take it."

Her brain finally kicked into gear and she stepped back. "No," she managed, and tried to close the door.

But he stopped her. His huge hand was on the door;

his huge foot on the step. He made his way inside and closed the door. "Sydney," he whispered, his eyes never leaving hers. "Sydney." He flipped the lock before slipping his hand onto her waist.

A noise came from her, but she couldn't stop his hands from pulling her to him. His lips landed on hers and an explosion happened inside her. An explosion of lust and sexual desire throbbed between her legs. She struggled to pull away, but gave in. Her hands clawed at him, his coat, his hair, his body, and they stumbled through the interior door and against it as it closed. Sydney struggled to unbuckle and unzip his pants, but when she did so, he spread her robe and lifted her onto him. With grunts and groans and gasps, they came in unison in the front entrance.

Sydney gasped for air and slid her feet to the floor. "That…wasn't…supposed to…"

His lips seared across her neck. "Yes, it was. Where's the bedroom?" He lifted her into his arms and carried her up three flights of stairs to her bedroom where they undressed and made love for the rest of the night.

*****

When Sydney woke, Bryan's head was resting on her chest. His arm was across her body, and her right arm was under him. She pulled it out and stretched her arms above her, her chest rising with the back stretch.

Bryan stirred, and lifted his head to rest it on her shoulder so he could look into her eyes. "Sydney," he murmured, while his hand slid over her body to come to rest on her breast. His fingers made circles around her nipple. "I enjoyed last night. We need to do it again."

"I enjoy sex, which that was," Sydney replied. "But I need to get out and do some things and you just need to get out." She rolled away, but he pulled her back.

"Let's do it again. Let's make love, Sydney."

She flung his hands off and gave him a scathing frown. "Get dressed, Byron. You can leave now." She walked into the bathroom and locked the door. When she finished and dressed, she found him fully clothed and lounging on the bed. "You should have left. I have things to do." She hurried down the stairs knowing he was following, as he was talking the whole way.

"So, when can we get together again? What about tonight? Are you busy? What about every night? We should date."

That stopped Sydney at the foot of the stairs and she looked over her shoulder at him. "No, we shouldn't." She unlocked and opened the front door.

"Sydney." He tried to shut it, but she wedged through.

"Listen, Byron," she snapped. "We had a one night stand, and that was it. That's all it will ever be. Now get out of my house, I need to leave." Sydney opened the vestibule door and found Amy getting out of the security car.

Amy looked up in surprise and slowly mounted the steps watching the scenario unfold.

"And how am I getting home?" Bryan asked stepping onto the stoop. "Can I get a lift?"

"Get a taxi," Sydney told him. "Just like you did last night. Now piss off, I have to talk to my assistant." She waited for him to leave, but he lingered.

"Sydney, I just…" He shook his head. "What the hell was last night?"

Sydney growled, shut the door, and led a stunned Amy down the stairs. "Come on. We'll leave instead." Amy got back into the car, but before Sydney did likewise, she said to Bryan, "Be gone before I get back." She got in and shut the door.

The driver took off down the street and turned the corner.

"Pull over here for a moment," Sydney said. When he did so, she added, "Can you get someone over here to follow him home? I want to know where he lives, what he does, and who he actually is. He needs to be looked into."

The guard got on the phone to his boss and a minute later hung up and took Sydney and Amy on their errands.

Bryan sighed and pulled out his phone, hitting the Uber app for a car. It would be a twenty minute wait. He pulled a beanie out of his coat pocket, slid it over his head, and tucked up the ponytail into it. He pulled up his coat's hood to cover his face, and sat on Sydney's stoop to scroll through his messages and social media. When the car turned up, he waved and called through the window before settling himself into the back seat. The trip was a fifteen minute ride, and he was dropped off outside a condominium building. He walked up two flights of stairs, entered his home, and locked the door.

Pulling off his hooded jacket, he hung it on the peg of the coat rack, then walked upstairs into the bedroom en suite and showered before dressing in a sweatsuit and padding back downstairs.

In the kitchen, he boiled the kettle for a coffee and made it strong, thinking about last night while he waited. When he had a big cupful, he opened the door to the coat closet under the stairs, reached up into the corner, and pulled a lever. The back of the closet opened and he entered the condo next door.

He'd bought both and connected them via a secret doorway, using the second as an office. He set his cup on the kitchen counter and removed his glasses, setting them on the counter against the wall. He removed the brown contacts and put them next to the glasses, then pulled off his ponytail wig and placed it on the dummy head on the counter. Finally, he removed his beard, wincing as it came off. He dropped it on the bench, rubbed his face, and ruffled his hair.

Heaving a sigh of relief at having all that off, he picked up his coffee and wandered through the open plan condo to the living room wall next to the kitchen. It was covered with enlarged images of Sydney Kingston.

*****

"You're leaving today? Sad to be going?" Amy asked as they came out of the pharmacy.

"Kind of." Sydney checked the receipt to make sure she'd paid the sales prices. "But at least I'll have a good long holiday in a nice sunny climate. Buy my dream house and hit the beach. And hope for no more stalkers." She put the receipt away and shoved the brown bag of pharmaceuticals into her tote. "I leave when?"

"At two. So, we have some time to get you to the airport for your flight and I will get the house packed up and cleared out for sale. How much are you hoping to get?"

"The realtor said twenty mill plus was possible. Considering who owned it back then."

"And who owns it now," Amy added. "Your book was the biggest seller of last year."

"Which one?"

"Both."

They laughed and Sydney added, "At least I'll be rid of the stalkers."

"And the Ryans," Amy said.

"And the Ryans." Sydney sighed. "Good times with some of them."

"And not with others."

"Did I tell you about Ethan? Or have I kept that a secret?"

"That he and Declan both turned up at separate times the night they told you about Lennie's murder, and how Ethan also turned up that Christmas, even though you'd broken up with him a year earlier." Amy sniggered in delicious delight.

"Yeah, crying like a drunk little woobie in need of a hug. Hell, he even proposed while blind drunk. Not a great look for a kid trying to be a man. I turned them both away, and reinforced the fact it was long over and in the past, even though I'd fucked Ethan a couple of times in those months after Nora. But I'd moved on and they should too." Sydney stopped and pulled her aside. "Listen, Amy, there's a lot that's happened in my life, mainly here in New York, that you don't know of or about. And I can't tell you because it's private or I was sworn to secrecy. Just so you understand."

"Of course." Amy nodded. "You're my boss, but not all of your life is my business."

"Exactly. Just so you know. There are things that happened that you'll never know. Okay?"

"You're the boss, Sydney. You saved my life. Your secrets are my secrets. Just a pity your men aren't my men." They laughed and walked on before she added, "At least most of the stalkers are locked up, and the lawsuits and Madam X's client list are over and done with. You can go off on holiday knowing you don't have to worry about them."

Sydney frowned in puzzlement. "Yeah, but we never did find out who sent me that letter I read in CC's office that day. The one with cut out letters from a magazine. What'd it say? *Die, bitch, die!* Landon never found out who sent it."

*****

Bryan stood in front of the wall of Sydney. Photos and posters of all sizes adorned every inch of it. Photocopies of letters he'd sent her, fan mail, publishing letters, and the invitation to his book launch were all pinned to the wall.

He sipped his coffee and pulled down a photocopy of a letter. He smiled at Sydney in every size, from photo shoots in magazines, to social media posts. Photos he'd taken of her brownstone, photos he'd taken of her out and about with Amy, Emerson, or on her own. Photos he'd taken at her functions, official photos, social media photos.

He drank another mouthful. Nice and strong, just how he liked it. Like Sydney. How he liked Sydney. Strong and hot.

He turned around and looked at the wall opposite. It too was full of photos and cut-outs of Sydney Kingston. And his desk stood proudly in front of it.

He walked behind his desk and set the coffee next to the framed photo of the two of them. It was a glossy colour eight by ten in a blue frame. He placed the photocopy beside his keyboard and sat down, ready to work.

He opened his laptop and waited for it to boot up, thinking back to the launch of Sydney's book, *Her Last Words*, when he'd seen her from across the room looking incredible, and she'd seen him. He'd eventually gone up to her and said hello. She just stared open mouthed and in shock. The things that happened that day…

He sighed at the memories and pulled up a Word doc for a new idea that had been brewing in his mind, a book about Sydney, a subject *all* of his novels were about, and sat considering what to call it.

It was January, already halfway through. He picked up the photocopy of a letter he'd sent to her via Pulsate. He'd made it out of magazine letters and it was simple and to the point. *Die, bitch, die!* Three simple words. God, how simple could a death threat be?

He chuckled. *And wouldn't you know, it was three*

years to the day we executed our plan. Me and Sydney, executing a plan so evil and maniacal it was beautiful. So, so beautiful. Just like her.

He dropped the paper and took a long swallow of coffee, looking at the photo of them on his desk. Happy, in love, together. He thought through the plotline. It wouldn't be hard to come up with. He'd already been living it. *They'd* already been living it.

He set down his cup, and with a wicked grin began to tell his wicked tale. He typed in the title. It was only three letters long.

HER

Underneath, he added, by Sean Ryan, writing as Bryan Jamison.

About the Author

L.J. has been writing since 2006, when her first of many novels, ***The Road To Vegas,*** was born. In 2016 she created the ***Porn Star Brothers*** series about three sizzlingly hot Australian born Greek Island raised brothers who became the hottest porn stars in '70s America.

L.J. lives in Australia, loves '80s music, disaster movies, and collecting Jackie Collins books as Jackie is her inspiration and mentor.

L.J. Diva is the adult pen name for author Tiara King. You can find more about Tiara on her website; follow her on social media, or visit her publishing house, Royal Star Publishing.

Socials

tiaraking.com.au/ljdiva

royalstarpublishing.com.au

Sign up for *Tiara's* Newsletter...

Make sure you're always in the know and never miss free exclusives, the latest news, book updates, and so much more with newsletters from...

tiaraking.com.au

Have you read these?

Or these?

NOVELS

Burning Desires
Anything for You
Falling for London
The Road to Vegas
Hollywood Dreams
The Billionaire's Dirty Little Secret

SHORT STORIES

The Body
The Perfect Plot
The Star of Your Own Crime Scene

www.ingramcontent.com/pod-product-compliance
Lightning Source LLC
Chambersburg PA
CBHW050600170726
48283CB00001B/44